*A*

# LEGACY

*of*

# BETRAYALS

*a novel*

## Judy H. Ray

ISBN: 978-1-7376736-0-6 (paperback)

ISBN: 978-1-7376736-1-3 (ebook)

This is a book inspired by true events, but it is fiction. The characters and dialogue portrayed in this novel are a product of the author's imagination.

Published by Judy H. Ray

Email Judyray4363@yahoo.com

Cover design by Damonza

*With love to my sisters and brothers Pat, Donnie, Jane, and Philip, we were stronger than we knew.*

*My three children Doug Ware, Kevin Ware, and Lori Ray, you are my joy in life.*

*Forgive others,*

*not because*

*they deserve forgiveness,*

*but because*

*you deserve peace.*

—MEL ROBBINS

# ACKNOWLEDGEMENTS

My sincere thanks go to my husband, Charlie, for his patience and support. He filled in the blanks with information about naval life and listened for years to changing scenes. A special thank you goes to my parents who lived a hard life but taught us all to appreciate and support the family.

A huge thank you to my brother-in-law Bud Reuffer for all the stories he could remember about dad and hours of editing. My sister Jane for her never-ending support and encouragements and my brother Don for his cheerleading on the side, thank you! My aunts and uncles, who added to the stories about Dad and Mom, helped me round out this tale. I only wish my sister Pat and younger brother Philip could have lived long enough to have seen it to completion.

A special thank you to my first critique group partners: Pat Stanford, Lyla Ellzey, and John Osborn. Your detailed and constructive comments gave this book depth and meaning.

My second critique groups met until our books were completed. Without their honest feedback my story would not have flourished. I am so thankful for Patty Daniels and Louise Rill.

I'm also grateful to my writing coach Heather Whitaker whose insight and expertise showed me how to bring this story to life, one transition after another. Your friendship and support has done more than you'll ever know.

For my beta readers, Carolyn Cane, Pat Spears, Jenny Crowley, Ellen Collins, Kate Kerr, Marcia Follensbee, and Susan Klinefleter who gave me rich feedback and encouragement, thank you.

My editors Joan Leggitt from Twisted Roads Publications

helped me transform this story, I can't thank her enough. And my thanks also goes to Janet Cowden from GalacticScribes, who spent hours upon hours making ensure the ship movements in the Pacific were correct in my story. Her pains taking efforts to make sure period details and were accurate, my sincere gratitude. She was always willing to research and help me with questions.

My deep gratitude goes to my teachers, Mary Jane Ryals and Laura Newton, two dedicated and talented women who inspired me to write and become a better reader and writer.

There were so many people who added their expertise to help me. Please forgive me if I've left anyone out.

# CONTENTS

# CHAPTER 1

# BOSTON, 1985

ON THE DAY of Ned's funeral, Luke was not satisfied with the eulogy he had written. He struggled to find a way to speak about his father that he could live with, and more than anything, not upset his mother. She had been through enough.

Claire and Barbara headed inside the chapel when Luke whispered to Claire, "I need a minute. You and Mom get settled, and I'll be right in."

Claire's eyes questioned him, but she nodded and followed Barbara.

Luke paced up and down the sidewalk beside the old stone building. He kept rereading his notes—this was not what he wanted to say. He realized people were starting to arrive. He knew several of the doctors, nurses, and hospital administrators he worked with would be in attendance, and neighbors who knew his family well. He could not lie about the past. At the same time, he did not want his father's past exposed.

After several minutes, Luke heard Claire call out for him "I'm back here, Claire."

Claire approached him. "It's getting close to the time to start. Are you ready?"

Luke shook his head. "No, not really." He blew out a breath. "This is so much harder than I thought it would be. I've put up with Dad the last few years for Mom's sake. I hated the man, and now I'm the one who has to tie his life up in a pretty package. This is just wrong."

Claire sat down next to Luke. "I can't imagine what you and your mother went through." She took his hand. "Luke, I know you. Whatever you decide to say will be right." She leaned over and kissed him. "I'll tell the preacher that you need more time."

After several minutes, the preacher came out and found Luke sitting on a bench in the small garden. "Luke, it's time. Are you ready?"

Luke looked up, shaking his head.

The preacher sat down next to him. "Talk to me. How can I help you?"

"How do I take ten minutes to tell Dad's story? You would've had to have been there from the beginning."

# CHAPTER 2

# LONDON, 1912

THE ROARING FIREPLACE did little to give seventeen-year-old Hillary Marie Dearborn's bedroom any warmth against the cold of London. She had committed an outrageous sin that resulted in being expelled from boarding school. Her parents refused to speak to her, and requested she remain in her bedroom until they summoned her. At times, she heard their loud voices. The words were not clear, but anger and shame penetrated the walls. Waiting for her parents to announce her punishment was torture; there was nothing she could do.

Most days, she sat in her window seat surrounded by soft pillows. Her mind would drift off to the summer before she'd left for school, a time when she'd been excited and ready for an adventure. Now, if she could only have the time back, she'd do it differently. Deep in her soul, she had an ache that would not cease. *How could I have been so gullible?* Every word he uttered she had believed. He was her knight.

She gently rubbed her belly, wondering if she could fulfill this child's needs. Her own mother was aloof and demanding—nothing pleased Mildred Dearborn. Hillary prayed she would not be like her mother. What if her parents would not let her keep the baby?

✧

Three weeks later, as the maid brought in her breakfast tray, her mother appeared in the doorway. Mildred Dearborn was a tall, statuesque woman who allowed other people's thoughts to drive her actions. She waited there until the maid left, then pulled an envelope from her pocket. "We've received word from your cousin, Gertrude Johansen, and her husband, Carl. They've agreed to let you come and live with them in America. I made sure they knew what they were taking on." Mildred kept her eyes averted. "Gertrude was always a well-mannered young woman—I'm surprised she agreed."

Hillary felt the fire of embarrassment rush to her face. "What? You're sending me away? To America? When may we come back?" She had to be dreaming. Her parents would not do this to her, not when she needed them most. "How does Father—"

"You used to be able to get your way with your father," Mildred Dearborn interrupted her daughter. "Not anymore. He wants nothing to do with a guttersnipe." She glared at her daughter. "Did you even think of what this would do to your father's business reputation, or our standing in the community?" Mildred shook her head as though she could get rid of this shame. "Your father is a deacon in our church. Hillary, did you do this on purpose?"

Hillary dug her fingernails into her palms so the pain would keep her from crying. "Please, Mother, let me tell you what happened. I want to talk to Father, too. This man told me he loved me."

"It doesn't matter what this man said. Don't you understand?" Mildred paused and turned to her daughter. "With a bastard child on your hip, we think you'll be better off in America. No self-respecting man in England would agree to marry you now."

"I'm sorry, Mother—I am." She dug her fingernails into her palms harder. "I thought he loved . . . ."

Mildred glared at her daughter. "We've done nothing but give you the absolute best and this is how you repay us." She stopped and took a breath. "We don't want to hear your excuses anymore. Your father has booked third-class passage for you. You'll need to pack. You're not returning, so pack all you can carry."

Hillary raised her head in time to see her mother heading out the door. The explanation, the apology, the *please forgive me* were all stuck in Hillary's throat. She wrapped her arms around her waist and rocked back and forth. How could they turn on her like this? She had no one. Sobs she could no longer hold back wracked her body.

Ten days later, Hillary was dropped off at the dock by the family's chauffeur. Struggling with her coat and suitcases, she made her way up the gangway to the White Star Line's RMS *Olympic*. The eight-day voyage would give her time to figure out what options she had if moving in with her cousins didn't work out. She could only imagine what poison her mother's letter had carried.

Hillary had never felt so alone—someone had always watched out for her. She turned to see if maybe her father had come to wish her a safe trip, or at the very least, say goodbye. But the throng of faces made it impossible for her to find him. Her relationship with her father had always been much closer than that with her mother. In the past, her father had given her an opportunity to tell her side of an issue when she and her mother had a disagreement. But this was different, and Hillary had to accept she would never have her father's support again. She wiped her eyes.

The second and third-class travelers pushed and nudged each other as they boarded the ship. On the pier, well-wishers cheered, "Bon Voyage!" and "We'll miss you!" and "Have fun!" At the same time, first-class passengers threw down streamers and confetti. Carts full of luggage belonging to the more elite fares crowded the pier. In the past, her bags had been in those carts, but now she had the burden of carrying her own belongings. The electric atmosphere should have been contagious, but Hillary kept her head down and refused to make eye contact with anyone.

*My clothes are getting tight.* Hillary tugged at her dress, but it didn't help. *Could this be a dream—a bad dream?*

She struggled down the six decks to the third-class cabins, where she would be sharing a room with five other women. As Hillary opened the cabin door, the stink of mildew mixed with sewer gases slapped her in the face. She covered her nose and mouth, then entered. There were two sets of three bunk beds stacked on each side of the small cabin, a lamp on a table between the beds, and six floor-to-ceiling length lockers.

The colorless cabin was a stark contrast to her soft-pink bedroom with a window seat full of pillows. Hillary knew her mother wouldn't have even stepped a bloody foot in this cabin, but here she stood. *Mother must be pleased with herself.* When Hillary opened one of the lockers, a fresh wave of sewer gases filled the room. She slammed the door shut, then sank to the floor sobbing.

The sad truth of what was happening began to settle in on her. She wasn't sure if she could do this alone. The ship's horn blasted and startled her. It was the fifteen-minute warning for guests to leave. Maybe her father came, and she just didn't see him. She grabbed her coat off the floor and dashed out of the cabin.

Hillary fought her way back up the six flights. She draped her coat over her shoulders and leaned against the rail. Deep down she knew she wouldn't see a familiar face, but she had to search the crowd. The ship's horn blew three consecutive times, the final signal for non-passengers to leave. The last of the guests scurried down the gangplank and the crew pulled the mooring lines, readying for departure. The engines growled as they pushed the ship away from the dock, letting off a stream of white smoke that layered itself on top of the fog.

She was their only child. How could they do this? Hillary reached into her pocket for something to wipe her eyes. She pulled out the handkerchief with the beautifully embroidered initials HMD in one corner. Below the initials were two delicate purple violets. Her mother made it for her sixteenth birthday last year. *I want this year back.*

As the ship shoved away from the pier, it caused the water to swirl around and churn up the bottom muck. Hillary shivered and rubbed her arms for warmth. She stayed on deck until the fog swallowed up her view, then headed back to the cabin.

Eight days later, the ship pulled into New York harbor. The second and third-class passengers from the RMS *Olympic* boarded the ferry to Ellis Island, where they lined up to be processed by the immigration service. Hillary gave her full name, her sponsor's name and address, and the amount of money she brought with her. Then came the physician's examination. Thank goodness the doctors were only looking for communicable diseases. She wasn't sure if the immigration agents would allow her entrance if they knew she was carrying a child, and she wasn't taking chances by asking questions or offering unrequested information. Hillary closed her eyes and pretended she was someplace else while she waited for her next interview. She felt strands of hair begin to escape the tight, black bun at the nape of her neck. Three hours after arriving at Ellis Island, she finished with the documentation and was cleared to enter the United States.

Before she left the island, she took a deep breath, determined to do what was necessary for her future in spite of her mother. Hillary slipped her coat on, picked up her suitcases, and boarded the ferry that transferred her back to New York's Battery Park pier. The cold fall air helped reduce the nausea she fought. She found her way out to the railing to get a look at the Statue of Liberty. Goosebumps covered her arms as the magnificent statue came into view.

When the ferry neared the pier, she began searching for her

cousins among the swarm of faces crowding the dock. *Will I even recognize them after all this time?* She didn't have to wait long though. In front stood a middle-aged couple holding up a sign with her name, and Hillary waved to get their attention.

As she approached the couple, she burst out, "Cousin Gertrude, Cousin Carl, it's me, Hillary." As the three hugged Hillary watched for any sign of disapproval from the two.

"How was your trip? I bet you're tired and hungry, right? I'm right, aren't I? You need a good home-cooked supper, right?" Gertrude took her suitcases and handed them to Carl as they made their way through the crowd, continuing with her rapid-fire questions. Hillary never answered most of Gertrude's questions, which didn't seem to faze her cousin. "So good to hear your accent too. It's been a while. Are you too old to be called Hilly?"

"No, I don't mind at all. May I call you Gert?"

"Of course," Gertrude said, giving Hillary a quick hug. "Hope your trip over wasn't rough."

Hillary remembered Cousin Gertrude Johansen as a woman who took charge and made decisions. She stood four feet eleven inches and was nearly as wide as she was tall. Gertrude had the same thick, black hair Hillary's family shared. *Efficient* was how she remembered Carl describing his wife, and he always let her have her way. Whether it was because he couldn't win an argument or he was tired of trying, no one in the family knew for sure.

Carl was tall and wiry, never had much to say, and seemed to prefer to stay in the background. Hillary knew they'd moved to New York City after Carl had been discharged from the British Royal Navy. They were to join his parents, who had migrated over earlier from Norway. She wondered if his gentle nature had changed. The couple, though complete opposites in personalities and appearance, must've jigsawed their marriage into working, as they had been married for over thirty years.

When they entered the third-floor walk-up apartment, the

scent of lemons greeted them. Gertrude showed Hillary to her room, then left to start dinner. Her small bed had a faded quilt— nothing even faintly resembling the room she had at home, but she knew Gertrude had given her the best she had. Hillary could still feel the rocking of the ship and became dizzy. She stretched out on the bed for a moment.

The next morning, Hillary awoke to a sharp rapping at her door. She sat up so fast that her equilibrium lagged behind her movements. *Where am I?*

Gertrude pushed open the door. "Good morning. How about breakfast? I know you're starving, having had no supper," Gertrude clucked. "Come on, upsey-daisy my dear."

"I missed your supper. I'm so sorry, Gert. I guess I was more tired last night than I realized." Hillary pulled her hair back and tried to smooth out the wrinkles in her clothes as she followed Gertrude into the kitchen. "Where's Carl?"

"Oh, he has to leave for work before the sun peeks over the horizon. Working on the docks, he meets the cargo ships first thing in the mornings. So now, Hilly, how about some tea?" Without waiting for a reply, Gertrude filled the kettle and placed it on the stove, then added more wood to keep the fire going.

From the kitchen window, Hillary watched several lines of laundry flapping in the morning's breeze. She hated to admit it to her cousin, but she missed home, her father, and her friends. Tears welled, but she wiped them away so Gertrude wouldn't notice.

Gertrude poured the hot water into her teapot and lowered a basket of tea leaves in to steep. "You had an exhausting week, I know. Now, I remember when we came ashore, I could've slept for days, maybe weeks. It'll pass—you'll see."

Gertrude pulled down two cups from the highest shelf in her cupboard. Each one had delicate lavender violets hand-painted on them. She placed them on the table where a honeypot and small glass pitcher of cream waited. "Hillary, your mother told me the reason for this move, but I want to hear what happened from you." Gertrude lowered her voice as if someone else might overhear them talking. "Our neighbors are nosey. They enjoy gossiping." She wrinkled her nose in dislike. "We feel it's necessary to tell them a little lie to protect you. Say you're a widow, no more. No one needs any more information." Gertrude poured out steaming tea for them both.

"Of course, I'll do whatever you and Carl think is best." After a long pause, Hillary continued. "I can only imagine what Mother told you, but the truth is I got involved with a married man. I had no idea he was married." She could feel her cheeks getting hot. Her voice wavered unnaturally. "He doesn't know where I am, nor does he care. My child will be born in December."

"So, he does know you're carrying his child?"

"Yes." She paused, unsure she could admit the truth aloud. "He has a family in France." Hillary gently touched her belly. Tears cascaded down her cheeks. Gert pulled a handkerchief from her apron and offered it to Hillary.

"This child," Hillary choked out, "is a casualty of a careless fling, according to him. He isn't going to risk losing his reputation for us. I've brought shame and disgrace to my family. I've made a shamble of things." Wiping her eyes, Hillary stared into Gertrude's round face and said, "I can't thank you enough for agreeing to let me come and live with you and Carl." Hillary's hands came together as if to pray. "I promise to help and work hard so we aren't a burden—you'll need to teach me to cook and clean. I'm truly grateful to you both."

For several moments, Gertrude said nothing. There was only the ticking of the clocks and noises from other families living in the building coming through the paper-thin walls in the kitchen. "Hillary, everyone makes mistakes. It's what you do next that defines you, right?" She placed her hands on the table and hoisted herself up. "Now, it's time to eat." She pulled out her cast-iron skillet, placed it on the stove, and began cooking eggs and sausage for their breakfast. She chatted on about what they would do to get ready for the baby. Gertrude's enthusiasm for the baby proved to be contagious.

Hillary leaned her head on the back of the chair and listened to all the plans her cousin had made for them. The tension eased from her shoulders for the first time since her nightmare began.

As the days passed, Gertrude and Carl continued to shower Hillary with love and acceptance. She grew more comfortable with the idea of becoming a mother. When the baby was born on December 19, 1912, Hillary named him Edmund Moreau Dearborn, and they called him Neddy. Hillary had insisted on giving the baby his father's surname as a middle name. Gertrude hadn't thought it was a good idea, but Hillary still held on to the hope that one day her son would know his father.

## CHAPTER 3

# BOSTON, 1922

**AFTER YEARS OF** working on the loading docks of New York City, Carl decided to move their extended family of four to Boston, Massachusetts, allowing him to change his career. Ship building was in his blood, and he felt the time was right. His mother was getting older, and living in Boston would allow him to buy a home large enough to bring her to live with them. He was sure his father would've approved. Young Ned didn't take news of the move well, but Carl felt the change would do them all good in the long run.

Their new neighborhood was in the suburbs south of the city of Boston. Sitting on the front stoop of their home, nine-year-old Ned stared out at the open field in front of their house. Leaving New York was hard, and he missed his pals. He didn't have his favorite ice cream shop where he and Uncle Carl would sneak off for a treat. He had no friends, no peanut carts, no ball parks, no nothing. With all the unpacking and helping his mother and aunt get settled, Ned hadn't even met any of the families in their neighborhood. Shaking his head, Ned decided New York was better than Boston.

His mother opened the front door and came down the stairs. He watched her adjust her hat and pull up her gloves. "Come on, Neddy, let's go exploring."

Ned jumped up and took his mother's outstretched hand, then the two started down the side of the dirt road. "Mum, can we go back to New York? Everything is so different here. Even smells different too," he said as he scrunched up his nose.

"You mean to tell me you miss the smell of Mrs. Horn's cabbage soup? I don't." She scrunched up her own nose mimicking his expression, then laughed. "We just got here. I'm looking for work, and you're about to begin a new school." She gave his hand a light squeeze. "You'll find new friends here, Ned. I promise."

Ned grimaced. "But I miss my old friends."

"We'll try to fit in a quick trip."

The two had walked nearly three blocks when two boys came running out of their house carrying something like hockey sticks, only straight. Both boys had bright red hair.

Ned dropped Hillary's hand.

The older boy stopped in front of Ned. "Hey, you're that new kid. I'm Red. This is my brother."

Ned nodded. "I'm Ned, and this is my mum."

Red glanced at Hillary, then turned to Ned. "Hey, ya want to play stick ball with us? I've got an extra stick you can use."

"Sure." He glanced at his mother, hoping she'd say yes.

"Where are you going to play?" Hillary asked.

"We'll be in the open lot across from your place." Red turned and pointed back toward their house.

"Go ahead, but Ned, let me know if you go anyplace else."

Ned agreed, Red ran back into his house for the extra stick, then the three raced back down the street.

~

By the time Hillary got back home, there were six boys in the field chasing after a ball. Gertrude stood on the porch and smiled as Hillary walked up the stairs. "This makes it all worth it, doesn't it?"

"Yes, for all of us. Ned makes friends so easily. Boston will become home to him in no time. I understand Carl's decision to leave New York was to have enough room to move his mother in with us. Not sure he meant it to be a fresh beginning for me, but I feel like it will be. I'll get a job, and no one will know about my circumstances."

"Make Ned your priority."

Hillary and Gertrude looked over at the boys running one way then the other. "Ned's new friend sure is loud," Hillary said. The two women grinned at each other, then took a seat on the steps, watching as the pack of boys grew in number and noise.

~

Shortly after the family settled in Boston, Carl brought his eighty-two-year-old mother, Brigitte, to live with them. Her health had deteriorated and she could no longer live alone. Brigitte wanted to finish her days out in the New York apartment where she and Carl's now-deceased father, Gus, had lived since their move from Norway. Carl insisted she would be better off with family to care for her. This was not a happy move for her.

Brigitte's rheumatoid arthritis left her upstairs and in bed on bad days, isolated. On good days, Carl carried her downstairs to the living room, where she sat in the wheelchair with only a small area in which to maneuver. With narrow halls and doorways, Brigitte's freedom was restricted to only two rooms.

Gertrude and Hillary saw to her needs throughout the day. In the evenings after supper, someone would read aloud, or they listened to Hillary play the piano. At the end of the day, Carl would carry her back upstairs.

Brigitte insisted on appropriate cleaning of the house, which meant doing it her way. All wall decorations came down for a thorough dusting, and windows had to be washed with white vinegar and water. Daily beating of the rugs, weekly scrubbing of the floors, monthly paste waxing rubbed into the floors, along with the routine polishing of the silver ruled the cleaning regiment. It all had to be done to her specifications and the demands never ended. Brigitte's complaints and requests kept Gertrude and Hillary perpetually worn out.

Hillary joked with Gertrude that Brigitte knew when a dust particle entered the house. "Better to laugh than to strangle your mother-in-law," Hillary whispered to Gertrude as they rubbed paste wax into the wood floor.

Gertrude put her finger to her lips for a hush. "Hilly, there's nothing wrong with Brigitte's hearing."

Hillary nodded and went back to her work. She knew Carl had promised his father before he died that he would take care of his mother for the rest of her life. Carl, being a man of integrity, would never go back on his word, even if he may have wished he could.

⌇

During a busy morning six months after Brigitte moved in, Hillary and Gertrude heard the bell Brigitte used ringing, demanding their attention. The two women dreaded what waited at the other end.

"Let me see to her, Gert," Hillary said, drying her hands. "Maybe I can fill in for you."

Gertrude looked up from the washtub full of clothes, and at a mound of the family's laundry yet to go. Her face was covered in a veil of shimmering sweat, rings of darkened material seeped under her arms, and a line of wetness outlined her spine. "Thank you," she said as she pushed away a stray lock of hair. "Have you heard when you'll be starting work at Mrs. Higgins's dress shop?"

"No, she is supposed to get back to me soon." Hillary pulled off her apron and mounted the stairs. She forced a smile, determined not to let the old woman upset her. She rapped on Brigitte's door, then entered the dreary room.

"Good morning, Mother Johansen. How're you feeling today?"

Brigitte turned when she heard Hillary's voice, lips pursed together in an unbroken line across her crinkled skin. "Where is Gertrude?"

"She's busy washing clothes. I offered to answer your call." Hillary remained in the doorway. Standing in front of Brigitte made Hillary feel as if she were facing her disapproving mother. Even though Hillary had never given Brigitte any reason to dislike her, she realized what Carl's mother thought of Ned and her.

Brigitte turned her head away and spat out, "This is my bath day and I want Gertrude! Not you!"

Hillary sucked back what she wanted to scream out. "I will let Gert know, but you may have to wait until she has finished the laundry. Or let me help you now." Hillary stood still, hoping for no reply.

Brigitte's cheeks twitched as she turned away from Hillary, then she turned back. "Do it now," she snarled.

Hillary left the room without a word and trotted downstairs to make bath preparations. She heated water in two enameled buckets, then picked up the basket of white washcloths, clean muslin bedding, and a freshly ironed nightdress for Brigitte, which she carried upstairs.

On her second trip downstairs, Hillary got the first bucket of hot water and dropped in a bar of Ivory soap. The soap floated on top of the water and knocked against the side of the bucket as she climbed back upstairs. A sweet, clean aroma drifted up to her.

Hillary pulled back the multi-colored braided rug before setting the bucket down, then opened the heavy curtains to let the morning sunlight in the room. She soaked the washcloths in hot water, then bathed Brigitte. She gently wrapped any joints that were red and swollen in a warm washcloth. She placed a towel over the area to keep the warmth for as long as possible. An unexpected groan of relief slipped out of Brigitte. Hillary kept her head down, but she couldn't suppress a grin.

Hillary used a new ointment the doctors recommended for treating Brigitte's bedsores. Vaseline's thick jelly consistency was supposed to protect and promote the skin's healing. But nothing seemed to help, and the oozing sores continued to fester. The damp air in the cramped room smelled of rotting skin. When the first bucket of water lost its steam, Hillary made her third trip down for the second bucket.

On one earlier bath day the water had cooled, and Brigitte had let her know, mincing no words, that cold water was unacceptable. Since then, Gertrude and Hillary always made sure the water never wholly cooled off, even at the expense of their poached hands.

When Hillary returned with the second bucket of water, she began singing hymns softly as she cleaned Brigitte's withering body. After she finished, Hillary carefully helped Brigitte to a chair to dress her in a fresh nightdress, then she changed the wet bedding. Next, she put the soiled washcloths, dirty bedding, and nightdress into one of the buckets, then gently helped her back to bed. Brigette never uttered a word.

"I will get you some tea and your pain medicine. Do you care for anything to eat?"

There was no reply. Brigitte's weight was down to eighty pounds, and her once thick, silky hair was now a stringy mess most of the time. Hillary opened the bedroom window, letting fresh air into the room. She picked up the buckets with additional dirty laundry for Gertrude to wash, and went downstairs for the fourth time.

For the rest of the day, Brigitte slept. Hillary and Gertrude took turns checking on her. When the bell rang again, the two women grinned at each other. "She's awake," they said in unison.

"Hilly, will you check on supper?" Gertrude pulled off her apron. "I'll see after Mother Johansen."

"Yes, and I better get Ned in for supper."

Hillary walked out to the back porch and leaned against the doorway while she watched Ned and his friend. They were climbing in a massive maple tree, her son moving from one limb to another with no fear. Hillary listened to the two boys bantering back and forth about a recent baseball game they attended with Carl.

Ned had the lanky build of his father, along with his hazel eyes, but he had his mother's thick, black hair. Even though he'd never met his father, he shared many of the same facial expressions and mannerisms. Hillary told her son his father died before he was born, and never went into more detail. She wondered why he never questioned her more. She wanted happiness, but having her own family and home seemed impossible. She needed someone to make her feel special. Men didn't want a ready-made family, especially one like hers.

Ned caught sight of his mother and a toothy smile broke out.

"Come in and clean up, please. It's supper time."

Ned nodded and came down the tree like a monkey, then came charging up to the porch. "Mum, do you think Uncle Carl would build a tree fort for Red and me?" Ned asked breathlessly. The smell of the outdoors swished past her as he bounded into the house.

"You'll need to ask him. Now go wash up for dinner, please," she called after her son.

Ned ran into the living room and stopped to talk to Carl, who was reading the paper. Hillary stood next to the table, listening to the soft tones of Carl and the eagerness of Ned's voice.

Carl had taught Ned how to carve wooden animals and play baseball, and at bedtime he read adventure stories to him. Carl connected with Ned as if he'd been waiting all his life for this one child. Hillary was happy for the two of them, but she feared she would end up living with her cousins' family instead of having one of her own.

Gertrude came downstairs and stopped beside Hillary to listen to the two male voices in the living room. The two women exchanged knowing smiles and went back to getting Sunday's dinner on the table.

∽

A few days later, Hillary started her part-time job in an up-and-coming woman's seamstress shop. She had to double her efforts to help Gert on the days she wasn't working, causing her days to be exhausting.

One afternoon, Hillary arrived home after work to find Gertrude upstairs with Brigitte, who was complaining that Ned was being too loud while she rested.

Gertrude was responding in a soft, reassuring voice. "I'll make sure Ned stays downstairs when you're napping, Mother Johansen. Now, I need to get supper ready. I'll bring your tray up shortly." Gertrude turned and saw Hillary standing behind her.

Before Hillary could say a word, Gertrude hooked her arm through Hillary's and steered her back downstairs without a sound. "What's going on?" Hillary asked in a hushed tone, trying not to get upset. "She's so cold toward Ned. He's just a child."

"I know. I'll ask Carl to speak to her tonight. But you need to speak to Ned. Maybe teach him to tiptoe when he's upstairs." Gertrude bristled with exasperation. "I can't tell you how many times I've been up and down these stairs today. There must be a better word to describe her than cantankerous, but I'm so tired I can't think of one."

∽

That evening, Hillary took Carl's place and read Ned a chapter of the adventure story they'd been reading while Carl spoke to Brigitte. After she'd finished the chapter, she put her arm around her son. "Ned, from now on, you need to stay downstairs when Grandmother Johansen is resting. She doesn't feel well, dear, so you must be quiet." She leaned over and kissed his forehead.

"Mum, why doesn't she like me?"

"Dear, it's not that she dislikes you. She's in pain all the time, and really doesn't mean to be ugly. Stay downstairs in the afternoon. And your friend Red can't come inside either. He is too loud." They both grinned. Red's presence was like an explosion of energy. "Ned, you need to be as quiet as possible when you're upstairs so you don't wake up Grandmother Johansen. Try tiptoeing and whispering, all right?"

"All right, Mum. I love you."

"Sweet dreams my dear." She gave him another kiss, then turned off his light and went downstairs.

Hillary caught Gertrude in the kitchen just as she was about to turn off the light. Hillary was bursting with news she had held in all evening.

"Gert, I met a man today, a handsome, mature Frenchman. I've been dying to tell you, but there wasn't a good time."

Gertrude pulled out a chair and sat down. "You did? Where? What do you mean mature?"

"He's older than I am, but I'm not sure how much. Anyway, let me tell you. I was working on Cora Kennedy's bridal gown in the front sales room this morning." Hillary sat down next to Gertrude and tried to keep her voice quiet. "When I looked up, he was watching me through the big display window. Then he came in and introduced himself, Philip Villier. He owns a restaurant, and it's pretty successful, according to Mrs. Higgins."

"Was Mrs. Higgins there?"

"No, she hadn't arrived yet." Hillary covered her face, then peeked out between her fingers. "Philip Villier's dark eyes melted my good sense—I froze. Nothing came out of me but poppycock." Hillary fanned her pink cheeks with a nearby piece of paper. "Gert, I don't know why, but this man is—well, he's different."

Gertrude reached for Hillary's hand. "Dear, I realize you're lonely. But you two haven't spoken more than a handful of words. I think you're being a romantic, Hilly. Come on, it's time we were in bed. We can talk more tomorrow."

Hillary winced. "You're right, Gert. It's just that I want what you and Carl have, and it seems as if it will never happen. I turn twenty-seven this year."

"It will happen, Hilly, but you need to be patient." Gertrude put her arm around Hillary's shoulders. "Let's go to bed."

∽

Hillary couldn't wait for Friday morning to come so she could get down to the dress shop. She had mixed emotions about the possibility of seeing Mr. Villier again, but the thought of having to explain about Ned to another person made her almost physically sick. She'd already lost several potential relationships. She had been honest regarding her son with the few men who had courted her, and each time it turned out worse than the last. They either wanted to bed her, or they did not want any part of her. Leaving New York was a fresh start for her, and her past needed to remain a secret.

Friday morning, Hillary couldn't keep her mind on her customer's dress. Every time the door opened, she pulled back the curtain. Around mid-morning, Hillary was squatting down on the floor to check the measurements on a customer's hem when she heard the shopkeeper's bell jingle. Without looking, she knew Philip had entered the shop. The back room suddenly felt stuffy to her and she needed to unbutton her collar.

"Why it's so good to see you, Mr. Villier," came Mrs. Higgins's voice from the front. "What may we do for you?"

Hillary accidentally stuck her finger as she tried to concentrate on both her customer's hem and the conversation beyond the curtain.

"Hillary? Is everything all right?" the woman asked, staring down at her.

"Yes, I stuck my finger. Again," she said in a hushed tone. "I'm nearly done. Sorry it's taking so long, Mrs. Evans."

From the front room came a deep voice. "Good to see you too,

Madame Higgins. I'd hoped, if I er, I might speak with one of your employees, a Mademoiselle Dearborn."

Hillary heard Mr. Villier's words and could not stop smiling. He was here to see her. She felt seventeen again. That special kind of tingling surged through her body.

"Mrs. Dearborn is with a customer. Is there something I can do for you, Mr. Villier?"

"No, no, this is a personal matter. I can come back if you wish."

"No, not at all, please sit down. I'll get Mrs. Dearborn for you." A moment later, Mrs. Higgins parted the curtains to the fitting room. "Mrs. Evans, would you please excuse Hillary for a moment?"

Hillary peered up with what she hoped was wide-eyed surprise for her employer. Her cheeks felt hot.

"Mr. Villier is here to speak to you." Mrs. Higgins gave her a disapproving glare. "I don't approve of my employees having personal visits during working hours. Make this conversation speedy, Mrs. Dearborn."

"Oh, yes ma'am." Hillary went to stand and dropped her pins. She scrambled over the floor to retrieve them. "Oh my gosh!" she gasped. She stood up and bumped into her customer. "I'm so sorry, Mrs. Evans." Flustered and excited, she tried to compose herself.

"Oh, for goodness sake Hillary, I'll get the pins. Button up your collar and see what the man wants." Mrs. Higgins bent down and started picking up the pins, shaking her head as she put them back into the box.

Hillary smoothed her dress down, buttoned her collar, and went out to the front sales room.

Mr. Villier smiled at her as she entered the room. "I hope I didn't interrupt you. But I was wondering if you would care to have lunch with me today?" He shuffled his hat from one hand to the other.

"What a lovely idea, Mr. Villier. I take lunch at noon, but only have a half an hour."

"Please call me Philip. I'll bring a picnic lunch and we can eat in the park across the street."

"That sounds lovely—I'll meet you over there." Hillary could feel Mrs. Higgins's eyes on her back.

"Wonderful. Until noon, Mademoiselle. Good day, Madame Higgins, Madame Evans." Philip tipped his hat and left the shop.

Hillary turned around to find Mrs. Higgins and Mrs. Evans staring at her. "Well, what did he want?" Mrs. Higgins asked.

"He wants to meet me for lunch in the park. Today!" She could not stop smiling. "Mrs. Evans, I'm so sorry for the interruption, come and let me finish your hem." The two women went back to the fitting room, leaving Mrs. Higgins speechless.

At noon, Hillary walked out to the front of the shop. It was strange, but Philip seemed so familiar. She told herself she was imagining it and pushed the thought from her mind. The weather felt perfect for a picnic. Thankfully, it hadn't rained. She glanced into the full-length mirror and pinched her cheeks. Mr. Villier was exciting and fascinating—all rolled into one unbelievable luncheon engagement.

She peered out the front window, and in between the tin lizzies puttering by, she caught sight of Philip as he made his way up the street. She took in a quick breath and felt a tingling in the pit of her stomach. He was so handsome, and he was interested in her. She'd been through this before and failed. It could not happen to her again. "Mrs. Higgins, I'm leaving for lunch now." Her hand shook as she reached for the door.

"Mrs. Dearborn, I want to remind you, you're a representative of my shop. Behave accordingly at your lunch in the park." Mrs. Higgins crossed her arms in front of her chest, almost as if she were angry it was not her going on this lunch outing.

Hillary bobbed her head. "Yes, of course, I will."

Mrs. Higgins was a widow, and Hillary figured she'd probably hoped to catch the attention of Mr. Villier herself. Hillary couldn't resist a smile.

She walked out the door and made her way across the cobblestone street. *Autumn is always so breathtaking in Boston.* Hillary scanned the fiery colors of the trees. The scent of burning leaves drifted through the park. Today would be special, Hillary was sure.

The first part of a relationship had always been tricky. Men didn't want her kind of ready-made family. She could hear Gertrude's voice, *Don't go into any personal information. Let it be all about the man.* Deep inside, Hillary wanted the relationship to be all about her. She craved the attention she thought a man would give.

Philip raised his hand when the two caught sight of each other. He beamed at her. "I'm so glad you could join me for lunch. I've a table set up for us, this way," he said, and led her down a path to a clearing near the edge of the park.

"Very thoughtful, Mr. Villier—excuse me, Philip. You've thought of everything." She blushed at her thoughts. She could almost feel his arms holding her, and the touch of his lips. It made little sense to her at the moment, but she felt as if Philip might be her last chance for happiness.

"Mademoiselle, I couldn't have you sit on the ground, now could I?" Philip had his wait staff set up the table and stay until both he and Hillary took a seat before they stepped out of sight. "I didn't know what you would prefer, so I brought samples of several spreads I've perfected over the years. I would enjoy cooking a meal for you one day, but today, with half an hour, I provide a casual lunch."

Hillary gazed around the table. "This is beyond my expectations. I'm overwhelmed." Every utensil sparkled, and the yellow and blue French country plates showcased the lunch Philip had prepared. "Oh my stars, everything is too perfect to eat."

"You flatter me. Let me tell you what I've prepared—a lobster roll, chicken salad, and ham spread. Which one would you like?"

"I love ham salad. Thank you, Philip."

"Wonderful choice, I also baked the bread early this morning, and the dessert is my favorite—a white chocolate mousse." He glanced up with a smile. "Why don't we begin with our salad?"

Hillary watched as he filled her bowl with the salad, then applied the dressing he'd prepared. He was in his element. She picked up her fork and took a bite. "Philip, the dressing is delightful. What's in it?"

"A special vinegar I have shipped over from France. So glad you like it." Philip smiled.

"Have you always enjoyed cooking?"

"Yes, my whole family is in the food industry, in one form or the other. We always cooked together before I moved to America. I miss them very much. Tell me, what business is your family in?"

Hillary's mind raced ahead—how could she redirect the conversation? Her family wasn't a subject she wanted to discuss. "My father is in banking. He and my mother still live in England. Do you have a large family?"

"Oh my, you must miss them as much as I miss my family. Yes, I've one brother and two half-brothers, all successful chefs. My papa and stepmother own a restaurant outside Montpellier, in the south of France. Have you ever been to France?" He didn't stop talking to let her answer. "One of the most fascinating places you'll ever visit. I promise you!"

"You said stepmother and half-brothers? Your mother?" she asked before she realized it was the wrong thing to say. "I'm sorry, I didn't mean to . . . ." She quickly covered her mouth with her napkin and looked down. This wasn't polite conversation.

"No, it's fine, Hillary. Father and Mother divorced while my brother and I were young—I don't ever remember living with him. I was away in culinary school when Mother died in a carriage accident. We reunited with my father and his family after her death."

"I'm so sorry for your loss." Hillary was instantly curious. Divorces were uncommon, and she wondered if he had a few secrets he didn't want out. She calculated that this might be to her advantage. Maybe there'd been another woman. She had to pinch herself not to smile.

"Thank you, but it was a long time ago. Now I have a big mix of a family, and we love to cook and eat together. I do miss my mother, but she would be happy for me. Do you have brothers or sisters?"

"I'm an only child. I would have liked a big family, but it wasn't meant to be." She took a deep breath. She didn't dare tell him the truth—not now anyway. "I live with my son and cousins."

"A son? You're, er—you were married? I'm sorry, I er, didn't know. But Mrs. Higgins did say Mrs.—" Philip appeared confused.

"I'm a widow," Hillary explained. Without hesitation, the lie slipped out of her mouth like butter sliding off a hot roll. She knew Gertrude wouldn't be pleased. "My son, Ned, is ten years old, and we've lived with my cousins since I left London in 1912." She couldn't tell him the truth, not yet—maybe never.

"And your husband?"

"He died months before Ned was born. My family sent me to America to live with my cousins." What she'd told him was partly true, and she could live with that for now.

"It had to be very hard. Suddenly finding yourself alone, and with a newborn, must've been very difficult."

Panicked by the idea he might want more information, she blurted out, "Have you ever married?" Another improper topic to bring up, but she couldn't have him ask her more about a nonexistent husband.

"Yes, I married after I finished culinary school, then my wife and I came to Boston. I was going to bring French cooking to America." He busied himself, straightening out his silverware. "She died from influenza four years ago. A most difficult time, to be honest. I understand your need to have a change in your life. It was kind of your cousins to open their home to you and your child."

"Yes, they've been very good to me." Hillary picked up a sandwich and ate. "This is excellent, Philip."

Philip grinned, then picked up his own sandwich and began to eat.

Hillary quickly asked, "Did you and your wife have children?" She felt like a complete ninny, revealing a total lack of polite conversation.

"No, we talked about it, but it wasn't to be. My wife couldn't carry a child; she was too delicate." He picked up his napkin and placed it in his lap. "I wanted children, and still do—maybe one day."

Hillary was reaching for her fork, but her hand jerked back at his words, knocking it to the ground. "Oh my stars . . . ." She could feel the heat in her cheeks. One of Philip's attendants rushed in and picked the fork up, then presented her with clean utensils. "Thank you." Hillary was mortified.

Philip put his hand on hers. "Not a problem. We have plenty. Now what were you about to ask?" He signaled to his attendants and again they stepped out of sight.

Hillary did her best to recover. "I was going to ask about your restaurant."

"A subject I love to talk about, thank you. The restaurant became a big part of my life when I lost my wife. I guess you could say we're a good fit for each other—I saved her, and she saved me." He paused long enough to pour Hillary a glass of sparkling water. They both automatically raised their glasses.

"Cheers," Hillary said. She drank her water and finished her sandwich, knowing she had made a disaster of this lunch. All she could think about was getting back to the shop before she embarrassed herself any more.

"Hillary, I don't want you to think me too forward, but I want to get to know you." He straightened up his silverware again, his eyes down.

Hillary hoped her mouth hadn't fallen open. She heard herself say, "I'd like that too, Philip. Why don't you come to Sunday dinner and meet my family?" She hoped she didn't show how desperate she was in rushing into a relationship.

"Sounds perfect—I'll bring a bottle of wine," Philip said. "What about your son? Will he be there too?"

"Ah, yes, Ned will be there too. Come over about four o'clock. We always eat at five on Sundays. My address is eighteen hundred Dorchester Lane. It's two blocks south of Mrs. Higgins's shop." She wiped her hands on the napkins. All her mistakes, on top of dropping a fork, and he wanted to see her again. She was thankful he couldn't hear her heart pounding.

"I'm acquainted with that area of town. Oh, what about my dessert?"

"Philip, I am so sorry, but I couldn't eat another bite. Thank you for such a wonderful lunch, and the good company. My cousin Gertrude will want to know what you put in your ham spread."

"Let me walk you back to Madame Higgins' shop." As they stood up to leave, Philip signaled his attendants "Please tell your cousin I'd be happy to share my ham spread recipe with her." He offered her his arm and escorted Hillary across the street.

Hillary felt as if nothing could spoil her day, not even Mrs. Higgins.

Later that evening, when Ned and Carl had gone to bed, Gertrude and Hillary sat in the kitchen to talk about Hillary's lunch with Philip.

"What did you talk about?" Gertrude asked as she shifted her chair, clearly uncomfortable asking. "Were you nervous?"

"Yes, but he made me feel so at ease. He's older than I am by many years, and more experienced. Oh, Gert, you're going to really like him." After giving Gertrude the details of the lunch, Hillary knew it was time to share her surprise. "Gert, I asked him to dinner—this Sunday." Hillary sat back in her chair, knowing her cousin would be excited to have the chance to meet Philip. Gertrude's face took on a strange expression. "Gert, what's wrong?"

"Tell me you're joking, Hillary. What in the world would I— could I—cook for someone who owns and cooks in a very successful restaurant?" Gertrude popped out of her chair and rushed over to the kitchen cupboard. She pulled out her *Fanny Farmer Cookbook* and began flipping pages.

Hillary covered her mouth and tried to stifle her laughter. Gertrude looked back at Hillary with wide eyes. She couldn't help herself and laughed too. "Hillary Marie Dearborn, you aren't amusing. I can't believe the predicament you put me in—honestly, Hillary."

A short while later they settled on roast beef with root vegetables, yeast rolls, fresh apple pie, and homemade vanilla ice cream. It would be fabulous. Hillary could smell the spiced apples and the richness of the roast beef as they planned the menu.

"Well, I guess since you haven't told me how you handled the subject of Ned," Gertrude tilted her head to the side, "it means you avoided the subject."

Hillary sank back into her chair. She knew this was coming. "I told him I was a widow. Yes, I lied. When the time comes to tell the truth—and it will, it always does—he'll walk away. Just like all the rest. Gert, I wanted this, whatever it is, to last a lifetime. Philip made me feel so special. I understand you're disappointed with me." Hillary wiped her eyes.

"We'll see, Hilly. You don't know this man. Remember to go slow, and wait to see what develops. I do wish you hadn't lied. It makes it harder when the truth comes out."

Hillary suddenly felt exhausted. "I think I'll go to bed now." She hugged Gertrude and went upstairs. She felt like she was on a seesaw—up one minute, then down the next.

❦

Sunday came quickly. Before Hillary knew it, she and Gertrude were frantically fixing dinner, setting the proper china on the dining room table, and scooting around the house with a dust rag. An arrangement of flowers brightened the center of the table. Brigitte decided she needed to be downstairs, so Carl placed her wheelchair in the already crowded kitchen.

Hillary pulled Gertrude aside, making sure no one else in the house could overhear her. "Do you think Mother Johansen will say anything? You know what I mean?" She kept glancing into the kitchen.

"No. It'll be fine, don't worry. She may judge you for Ned, but she wouldn't sabotage your future," Gertrude reassured her cousin.

"I hope you're right, Gert, because I'm not as sure as you are. She doesn't approve of me."

"Come on, we've got things to do."

∽

Later that morning, Carl and Ned went outside to get the ice cream started. "Uncle Carl, why is Mum so jumpy today?" Ned asked, while he turned the handle on the ice cream maker.

"Women, what can I tell you, Neddy, my lad? They're different creatures than us men," Carl said as he sprinkled the rock salt on top of the ice.

"What's so special about this man? Seems like a lot of fuss over a dinner guest." Ned watched his mother and Aunt Gertrude working in the kitchen. "Must mean he's special, right?"

"Ned, my lad, we must wait and see," Carl said. He put his hand on Ned's head and ruffled his hair.

## CHAPTER 4

# BOSTON, 1923

OVER THE NEXT year, Carl and Ned organized a baseball team so they could join a league in order to play other teams in the surrounding area. After a very exciting initial season, their team made it to the playoffs, and they had a good chance to win a first-place trophy. Everyone in the neighborhood was excited with the prospects of beating the west side team.

Ned ran into his mother's bedroom expecting to see her getting ready for the game, but instead she was getting all dressed up. "Mum, what're you doing? Aren't you going with us to the game?"

"No, Philip is preparing a special dinner for me, dear." She continued dressing. "Today is the anniversary of when he first opened his restaurant. He's making me the first meal he ever cooked. Very exciting, don't you think?"

"But this means you'll miss my baseball game." Ned flopped down on his mother's bed, rolling over on her new dress. "You haven't been to any of my games this season."

"Ned! Look what you did. Get off my dress, dear, or I'll have to iron it again." Hillary picked up her dress and checked it for wrinkles. "Be more careful when you're in here."

"You're gone all the time. Why tonight?"

"Oh, Ned, please go play, I'm trying to get ready. Philip will be here any minute." She brought out her new shoes and held them next to her dress. "I'll go to your next game."

"This is the playoff." Ned got up and left his mother's room with his head down.

Ned found Carl in the shed getting the team's gear together. Carl looked up and said, "There you are. Ready to go?"

Ned climbed up on a nearby stool and sat quietly for a few moments. "I don't want to play tonight."

"What? Our star pitcher doesn't want to play against the slimy west-siders?" Carl turned around, cocking his head. "What's up, lad?"

"Mum's not coming."

"I heard that too." Carl sat down on his stool. He seemed to be waiting for Ned to speak.

"I don't like Philip." Ned made a face, making Carl laugh. "She's always with him. Why?"

"What can I tell you about the heart of a lady?" He stood up and patted Ned's shoulder. "I think she's happy, Ned, and it's been a long time coming for her."

"You mean since my dad died?" Ned watched his uncle, hoping he'd talk more about his father. He wanted to know more, but felt the subject was forbidden.

"Well, uh . . . yes. Come on, Ned, it's time to go. We've got a baseball game to win." Carl smiled and picked up the equipment bag he'd been putting together.

Ned climbed off the stool, still unconvinced his mother couldn't have come to his game.

❧

The next morning, Hillary found Gertrude in the kitchen getting breakfast ready.

"Good morning, Hilly. Did you have a good time last night?" Gertrude asked, glancing up briefly as Hillary entered the kitchen. "You were late getting home, must've enjoyed yourselves." She stirred the oatmeal, then placed a lid on the saucepan. "You missed a good baseball game. Ned's team won."

Hillary said nothing, instead wiggled her fingers on her left hand so Gertrude could see her ring.

"Oh my stars! Hilly," Gertrude gasped, "It's lovely." Her eyes glistened with tears. She wiped her hands on her apron, then took Hillary's hand in hers. "Beautiful, dear, just beautiful!"

Carl walked in the room. "What're you two up to so early in the morning?"

Hillary held out her left hand to show Carl her ring. "I'm so excited. Philip asked me to marry him last night."

"We expected this, didn't we Gert?" He glanced over at Gertrude.

"We're supposed to tell everyone at dinner tonight. But—well, come look at this ring. Isn't it beautiful?" Hillary stared down at her ring and once again felt the tingle of amazement.

"I can't imagine this house without you and Ned here," Carl said, but then paused as Gertrude wiped her eyes. "Aww Gert, ole gal there'll be no tears. We've always wanted this for Hillary." He walked over to his wife and pulled her into a hug before speaking again. "What about Ned? How do you think he'll handle the news?"

"I hope he's all right with it. He and Philip have spent very little time together." She glanced at Gertrude. "I'll never be able to thank you for all you've done for me—for us."

"We'll always be here for you, Hilly." Gertrude said. "Have you set a date?"

"No, but Philip said he wanted the wedding to take place soon. He wants to take me to France to meet his family, then go to London to meet my family."

Gertrude didn't say a word.

Hillary let out a small sigh. She knew the truth had to be told to Philip. "No, I haven't told him . . . ."

At that moment, Ned walked into the kitchen. "Tell me what, Mum?"

Gertrude gasped. "Oh! Ned, you startled me." She turned around and hugged him. "Hillary, did you know Ned's team won last night? And your son threw ten strikeouts."

Hillary tugged off her ring and slipped it into her apron pocket. She had forgotten all about Ned's game. To cover her blunder, Hillary clapped her hands in celebration. "How wonderful, Ned. Now sit down and I'll get you a hero's breakfast." She turned in time to see Gertrude and Carl give each other anxious looks over Ned's head.

"Aww, you never tell me what you're talking about," he said, taking a seat at the table.

Carl ruffled Ned's hair, kissed Gertrude, and collected his lunch box.

"Whew, Mum did you see Uncle Carl and Aunt Gertrude kissing?" Ned howled. Hillary let out a nervous chuckle.

"I'll see you all tonight," Carl said.

After Ned left for school, Hillary and Gertrude poured fresh cups of coffee. "Gert, I tried to talk to him last night, but he didn't want to discuss serious matters." She avoided eye contact with her cousin. "I've been thinking about not telling him. Honestly, Gert, he'd never know the difference."

"What?" Gertrude sat forward in her chair. "Hillary, you can't begin a marriage with a lie. Please tell me you aren't serious. If you don't tell him, you'll always worry that he'll find out. Marriage is hard enough, please don't make this mistake."

"I'm, uh, I will tell him. It's just that it'll end everything. Gert, my mistake has hung over my head like an ax always waiting to fall." Hillary turned away and touched her apron pocket to feel the ring beneath the cloth. "And now when the stakes are the highest, I'm going to be punished again."

"A mistake? Is that all Ned is to you?" Gertrude stared at Hillary.

"Gert, you know that's not true. I love Ned." Hillary held her head in her hands.

"Hillary, I'm concerned that Ned won't take the news well. Have you noticed that even during dinner, the talk is all about the restaurant or something that Philip thinks is interesting? He doesn't let Ned get a word in, much less Carl or me. I suggest it might be wiser to speak with Philip before you tell Ned. In case . . . ."

Hillary shook her head. Gertrude's words stung, but Hillary couldn't deny the truth in them. She lifted her head and murmured, almost to herself, "Philip said he wanted children. But I'm sure he didn't mean someone else's." Hillary pulled the ring out of her pocket and slipped it back on. "It's beautiful the way it sparkles back at you. Isn't it?" This was something she'd always dreamed about, and now it was within her grasp.

Before Gertrude could reply, Brigitte's demanding bell rang.

"We can talk later tonight, dear." Gertrude started up the stairs, then stopped and turned back to Hillary. "Hilly, this marriage must be right for you, for Philip, and for Ned, or there'll be problems."

Hillary knew in her heart that Gertrude was right, but she wanted to simmer in the happiness she felt now. The truth would have to be dealt with, but not today. She moved her hand one way then the other as sunlight brought out the twinkling of the diamond.

꿏

Philip arrived later that evening with a bouquet of flowers for Hillary and a bottle of wine for toasting their engagement.

"Please, come in." Carl held the door open.

"Hillary and I have exciting news, Carl. Where is the family? Where's Hillary? We want to share it with all of you." Philip's face was flush with excitement.

"She couldn't hold it in—she told us this morning. Congratulations!"

His face dropped like a stone in water. "What? She didn't wait for me?"

"Women and weddings, she wanted to share her happiness."

"I guess so. Where is the bubbling bride-to-be?" His question was laced with sarcasm.

Hillary came down the stairs in a soft-pink dress, her hair braided back into a bun. "I knew I heard your voice." Philip stiffened when she touched his shoulder.

"Dear, you didn't wait for me to tell our news." There was a coldness in his voice.

Carl excused himself and walked out of the room, taking the flowers and the bottle of wine with him.

"Philip, I couldn't wait. They're so happy for us. I'm happy. Please, don't be angry. My ring is so beautiful. I had to show Gert."

"I want it to be *us* sharing *our* good news in the future."

"You're right, dear." Hillary leaned over and softly kissed his cheek. "Philip, I want to hold off telling Ned until you and I have discussed a few issues. Do you mind?"

"Whatever you want, *ma cherie*," he said, raising her hand to his lips. "Where is your ring?"

"Until we talk, I didn't want to wear the ring in front of Ned."

Philip grimaced. "We'll talk first, then we'll tell him together. How does that work for *ma chérie*?"

Hillary smiled and took his arm, and they joined the family for dinner.

Over the past year, Gertrude had conquered her fear of cooking for Philip.

"Gertrude, what scrumptious dish have you made for us tonight?" he asked, pulling out the chair for Hillary.

"A recipe my Irish grandmother taught me," Gertrude replied. "Shepherd's pie—hope you enjoy. I'll share my recipe with you."

"A favorite of mine as well, and it smells so rich. I'm anxious to taste your grandmother's pie. Let me tell you about my French *grand-mère*."

Hillary caught Carl giving Gertrude a look of dread she'd seen many times over the last year. They didn't understand Philip. Eating didn't seem possible for Hillary, and she hoped no one would notice her pushing food around her plate.

After dinner, Carl and Ned hurried out of the kitchen to work on a school project of Ned's, and Hillary cleared the table.

"Philip, let me help Gert clean the kitchen, and I'll meet you in the backyard soon." She kissed his cheek, then prayed he would understand when she told him the truth about Ned's father and not walk away.

⤫

When the dishes were finished, Hillary found Philip sitting in one of the chairs Carl had built. The family's vegetable garden thrived. The massive maple at the back of the yard almost hid Ned's tree house. There was a sense of serenity Hillary hoped Philip would feel too.

"I see why you enjoy it back here." Philip stood to greet her.

"Carl and Gert have created something special for the family. I hope you and I will have as lovely an oasis as they have." She touched his cheek gently and sat down next to him.

For a few minutes, neither of them spoke. Hillary was deep in thought about how to confess to Philip. She knew it had to be done.

Breaking the silence, Philip asked, "So, what do you want to discuss?"

"Ned, for one."

"What about him?" Philip picked up a blade of grass, not looking at her.

"I need to tell you a few things about my past I haven't shared. Mainly because I couldn't foresee where our relationship would go."

37

Hillary stalled for a moment, trying to gather the courage needed. "It's caused me many sleepless nights."

"You've had sleepless nights? What does this have to do with Ned?" Philip dropped the blade of grass, then began to pick his fingernails without a glance her way.

"There are subjects I haven't talked about." Hillary felt her muscles tense, and worried she'd throw up the little she had eaten.

"Are you saying you've secrets? *Ma chérie*, you should realize by now that you can tell me anything. Why, we've shared so much about ourselves over the past year, what could you've possibly left out?"

"I wouldn't say secrets. However, I haven't told you everything, and if we're to get married, I want you to hear the whole story. It's a bit complicated, and not something I'm inclined to talk about. That's another reason I haven't told you before now." Hillary paused as she tried to ease into her confession. She had to do this, but the words stuck in her throat.

Philip sat sideways in his chair facing her. "Well, by all means, fill me in on your past. I'll stop you if I've heard it before." He crossed his arms over his chest, clearly bored with the conversation. "Now, this is about Ned, right? Or is it about you?"

She ignored his tone, but stopped for a moment to collect her thoughts. "When I was younger, I was foolish—and very naive." This part of her life always caused her pain. She could never get past how she was deceived. "I met a man while I was attending boarding school. I didn't realize he had a family. If I'd known . . . ." She attempted a deep breath, but there wasn't enough air in the backyard.

Philip's face hardened as he sat up straight in his chair. His shoulders squared, and a crease formed on his forehead. "Go on," he encouraged. All sarcasm was gone from his voice.

"We fell deeply in love. Or so I thought." She rubbed her arms, then took a deep breath in an attempt to stay calm. She felt the deep blush of humiliation creeping up her throat. "I wanted to believe we were deeply in love, is more the truth. When I found out . . . I was . . . ." She braved a glance at Philip's face. An ache in her chest caused her to stop.

Philip's eyes narrowed. His face registered his understanding of what she was trying to say. "Are you telling me your son is the product of this affair?" He paused, turned away, then turned back. "So, this means you aren't—or weren't—a widow? You were never married?" He reached over and lifted her chin, insisting she face him.

"Yes. I mean no. We—Carl, Gert, and I—told everyone the same story to protect Ned." She felt her face become hot as the truth tumbled out. "Ned doesn't know the truth, Philip. He believes his father died before he was born. It's the same explanation I gave you at our first luncheon."

"To protect Ned? It was to protect *you!*" Philip shook his head. "You're not the person I thought you were."

Hillary's lips trembled. "That's not fair, Philip. You don't understand. I was very young, and thought this man loved me. I paid a very dear price for my foolish behavior. My family has disowned me. The man wanted nothing to do with my child, or me, when I told him." She gulped and fought the tears that insisted on rolling down her cheeks. Her heart was slamming against her chest. "I lost my family, everything dear to me. Don't you understand I lost everything, on top of—"

"Hillary, what did you expect would happen? Your innocent parents wanted to educate their only child, and this is how you repaid them? Didn't you think of the repercussions?"

"I never thought I'd end up an unwed mother, and the man I thought loved me—didn't. Philip, this man lied, and like a fool, I believed every word he spoke. I was seventeen years old and away from home for the first time. Lonely." She stared down, not daring to look at Philip. "My parents have never seen their grandson, and have no desire to. Our correspondence ended when I came to

America. I've no idea if they're even alive anymore." A sob slipped out of her. Then she felt an odd sense of relief. The truth was out. "I couldn't tell you, Philip. I thought as you became acquainted with Ned and saw what a sensitive child he is, you'd love him too." She pulled out her handkerchief. "Please."

"How could you lie to me? You allowed me to fall in love with you without telling me the truth. Didn't you trust me?" Philip's voice continued to get louder. He stood up and paced back and forth, his hands shoved deep into his pockets. His eyes avoided hers.

"I wanted to tell you, but this isn't a subject one brings up while courting. I didn't know where our relationship was going. I didn't think—" She twisted her handkerchief first one way and then the other.

"Hillary, you didn't *think* is an understatement. Your dishonesty has . . . ." He stood in front of her. "I don't know you at all." He paused, glaring down at her. "You expected this man to leave his family because you got *yourself*—you should've told me the truth from the beginning instead of waiting until days before we married. I don't think I can look at Ned and not think about your whoring-around days."

Hillary gasped. She knew she should never have told Philip the truth.

"I'm leaving. I don't want to hear any more."

"Please, Philip, don't leave like this," she cried. "I love you. This is why I didn't tell you before now. I knew what would happen."

Philip took long strides away and didn't look back.

Hillary was hit by a deep ache in her stomach and doubled over sobbing. Afraid someone might see her, she slipped back into the house. Carl and Gertrude were busy with Ned in the kitchen, who was doing his homework, which allowed her to pass upstairs unnoticed.

A few hours later, Gertrude knocked on her bedroom door. "Hilly, may I come in?"

"Yes."

Gertrude brought a small tray with a pot of tea in with her. She placed it on the dresser and pulled a chair up next to the bed. "Tell me what happened."

"What happened?" Hillary sat up, shaking her head slowly from one side to the other. "I have paid the ultimate price for being foolish. I wish I hadn't told him." She wiped her eyes. "Oh Mother would be so pleased. He said he couldn't look at Ned without thinking about my *whoring-around days*." Fresh tears flowed down her face. "He didn't even attempt to understand what happened. How many times do I have to be punished for my sins? I should've gone to my grave with this—he never would've known the difference."

"Oh, Hilly, you had to tell him the truth before you married him."

"No, I didn't. Philip didn't need to know." She paused. "I'll never have a family of my own. All I ever wanted was to have someone love me. I've lost everything—again."

Gertrude reached for the wet washcloth she'd brought and handed it to Hillary. "Dear Hilly, you'll always have family with us, and Ned loves you so much."

Hillary didn't respond. She knew Gertrude would never fully understand how she felt.

Gertrude poured a cup of tea and placed it on the nightstand. "Here, dear, drink some tea. We'll get through this together, as we've done throughout the years. One day at a time, Hillary. You're a strong woman."

"I don't want to be strong, Gert. I'm tired of being strong."

"No, you don't have to be strong tonight. But let's wait and see what the sun brings up with it in the morning, shall we? I can't guess what Philip will do. This is a lot for him to sort through, along with a bruised ego. Things he thought were true weren't. You have to admit it's a bit of a shock. But if he loves you, and I believe he does, he'll be back." Gertrude reached over and hugged Hillary.

"I'm going downstairs to get Ned to bed. You get some sleep, and I'll see you in the morning."

Gertrude stood up and smoothed out her apron. "My mother always told me not to solve problems at night. Everything looks worse until the sunlight has had its say."

## CHAPTER 5

# BOSTON, 1923

FOR WEEKS AFTER Philip left Hillary in the garden, she clung to the hope he would reconcile with her, but it didn't happen. Heartbroken and discouraged, she hired a courier to return her cherished engagement ring. Still, she was determined not to let this loss ruin the upcoming holidays, so she decided to make Ned her focus now and to move forward.

≼

On December twelfth, a week before Ned's December nineteenth birthday, it was the family's tradition for Ned and Carl to harvest their Christmas tree.

Ned flew down the stairs, pulling on his winter jacket. "Mum, I'll help you bring up the Christmas decorations when we get back."

"Slow down and put your boots and gloves on." Hillary watched as her son yanked on his winter gear. "You two bring us back a beautiful tree."

Ned saw the sadness in her eyes and ran over to hug her before flying out the door after Carl. "Yes, ma'am." He'd bring back the best tree they had ever had, and that would make her smile.

✄

Ned and his uncle walked several miles from the house to find the perfect tree. The three feet of snow that had fallen since Thanksgiving made navigating their way in the deep snowdrifts difficult. Carl found a spot where a huge tree had fallen and suggested they rest a minute. Silently, the two took in the beauty of the forest and the fresh scent of the pines. As he waited, Ned blew out puffs of white breath and watched them sag out of shape in the air. He decided now was the time to talk to Uncle about his mother.

Ned twisted a piece of yarn from his mittens. "I've heard Mum crying at night." His voice was soft, and he glanced up at his uncle to see if he had been heard. "Why's she so sad?"

Carl didn't say anything at first. "Ned, she and Philip decided not to see each other anymore, and she's not happy. But she'll be all right."

"Did I do anything wrong?" Ned kept his head down. He really didn't want to hear what he'd done wrong. "All Philip talks about is his restaurant or his family. He's not very interesting."

"Yes, Philip does talk a lot about his restaurant, and he's proud of what he has accomplished. I'm sure he misses his family."

"But you don't talk about shipbuilding all the time."

"People are all different, Ned. Don't judge Philip too harshly." Carl wrapped his arm around Ned's shoulders. "Courting is a way to find your partner for life. He and your mother must've felt they weren't right for each other." Carl pulled Ned into a sideways hug. "Besides, what could've my star pitcher done wrong?"

Ned had to think about what his uncle had said, but for now he accepted the assurance Carl provided.

✄

Before supper that evening, Ned stopped his mother in the hallway and whispered, "Will you help me wrap the gifts I made for Uncle Carl, Aunt Gertrude, and Grandmother Johansen?"

She touched his face. *He's getting tall.* "I'd love to, Ned. First I need to help Aunt Gertrude with dinner, and Grandmother Johansen needs help to eat, so how about we wrap your gifts afterward?" Hillary checked to make sure no one was listening. "What did you make for them?"

Ned's eyes sparkled with the conspiracy of keeping Christmas secrets. "Uncle Carl showed me how to carve animals and birds from wood this summer. So I made two birds, one for Grandmother Johansen and one for Aunt Gert, then a sailboat for Uncle Carl. Aunt Gert helped with the sail, but I did the rest. I'm not telling you what I made for you."

"Of course not. You wouldn't want to spoil my surprise, silly." They grinned at each other. "I can't wait to see them. Why don't you put them in my room, and we'll wrap everything after chores?"

He beamed at her praise and bounded up the stairs to move his gifts.

Hillary walked into the kitchen. "Ned is so excited for Christmas this year."

Gert smiled and placed a pot of tea on Brigitte's tray. "Yes, he's such a giving and thoughtful child."

"Are you ready for me to take Mother Johansen's supper up?" She stopped by the stove and stirred the creamy clam chowder. "Yum, the chowder smells good."

"Thank you, Hilly." Gertrude placed a small tin of pills next to the tea. "Just about ready. Here's her medicine for the evening. Tell her I'll be up to read after I finish in the kitchen."

"What has the doctor said? I don't see any improvement."

"Well, he claimed there wasn't much he could do for her at eighty-five. I'm not sure if I agree with anything he has said or done, but he's the doctor, not me," Gertrude said, raising her eyebrows.

"Makes me feel sad, thinking of the condition she's in now. She doesn't seem to have the same spitfire determination." Hillary picked up the tray. "But that might not be all bad."

Gertrude agreed, then bent down to slide a pan of yeast rolls into the oven. "Brigitte and Gus loved this time of the year. Their marriage wasn't perfect, but they both respected and loved each other. That's important."

*Don't start, Gert.* Hillary didn't want to get into a conversation about Philip, not tonight anyway. She picked up the tray of food and headed upstairs without commenting. With a knock on Brigitte's door, she waited, then entered the room. "Good evening, Mother Johansen. I've brought your dinner."

Brigitte turned away from Hillary. "I'm not hungry right now. I'll eat later."

Due to arthritis, Brigitte's hands had become gnarled hooks. The joints in her middle fingers looked as if squirrels had hidden their acorns under her skin, causing a repulsive and unnatural appearance. Her thumbs moved, but the disease kept the top joint from bending. Either Gertrude or Hillary had to assist her with meals, and many of her daily needs.

Hillary placed the tray on the table next to Brigitte's bed. "It's your favorite—clam chowder. Let me help you sit up."

"Why aren't you off with your beau?"

Hillary knew Brigitte had heard she and Philip were no longer courting. Was this her way of adding to her misery? "We aren't seeing each other anymore. You're aware of that." Hillary teared up. She didn't want to discuss her lack of success finding a husband with anyone, especially not Brigitte.

"Hillary Marie Dearborn, you need to find a man who'll love you more than himself. Philip wasn't good enough for you and he's too old for you. You need a man your own age." She turned away from the light. "Go away and let me rest. I'll eat when I'm ready."

Hillary gasped. She didn't trust her voice to reply. It was the first time Brigitte had said anything remotely civil to her since she moved in two years ago. She sat next to the old woman, listening to her shallow breathing. Then she stood. "I'll be back to check on you."

Brigitte's eyes remained shut. Hillary wiped her eyes before she went downstairs. The last thing she needed was Gertrude's questions about why she was crying.

✍

When Hillary came down the next morning, Carl and Gertrude told her Brigitte still was not doing well. A loud knock on the front door caused the three to flinch.

Gertrude placed her coffee cup on the table. "Who is that at this time of day?"

Carl stood up. "Let me find out."

The delivery man at the door held a package. "This is for Hillary Dearborn." The young man handed him a form to sign, then the package.

Carl walked back to the kitchen. "It's for you, Hillary."

Hillary's forehead wrinkled. "Me?"

A small envelope fell out as she tore the wrapper away from the box. Inside lay the engagement ring Philip had given her months ago. She gasped, then read the note aloud. "Hillary, let's start over. Philip." Hillary couldn't believe what she had just read. He wanted her back. More than anything, Hillary wanted to reconcile with Philip, but knew her cousins would think she was naive. She covered her mouth and stared at the ring laying in the box.

Gertrude reread the note as if she didn't believe the words Hillary had read. "Oh my stars."

Carl shook his head in disgust. "I'll see you all this evening." He picked up his lunch and coat and left.

Gertrude stared at Hillary. "You can't seriously be—" She stopped as Ned walked into the kitchen.

"What's that? Did you get to open a present early?" he asked, pointing to the box the ring came in. "Can I open one too? Pleeeease?"

Hillary slipped the ring and note into her apron pocket, then threw away the box and wrappings.

"Ned, we'll talk about you opening a present later, Hillary said. "Right now, you need to eat your breakfast and get off to school before you're late."

"Aww, Mum, I want to open one gift. That's all, one present. Pleeeease."

Gertrude gathered the teapot and headed toward the stairs. "I'll see if Mother Johansen feels like a little breakfast. Ned, have a good day at school. Maybe tonight we can talk Mother into letting you open a present."

"Yeeeaaah! Thanks, Aunt Gert."

Once Ned was out the door, Hillary pulled the note out of her pocket and studied the beautiful penmanship, then slipped on the ring.

When Gertrude returned to the kitchen, she placed the teapot on the table with a thud. "You put that ring back on? Does this mean you'll take him back, with all he said about you and Ned?"

Hillary flinched and pulled the ring off. "It's so beautiful. I just wanted—"

"It's my opinion, but I think you saw his true colors when he walked out on you."

"Gert, you're too hard on him. I should've listened to you from the beginning." Hillary pulled out the small black box from the trash bin and placed the ring and Philip's note inside. "Our relationship might have been different if I had."

Gertrude got up and refilled her coffee cup, but didn't comment. For a few minutes, neither of the women spoke.

"I have to work today. I'd better get ready, or I'll be late." Hillary turned back to the kitchen. "I hope Brigitte is better today."

"Me too," Gertrude said, untying her apron. "She's given up on living."

"I hope not, Gert." Hillary reached out and touched Gertrude's shoulder. "I hope not."

❧

That afternoon, Hillary heard Philip's voice and dropped the fabric she was holding. Second chances rarely came her way. With her heart pounding, she took a deep breath.

Mrs. Higgins looked up from her desk. "Well, Mr. Villier, it's been a while since you last visited us," she said. "What can we do for you?"

"I want to see if Mrs. Dearborn is available for lunch."

Coming out of the back hesitantly, Hillary said, "Hello, Philip."

They stood staring at each other. When a customer walked in, Mrs. Higgins jumped up, welcoming the interruption. "You two have a lovely lunch," she said, moving past them to assist her customer.

"Let me get my coat." Hillary didn't think she could eat a bite. Could it be true that Philip knew her secret and still loved her? She thought she must be dreaming.

Outside, they walked side by side to a restaurant they'd frequented many times. The waiter recognized them and ushered them to their usual table. They sat next to the window with a view of sailboats bobbing on the icy water.

Hillary tried to read Philip's face. "How have you been?"

"I've been well." He paused. "No, that's not true. I've missed you, and feel terrible with how I left you. I want to start over, if you're willing."

She reached across the table and put her hands over his. Touching him felt so natural to her. "I've missed you too. We need to talk about my past and Ned. You need to understand what happened."

"Hillary, can we leave this situation in the past and forget that portion of your life?"

49

"If that's what you want." She turned her head away and watched the boats bobbing on the water. Hillary wasn't sure Philip could pretend she'd never been with another man. This wasn't the way a marriage should be, according to Gertrude. Hillary had her doubts too.

"I would still very much want to marry you, but . . . ."

The expression on his face made her stomach twist. "But what, Philip?"

Philip's eyes locked onto the salt grains scattered on the table. "I want to marry you, Hillary, but I don't think I can accept Ned."

She yanked back her hands as if they'd been burned, then sat back hard in her chair. For a second, she couldn't be sure she'd heard him correctly. "Philip, no! I can't do that. This is my fault, not Ned's. Can you imagine how this would hurt him?" Hillary shook her head. "I don't believe you'd ask me to give up my son."

"What about your cousins? You said they weren't able to have a family, and Ned filled a void for them. He wouldn't have to leave his home where he is comfortable and well taken care of. You'd still see him regularly. Just—not live with him." Philip seemed to be pleading his case.

"How do I even approach Gert and Carl with this?" She folded her arms on the table. "Ned wouldn't understand, Philip."

"Hillary, you've a choice. Marry me, or stay with your cousins. But I have to be honest with you—Ned will never be my son. I don't think—"

"You don't think what?" She wasn't sure she wanted to hear anymore.

"I will always see him as a reminder of your past."

Tears slid down Hillary's face. "Philip, I need to think." Her heart was being torn in two, and it hurt to breathe.

Reaching for her hands, Philip said, "Take a few days if you need to. But know, I believe we could be very happy together."

◈

On her way home from work, Hillary tried to make sense of her conversation with Philip, and questioned her motives for needing to be with him. Give up her son? There would never be an easy answer. In her heart, she loved Philip, but was that enough?

When she got home, Carl, Gertrude, and Ned were sitting around the kitchen table. Carl was teaching Ned how to carve wood using a new technique. Hillary stood watching the trio. The bond among the three was everything she'd wanted with her parents.

Hillary never measured up to her mother's expectations. She realized that Philip's disapproval of her disgrace would be taken out on Ned. She would never allow that to happen. Ned was better off with the love and attention her cousins would give him. She'd sacrificed her whole life for Ned, and not being a mother to him would be the hardest decision she'd ever make.

She told herself that living with her cousins was a much better environment for Ned. And she would still be near, still see Ned every day, much like now. A thought struck her. Would her marriage to Phillip be an avenue to repair her relationship with her parents? Philip would fit into their world. Maybe it would work. She nodded to herself. Yes, she would make this work.

⌒

Before dinner, Ned was heading upstairs when he heard his mother talking to his aunt.

"Gertrude, I need to talk to you and Carl tonight regarding Ned."

Ned stopped and stepped back into an alcove in the hall.

"You can't tell me now?" asked his aunt.

"No, and I really want to wait until Ned is in bed."

A smile crept across Ned's face. It had to be about a special birthday or Christmas gift. Ned had to find out what they were planning. He silently clapped his hands together. What had his mother gotten him?

"I'll let Carl know."

Ned grinned, then slipped silently upstairs. All that practice tiptoeing around Grandmother Johansen would help him today. He was bursting to find out what they were planning. The suspense made waiting almost impossible for him.

That night, after Carl had finished a chapter of *Treasure Island* and they'd said their good nights, Ned waited until he heard his uncle go down the stairs, then snuck out of bed. He knew where the floorboards squeaked and spider-crawled over them. Sitting back in the shadows so no one would see him, he waited with his legs pulled up to his chest and his arms wrapped around them. His mother had told him a new bike this year was too expensive right now, but maybe she'd changed her mind. He heard the grown-ups pulling the chairs out around the kitchen table, so now he could move a little closer without being seen.

"I met with Philip today for lunch. We really had a good talk," his mother said. "He told me he still loves me and has forgiven me for lying to him. But he made it clear he couldn't accept Ned as his son. He said Ned would be a daily reminder of the disgrace an illegitimate child brings to the family."

Ned heard his mother's words, but he didn't understand. *Could not accept me as his son? Why not? And what's illegitimate?*

He heard Aunt Gertrude gasp. "Hilly, I'm sorry. I realize how much you care for Philip."

"No, no, Gert, you don't understand. Philip still wants to marry me. He just doesn't want Ned."

Ned's stomach clenched—his mother's words a punch in the gut, and he covered his mouth so no sounds would come out. *Why didn't Philip want me? What had I done?*

"Are you telling us you're thinking of marrying this man? Abandoning Ned? What?"

Ned hugged his legs tighter. *Abandon me? Why?* He and his mother had been having so much fun together since Philip wasn't around. Each day, he looked forward to her helping him with his homework, going for walks, and trips to the ice cream parlor. Even dinners were more fun. Everyone laughed and talked. He remembered Carl's words that his mother and Philip decided not to see each other anymore. What had changed? In his head, he kept hearing his aunt say, *You're abandoning Ned? She wouldn't really leave me, would she? What did it mean to be illegitimate?* A fresh wave of pain washed over him, and before he might give away his presence, Ned crept back to his bed. He circled up into a ball, pulled his pillow over his head, and sobbed until he fell asleep.

⤶

Hillary tried to make her plea clear. "Gert, if you and Carl would take Ned, I'd be able to marry Philip. This marriage might even restore my relationship with my parents. I'd be a respectable woman. No one would look down on me again, especially when I become Mrs. Philip Villier."

Carl sat back in his chair. "Hillary, we love Ned, but giving up your son to marry a—"

"Carl, I love Philip. This is the only man I've met who would even consider marrying me, and he knows the truth. I want a marriage like you and Gert have." She pressed her hands together. "What is my future if I don't marry Philip?" She waited for a few seconds. "As a single, unmarried mother, if I didn't live with you and Gert, there's no way I could support myself and Ned. Don't you understand my future is secure with Philip? I'll never want for anything."

Carl shook his head. "You'll never have what Gert and I have—if you marry this man." Carl stood up. And for a moment he didn't say a word. When he spoke, the words seemed torn from him. "Gertrude and I have to talk. People our age don't take on raising a child. We have our hands full with my mother and all the circumstances surrounding her." He glanced at Gertrude, then looked straight into Hillary's eyes. "Excuse me, but I'm done talking tonight. I'm going to bed."

53

Both women watched as he left the room, his head and shoulders bent forward as if he were carrying a heavy weight.

"Hillary, I can't believe you would abandon Ned for such a pompous man." Gertrude pushed herself up and followed Carl out.

Hillary didn't understand why her cousins would stand in the way of her happiness. She'd still see her son. Nothing would be different, except she'd have a husband and happiness.

؈

The next morning as Hillary headed downstairs, she couldn't smell the coffee. It was too quiet. No lights were on in the kitchen. Carl's lunch box stood empty, the coffee pot sat in the sink, and no breakfast was started. *Where is everyone this morning?* She turned around as Gert came down the stairs. Her eyes were red and swollen. "Gert, what's wrong? Please, tell me this isn't about our conversation last night."

"It's Brigitte. Carl has gone for the doctor. She's taken a turn for the worse."

Hillary reached out and grasped Gertrude's hands. "Is there anything I can do?"

"Breakfast hasn't been started." Gertrude pushed her hair out of her face. "And Ned needs to get up, or he'll be late for school." She rubbed her forehead. "Oh, and coffee, Carl will need some when he returns. We've been with her most of the night. I think this is the. . . ."

"Don't worry, Gert. I'll take care of everything down here." Hillary felt a cold shiver run through her body as she began the usual morning ritual, then headed upstairs to wake her son.

A half hour later, Carl returned with the doctor as Hillary was preparing breakfast for Ned, who sat unusually quiet and distant. The two men went upstairs without a word or a glance their way.

Ned's forehead wrinkled as he looked up at her. "Why's the doctor here?"

"Grandmother Johansen is sick," she said. "Eat your breakfast

54

and get off to school. It's your last day before Christmas holidays. You don't want to be late."

"Is she going to be all right?" He turned back toward the hall stairs.

"I don't know, sweetheart. The doctor's here, and he'll help Grandmother all he can." Hillary rubbed Ned's back lovingly. She felt him stiffen and pull away from her touch.

After Ned left for school, Hillary washed the dishes and cleaned off the table. Every so often she'd glance at the ceiling. Maybe this would be a blessing for all of them, if Brigitte didn't pull through. *She'd be out of pain, Carl and Gertrude could adopt Ned, and I'd be free to marry Philip.* There was hope.

A short time later, Carl and the doctor came downstairs. She overheard the doctor talking.

"Carl, it won't be long. I've left some stronger medication for pain for your mother, but there's nothing I can do for her at this point. I'm sorry."

Carl said nothing.

When she heard the front door close, Hillary walked out of the kitchen and found Carl adding wood to the fireplace in the living room. Each log sent sparks flying up the chimney. She thought his movements were mechanical and stiff.

"How is your mother?"

He shook his head. "There's nothing the doctor can do. He thinks she had a stroke last night." Then he turned, walked past her, and trudged back up the stairs.

"I am so sorry. I'll bring up a tray for you and Gert when the coffee is done." She waited until Carl had closed his mother's bedroom door before she went back into the kitchen.

Gertrude and Carl stayed with Brigitte until late afternoon. When they came downstairs, Hillary asked. "How is she?"

Carl rubbed the back of his neck. "She's gone." Then he pulled on his coat and left the house.

Gertrude teared up and sat down on the edge of the couch. "Carl is notifying the funeral home and the pastor. We have decisions to make for the funeral, but she's out of pain. I guess you have to count your blessings at a time like this." Gertrude paused. "She'll be with Gus again for Christmas. All her problems are over."

"It's a good thing, Gert." Hillary gave her cousin a long hug. *I'm counting my blessings.*

## CHAPTER 6

# BOSTON, 1924

THE JOY OF the Christmas holidays was marred by the funeral for Mother Johansen. Carl had fulfilled his promise to his father to care for his mother until the end. The four of them wouldn't miss Brigitte's demands and illness, but her absence affected them in different ways. Gertrude and Hillary often had too much time on their hands, Ned still tiptoed when he was upstairs, while Carl grieved silently.

During the weeks after Christmas and on into the early days of 1924, every time Ned walked into a room when his aunt and uncle were discussing something in hushed tones, he got the uncomfortable feeling they were talking about him. He decided to talk to Red instead of Uncle Carl about what he'd overheard, and get Red's take on what was happening at home. Red was older than he was and would know what to do. If he could have talked to his uncle, Ned would have preferred to, but he felt his uncle would be unhappy with him eavesdropping on adult conversations.

On the way home from school the next afternoon, Ned asked Red, "Hey, you ever overhear a conversation you're not supposed to?" He glanced over at his friend.

"Yeah, sure, a million times. So, what'd you hear?" Red kicked a pinecone out of his way.

"I, uh, I thought it was going to be about my birthday present, but it wasn't."

"Yeah—so?"

Ned blurted out the words, "Mum's boyfriend doesn't want me for his son." Saying the words out loud to someone sounded even worse than when he'd first heard them. "And lately, if I walk in the room and my aunt and uncle are talking, they just stop. What's illegitimate mean?" He wanted to tell Red about his aunt saying his mother was going to abandon him, but he couldn't get the words out.

"It means your mom and dad weren't married when you were born. Red stopped and looked undecidedly at Ned. "Are you talking about yourself? You're illegitimate?" Red hesitated then cocked his head to one side.

Ned's cheeks began to burn, and he could find no words.

"Some would say you're a bastard, but I'd say you're lucky." Red searched for another pine cone to kick. "Hell, you don't want him as a father either, so in my book you're even. The man sounds like a real prick. Who cares what he wants."

"My mum told me my dad died before I was born. She lied to me? I don't understand. Everyone is acting funny at home, as if something big is going to happen. Know what I mean?" He was more confused than ever and felt somehow this was his fault.

Red kicked another pine cone out of their path. "Forget them, Ned. They all lie. You're better off with no old man around to beat you like I have. Ever thought of running away?"

"Where would I go?" The thought had crossed his mind, but he loved his family until all this came up.

"My attic is a great place."

That was the last place Ned wanted to go. "I'll think about it, but don't say anything to anyone, all right?"

"No way would I snitch on you."

Ned didn't feel any better after talking to Red. Was he really a bastard? His mother had always told him not to lie and yet she had. He needed to talk to his uncle. But for now, he would wait.

❧

Months had passed since Hillary approached Carl and Gertrude about adopting Ned. They hadn't said anything else to her, and Philip had been urging Hillary to talk to Gertrude alone. She was afraid Philip wouldn't wait much longer.

One morning after Ned left for school, Hillary lingered at the kitchen table, watching Gertrude wash the dishes. "Gert, come have a cup of tea with me." She had to convince her cousin. Hillary felt Philip's patience was running out—he'd made his demand clear.

Hillary glanced up and saw Gertrude wipe her hands.

"I've expected this talk. You're eager to move on with your life."

Hillary fidgeted in her chair. "I am, but only if you and Carl will—"

Gertrude's exasperation broke loose. "Hillary, can you honestly tell me you've thought out what you're doing? Not just to Ned, but to yourself as well. Philip has never had children. He has no idea what he's asking you to do. Marriage is not an easy union, then to add the pain of giving up your child . . . . Do you realize the hurt it will cause Ned?" Gertrude leaned forward, and with hands together she appeared to be praying. "I know you love him."

"I do love Ned, and I've done nothing but think about my future, and my son's." She took in a breath, and giving herself a moment, she blew it out slowly. She wasn't sure her cousin would understand. "No one wanted me, Gert. No one except Philip, and he even knows my past." Hillary brushed unexpected tears off her cheek. "Ned will have a better life with you and Carl—better than I ever had with my parents."

"Your parents loved you, Hillary, especially your father. Your mother couldn't show affection, but losing you had to have hurt her. Think about how much she hurt you by sending you away. Can you do that to your son? Please reconsider this."

Hillary sat back hard in her chair. "Philip will never accept Ned. What kind of life would that be for my son?"

"Hillary, what kind of man is he to blame an innocent child? What kind of husband will he be? Think, Hillary," Gertrude pleaded with her cousin.

"Philip's a good man, Gert. I won't want for anything." With a deep sigh, Hillary took hold of Gertrude's hands. "I'm sacrificing my chance to be Ned's mother so he can have a better life. Don't you see this?"

Gertrude looked down for several moments. Without moving, she said, "I know you well enough to realize when you're not going to take my advice. Nothing I can say will make a difference. I'll speak to Carl again—but I won't promise anything."

Hillary felt the tension release from her shoulders. "Oh, thank you, Gert. I'll be forever grateful."

Gertrude started to respond, then stopped, as if the words had dried up inside her.

∽

Weeks later, in uncomfortable silence, Hillary sat with her cousins in the reception area of Mr. Truman Howell's law office. She wanted to cover her ears to block out the constant striking of the Underwood typewriter. The only relief from the continuous pecking was the shrill ring of the telephone, causing her to flinch each time it rang. She understood it was her cousins' devotion to Ned that made their decision, not her future happiness. Etched in her memory were Carl's words: *she'd never have a marriage like theirs.* Determined to prove him wrong, Hillary pushed all doubts from her mind.

Everyone flinched when the secretary's buzzer went off. She walked around her desk and opened the lawyer's office door. "You may go in now."

Mr. Howell was short in build with an overfed belly. The ruddiness of his complexion suggested he had had one too many sips of bourbon. Carl had researched his background and discovered Mr. Howell had an excellent record of success.

As the lawyer stood, he placed his chewed cigar in an ashtray on his desk. "Welcome, Mr. Johansen. Please take a seat and tell me what I can do for you today." He reached out and shook Carl's hand, then gave Gertrude and Hillary a stiff nod.

The stench of cigar smoke caused Hillary to need to cover her nose with her handkerchief. She took the seat between Carl and Gertrude.

"This is my wife, Mrs. Gertrude Johansen." Then, Carl gestured toward Hillary. "And my wife's cousin, Miss Hillary Dearborn. We're here to have paperwork drawn up in order to adopt Miss Dearborn's son." Hillary kept her eyes lowered.

Mr. Howell cocked his head to one side and watched the trio for a few seconds. "Well, this is a strange request for an older couple. I assume it's for financial reasons." He kept looking at Hillary, making her feel uncomfortable. "Usually this is a happy time for a family. How old is the baby?"

Carl shifted in his chair. "Mr. Howell, should we find a more seasoned lawyer, or can you handle this adoption?"

Mr. Howell's face morphed into a clay mask. All the formal politeness left his voice. "Yes, I can. We need the baby's birth certificate and some information from both parents. That brings me to the next question. Where is Mr. Dearborn?"

Hillary cleared her throat, delaying what she knew would bring on more humiliation. Should she lie, or tell the truth? Her mind spun. "The father is deceased." Hillary could see Gertrude's head bow down. Carl didn't flinch.

"So I was correct. This adoption is due to a financial situation." He reached forward for the button to call in his secretary. "We'll get the necessary information from you so we can fill out the forms." He turned toward Hillary. "Do you have your husband's death certificate with you?"

Hillary wiped her hands on her dress to soak up the sweat. "No, I don't."

Miss Francis opened the door, and Mr. Howell gave his head a slight shake. She backed out without a sound.

Mr. Howell sat back in his chair. "What aren't you people telling me?"

Carl shifted in his seat. "Mr. Howell—"

Hillary put her hand on Carl's arm, stopping him. "Mr. Howell, the truth is I, uh, I never married. The father won't ever acknowledge my child. I want my cousins . . . ." She turned away, unable to speak. She reminded herself this was what she wanted, and that she was doing what was best for Ned. It was the only way.

"Well, this changes our approach. It might take a little longer, but now I have the facts." Mr. Howell paused. "I know all the facts, right?" He stared at Hillary without blinking. His voice took on an icy tone. "I want to make myself clear. You don't need to lie. I do, however, need the truth." Then he glared at Carl and Gertrude. "I'm neither the judge nor the jury. I want to say I care. But I don't."

Hillary's eyes cut over to her cousin, but Gertrude kept her head down. Carl made no reply. This adoption went against the fabric of his and Gertrude's souls. *Would they ever forgive her?*

"We must get the father to agree to give up his rights to his baby. Do you know how to reach him? Or who he is? I rarely handle these unsavory cases, but I see you're trying to right your wrong," Mr. Howell said. He kept pushing the tips of his fingers together as he spoke.

Hillary sucked in air and could feel the rush of humiliation race up her neck. "Sir, the father gave up his rights eleven years ago. He won't admit Ned is his son, and he won't sign any paperwork, and I won't—" She wanted to say more, but no words came out.

Mr. Howell stared at Hillary. "Is the boy retarded or simple?" He shifted his stare from Hillary to Gertrude, then back to Hillary. "I've heard it can be the case with children from unmarried mothers."

Gertrude's head jerked up. Her words came spitting out of her mouth. "He is not!"

"Mr. Howell," Carl said. His voice, though not loud, let the lawyer know he was a step from losing a client. "The father lives out of the country and won't interfere in this adoption. Can you handle this or not?"

The room fell silent, but the tension arced among the four. Mr. Howell pushed the button for his secretary.

"Miss Francis, please show Mr. and Mrs. Johansen and Miss Dearborn to the conference room. Bring in the forms for a name change and an adoption. There is no father in this case." He turned to Carl as his secretary opened his office door. "I believe I can help you, but it will take a little longer and the cost will be higher, due to the extra paperwork involved. I'm sure you understand."

Hillary winced as she reached for Gertrude's arm. She knew the cost of this adoption was already stretching the family's resources to its limit.

Mr. Howell stood up, signaling the meeting's end as he took a step back from his desk.

Gertrude turned to Hillary and took her hands. "Are you sure you want to do this?"

Unable to speak, Hillary nodded.

Mr. Howell turned to Carl. "Miss Francis will get things started. If I need more information, I'll have her contact you." He slid his hands into his trouser pockets.

Carl led Gertrude and Hillary back to the reception area. Suddenly, he turned around, went back into Mr. Howell's office, and closed the door. Hillary could hear the men's voices, but couldn't make out their words. Carl hadn't approved of her decision, but he also wouldn't allow anyone to be disrespectful to his family, as the lawyer was no doubt finding out. Hillary's lips pressed in a tight smile. Carl was a good man, and with his guidance, Ned was sure to become one too.

⤺

Weeks passed before the legal paperwork was completed; they now had to tell Ned. Carl had insisted they soften the adoption and explain it as a mere name change. Throughout the afternoon, Hillary rubbed her arms and paced around the kitchen doing unnecessary chores. Once or twice Gertrude glanced over at her, but never said a word. Hillary knew Gertrude and Carl loved Ned, and he loved them. She reminded herself again that this was best for Ned.

⤺

That night after dinner was over, everyone stayed seated at the table. Ned could feel the tension in the air. Something was going to happen. He had to escape. "May I be excused?" he asked as he stood up.

"No, Ned, we want to talk with you," Hillary said as she gathered the dishes from the table and placed them in the sink full of water.

Ned turned to Carl, his eyes narrowed. "Am I in trouble?" But he knew he wasn't.

Carl shook his head. "No, you're not in trouble, Neddy." He took a breath. "Your mother, Aunt Gertrude, and I . . . well, a few weeks ago, we began the paperwork to change your last name to Johansen."

"Why?" Ned looked from his mother to his uncle. "I don't understand. Mum and I won't have the same last name?" He realized this is what had been going on. But they weren't telling the truth, even Uncle Carl. All he wanted was to get away from all three of them. *Say it!* he wanted to scream. *She's getting rid of me!*

64

Hillary abruptly stood up. "Let me get that dripping faucet." She left the table and pushed on the faucet. But instead of coming back to the table, Hillary stayed by the sink.

Carl continued as if nothing had happened. "Aunt Gertrude and I have chosen you to carry our name and become a part of our family. Your mother has agreed."

Ned's eyebrows squished together. He rubbed his hands together as hard as he could, hoping to rid himself of the pain he was feeling. "I thought I already *was* a part of your family." He wanted to tell them he knew what was going on. Anger was building up in him. For the first time in his life, he didn't trust the three people he loved the most.

Gertrude reached across the table and patted Ned's arm.

He flinched.

Gertrude quickly pulled her hands back. He saw her glance at Uncle Carl. "You are, dear, but now you'll have our last name and be able to pass it to your children. Keeping our name from dying out is important to us."

Ned sucked on his lower lip, then shook his head. "I still don't understand. What does this mean?" He wanted them to say it out loud.

"Well," Carl cleared his throat, "ah, we're adopting you. What I mean is, well, we'll be your legal parents."

"Adopting me?" He wrinkled his forehead. "Isn't that for kids with no parents? I've got Mum. She's my family." He ground his fist into his palm, hoping not to cry like a baby. They were all lying to him.

Hillary added. "What do you think? Your new name will be Edmund Moreau Johansen. It's pretty snappy. Don't you agree?"

Ned shrugged, then unable to help himself, he glared at Hillary. "You're still my mother, right?"

"Yes, always."

"And now," he paused, trying not to give away that he already knew what was going on, "Aunt Gertrude will be my mother too, and Uncle Carl will be my father. This makes no sense. What do I call you?"

Gertrude folded her hands on the table. "You can call Uncle Carl, Pa. How does it sound to you?"

"All right, I guess." Ned played with the hem of his shirt. "My baseball glove says Dearborn. What about school, and Red, what do I say?"

"I can fix your glove, Ned," Carl said. "And we've notified your school."

Ned stared at his uncle in disbelief. They had talked to the school before telling him. He felt his body sag.

Gertrude continued, "How about you call me Ma Johansen, so we know which mother you're talking to?" She smiled at Ned. "You're pretty special having two mothers that love you to pieces."

Ned saw Carl give his mother an icy glare. He couldn't force out a reply.

Carl put his hand on Ned's shoulder. "Maybe you should think about this, and we can talk later."

Ned glared at his mother. "I liked my old name. But Johansen is better—I guess. May I be excused? I told Red I'd bring his bat and glove back tonight." He had to get away from all of them. They lied to him, and he knew his mother was getting rid of him.

Carl stood up. "Sure. But straight to Red's house, then back home. It's a school night, *son*."

Ned scrambled out of his chair without a word and disappeared out the back door. He wanted to hate his mother, but then . . . maybe he had done something to cause this, whatever it was. He ran as fast as he could to Red's house, leaving the bat and glove on his porch. It hurt to take a breath. All he wanted was for everything to go back the way it was in New York. Everyone was happier before his mother met Philip. Now, it seemed his family would never be happy again.

❧

When the adoption papers arrived, Hillary and Philip began to plan their wedding and an extended honeymoon in France. This wedding was more than Hillary had ever hoped for. Philip paid for her dress and flowers. She nodded to Gertrude and Carl as she and Philip entered the courtroom, but she didn't attempt to speak to Ned. She didn't want a scene made. Not on her special day.

Ned had turned to watch his mother walk down the aisle, her cold blue eyes sparkling. She didn't even appear to see him standing with Uncle Carl and Aunt Gertrude. Hillary smiled throughout the whole ceremony. Ned wanted to scream at his mother to please love him again. But he knew it wouldn't do any good.

After Hillary and Philip exchanged their vows, they all went to Philip's restaurant for champagne and cake. Ned tilted his plate, allowing his piece to slide onto the floor, then ground it into the carpet. He walked off and sat as far away as possible. White icing lined the rim of his shoe.

Ned saw Hillary pull Gertrude aside and whisper something in her ear. She held onto his aunt's arm. He didn't care what they had to say—his mother wasn't a part of his family anymore. She never would be again.

❧

Three months later, Hillary and Philip returned from their honeymoon in France. Gertrude, Carl, and Ned met them at the Boston port.

Hillary was pale and felt sick, but her excitement about being home helped her to overcome her unrelenting nausea. She watched Ned from the top deck of the ship. He had shot up nearly as tall as her cousin while they were away. She wanted to talk to Gertrude to find out how Ned had adjusted, but she doubted there would be an opportunity tonight.

Philip took the bags of presents they had brought back and helped Hillary down the gangplank.

"Hillary, I'm eager to get to the restaurant. Please, let's not stay at your cousins too long."

Distracted, Hillary replied, "Look how big Ned has gotten, Philip. I'm so glad to be home."

"Hillary, did you hear what I said to you?" Philip's lips pressed together in an unflattering line.

"Yes, Philip. We won't stay long." She glanced at Philip, then her attention darted back to her son.

Ned stood behind Gertrude and refused to face—or even speak—to Hillary. Gertrude gave him a gentle nudge, but he hung back as the couple approached.

Hillary watched the interaction, trying to make sense of her son's behavior. "Neddy, I've brought you some presents. I've missed you so much, dear."

Ned stared down, refusing to respond.

Tightness stretched across Hillary's chest. She hoped someday she'd be able to talk to him and help him understand her reasons for giving him up.

Gertrude hugged Hillary, then said, "Can't wait to hear all about your trip, and I've made supper—"

Philip held up his hand. "Gertrude, your offer is very thoughtful, but we can't stay for dinner. I need to get to the restaurant."

"But you've just gotten home. Can't whatever it is wait until tomorrow?" Gertrude turned to Hillary. "You don't need to rush off too, do you?"

Hillary felt herself caught in the middle of the two strong personalities. On one hand, if she went to her cousins' house, Philip would think she was betraying him, and on the other, if she didn't, she would appear weak to her cousin. "I'm, uh . . . ."

Philip's face took on a stony stare. Hillary knew enough about her husband to recognize that he was getting impatient.

"Your trip must've been exhausting," Carl said, filling the silence. "We can catch up later. Philip, let me help you collect your luggage and we'll be on our way." The two men walked on ahead as the women followed, with Ned lagging.

The crowd and the noise of the port, with all the passengers searching for their families, caused memories to flood back to Hillary. So much had changed since she first set foot on Ellis Island in 1912. Reflecting how she had a new life once again, she looked around and drew in a deep breath of salty air.

"You're very pale, Hillary. Did the ship run into rough weather?"

"No, I've been on the verge of coming down with something for a week. I'll shake it off now I'm home." Hillary smiled. "Sorry we can't stay for one of your dinners. I'll be over tomorrow, and we can talk."

Hillary looked to Gertrude for a reply, but her cousin just gave her a nod and kept walking.

⌀

The next day, Hillary arrived at her cousins' home before noon. She hadn't slept well that night, causing dark circles to intensify under her eyes. Her nausea had subsided some, but she still wanted no food. Philip had left early that morning to start taking inventory at the restaurant, telling her he wouldn't be back until after the supper hour, and not to wait for him. She had planned to stay with Gertrude and wait for Ned to get home from school. Maybe he would talk to her when no one else was around.

When Gertrude opened the door, she and Hillary exchanged hugs. Gertrude then led her to the kitchen where, after a cup of hot tea in the familiar surroundings, Hillary felt the tension ease in her shoulders.

Gertrude folded her hands around the china cup. "Hillary, how're you feeling? You know, picking you up from the docks reminded me of when you first arrived in New York. You were pretty queasy then too, remember?" Suddenly Gertrude's mouth dropped open, and she lifted a hand to cover it. "Are you . . . ?"

"I don't know." Hillary bent her head down, unable to face Gertrude. "It would thrill Philip. It's a possibility, I guess."

"How about you, Hillary?" Gertrude leaned forward. "Would it thrill you?"

"You know I'd love to have children, but it's too early in our marriage. I need a little time to get used to being married first. I'm not sure how I feel." She pushed back the stray hairs from her face and stared down at the table. "I'm afraid Ned will think I'm replacing him. More children would be nice, but not now. His reaction yesterday broke my heart."

"Yes, it surprised me. He was so standoffish—but so much has taken place in such a short time. Maybe we all need life to smooth out for a while." Gertrude rubbed the back of her neck. "If you're with child, I wouldn't tell Ned right away. Spend time with him and try to get him talking again."

"You're right, Gert. Thank you, I will." Hillary leaned forward. "How's he been?"

Gertrude took a sip of her tea but didn't reply.

Hillary sat back in her chair and tried to read Gertrude's face. "Tell me what's been happening. Please, Gert."

"He's had problems in school, but Carl has been working with him. He got into some fights—"

Hillary gasped. "Fights? Ned got into fights?" He had always been such a level-headed child. It made no sense to her.

"Yes, he had a hard time with your leaving, and the adoption made little sense to him. He was angry, and I'm sure he feels abandoned." Gertrude put her hands on her hips. "Well, what did you expect?"

Hillary bent her head down and tried to rub away an ache that started pounding in her temples. "What have I done?" She prayed she wasn't with child.

"What? You knew your marriage wouldn't be without problems. Why're you so surprised?" Gertrude got up from the table and filled the teakettle with more water. "Did you think because you were happy that your son would be too?" She placed the kettle on the stove with a thud. "I'm angry too, Hillary. So is Carl. We want to support you, but . . . ."

Hillary dropped her head into her hands and began to sob. Gertrude pulled out a handkerchief and handed it to Hillary.

"Gert."

"Go home, Hillary, and rest. I'm sure you're still feeling the effects of the long trip. Ned will be fine. He's from good stock. We'll talk more after you get rested."

The two women gave each other a stiff hug, then Hillary left. As the door closed, Hillary felt an aching throughout her body. She worried her son would never want to see her again.

ᗡ

Later that evening, Hillary stared in the mirror at her swollen eyes and ghost-like pallor. Philip would be home at any moment, and she needed to convince him that Ned had to come and live with them. He couldn't see her in this state—he'd blame Ned. So, with makeup applied, she sat waiting in the living room with her needlework.

Philip burst into the house. "Hillary, I have the best news to share with you!" He pulled her into his arms. "I've had an offer from an investor to buy my restaurant." His smile spread from his mouth to his eyes. "Isn't this exciting?"

"What? What will you do without the restaurant?" Her mind went blank and she broke out of his arms. She wasn't sure she'd heard Philip's words correctly.

"We're moving to California, and I'll open a new restaurant. What do you think?" Philip poured a glass of red wine for himself.

At first, Hillary couldn't say a word. It felt like there was no air in the room. She couldn't breathe. The thought of leaving her family had never occurred to her. "What do you mean, move to California?" She walked to the far side of the room, sat down, then got up again. "No, I can't move, Philip. We just got back. You said I'd still be near Ned after we got married. No."

"Hilly, this is a business opportunity I can't pass up. It's the best thing, for our family to make this move." He put his arms around her and held her close to him. "We're moving. Ned will adjust, and he can visit us."

"I think I'm with child, Philip." Telling her husband like this wasn't at all what she wanted. "I don't know for sure."

"What? Hillary, oh, *mon amour*! A child! This is a phenomenal day." He turned her face up to his and kissed her passionately. "I can't wait to tell my family. You have given me the most fabulous news. What a night!" Philip brought her hands up to his lips and kissed both. "First, I'm given an outstanding price for my restaurant, then I find out I will be a father. We must celebrate." He whirled her around as if they were in the middle of a dance and kissed her neck.

Hillary pushed away from him and defiantly folded her arms across her chest. "I want to stay near Gertrude during this time. Please, Philip, put off this move." Tears threatened to overflow. "I can't cope with all these changes. Please, Philip."

"Now, Hillary, let's be sensible about this for a minute. I can and will make an enormous amount of money with this sale. I've worked hard all my life, and now is my payoff." He pulled her to his chest and wrapped his arms around her. "It'll take me months before I'm ready to move. So you'll stay near Gertrude—for now, but make no mistake in thinking I'll change my mind. We are moving. The sale of my restaurant will allow me to live as I've always wanted."

Hillary sagged against him. How would she tell Gertrude? And dear Ned, how could she leave him again?

## CHAPTER 7

# BOSTON, 1924–25

IN THE WEEKS that followed the honeymoon, it was vital to Hillary that she reconnect with Ned before he learned she was pregnant. She was sure he would be more upset with her once he found out. Her morning sickness made it a struggle to get over to Gertrude's house by noon. And as soon as school was dismissed, Ned was off with his buddies. Hillary felt he was doing his best to stay away from her.

Sitting in Gertrude's kitchen waiting for Ned to return from school one afternoon, Hillary fumed, "Gertrude, he won't talk. I try to help him with his homework—he wants Carl. I've tried all his favorite games, and he won't play, or I come over and he's off with that Red. You know, I think I smelled alcohol on Ned's breath the other day. I think Red is a bad influence on Ned. Have you noticed it before?"

"Hillary, Ned isn't even twelve years old—he isn't drinking alcohol. What're you thinking?" Gertrude stared at Hillary as though she'd lost her mind.

Hillary threw up her hands. "Maybe you're right, and I was imagining it. Still, things are so awkward between us. And if he finds out I'm carrying another child, well, I'm afraid he'll think I'm replacing him. Not to mention the fact that we're leaving without him. Oh, Gert this is such a mess."

"Get him talking about baseball. You know he loves the sport. We can't get him to stop talking about the game," Gertrude said as she chopped vegetables by the kitchen sink. She stopped and turned back to Hillary. "Oh, what about going for ice cream after dinner? There's a new parlor down from Philip's restaurant. He loves ice cream."

"Oh that's a good idea. I'll try it today. Thanks, Gert." She glanced down and patted her belly. "Hope this little one will love ice cream too. Ned and I have good memories of Carl making his special fruity recipe." When she raised her head, Hillary saw Ned standing at the kitchen's screen door. She gasped. *What had he heard?*

By the time Gertrude whirled around, Ned was running away from the porch. "Go after him," she cried. "Now!"

✎

Ned had angry tears running down his face. It was bad enough that she'd gave him up for adoption. But she said she'd live close by— and now she was leaving him. How could she do this to him? She was his mother. And she was having another baby. He scrambled up into his tree house and rested his head against the huge tree. What had he done?

"Ned, please come down," his mother called from below.

He choked back his emotions long enough to ask, "Where? Where're you going?"

"Philip has bought a new restaurant in San Diego, California. Do you remember where on the map California is, dear? Come down, Neddy, so we can talk."

"I can't go with you?" Nothing made sense. "I heard you tell Ma you were leaving without me. Why?" The crying was making his head pound. "Is it because Philip doesn't like me because I'm a bastard?"

Hillary gasped. "Oh, Ned! Where did you hear that? Please come down so we can talk. I can tell you're confused."

"You had them adopt me so you could get rid of me. I heard it from you." He heard her gasp again. Her talking made him want to get as far away from the sound of her voice as he could. Ned opened the slatted door of his tree house and grasped the rope swing Carl had made for him, then swung out away from the platform. He jumped to the ground and ran, unsure of where he was going, as long as it was far away from her.

⤜

As Hillary's pregnancy advanced, her physician placed her on strict bed rest. All hope of restoring the relationship with her son ended. Philip blamed Ned for the problems Hillary was having with her pregnancy, and Hillary blamed Philip. She begged her husband to reconsider taking Ned with them to California, but he refused.

Hillary delivered her second son, Arthur Carlton Villier, on September 24, 1925. Instead of his mother's fair skin and sea-blue eyes, Arty had his father's deep olive complexion and brown eyes. Everyone, even Carl, couldn't get enough of the baby's joyful nature. One day during a visit to her cousins', Hillary watched Ned's face harden as Carl held the gurgling baby.

Carl tickled Arty under the chin. "Come here, Ned, and see your baby brother. He will be a catcher for sure. Come see his hands and long fingers." The baby had wrapped his hand around Carl's pinky and wasn't letting go. "Look at his strength. He's so strong." Carl smiled down at the tiny bundle in his arms. "I remember when you were this small."

Ned didn't move closer, but instead asked if he could go to his room.

As the weeks went by, Hillary watched Ned's jealousy and anger grow as Arty received love and attention from the whole family. Helpless, she could do nothing without the risk of upsetting Philip.

∽

In early November 1925, the Villiers were set to make their move to California. Ned didn't want to see his mother leave, so running away made perfect sense to the soon-to-be thirteen-year-old. Hours before the trip, Ned watched as Gertrude left the house to help Hillary get the baby ready. Now it was time for him to escape. His treehouse had become his retreat. He felt safe up in the branches. Not long afterwards, Ned heard Carl call to him.

"Come on down, lad. We need to see your mother off."

Ned peered out through the slatted wall. "No. She doesn't love me."

Carl lumbered up the tree and sat with his huge legs dangling off the platform. "Neddy, I realize this is hard to understand, but—"

"Why can't I go too? Philip doesn't even know me. He's hardly spoken to me other than asking me to pass him food at the dinner table." Ned came crawling out of his hideaway and sat next to Carl. "I want to go too." He waited for his uncle to make his world right again.

Carl put his arm around Ned and held him close. "I know, lad. I know."

Minutes later, the two climbed down and walked to the train station together. Ned used the back of his hand to wipe his face.

When they arrived, Ned stood away from the boarding platform, where Aunt Gertrude was helping his mother. He refused to hug his mother or say goodbye. Philip, holding Arty and gently patting his back, gave Ned a disgusted stare. When Ned turned away from Philip, he saw Carl's most angry face focused on Philip. Pa didn't like him either.

Ned reached for his uncle's hand—no, his pa's hand—and the three Johansens stood and watched the train roll down the tracks.

∽

In 1928, three years after the Villiers moved to California, Hillary's third son, David Douglas Villier, was born. From the accounts Ned heard, this son did nothing but cry and spit up. Which pleased him completely.

Any problems his mother was having gave him enormous pleasure. After the birth of David, he wouldn't accept gifts, letters, or news of his mother. In his mind, she'd replaced him with two sons, creating a new life for herself without him. He would do the same. Fights at school became the outlet for his frustration. This often caused Ned to be suspended from school. Many times, Carl had to listen to angry parents complain that Ned had blackened their son's eye or busted a lip in a fight. Gertrude told Carl that she thought Ned was drinking, as crazy as it sounded for a fifteen-year-old.

Carl kept Ned busy with chores whenever he got into fights. There were always long talks while they chopped wood or performed some other physically exhausting job his adopted father would assign as punishment. Ned loved Carl, and hated that he was disappointing him. But his growing self-hatred would only turn his anger into more fights. He was afraid that Pa would end up leaving him, as his mother had.

## CHAPTER 8

# BOSTON, 1930–1935

CARL HAD INSISTED that Ned join the U.S. Navy Reserve when he was a senior in high school. Several years later, in March 1935, then twenty-two-year-old Ned graduated from apprentice to journeyman while working for Terkelsen's Tool & Die Company.

One Saturday morning, Ned was sitting at the kitchen table when Gertrude came into the kitchen with a pile of laundry in her arms.

"Ned, please open the porch door for me?"

He groaned as he rose and opened the door. "I'm going with Red and the gang to catch a doubleheader at Fenway Park."

"Wait a minute, you promised to help Pa get the storm windows down today. He shouldn't be doing this alone. It's too dangerous for him to get up and down ladders with those heavy glass windows. He needs your help." She dumped the laundry on the floor next to her second-hand wringer washing machine. Sweat stains had already appeared on her dress. "Ned . . . ."

Ned craned his head back and squeezed his eyes shut. "Ma, not today, of all days. The Reds are playing the Yankees." He would have liked nothing more than to tell her what she could do with her storm windows, but he wasn't ready to cross that line.

Gertrude's patience appeared to bottom out, as it usually did when she had to take a stand against Ned. "I want it done today."

"Whoa, you two," Carl said as he was entering the kitchen. "Ned, tell Red you'll be late to the game."

Ned's jaw clenched, and he turned his head away. *Damn.*

Carl sat down at the table across from him. "You and I will get the chores that Ma wants done then we can catch the second game. How does that work?"

It had been quite some time since Carl had joined Ned at a ball game. "You'll come with me for the second game? Well, all right. I'll go tell Red we'll be there late."

"You better be right back." Carl rubbed his jaw. "Gertrude, make me an appointment with the new dentist. This tooth isn't getting any better. Now my whole jaw is hurting."

"I told you, you should've gone last week," she called from the porch. "I'll take care of it for you."

❧

Gertrude stood next to the washing machine and watched Ned run out of the backyard. She shook her head and went back into the kitchen. "You've a way with Ned like no one else. He adores you."

"Can my best girl get me a cup of coffee?" Carl smiled at his wife of nearly fifty-five years. "Ned's a good Joe—be patient with the lad."

After getting Carl's coffee, she untied her apron and hung it on the back of the door. "When Hillary left, Ned was a mess, and if it weren't for you . . . well, I don't know." Gertrude poured a cup for herself. "He's done well at Terkelsen's. Who knows what would have happened to him if you hadn't been there for him."

"Gertrude Johansen, you've been a better mother to him than the one that God gave him. He's lucky he had you when she left." Carl paused. "I know he got the job because Terkelsen owed me a favor, but from the way Ned has thrown himself into that job, I figure now he owes me another." Carl raised his eyebrows and gave his wife a slight nod of satisfaction. "He has an employee who is sharp and pays attention to details like no one else I've ever come across. Ned will do well." Carl held his cup with both hands. "Especially if President Roosevelt can get the economy going. Jobs should be plentiful in this trade—Ned should make a decent living."

Gertrude placed the dirty dishes in the sink, then turned back to Carl. "I'm worried about the possibility of us getting pulled into a war with Germany."

Carl sighed. "You know, when I least expect it, I'll have a nightmare about the Great War again." His brows knitted together. "Roosevelt is staying out, but there's a lot of speculation about his real intentions. At least Ned has training from the navy reserves." He took a sip of his coffee and turned around to face Gertrude. "He'll know how to shoot a gun. A war might get this country out of our financial mess."

"Roosevelt wouldn't do that, would he?"

"There's a lot of talk, and most think this Hitler character is dangerous. The president will take a stand eventually. I don't think neutrality is the answer."

❧

A few minutes later, Ned opened the back door. "Pa, let's get going. I'd like to see the second game today."

"I'm coming, Ned. We'll start in the back. Bring the ladder with you," Carl said. As he passed Gertrude, his calloused hand gently touched her arm. "It'll work out, my dear, whatever happens. Don't forget about making my appointment. The pain isn't letting up today."

"I told you I would."

Carl bent down for an unexpected kiss on her cheek. "You're a good wife." The two grinned at each other.

✍

That afternoon, Ned and Carl took the forty-five-minute train trip to Boston's Fenway Park. During the ballpark's renovations in 1934, a fire had destroyed much of the stadium. The owner, Thomas Yawkey, promised fans opening day would take place on time, and true to his word, the field was ready.

Ned grinned and slapped Carl on the back as the two entered the stadium. He felt at home; Fenway was his world. From the smell of the hot dogs roasting to the singing of the National Anthem to the jeers of the spectators for poorly called plays, he loved baseball. Solid white lines in that diamond shape against the red clay screamed *Play Ball!*

Unable to find seats with Red and the gang, Ned and Carl sat down the first base line in right field. The owner had built a twenty-five-foot wall in the outfield named The Wall to keep spectators who didn't pay for admission from seeing the game. It worked, but if truth be told, there was no more space to expand the ballpark.

Fenway was loud, and the crowd was eager for a win against the New York Yankees. Ned sat forward in his seat watching the pitcher read the signal from the catcher. "That damn Ferrell is playing small ball. I hate it when a coach plays it safe. We need this win! He's got to be more aggressive! The Yanks will take advantage of his poor strategy."

Carl rubbed his jaw. "I'm eager to see Lou Gehrig play. He's one of their so-called golden boys. But you know how they can brag."

"Pa, what's wrong with your jaw?"

"I've got a bad tooth. It hurts for a while, then goes away. But it's not letting up today. Ma's making me an appointment for next week."

"Good." Ned's attention slipped right back into baseball mode. "I wished we'd seen the first game, instead of hanging off ladders all morning." He gave Carl a sheepish grin.

Carl had introduced Ned to baseball, hoping he would play the game, but Ned wasn't athletic. However, he did become an ardent baseball fan, which he knew pleased Carl.

"I wonder if the Babe will hit a home run."

Carl laced his fingers together behind his neck and leaned back. "Makes for a good game, don't you think? How about a hot dog and beer? It'll be my treat for helping me out this morning."

"I never turn down a good meal. I'll get the food since you're paying, old man." Ned smiled and took the money Carl handed him, then charged up the stairs.

Three hours later, the two headed for home. A better day would have been a sweep against the Yankees, but that was baseball. The train was full of fans arguing about the umpire's poor eyesight when two Yankee fans got into a fistfight with Red Sox fans. Ned realized the day had worn Carl out, but he'd treasured their time together despite the loss. The two stood for the first few stops. It was a relief when the arguing Yankee fans got off, and Carl and Ned could sit down.

After they settled back, Ned pulled his ball cap off and ran his hands through his hair. "Pa, what do you think about those rumors we're hearing about Germany?"

"I can't imagine another war, but it's a possibility. The thought of another war—" Carl gave a slight shake of his head. "It's not been even twenty years since we were in the war to end all wars."

"Glad I'm in the navy. Never been one to sleep in the mud." Ned settled back in his seat, twisting his ball cap.

"War is war—on the water, in the air, or on land. It won't be pretty no matter where you find yourself. It changes a person. You're never the same." Carl's gray eyes didn't blink, and the two fell silent.

Ned didn't want to hear about the war again. He pulled his cap over his face and rested his head against the window.

A woman's shrill scream jolted Ned out of a sound sleep. He looked down and found Carl sprawled in the aisle. Ned jumped up and knelt down beside his father. "Pa, what's wrong?" There was no answer. Ned yelled, "Help! I need help!"

The conductor and a car attendant came running down the aisle. "What's going on?" they asked as they pushed past the other passengers standing in the path.

"Stand back. Give the man air," the attendant shouted as he knelt down next to Carl. "Son, move back and give me some room."

Ned automatically reacted.

The man pulled back Carl's coat sleeve to find a pulse, then opened his coat and put his head on Carl's chest. He turned back to the conductor. His expression gave the bad news.

This wasn't happening. It couldn't be. Ned yelled, "Do something! My father—"

Carl's mouth hung open, his eyes unseeing.

The attendant used his gloved hand to close Carl's eyes "I'm sorry, son." He sat back on his heels. "He's gone. There ain't nothing no one can do for your dad."

"Gone? No! We need a doctor. There has to be something! Help us! We need help here!" He pushed the attendant away from Carl's body. This wasn't happening. It couldn't be happening. Ned's body trembled as if he were cold, but he wasn't.

By now the car was full of onlookers whispering about what they had seen. The conductor turned to the attendant, then he disappeared down the aisle. Two men pulled Ned to his feet and sat him back down. Moments later, a white linen tablecloth covered Carl's body.

The conductor moved out of the aisle and took the seat across from Ned and leaned in. "Son, listen, your dad's gone. Is there someone we can contact for you?"

"Oh my God! Ma." Ned couldn't focus. It all seemed unreal. He'd never felt so helpless.

∽

Carl's funeral took place weeks later. Ned's new girlfriend of just over a month, Barbara Barron, accompanied him to the funeral. She was petite, with thick black hair. Ned's best friend, Red, had introduced the couple. They'd been dating for a month when Ned decided she was the one.

When Gertrude and Ned returned home, mourners crowded the house and food overflowed from the kitchen to the dining room. It all became too much for Ned and he slipped out to the backyard. He sat in one of the chairs Carl had built and pulled out a silver flask half-full of whiskey. He couldn't stand to hear another person tell him how sorry they were about Carl. The liquid burned as it slid down his throat, but the pain felt good. With his head back against the chair, he waited for the alcohol to comfort him the way nothing else could. He didn't want to feel.

"Ned," Barbara said, then sat down, putting her hand on his arm. "Your mother is here, and, uh . . . she wants to see you."

Startled, Ned sat up straight, then glanced back at the house. "What? Ma needs me?"

"No, Ned. Your, uh—your other mother. Let's go back into the house."

He smirked. "Is the whole family here?" His body tensed up, and that black feeling surfaced. "This is exactly like her, swooping in to save the day."

"No, I think she's by herself. Come on, Ned. I'll go with you." She stood up, nervously rubbing her arms.

He'd imagined seeing his mother again one day. Conversations had run through his mind of what he would say to her, how she'd hurt him. But today wasn't the day. "I don't want to see her."

They heard the side door to the porch bang and turned to see Hillary heading toward them.

"Ned," Hillary said as she entered the backyard, "I thought I'd find you here. We used to—"

He saw his mother stop when she noticed Barbara was with

him. She'd aged, but still had the same cold blue eyes. Ned didn't wait for his mother to continue. He reached out and gently touched Barbara's arm. "Barbara, please excuse us for a minute."

"Sure. I'll be inside with your, uh . . . ." Barbara trailed off, then smiled weakly at Hillary as she passed.

Ned grimaced. "Mother." He motioned for her to sit.

"Not much has changed out here." She walked a short way into the yard, but remained standing. "I always came out here when I needed a peaceful moment. You look good, Ned."

He sat forward in his chair, shoulders crowded up against his neck and hands clasped together. "Why're you here?"

"Gertrude asked me." She paused. "I loved Carl too, Ned. He and Gert did more for me than you know." She walked back and sat down in the chair next to her son. "Please, can't we talk? I'm sorry—"

"Yes, you are . . . sorry, I mean." Disgusted with her, Ned stood up. He had to get away. "And late. In fact, you're too late."

"Please, don't leave. Let's talk this through." She stood up, her arms held out. "There are things you think you know, but you don't."

"Mother, what I know is you dropped me like a piece of used-up trash when I was twelve. For what? So you could marry a pompous ass. You know I heard you talking to Ma and Pa before you got married. I'm fully aware of the truth." He paused when he saw the pain in her face, feeling an unexpected—and undesired wave of sympathy for her. In a low voice, he added, "I was listening that night because I actually thought you—my loving mother—were trying to figure a way to buy me a bike for Christmas."

Hillary opened her mouth to say something but nothing came out.

Ned tried to take a breath, but felt a suffocating lack of air. "You moved across the country from me, made a new family. A new life. I was just a kid. What did I ever do that was so wrong?" He wanted to hit her, fists clenched so hard his hands hurt. "All these years you never bothered to come around. You didn't have—" His face was hot, and sweat dripped down his shirt. "I'm not sure at this point who I despise more, you or—"

"Ned, stop." She took a step toward him. "We have to talk—you don't know the whole story."

Ned raised his hand to keep her from getting any closer to him. "Don't know the whole story? Yes, unfortunately I do," he snarled as he pulled out his flask. "Stay. Away. I don't want to hear your excuses. You made your choices. I get it. I was in the way—a bastard child you were ashamed of." He took a long swallow of the whiskey, then left her staring at him as he staggered out to his old tree house. He managed to climb up to the main platform and used the massive trunk to support himself. Ned could feel no sense of satisfaction after his confrontation with his mother. A sudden wave of nausea washed over him and he vomited over the side before falling to the floor. Lying on the platform, he curled into himself as tears streamed down his face. *Pa!*

The evening turned brisk and quiet before Ned climbed down and headed back to the house. A pale light in the hallway allowed him to see Gertrude sitting at the kitchen table.

"Ma?" he asked, placing his hand on her shoulder. "You must be exhausted."

Gertrude placed her hand over his. "I can't—I can't believe he's gone."

Ned knelt down beside her chair and wrapped his arms around her. The two sobbed. Neither wanted a world without Carl.

꙳

Four and a half years later, on November 22, 1939, Ned and Barbara got married in the living room of Gertrude's home. Barbara's parents and Gertrude watched the two take vows to love, honor, and obey. They hadn't invited Hillary. Barbara gave up her nursing job not long afterward, and they moved in with Gertrude. She taught her daughter-in-law how to cook Ned's favorite meals and some shortcuts to cleaning house. The two became more than a mother-in-law and daughter-in-law, they became friends.

Over a year later, on a bleak Saturday, Ned received orders from the U.S. Navy to report to active duty. Thankfully, he'd be stationed at the Naval Air Station in Squantum, Massachusetts, which was less than one hundred miles from home. Ned and Barbara sipped coffee with Gertrude as they made plans. "I'll try to get home on weekends if I don't have to be on duty. This won't be bad." Watching their faces, he knew this wasn't easy for either of these two women since they had both depended on men all their lives.

"Don't worry about us. Ma's going to teach me to sew while you're gone. We'll be fine, won't we, Ma?"

Gertrude wrung her hands. "Please, come home whenever you can."

The young couple spent Ned's last night at home making love and planning their future. Ned couldn't wait to be on his way. Even though he loved Barbara and hated to leave her, he wanted to do his part for his country.

On the morning of November 30, 1940, the family said their goodbyes. "I'll be in touch as soon as I find out what the navy has in store for me. Take care of each other. I love you both." Ned knew the United States was only steps away from war with the events that were taking place in Europe, but he didn't share his feelings with his family. They would know soon enough.

## CHAPTER 9
# N.A.S. SQUANTUM, 1942–43

FOR THE PAST two years, Ned had been stationed at N.A.S. Squantum, but he was itching for something more involved since the Japanese had attacked Pearl Harbor. He received leave for the Christmas holidays and looked forward to seeing the love of his life. But the two-week leave proved to be anything but good. Gertrude didn't approve of his drinking and had made herself clear on the subject—he was not to bring whiskey into her house.

They also didn't agree on President Roosevelt's approach to the war in Europe. Ned believed the president was doing the right thing. Gertrude thought the war in Germany wasn't American's problem and caused an influx of migrants from Germany; she believed they should concentrate their efforts on Japan. Their arguments got so heated he had to leave the house and not return until she was in bed. On those nights, Ned hung out with his friend, Red, which led to heavy drinking. Barbara wouldn't give him any space while he was home, and resented his time with Red. So when 1943 came in, he was more than ready to return to the base, live according to his own rules, and resume navy life.

During his time at N.A.S. Squantum, Ned helped keep Patrol Bomber-Y, known as PBYS (a code name used by the manufacturer-Consolidated Aircraft for flying boats) flying. More than anything else, Ned wanted to do his part for the war effort, and he wanted it to be more than just keeping these water birds in the air. When he arrived on base, he stopped by the package store for a few bottles of his favorite, Imperial Whiskey, before he checked in at the duty office to pick up his mail.

As he turned to leave, the duty officer handed him a special delivery envelope. "Johansen, you'll need to sign for this one." He held out a clipboard and a pen for Ned. "Did you get new orders?"

Ned placed the bottles of whiskey on the counter, then noticed the envelope's return address, The Department of the Navy. "God, I hope so." He slit open the top, pulled out his transfer orders, and started reading.

"Where're ya going?"

Ned didn't reply right away, then looked up with a grin. "I've been assigned to the Blue Ghost. She is the Lady Lex back from the dead. Hot damn! Guess who's celebrating tonight?"

"Congratulations. Give 'em hell, sailor."

Ned headed to his barracks, unable to believe his good luck with the new assignment. His orders were to report to the USS *Lexington* (CV 16) for a three-month shakedown cruise in the Caribbean. He held out the three large bottles he'd gotten at the liquor store—these beauties had to come with him. But with strict navy rules against alcohol on ships, he wasn't sure how to solve the problem. He explained his predicament to one of his buddies, who suggested cleaning out mouthwash bottles. After a quick trip to the PX, he was set, and the replacement bottles worked like a charm. As long as no one actually checked the contents, they looked totally believable. Ned was excited to be leaving, and decided not to call home until he got to Norfolk. A call home would be a chance for Ma to give him another lecture on the evils of drink, something he could do without.

During Lexington's time in the shipyard, Ned had flown down to Norfolk to help install the hydraulics systems. The ship was a virtual floating city with a company of nearly two-thousand eight-hundred crew members and officers. His orders were for three months, and best of all, he had to report in two days.

Ned caught a cargo flight out a day later. When he checked in with the duty officer, he had a message to meet with James L. Ware, Lieutenant Commander, USN, at 0900 the next morning. A smile spread across his face. Ned had enlisted in the Naval Reserves in his senior year of high school, and with the tool and die training he'd received at Terkelsen's shop, he felt he was a top pick for Chief Warrant Machinist. *Time to celebrate.*

The next morning, blurry-eyed and nauseated, Ned reported to Lt. Commander Ware's office. He guzzled coffee and took several aspirin before he left the chow hall, but the medicine was only able to muffle the pounding in his head.

It took all his strength to snap to attention and keep his back ramrod straight, his focus forward, while waiting for the Lt. Commander to acknowledge him. He'd heard the Lt. Commander was a teetotaler. This meeting had to go well—his career depended on making a good impression.

"Johansen, take a seat." The Lt. Commander gave him a quick once-over. "Celebrating last night?"

"Yes sir, a little," was all Ned could manage as a reply. He felt as if he could throw up at any moment. Hoping this meeting wouldn't take long, Ned held on to the arms of the chair as if they would save him from hurling.

"Better watch your drinking. At any rate, I have good news. The president has agreed to our recommendations and your request for a promotion to Chief Warrant Machinist." He opened Ned's service folder and handed him a copy of the promotion. "Johansen, we expect a lot from you."

Ned struggled to keep his composure, but he did manage to give the Lt. Commander a proper acknowledgment. "Thank you, sir."

"There won't be an official swearing-in at this time, but there's a party at the Officers' Club for all of the newly promoted." The Lt. Commander paused. "Johansen, I won't tolerate any drunken behavior from my officers. Do I make myself clear?"

The Lt. Commander's eyes narrowed, and Ned was afraid the man was having second thoughts about the promotion. Ned could feel his hands getting sweaty. He was sure this was the intended reaction. He forced a firm, "Yes, sir."

The Lt. Commander nodded and said, "My aide has a package of information. See him if you have any questions. We're done here, Chief. Congratulations on the promotion." He dismissed Ned and went back to the mountain of paperwork without another upward glance.

Relieved, Ned stood up. "Yes, sir." Now that he was a naval officer, his whole life had taken on new meaning. His stomach calmed down as he took the packet of information from the aide and left the office.

By the time Ned found the nearest open phone booth, the muscles in his face hurt from grinning. He wished he could tell Pa, but calling Barbara would work. He picked up the receiver and dumped a few coins in the box. Ned counted the rings before his wife picked up.

"Barbara, I've been promoted to Chief Warrant Machinist! I'm a naval officer now! What d'you think?"

"That's fantastic, dear! I'm so proud of you. Do you have new orders?"

"Oh man, do I have orders! How about a shakedown cruise of the Lexington. In fact, I'm in Norfolk, Virginia now. Get this—she's going to the Caribbean for three months. How 'bout that? I'll get my training there, then we'll have to see what's next."

"Oh, Ned, the Caribbean! It sounds exotic and warm. Boston is expecting to have freezing temperatures tonight. It would be glorious to be warm at this time of the year." Barbara laughed. "I don't mean to sound dumb, but what's a shakedown cruise?"

"Sorry, it's the first time a ship goes out after it's built, to check for problems. All systems are tested several times before the navy accepts the ship, and every system failure has to be documented. It's a great opportunity for me to get experience and training."

"Hey, you're in Norfolk now?" Barbara paused. "Can you get home before you leave? I miss you so much, and well, I feel bad we left on bad terms. I'd really like you to come home, even for a day—if it's possible."

Ned's mouth fell open. *What the hell?* He realized she had no understanding of what this promotion meant to him. Or what it meant to him to go to war. He had no words of comfort for his wife.

The operator cut in. "To continue your call, it will be twenty-five cents, or the connection will be terminated in thirty seconds."

Looking down at the pile of dimes and nickels he held in his palm, Ned said, "Sorry, Barbara, I don't have any more change. I'll call when I can. Love you." As the call disconnected, he heard her voice, but not her words.

∽

The first month of the cruise started as Ned had expected. Every system on the ship was tested and retested, then documented. Extreme boredom had set in and he'd already drunk nearly two-thirds of his stash. He had to try harder not to drink so fast—the liquor needed to last two more months.

Ned's job required tedious paperwork on all of the failures and repairs that took place. He found it increasingly difficult to concentrate without the aid of his doctored coffee. When Ned could slip away, he stayed on the flight deck, watching the planes take off. The noise could be deafening. He couldn't imagine what the rush of adrenaline would feel like from landing a Wildcat on a postage-stamp-sized runway on a rolling sea. His pride in his country outweighed everything he'd ever done in his life. He understood the reason for this war.

By June 2, 1943, the Lexington was in the Gulf of Paria off the coast of Venezuela, two months into its three-month deployment. The F4F Wildcats had been out flying training missions for the past hour, and Ned was finishing his reports when one of his crew came running in and slid to a stop in front of his office.

"Chief, there's been a crash," the young sailor said between breathless pants.

Ned's head jerked up. "What? Who?" Without waiting for a reply, he got up, and the two men rushed up to the flight deck.

Dozens of sailors lined the side of the deck to watch as rescue boats headed out to find the pilot. Ned saw his roommate, Ross Paxton, coming down from the bridge. Knowing he would have the straight scoop, Ned ran to catch up with him. "Hey Ross, what happened?"

Ross shook his head. "All we're sure of is that the pilot reported a severe oil leak and had to make a water landing. The other pilots watching said they thought he got out."

The wind had picked up and the two men had to hang on to the railing as the ship dipped and came up on a wave. Ross and Ned ducked as sea spray washed over the deck. Ross yelled above the wind, "Don't have any more information than that at the moment. I'll let you know."

"Do you know who?" Ned felt his whole body tense up. He'd gotten acquainted with several of the pilots and couldn't stand the thought that one may have died in a training exercise.

"Yeah, it was Nile Kinnick. There're all kinds of speculations, but we're not sure of anything except he called in a serious oil leak.

What a damn shame. Did you know the kid is only twenty-four years old? Hope he survived. He won the Heisman Trophy when he played for the University of Iowa." Ross shook his head as if he was trying to get the image of this young man out of his mind. "I've got to go."

But Ned barely heard Ross's last words. Nausea had gripped his stomach. He and Nile had often talked about football over the past few weeks. He had liked the young pilot's humble, Midwest manners. No cockiness or God-like complex, Nile was an unassuming young man with a promising future. *He can't be dead.*

Ned paced back and forth by the railing. He dashed down to his cabin and grabbed Ross's binoculars. He found his doctored coffee, took a big gulp, then made his way back to the deck. Hours later, the search ended due to worsening weather conditions closing in on them. The rescue boats searched for hours, but Kinnick was never found. A black gloom fell over Ned as he left the flight deck. He couldn't wait to get back to his bunk to numb his feelings. *This was a fuckin' training exercise—no one should have died.*

᷍

The *Lexington* returned from the Caribbean three months after departure, arriving in Boston on June, 8, 1943. Ned had orders to report on July 15th for another three-month deployment on the USS *Princeton* (CV 23) for more training. It was time to go home for a short visit. Barbara had continued to write about Gertrude's failing health, and his conscience began to weigh on him.

᷍

It was a bright summer day when a yellow taxi pulled up in front of his childhood home, and he sat staring at the two-story brick house. He didn't realize until that moment how much he'd missed this place. Ned reached up and rubbed the tightness that spread across his chest.

The driver pushed his straw fedora back on his head and turned around. "Hey, buddy, is this the right place?"

Ned smiled. "Yeah, it's the right place. I've been at sea, and it sure looks good."

The taxi driver checked his watch. "Yeah, I figured as much, but I gotta get another fare to pick up. Youse know what I mean?"

Ned opened the car door and handed the driver his money. "Yeah, sorry, it's good to be home. Kinda took me by surprise." He popped a stick of gum in his mouth, hoping to hide any residue of his last drink. Getting the family upset right now wasn't how he wanted this visit to go.

The front door flew open and out ran a barefooted Barbara. "Why didn't you tell us you were coming home?"

Ned laughed. "I wanted to surprise you and Ma." He encircled her in his arms and whirled her around like a child. "It's so good to have my arms around you." It amazed him how emotional he felt.

They stood in the front yard in a tight embrace, both enjoying being held by the other, then went into the house.

Gertrude sat in the living room covered with a blanket. "Ned, oh my Lord, you're home." She removed her glasses to dab away the tears. "You should've told us you were coming."

Ned stopped in the doorway at the sight of a much older and frailer Gertrude than the one he had left. Barbara had warned him about Gertrude's condition, but until he saw her, the reality of his mother's condition hadn't registered.

"What's going on with you, Ma? How're you feeling?" He knelt down next to Gertrude's chair, hugged her, and gave her a kiss. Instead of the clean scent of Ivory soap and lavender, she had a faint smell of urine and sour body odor. "Ma, you of all people know I'm not good at communicating." He pulled back and sent a questioning glance to Barbara.

"Ned, you look good to these old eyes." Gertrude smiled. "Now, how long can you stay?"

"I have to be in Philadelphia on July 15th, so I have a little time with my girls."

Barbara dropped down on the arm of Gertrude's chair. "That's not very long." Her shoulders slumped, and she didn't attempt to mask her disappointment. "I would've thought the navy would have given you more time off before they send you—"

"What's next for you, Ned?" Gertrude asked as she patted Barbara's arm. "We're grateful to have you home. There're so many who won't be able to get home."

"I'm assigned to the USS *Princeton*. Leave in July, so I can spend some time home on the weekends." He released Gertrude's arm and pulled up a footstool. "It's more training for me. We're going to Pearl Harbor and then I will be assigned to the USS *Cowpens*."

"What a strange name for a ship," Gertrude said. Her forehead knotted with worry lines. "Any idea where you'll be going?"

"Of course, there's all kinds of scuttlebutt, but my guess is that we'll join the Third Fleet and follow them." He tried to keep the excitement out of his voice. He wanted to be here with his family, but more than anything, he wanted to be aboard ship, fighting for his country. At the same time, he didn't want his family to worry. "The brass keeps all that information pretty quiet. My guess is they won't know either till we're out to sea." He rubbed his mother's arm and realized it might be the last time he'd see her alive. "Enough of this kinda talk—what's for dinner?"

❧

After a few weekends of living nearly sober with his family, the sight of the USS *Princeton* was a relief to Ned. His surprise visit had allowed him to make amends with his mother and Barbara, and his conscience was somewhat clear, although there'd been a twinge of guilt when he'd snuck out to the garage for a drink. But what they didn't know wouldn't hurt them.

After the USS *Princeton* arrived in Pearl Harbor, Hawaii he packed up and transferred to the USS *Cowpens*. He saluted the flag as he stepped aboard. Nothing had ever felt more right to Ned. He was proud and ready to serve. Everything he'd done up to this moment was to get him ready to defend his country. He walked her flight deck with his shoulders pulled back and hat squarely on his head.

The ship's nickname was the Mighty Moo, an eleven-thousand-ton light aircraft carrier. She had a full complement of fifteen-hundred and seventy crew members and officers. Forty-five F6F Hellcats lined her deck. His first order of business was to drop off his gear and get down to the machine shop.

The two-man quarters were a tight eight-by-ten-foot slot. A set of bunks filled up the back of the cabin, with two drawers beneath. He placed his duffle bag on the bottom bunk and tossed his folded clothes in a drawer. He needed a place to put his mouthwash bottles where they wouldn't be noticed. He hadn't been able to bring as many as he wanted, and hoped he would have enough. Could he pace himself? This was the question that worried him the most.

Ned pulled out a small wedding picture of Barbara and put it on the desk that faced the child-sized metal sink. At the other end, there was just enough space for two metal lockers to hang up uniforms. He made a secure rack behind his uniforms for the four bottles and took one with him down to the machine shop.

On the door to the machine shop hung a sign, *The difficult we do right away*, with a picture of a caliper in the center. On the bottom the sign read, *The impossible will take a little longer*. Ned smiled and pushed open the door. *That's right.*

An overpowering scent of oil and metal filled his sinuses. This smell sent him sailing back to when he worked at the tool and die shop. He was impressed with the ship's organization in the compact space. The machines had yellow lines on the floor outlining their footprint. Only so much room on a ship, and every inch mapped out for efficiency. Drill presses, a huge lathe, and rows of toolboxes sat on the workbench. There was a drafting table equipped with lights to lay out schematics of equipment that might need repairs. The men working around the shop looked like they had plenty of room to do what they needed.

When the crew noticed that Ned had entered the shop, a call went out, "Attention, Officer on deck." All the sailors stood at attention as Ned made his way to his office in the back of the shop.

"At ease," he called out to no one in particular. The order for attention when he walked into a room was still a pleasant surprise. He smiled and took a seat at his desk. His crew consisted of twenty-five raw recruits, from the looks of their young, barely-old-enough-to-shave faces.

His nearly closet-sized office had enough room for a dull gray metal desk and two chairs. He found the service records of his crew in the bottom drawer of his desk. He pulled his mouthwash bottle from inside his coat and placed it underneath the papers, then locked the drawer. Stacks of repair requests for the Hellcats and various areas of the ship screamed for attention. He couldn't wait to get started.

❦

The Mighty Moo's first taste of combat took place October 5-6, 1943, with a strike on Wake Island. Despite the destruction and human carnage Ned had witnessed, he still wanted to be a part of the fight for his country.

While at sea, Ned's crew managed to repair the damage to the ship caused by enemy fire. He struggled to keep his mind on the task at hand and tried to ignore the sounds of gunfire and torpedoes swishing past the hull of the ship. Carl's words, *War changes a man,* came back to him when he first saw human flesh mangled from enemy bullets fired by men like himself who were also fighting for their country. Fear of being blown up or seeing any of his crew killed seeped into his dreams. His hands shook, and any loud noise set him on edge. He desperately needed a larger stash of booze if he was going to survive. There was no other answer.

The USS *Cowpens* returned to Pearl Harbor to prepare for strikes on the Marshall Islands that November. They launched air strikes on Mille and Makin atolls November 19-24, then returned to Pearl Harbor December 9th. Once the ship pulled into port and they were cleared to go ashore, he and his cabin mate, Ross Paxton, headed to the Officers' Club for a drink.

Ross was a quiet man most of the time, and kept his thoughts and feelings to himself. His crew called him Grumpy, although he was anything but grumpy. He enjoyed sitting at an all-night poker game even if he came back broke or owing next month's pay. Many times, he owed more. On the rare occurrence Ross came back a winner, he usually had bookies to pay off. But the euphoria of the win was always enough to bring him back to the tables. From the first time they met, Ned and Ross had a strong connection. The two men struggled from serious addictions that the war only intensified.

Ned craved the O Club's dark, den-like atmosphere. It was the only place that silenced the sounds of the roaring planes and the pounding of bullets ripping into the steel sides of the ship that echoed in his mind whenever he'd let his guard down. Never before had he seen planes slide off the deck or smash into each other and burst into flames. Ned had met many of the pilots, and whenever he witnessed one being killed, he'd hear their screams in his dreams. He would shake his head to get their images out of his mind, but the smell of burning flesh remained. When the first few beers didn't help, he switched over to straight whiskey. After a few shots, the visions began to blur.

∻

A dreary five months after Ned's surprise visit home, Barbara stared out at the gray, overcast sky while she sat beside Gertrude's hospital bed and held her hand. The massive stroke she had suffered a week before had left her in a coma. Barbara had never met anyone as selfless and giving. She struggled to hold back her grief as Gertrude took her last labored breath. "Goodbye, sweet friend." She gently smoothed back Gertrude's white hair and kissed her forehead. "I love you."

The doctor leaned over the bed and touched Gertrude's neck to feel for a pulse. He stood up and placed his hand on Barbara's shoulder. "She's gone." He gently patted her. "I'm sorry. I wish I could've done more."

Boston's beautiful, white snow was all gone, replaced with muddy slush. Trees stood naked in the wind except for tiny icicles dangling from their branches. Barbara shivered as she left the hospital. She had to make the final arrangements—alone.

The Department of the Navy advised her that Ned was out to sea, and they couldn't get the message to him until he returned to Pearl Harbor. They wouldn't tell her where he was or when she would hear from him. He wouldn't be home for the funeral.

Barbara knew she needed to contact Hillary, but dreaded the call. Still, both Carl and Gertrude had done so much for Hillary, and she should be told. She made the call to her mother-in-law, regardless of her husband's hatred for the woman. She and Hillary would attend the funeral together.

⚓

Several weeks after Gertrude's funeral, the phone rang very early in the morning. Barbara dashed downstairs and grabbed the receiver.

"Barbara, I just got the news about Ma. I'm so sorry I couldn't get home." Ned's voice caught, and without seeing his face, she felt his pain.

"It was peaceful, Ned. She was ready to go. Life didn't have the same meaning without Carl." She paused and smiled. "You should've seen all the flowers. She would've loved them." Barbara waited for a second before asking, "What about you, can you get home now?"

"Good God, Barbara, *no*. We're in the middle of a war. I can't take leave." He took a deep breath. "I don't mean to be harsh. I haven't had much sleep, and this news really . . . ." He paused a moment. "Listen, I realize this is a lot to put on you, but I want you to sell the house and move to San Diego. This way, when I have time off, I can catch a military hop over to the mainland to see you. Pa's lawyer can handle all the paperwork. Got it?"

Barbara made a quick survey of the house Ned's family had lived in for decades. She knew every closet in the house overflowed with stuff Gertrude and Carl wouldn't throw out. She was glad she and Ned were on the phone so he couldn't see her face. *I'm supposed to do this alone too?* "Are you sure you don't want me to just close up the house? We could come back and live here later." She saw Hillary standing in the kitchen doorway. "Oh, um, your mother is here with me now. She came for Gertrude's funeral." Barbara waited a few seconds to see if she could gauge his response. "Without you here, I was lost. She's helped me so much." She smiled at Hillary.

"*Who's* with you?" Ned took a deep, audible breath. His voice had an irritation to it, and Barbara knew he was mad. "Never mind. It's good you weren't alone. Listen, I don't want anything in that house. Sell everything."

"Wait. Aren't there things of Carl's you might want to keep?" The phone went silent. "Ned, are you there?"

"Barbara, you need to come to San Diego. That's all I want out of the damn house. Just get here soon, understand?"

Barbara heard a desperate tone to his voice that had never been there before. "Yes, I understand. How're things going aboard ship?"

"About what you'd expect—loud, then quiet and boring. We're heading out to sea again very soon." He paused. "Try and get out here pronto. I've got to go. I love you, and will call as soon as I can."

The phone went dead before she could ask how to reach him when she got to San Diego. "I guess you realize that was Ned. He's glad you're with me."

The corners of Hillary's mouth formed a smirk, but she didn't say anything.

Barbara knew she was not fooling anyone, and was glad Hillary didn't ask anything about the conversation. She didn't want to lie.

"Come on, I'll make coffee," Hillary said, as she tied the belt on her bathrobe and headed for the kitchen. "I don't think either one of us will get any more sleep this morning."

Barbara followed her and took a seat at the table. "I could use a cup of coffee." She rested her chin on her fist and watched gratefully while Hillary took over the kitchen. "Ned wants me to sell the house and move out to San Diego. He was very insistent about not coming back to this house." She waited to see if Hillary would say anything. "He said he didn't want anything of Carl's or Gertrude's, but I bet that isn't true. What do you think, or are you aware of anything he might want?" She paused to give Hillary time to think. "I've no idea what I'm going to do with all the furniture. Do you want any of Gertrude's things?"

Hillary shook her head "Gertrude's taste was a little old-fashioned for me. But thank you for the offer." She filled the coffee pot with water, then stopped. "I know Carl had some tools he brought over from England that Ned might like. As for the rest, this is an old house with too many memories for Ned. Starting new might be for the best."

Barbara wanted to ask about the memories, but didn't feel comfortable. She would wait for a better opportunity.

Hillary placed the coffee pot on the stove and turned back to Barbara. "I'll help you sort through Carl's tools. They would have real meaning for Ned." She smiled again. "Too, the tools might come in handy when you two have your own home. Carl taught Ned a lot about home repair." Hillary paused. "Did Ned tell you that Carl taught him woodcarving? They used to carve on the back porch for hours. What a mess." She slowly shook her head as if she were picturing the two men together. "I'm sure there're other things we can pick out also." Hillary smiled. "Ned wasn't always this angry."

Barbara didn't say anything, and hoped Hillary would continue. But she didn't. "Would, uh . . . would you consider staying on and helping me? I know that's asking a lot of you, but I feel so overwhelmed." Barbara rubbed her forehead, trying to imagine how she was going to handle dismantling this entire house.

Hillary pulled down two white cups. "I'll have to talk to Philip, but I can't see why not. He's busy with his restaurants, and the boys are in school." She checked the color of the coffee as it pulsed up in the glass top. "We live in San Diego. After the house sells, why don't you stay with us until you find a place to live? It would give us a chance to get to know each other. You haven't met Ned's half-brothers, or my husband. What do you say?" Hillary's face lit up with her first genuine smile since arriving.

Barbara knew accepting Hillary's offer would lead to trouble. Ned wouldn't want her around Hillary's family under any circumstances, but she was so alone. "I don't want to be any trouble, but, well, your offer sounds good. I, um . . . I haven't been outside of Boston before. The thought of going to the other side of the country is kind of scary. Thank you." Barbara bent her head and rubbed the ache in her tight neck muscles.

"Settled. We'll make it fun," Hillary said. "*Where* do we start in this old house? If I remember correctly, Gertrude hung on to everything, and so did Carl. They both told me, 'You never know if you might need it later.' "

Barbara laughed nervously. "I can hear Gertrude saying that too." She looked back toward the hall and could still hear the desperation in Ned's voice, how broken he'd sounded. Was it the loss of Gertrude that had hit him so hard—or was it the war?

෨

The USS *Cowpens* left Pearl Harbor with Task Force 58, January 16, 1943, for the invasion of the Marshall Islands. They made air strikes on Kwajalein and Eniwetok January 29- 31st. The USS *Cowpens* used

Majuro Island as a base and struck the Turks February 16-17, then the Marianas in late February before heading back to Pearl Harbor.

On March 4, 1944, the *Cowpens* arrived in Pearl, and Ross and Ned headed to the O Club the next day. There was always a poker game waiting for Ross, and the booze flowed.

Ned adjusted his hat and hailed a transfer Jeep. "No walking for me. I feel like my legs don't know how to respond to solid ground."

"Have a couple of shots, and you'll be fine," Ross said, climbing into the back.

"Don't let me forget to call my wife tonight." Ned held on to the dashboard as the Jeep took off. "I want to find out what my folk's house sold for, and if she's found a place for us in San Diego."

"If I can stay sober long enough to remind you." Ross grinned at Ned. "You know there must be ten women to every man in port. Maybe more. I think you're crazy to have her so close." Ross shook his head. "I'm not asking Louise to come out. She cramps my style." He laughed as he punched Ned in the shoulder.

Ned didn't reply. He had the real deal in Barbara.

An hour later, with a few drinks in him, Ned got up from the bar. "Ross, ole buddy, I'll be back." He staggered out the door and found a bank of pay phones not far from the club. Digging into his pockets, he pulled out a handful of change.

When his home phone number in Boston didn't go through, he asked the operator if she could find the home phone number for a Philip Villier in San Diego, California.

A man's voice answered. His heart sped up and he tried to swallow. "Hello, this is Ned Johansen. May I speak with my mother?"

There was no reply, but Ned heard a man's muffled voice. "It's Ned."

Hillary's excited voice boomed through the phone. "Ned! Is that you? How are you?"

"Yes, Mother." He could feel pounding in his chest and sweat forming on his forehead. "I'm . . . uh . . . I'm trying to reach my wife." The last time he'd talked to Hillary was at Carl's funeral. Suddenly he was in desperate need of another drink.

"Yes, she's living with us until she can find a new home for the two of you," Hillary said. "She must've told you."

"I want to speak to her, please."

"Oh dear, she and Arty are out apartment hunting. Is there a number where she can reach you?"

"Who?" he asked, pushing back his hat. "Who's my wife with?" *What the fuck?*

"Your brother, Art. He knows the neighborhoods around the base, and offered to take Barbara around to find an apartment."

Ned slammed the phone down. *That bitch is out with another man!* Rage took over. Without thinking, he turned around and punched the brick wall next to the phone. Pain exploded in his hand, and he dropped to his knees.

When Ned could stand up, he cradled his hand and went to find Ross.

The sick bay doctors told him he'd broken several bones in his hand. With a cast on his hand and splints on his fingers, Ned wasn't sure who he was angrier with—himself or his wife.

"These need to be removed in six weeks. Here are some pain pills." The doctor sat back in his chair. "Some sound advice? Don't go punching brick walls anymore, sailor."

It was several hours later when Ross helped him out of the Jeep and the two staggered toward the ship. "You're a dope. You realize that, don't you?" Ross told him.

Ned didn't reply, but simply adjusted the bottle of booze he and Ross had hidden in Ned's sling.

The next day, Barbara and Ned's half-brother Art borrowed Hillary's red convertible once again. The influx of military families around the San Diego area was making it almost impossible to find an affordable apartment. She was sorry that she'd missed Ned's call the day before, but realized that she was actually more excited to be out again—with Arty.

She had a twinge of guilt for enjoying her time with Hillary's family. Ned would never fit in with them, but she also understood a little more about why he was so angry. Watching Hillary dote on her two boys and husband bothered Barbara. What would Ned have been like if Hillary had taken her son with her? Maybe she could help Ned give his mother a second chance. It was something she'd work on when he came home.

She glanced over at Ned's half-brother. Arthur Carlton Villier was six foot four, lean, and athletic. His hair was midnight black and combed straight back. The Brylcreem in his hair gave it a high shine. He had Philip's cocoa brown eyes and olive skin. Handsome, charming, and dangerous all rolled up into one incredibly available man. Barbara was lonely, and being with Art felt delicious despite their nearly ten-year age difference. He showered her with compliments and attention, something that didn't come naturally for Ned. She wished for a moment that Ned were more like his younger brother.

Art turned to Barbara and found her staring at him, and he smiled. "There're some apartments Mother wanted me to show you down near the base."

"Geez, I don't think there is anything down there Ned and I can afford. Are you sure it's near the base?"

Art laughed. "Mom owns a few places you might be interested in. She said she'd give you the place at a price you can afford."

"That's so sweet, but my husband—"

"Ned needs to get over it. His mother, excuse me, our mother can well afford it."

"Art, there is a lot to their relationship I don't think you know," Barbara said, then stopped. She felt herself becoming defensive, and besides, she didn't want to share anything that Ned wouldn't want his half-brother to know. "Let's drop this conversation if you don't mind. It's such a beautiful day, and I'm anxious to see the apartment."

"You got it, doll." He reached over and squeezed her hand. "My brother sure is a lucky man."

Butterflies filled her stomach when Arty didn't release her hand.

⟡

After weeks of searching for a suitable home, Barbara had no other options but to agree to rent the apartment near the base from her mother-in-law. It was time she got back out on her own. If Hillary or Philip knew she and Arty had been having sex under their roof, it wouldn't be good. Their affair had started off innocently. The sweet kisses and gentle petting didn't last, and their passion built until one night Arty slipped into her room.

She realized too late that she'd let Hillary manipulate her as if she were a naive schoolchild. Barbara understood that if Ned found out what had happened, there would be hell to pay. He'd warned her how controlling his mother could be, but worst of all, she had broken her wedding vows.

In bed in her new apartment that first night, she replayed the conversation she'd had with Hillary. "Barbara, dear, I wish we could be honest with Ned. But he wants nothing from me. Trust me. We have to do this my way," Hillary had said as she held out the keys to the apartment. "Ned's been this way since he was ten years old. Nothing we say will make a difference. He's a mule."

Hillary had struck a nerve in Barbara when she criticized Ned in front of Arty. Without thinking, she asked, "Hillary, since you brought it up, what happened when Ned was ten? Ned and Gertrude told me a little, but you have the whole story. What happened?"

Hillary hesitated. "We don't need to dig up ancient history." She glanced over at her son. "Just agree with me on this, please." She busied herself with the apartment keys. "Besides, how's he going to find out? You send your rent check to the manager of the apartments. My name doesn't appear on any of the rental agreement paperwork." Hillary again held out the keys. "I'm hoping my relationship with you will help me work my way back into his heart. Please, do this for the family."

Barbara wondered if Hillary had Ned's best interest in mind, or her own. "He can see right through me. It's as if I have *liar* tattooed across my forehead. He'll find out, Hillary."

Hillary laughed. "I've never heard it put like that, dear. Trust me, it'll be okay. I'll get to help my son, which is something I've always wanted to do, but he's never let me."

Barbara took the keys that Hillary held out. "I'm not sure this is the best way to mend your relationship with your son. I'm concerned about what will happen when the truth comes out." Barbara worried what strings Hillary would attach for not paying the full rent. This was a mistake, but she needed to get out of their house before the truth was uncovered.

Hillary hugged her daughter-in-law. "It'll be okay. You don't have to say anything."

After several hours of going back over their conversation, how Ned would react wasn't the only thing to upset Barbara that evening as she crawled into bed. She picked up her small calendar and counted the days since her last cycle. *I'm late, and I'm never late. Maybe this move and nerves have upset everything. Do I tell Art? No, I'll wait. Maybe I'm wrong, and worrying makes everything worse.* She placed the calendar on her bedside table and turned off the lights.

## CHAPTER 10

# PEARL HARBOR & SAN DIEGO, 1944

THE USS *COWPENS* returned to Majuro in April and supplied patrols during raids on Palau, Yap, Ulithi, and Woleai. That damage meant Ned's men had to work in around-the-clock shifts to make the repairs. Often, they had to create a part for a machine to make the fix. Ned would mentally transport himself back to Terkelson's shop to escape the madness.

This was the first time they had experienced the intense Kamikaze attacks. They watched pilots so determined to kill that they would sacrifice themselves. Ned wanted to live, and could see no glory in the Kamikaze warrior approach to serving his country.

Most of Ned's crew had become seasoned sailors, which made his job better in some respects. He had to hold himself together, and that was getting more difficult. He had twenty-five souls he was responsible for, and the fear of losing one of them haunted him.

In Ned's dreams, he kept seeing a Kamikaze pilot heading

toward him with no hope of escape. He would wake up covered in sweat and shaking. His hands trembled, and he craved the only thing that would hold him together: whiskey. He ran his hand over the frame of his wedding picture, but it brought little comfort.

To keep the nightmares from coming, Ned fought sleep, but all it did was make the dreams worse. His weight dropped, food made him queasy, and cigarettes perennially hung from his yellowed fingers.

The Cowpens operated out of New Guinea during the invasion of Hollandia. It took part in air strikes on Truk, Satawan, and Ponape, then went back to Majuro for training.

On July 10, 1944, they headed back to Pearl. As soon as they were in port, and Ned and his cabin mate could leave the ship, they made their way back to the O Club. They waved to the bartender as they entered. It was noon, and only two bar stools stood open—not their usual spots—but today it didn't matter.

"Good to see you boys back and in one piece. What can I get you?" the bartender asked. "How many Japs did you kill?"

Ned wanted to knock the bartender's head off. "Not enough. Now get us two shots, or we'll shoot you." *Stupid shit!* Ned felt his muscles tense up and his fists clench. Carl's words echoed in his mind—he wanted to fight—anyone. Pa was right. The war had changed him, and he was afraid of what that transformation would actually become.

The bartender held up his hands. "Sorry. Don't get so sore. I'm just glad to see you two."

Ned and Ross ignored him and raised their glasses. "To life." They clicked their shot glasses together.

They swallowed the amber liquid and ordered more. As if speaking would break the calm, the men sat silent, lost in their own thoughts.

After a few minutes, Ross slipped off his bar stool and slapped

Ned on the shoulder as he passed by. "I think there's a poker game calling my name. I feel lucky."

Ned watched as Ross strolled off, and called after him, "You always feel lucky."

A short while later, someone sat down in Ross's seat.

"Hey, don't I know you, sailor?"

Ned slowly turned his head to see who had spoken. There sat Barbara's cousin, Donald Barron. The two men had been close friends from the time they first met at Barbara's house. Donald stood six foot five and had the frame of a heavyweight boxer, but he was a complete pussy. He had the same dark, wavy hair as Barbara, but he and Ned shared something stronger than blood lines—they shared the same addiction to alcohol.

"I'll be damned, Donald! Where the hell did you come from?" They shook hands as Ned jumped up from his stool. Donald reached around him and bear-hugged Ned, lifting him off the floor.

Ned stared in disbelief. "You're an ugly sight for my poor eyes. Son of a bitch, how the hell are you?" But here he was, right next to him, big and ugly—a gift from the gods.

The two men sat down as Donald held up his hand and ordered two shots. "I'm fine, trying to stay alive like everyone else. Good to see you too. What ship are you assigned to?"

"The USS Cowpens—better known as the Mighty Moo. And you?" Seeing Donald was a lifeline to Ned, someone from home. He couldn't believe his dumb luck.

"I just got to Pearl. My orders are to report to the USS *Enterprise* in the morning. Not sure when we leave, but it should be within the next few weeks. Lots of repairs still to be done." Donald rubbed his hands together as if he couldn't wait to get started. "Hey, how's my beautiful cousin Barbara doing? Mum tells me Aunt Judith is worried about her daughter—so far from home." He fluttered his fingers in the air, mocking his mother.

"Worried? Why?" Ned said. The lines in his forehead deepened, and he straightened up on the stool. "She's supposed to be moving to San Diego and finding us a place to live while living with my mother—this can't be good."

"Oh yeah, Mum said she'd found a swanky apartment down near the base," he said as he raised his glass. "Exclusive area, I'm told." Donald held out his pinky finger and downed his drink. "How'd you pull that off?"

"Swanky?" Ned's eyes were bloodshot, and his words slurred. "Anything more?"

"No, that's all." Donald threw back another shot.

"This sounds like the meddling of my mother." Ned slammed his hand on the bar, making the shot glasses jiggle and attracting stares from the others at the bar. "I should have known Barbara would get tangled up—"

"Whoa! Don't get so upset. I'm not sure Mum got it right. Speak to your wife first. Let's have another shot—on me." Donald held up two fingers for the bartender.

Ned couldn't shake Donald's words: *a swanky place*. But he had a more immediate need. He'd warned Barbara not to accept help from his mother, and she refused to listen. He would take care of that problem later. Right now, he had the man, he felt could help him with his survival. "Donald, ole buddy, do you realize what's wrong with these fuckin' ships? There's not a drop of whiskey anywhere, and there is only so much you can sneak on board. It's a problem I have to, excuse me, we have to resolve. Got any ideas?"

"Boy, do I have the answer to your problem." Donald slid a shot glass down to Ned. "Have ya ever tried moonshine? It's simple to make. Or so I'm told, anyway. I've got this buddy and he makes it all the time."

"No. Bet it tastes like gasoline." Ned smirked. "Still, you'd have to get it aboard ship without getting caught." Ned raised his eyebrows in doubt.

"No. Not a problem, 'cause you make it aboard ship." Donald

sat up straight on the bar stool with a grin on his face. "Bet you never thought I'd say that, did ya?" Donald held up his hands for the bartender. "My buddy says the first sip bites like a snake, but the second one swallows smooth as honey." Donald chuckled, showing his perfect white teeth. "Hell, it's an adventure."

Ned stared into his empty shot glass. "These battles are getting to me. I've never experienced anything like this in my life. These Kamikaze fuckers want to die and take you out with them. Why?" He rolled his shot glass one way then the other. "If we make this moonshine, I'd have a constant supply and might survive." Ned didn't want to admit any kind of weakness, but he had to get help. He kept staring at his glass. "It doesn't matter what the shit tastes like."

"Stop right there. I've got your back. I'll get the recipe and fix you right up. Let's meet back here tomorrow, and we'll make plans for Operation Righting the Navy's Wrongs." Donald held up his glass for a toast, but it was empty.


Weeks after moving in, Barbara invited Hillary and Art for a tour of the updated apartment. "This is my first home." She smiled at her mother-in-law. "I need to thank you and Arty for all your help."

It was a cozy, five-room apartment, two bedrooms with a bath in between, a living and dining room combination and a good-sized kitchen. Art helped her paint all five rooms a soft winter's white, and they had all the wood floors refinished. He hung curtain rods and pictures, and laid rugs. The two spent many hours together searching second-hand furniture shops for pieces to refurbish. She found herself waiting for Arty, and she moped around on days he had class. He made her feel special, but it scared her to think she might be falling in love with him.

Hillary scanned the room. "You've done a stunning job of

mixing old pieces with new ones. I should have my friend come and take pictures for her magazine. Ned'll adore living here."

Art turned and let out a laugh. "Yes, until he finds out who owns it, then all hell will break loose."

"I'm sorry. I wish things were different between the two of you." Barbara wanted to know the truth, but with Arty there, she realized Hillary wasn't going to say anything.

Hillary held up her hand. "Say nothing to him. There's no way he'll find out."

Art laughed. "That's not true, Mother. I've never met Ned, but I'm sure he isn't dumb." Art turned from the window and stared at Hillary and Barbara. "This is a time bomb waiting to go off, and you two are kidding yourselves. We've covered all of San Diego, and he won't find any place as close to the naval base as this one, and especially at Mother's discounted rent. Let him have his temper tantrum. I'd like to see him do any better."

Art didn't understand the depth of Ned's feelings, but Barbara knew his mother did. Still, Hillary seemed determined for this charade to work.

Barbara shook her head. "Art, you're right on the one hand, but Ned would rather live on the street than accept anything from—" She stopped and could feel the heat on her cheeks when she realized what she was about to say. "Hillary, I don't want to offend you. You've been so kind, but you understand what I'm saying."

"I do. Let's keep quiet, and we'll handle Ned if he finds out," Hillary said. She gathered her purse and coat. "See you two tonight for dinner, right? Six-thirty for drinks and seven-thirty for dinner. Don't be late. Chef has a fabulous seafood dinner planned for us. It'll be yummy."

"Thank you again, Hillary." Barbara hugged her mother-in-law and walked her to the door. "We'll be on time."

Hillary turned back to Art as if to say something, but instead she just waved and left.

Barbara walked back into the living room. "She knows, doesn't she?" She dropped into the leather club chair nearest her. "I don't know how, but she does."

Art laughed. "Oh, come on, doll. You're letting your guilt show."

"Art, has your mother said anything to you, uh, you know . . . about us spending so much time together?" Barbara sat forward in her chair. "Would she say anything to Ned? Oh, God!"

"No, silly girl, she's been so obsessed with having you here and the hope of restoring her relationship with Ned—I doubt she's paying any attention to us."

Barbara covered her face. "No, now be serious. Do you think she'd ever say anything to Ned?"

"No, I don't." He walked over to her and pulled her up. "Come on, doll, let's visit your newly decorated bedroom before heading to Mother's. Don't ruin the moment by overthinking." He grinned and kissed her neck.

She leaned into his body and let a small groan escape. "Art, what're we doing?"

"Silly girl, we're playing like rabbits, and having an excellent time too." He took her hand and led her into the bedroom.

Later, Barbara stepped out of the shower and wrapped a towel around her wet body. She picked up her dirty clothes and dropped them in the basket. She could still smell Arty's cologne on them. There was enough time to dress and get to her mother-in-law's house for dinner. They would probably miss cocktail hour, but she couldn't do anything about it now. As she brushed her hair back into a long ponytail, she stared at the mirror. *I'm crazy getting involved with him. What am I going to do if I'm pregnant? Do I tell Arty? Would he tell his mother or, worse yet, tell his brother?* There were no answers back. She snapped off the light and walked out of the bedroom.

"Arty, are you ready?" she asked. "We'll be late again."

Art came into the bedroom, bare-chested and holding fresh

drinks. "You worry too much. Mother will be fine if we're a little late." He smiled and unbuckled his belt. "Come here, doll, and let's test your bed out again before dinner. It'll stimulate your appetite." A gleaming white smile spread across his face, and he raised his eyebrows as if to tempt her.

"No, we have to go now." Barbara pulled on her dress and slipped into her flats. Art had nothing to lose in this relationship, which caused his attitude to be a little too casual. *I'm a fool, and he's a dope.* She picked up her purse and checked the mirror as she headed for the door. "I won't give your mother any more reasons to think something is going on between us. I'm sure she's disappointed enough in me."

"Okay, okay, let me put my shirt and shoes on, and we'll head out. Your guilt makes you no fun."

The phone rang, and Barbara went to answer, but Art reached it first. "Hello, the Johansen's residence." He was silent for a few seconds. "Hey, brother." He paused again. "What's that?" Art's mouth fell open. "Well, okay, hold a minute, and I'll get your *wife*."

Barbara covered her face. She couldn't move. Her worse nightmare had come true.

Art held the phone out to her, urging her to take it from him.

Barbara slowly walked over, took the phone, and squeezed her eyes shut. "Hello, Ned?"

"Who in the hell was that?" he asked. "Is being around my slutty mother rubbing off on you?"

"Wait a minute. Art has helped me find an apartment in a city I know nothing about. He helped me move in and get *our* home settled. I would have been lost if it weren't for your mother and her family." She couldn't look at Arty, but knew he was watching and listening. "He came to get me so I could have dinner with your mother." Her tone wasn't convincing anyone. She turned in time to see that Art had walked out of the room. "Can we begin this conversation over?"

Ned didn't reply right away. "You're right. Sorry. I just don't like you getting so close to Mother."

Barbara felt herself shaking. *Had she convinced him?* "Hillary has helped me so much, Ned. Our home is lovely and waiting for you."

"I heard it was a swanky apartment. How did you pay for it? And it better not have taken all the money we got from selling my parent's house." He paused. "Tell me you haven't spent all our money on renting an apartment."

Art gave her a look, then pointed to his watch.

"Ned, that's not true. Who told you that?" *Did Hillary tell him?*

"It doesn't matter who told me. Is it true? My mother has a way of causing trouble, and I suspect that's where all this stemmed from."

"Please don't say things like that. Your mom and her family have been here for me." She saw Art smiling and moving his hips in a humping motion. She turned her back on him. "Let's not spend the little time we have fighting. Please. When will you get time off?"

"Next month. Can't give you an exact date, but I should have a better idea after this next deployment. I love you, Barbara. I'll be over as soon as I can. Oh, before I forget, I ran into your cousin Donald. We're getting together again tonight at the O Club."

"Oh, my, how is Donald? Be sure and tell him hello for me."

"He's great. Listen, I gotta go. Guys are lining up to use the phone. I'll call when I'll be over. Love you."

"I love and miss you, Ned. Be safe." She hung up the phone, then covered her face with her hands. "Listen, Arty, I can't do this anymore." She didn't wait for him to reply and walked into the bathroom, closing the door.

Art knocked. "Come on out. We need to go. I get it, playtime is over. But you gotta admit it was fun."

Barbara walked out and picked up her purse. *I have to tell him. I can't hold this in anymore. Oh God, what if he wants this child? What if he tells Ned? I can't do this alone.* "Arty, I, uh—I think I'm pregnant."

Art's face froze, and he stared at her. "You *think*! When will you *know?*" He dropped into a chair and leaned forward. "When will Ned be home?"

"He doesn't have a date. He'll call me after this next deployment." Barbara bit her bottom lip. "Arty, I've been sick in the mornings and have missed my cycle this month by a week." She fiddled with her wedding rings. "I thought it might've been the move. Everything felt off, but I'll make an appointment with a doctor on base and get a confirmation."

"*No!* Don't go to a doctor on base. Let's find a private physician." Art popped out of the chair and began pacing the room. "If Ned comes back soon, and we play our cards right, we could make Ned think it's his kid."

Barbara began to cry. "Ned will see right through me."

He walked over to her and pulled her into his arms. "We'll get through this. Don't worry." Art leaned down and kissed her.

"Oh God, we should've never done this. It's wrong in so many ways. We have to end this relationship now."

Art kept his arms around her. "I figured it would end, but not this soon. I wish I wasn't falling in—"

Barbara pulled away from him. "What?" *Do I feel the same?*

"Nothing, just me being sentimental. Come on, we're late for dinner." Art took her by the arm and led her out of the apartment.

Mixed up and miserable, Barbara let the subject drop.

✎

Ned and Donald met with Ross the following night at the O Club. They knew they had to talk Ned's cabin mate into joining the group to make their plan work. Ross had the authorization to bring equipment aboard without getting questioned. He was the key to the success of this adventure. The problem was that he was a bit of a rule follower.

The three found a booth away from the nosey bartender. The place was packed, so they needed to lean in close to hear each other. A layer of hazy cigarette smoke hovered just above their heads.

Ned sat across from Ross and stared intently at him. "You know the problems I've been having—well, Donald has a solution. But to make this happen, we need your help."

Ross shook his head. "What are you talking about?"

"I get pretty worked up after battles, and a little hooch makes all the difference." Ned glanced sideways at Donald. "There're only so many mouthwash bottles you can smuggle on at one time." He put his hand on Donald's shoulder. "My cousin has a solution."

Ross eyed Ned with suspicion and stated, "You get caught doctoring your coffee and you could find yourself in a lot of trouble." He sat back in the booth. "Everyone is rattled after an attack, but it passes."

Donald smirked. Clearly, he was getting impatient to get on with the discussion. "Ross, what we want to do is to construct a still aboard ship and give my man here some peace."

Ned craned his head back in frustration. This wasn't the way to convince Ross of anything. "If we could do this, Ross, it would be my saving grace."

"What the fuck are you two thinking?" Ross shook his head. "I'm not getting mixed up in this."

Donald held up his hand. "I got a buddy that's made it and says it's a snap." He pulled out two sheets of paper. "Here are the items we need and the instructions to get started." He handed the supply list to Ned. "Check it over and tell me what you can't get. I'll get my buddy to help me find anything you can't. He's been cooking this shit for a while."

Ned and Ross went over the list. "I see no problems," Ned said.

Ross shook his head. "Here's a problem to solve. Where in the hell do you set the still up? The stink and the noise will be a real problem. Have you two thought about this?" He ran his fingers through his cropped hair.

Donald laughed. "There's always one worrywart. First, get the supplies, then we'll find a place to set up."

"How long does it take before it's ready?" Ross asked. "The

longer it takes, the more of a chance you'll get caught." He took a sip, then sat forward in his seat rolling his shot glass between his palms. "You two understand you could be busted down to nothing! I don't want any part of this crap."

Donald stood up, apparently ignoring Ross's warning. "I'm going to the bar. What can I get you girls? How about shots all around—to righting the navy's wrongs?" He pumped his arm high in the air as he made his way to the bar. "Coming through, coming through."

Over the next hour, the three talked about how the setup could go, what supplies were needed, and precautions that were needed. Ross threw in all the possible flaws there were in their plans.

Donald started to get up. "I need to use the head. If you ladies will excuse me."

Ross turned to Ned after Donald had left the table. "Ned, this is crazy. Donald has nothing to lose if *we* get caught—he's on a different ship. I'll bet we get caught and thrown in the brig before the shine is ready to drink. We have to think this through. Louise will kill me, if the navy doesn't!"

Ned smiled. Ross had finally used the word *we*. He was in. Ned crossed his arms on the table. "Come on, let's give it a go. If we get caught, it's all on me. There're times after a battle my nerves are so rattled that I can't think straight. My hands shake for hours, and any noise sets me on edge. A little hooch would be just the ticket." Ned bowed his head and rubbed his eyes before he looked up. "I believe it's true for you too."

When Donald returned, he slid into the booth. "What are you two girls whispering about—me?" He looked from Ned to Ross and back. When no one spoke, Donald asked. "Well? Are we ready to do this or not?"

Ned frowned. "Ross here doesn't think this is a good idea. Afraid we'll get caught and busted down to nothing but head cleaners." He rubbed his shot glass between his hands and waited to see if Ross would cave in with a little more pressure.

Ross sat staring into Ned's face, his eyes hard, but he didn't argue, either.

"Well, he's probably right." Donald laughed so loudly people turned and looked at the three men. "It's an adventure, Ross ole buddy, and if you don't want to come along, that's okay. But remember, if you don't help—Ned, my man here—won't share." He laughed again.

Ned knew Ross was right about the risks, but with each battle, it took him days to recover. He couldn't sleep, and when he did, night terrors ripped through his dreams. Food made him sick. This had to work. "So, what's it going to be Ross?" Ned asked.

Ross bent his head down before he frowned at his co-conspirators. "Okay, I'm in, but this is totally against my better judgment."

After several more shots, the three decided that moonshine on the Cowpens was a great idea. And the perfect location for the still was Ned's machine shop's storage closet. The smell and noise wouldn't be a problem there. Ned knew he wasn't the only one with a key to the supply closet, and that worried him some, but he kept that fact to himself. And after a few more rounds, even that little detail didn't bother him anymore.

Weeks later, Barbara and Art walked into the office of a doctor in Alameda, California who was recommended by friends. Art felt this was far enough away from San Diego that they wouldn't run into someone they knew. Barbara kept fidgeting with her purse, first up in her lap, then down on the floor. She flinched whenever the door opened as more patients arrived. Ned should be the one with her, not Art. The ugly truth was like a blinking neon sign she tried to ignore, but couldn't. She wanted the last three months back.

A tall, willowy nurse holding a clipboard stood in the doorway leading to the exam rooms. "Mrs. Villier?"

Barbara had agreed to say she was Arty's wife, but he had to nudge her when the nurse called for Mrs. Villier. When she stood up, she wasn't sure if she would throw up or not. Her legs were weak and rubbery as she made her way up the aisle. With every step she took, all she could think about was turning around and running out.

When Art rose to follow Barbara, the nurse shook her head. "Sorry, Mr. Villier, this is for the moms and their doctor. I'll call you when you can join your wife."

Relieved Art wasn't joining her, Barbara turned back to him to let him know she was okay. She wiped her sweaty palms on her dress as she took a seat in the doctor's private office. With a quick prayer that she wasn't pregnant, Barbara tried to relax. Maybe everything would work out.

Dr. Heath entered a few seconds later and sat behind his desk. "Good Morning, Mrs. Villier? Did I pronounce your name correctly?" He reached out and shook her hand. "I understand you think you might be pregnant." He removed his glasses. Barbara watched as he got comfortable in his chair, something he must have done a thousand times.

The words wouldn't come out. Tears began to slide down her cheeks.

"Oh, my, this isn't good. Here, here, let's find out what's wrong." The doctor got up and handed her tissues, then sat in the chair next to hers. "Tell me what's going on. First-time moms get a little emotional. All this is normal."

Barbara wiped her nose and eyes. "I'm not Mrs. Villier, Dr. Heath. My husband is aboard a ship in the Pacific, and I've made the biggest mistake of my life." Too ashamed to look at the doctor, Barbara couldn't bring herself to face him.

"I see, oh my, this explains the tears. My dear, I've been told mistakes happen, but they don't define you. What is your name?"

"Barbara Johansen. My husband is fighting in the war, and I'm here . . . cheating on him." She bent her head, not able to hold back the sobs any longer.

After a few seconds, the doctor pulled out another tissue and handed it to Barbara. "Well, let's find out if you're pregnant, then talk about your options. There're women out there who would love to adopt." He walked around his desk and touched the buzzer. When his nurse entered, he said, "Please take Mrs. Villier to the exam room." The doctor winked at Barbara when she looked up.

When the exam was completed, Dr. Heath had Art join them in his office. "Your baby should be here in mid-to-late December."

Art smiled and reached for Barbara's hand. "Wonderful."

Barbara pulled her hand away from him. "I told Dr. Heath our situation."

Art's smile vanished. He stared at Barbara in total disbelief.

Dr. Heath didn't wait for Art to respond. "You two can do one of two things, legally that is." The doctor took off his glasses. "You can have the child and put it up for adoption—or keep the child. There is a lot to think about either way you go. If I can be of assistance, I'll be glad to help."

The doctor sat forward in his chair and clasped his hands together. "In the meantime, get some rest, try not to worry, and make another appointment for a month from now." The doctor stood up, walked around his desk, and took Barbara's hands in his. "Mrs. Johansen, take your time with this decision. Whatever you decide, it will be with you for a lifetime."

Barbara thanked him.

Neither Barbara nor Art spoke until they pulled up in front of her apartment. Her thoughts had wandered all over the place. *Should I keep the child? Abortion was one avenue. No, I can't do that. Could Ned be fooled into thinking it was his child?* Nothing sounded right.

"Art, I appreciate you taking me today, but I want to be alone. Okay?"

"Sure, doll, I get it."

Barbara touched his hand, then got out of the car. When she'd made it inside and closed her apartment door, the reality of what she'd done hit her in the face. All she could think about was how she'd ruined her marriage, and on top of everything, brought an innocent life into the mess.

The phone rang, and she grabbed a tissue before answering.

"Barbara, is that you? Are you crying?"

As soon as she heard her mother's voice, she nearly lost her own voice, "Mom, I, I, uh—I need you. I've messed up badly."

"Calm down so I can understand you, dear," Judith said. "What's wrong? Has something happened to Ned? Do you want me to fly out? I'll be there as soon as I can."

Struggling to stop crying, Barbara heard herself say, "I'm pregnant, Mom."

Judith Barron didn't speak for a moment, then asked, "Whose child is it?"

"Ned's half-brother's." Barbara choked back sobs. "I've messed up, Mom. Ned will never forgive me."

"What?" Judith took in an audible breath. "Barbara, his half-brother? Oh my stars. I'll catch the next flight out. We'll figure this out. I guess my next question is, does Hillary know about this situation?"

"No, but I'm afraid she thinks something is going on between Arty and me. Do I need to tell her?"

"Not now, but yes, she deserves the truth."

Barbara gave her mother her new address. The two talked for a few minutes longer, and when they hung up, Barbara went to bed. This couldn't be happening, and yet it was. She knew Ned would figure this out and was terrified of how he would react.

## CHAPTER 11

# PEARL HARBOR & SAN DIEGO, 1944

**JUDITH ARRIVED IN** San Diego several days after the disturbing telephone conversation with her daughter. She collected her baggage, then hailed a taxi. She knew what her daughter had to do if her marriage was to survive. But she didn't have the contacts in San Diego, and Judith wasn't comfortable making these kinds of arrangements with people she didn't know. Barbara had to return to Boston, get an abortion, then start over. *What kind of monster am I?* She cringed. For Judith, being a grandparent would be the joy of her life. She stared out the taxi window but saw nothing.

The driver stopped the taxi in front of a five-story white apartment building. "It'll be four dollars, ma'am. I'll get your bags."

Judith got the money out of her wallet as the driver pulled her luggage from the trunk. The neighborhood had royal palm trees and flowering hibiscus lining the streets. Sandwiched between high-rises were restaurants and boutiques. "Beautiful area, isn't it?" she said as she handed him a five-dollar bill. "Keep the change."

"Yeah, it is, but it's a little too rich for my blood," the driver said as he took the money and tipped his hat.

She had turned to walk up the steps when a doorman in an elaborate uniform came out to greet her. "Ma'am, let me take your bags. Who're you visiting?"

Judith released her suitcases. "Oh, um—Barbara Johansen, she's on the fifth floor." She regained her composure and added, "This is a pleasant surprise."

"Is this your first trip to San Diego?" The doorman smiled as he took her luggage. "Please, follow me."

"Yes, it is." Her eyes darted around, taking in the lush environment.

They went through massive, wrought-iron gates to the main lobby. As soon as she entered the foyer, fresh air greeted her. The doorman handed her bags to a bellboy and tipped his hat to her, then turned to take his place back at the front door.

Beautiful white marble flooring echoed the clicking of her high heels. There were chairs and love seats covered in vibrant green and white striped fabric staged in front of the concierge's desk. Fresh flowers decorated the side tables and scented the air. Everything screamed, *It's expensive to live here.* If it hadn't been for the bellboy calling to her, Judith would have missed the elevator since she'd been so consumed with the building's opulence.

As the elevator doors opened on the fifth floor, the bellboy went ahead of her and knocked on Barbara's door. When she opened it, he placed the bags in her foyer. Judith held out a tip and thanked him as he left. Barbara came out into the hall and immediately hugged her mother.

"Come on. Let's see your new home, shall we?" She'd always been able to take care of all her daughter's problems with a Band-Aid and a kiss. But that wouldn't be enough this time. Arm in arm, the two entered the apartment.

"Would you care for anything to eat or drink?" Barbara moved her mother's luggage out of the foyer. "How was your flight?"

"Thank you, nothing right now." Judith nodded while she sized up the apartment. "Flight was okay. Your home is lovely, dear." Judith put her purse and coat down on a nearby chair. "Is it me, or does this apartment seem above the pay range of a serviceman? I don't think *I* could afford to live here."

"It's as pricey as they come, believe me. Hillary owns the apartment. She reduced the rent so we could live here. Otherwise, I'd probably still be hunting for somewhere to live. The demand for houses and apartments is far beyond what is available."

Judith sat down on the couch and slipped off her shoes. "Does Ned know about this arrangement with Hillary?"

"Yes and no. Ned isn't aware that this apartment is Hillary's, if that's what you're asking. He knows I found a place near the base. Hillary wanted to help Ned. After all, he is her son, but with his attitude toward his mother—we decided not to tell him." She took her mother's coat and hung it in the hall closet. "I think it's better for Ned this way."

"I don't believe you're giving Ned enough credit for knowing when something is fishy." Judith couldn't believe her daughter was actually taken in with Hillary's deception. "Barbara, he'll figure it out the minute he comes in the front door. And if not then, how about when that dandy doorman takes his bags? He's not stupid." Judith stood up and paced.

"Mom, there's a housing shortage, and I wanted to be close to the base. Ned would never have agreed." Barbara sat at the other end of the sofa and played with the tassels on the pillow. "Hillary wants to get back in Ned's good graces more than anything in this world."

"So you agreed to leave out the most obvious of facts?" Judith stopped pacing. "Does she know about your situation?" She pointed at Barbara's belly. Judith felt if her daughter would agree to an abortion, maybe she shouldn't tell Hillary the truth. "You're aware this baby could ruin any chance of a happy ending for those two if Ned finds out the truth. Have you thought this through? Would Hillary's son—what's his name? Would he tell her?"

"No, I don't think Arty would say anything, and no, I haven't told her." She tucked her feet up underneath the pillow. "It's not in Arty's personality to take responsibility for anything. I'm not sure how she'll react when she finds out."

"Forget *Arty*!" Judith felt as if she wanted to shake her daughter to wake her up to the real world. "What's *your* plan?"

Barbara ran her fingers through the fringe on the couch pillow. "Well, Arty suggested that if Ned comes home soon, I could wait for a couple of months, then send him a letter saying I was pregnant." She wiped her eyes. "But if he doesn't come soon, I don't know."

"Barbara, how's that going to work? Ned knows it take nine months before a baby is born. You're *not* thinking. What if he gets another opportunity to come home and finds you very pregnant, or better yet, giving birth? What then?"

She shook her head. "I can't tell him."

Judith drew a deep breath and decided now was the time to discuss her solution of an abortion. "I've a suggestion, and it's not pretty, but I can make it happen." Judith could feel her pulse speeding up. She could see no other option if her daughter's marriage was to survive. "I think you need to return to Boston with me. I've connections, and can make this all go away. Safely, too."

Barbara sent the couch pillow flying to the floor. "What? Mother, are you seriously suggesting?" She pulled her knees up close to her chest. "I can't do that, and I don't believe you could even suggest such a thing."

"Then be honest with your husband and tell him you made a mistake. He will find out. It would be better to hear it from you than your mother-in-law. There's no telling how she'd spin this situation." Judith spoke harsher than she intended. She was so disappointed with her daughter, but convinced in her own mind that she knew what was best.

"No, I'm not going to."

"Are you in love with this, *Arty*?" Judith steeled herself for the reply.

Barbara shook her head. "Mother, I was lonely. Away from you and my friends for the first time. Arty was, well, very attentive, and is probably the most handsome man I've ever seen." She paused. "I didn't mean for it to happen."

Judith could hear the regret and sadness in her daughter's voice. Sympathy wouldn't help. "Barbara, the fact is you did, and if you don't tell your husband the truth, it will *always* hang over you."

"*No* abortion! And *no,* I will not tell Ned. That's final, Mother. I thought you came here to help me." Barbara looked up at her mother. "When Ned comes home, which I hope will be soon, I'll pass this child off as his."

The two women stopped talking.

Judith sat back on the couch, letting a few moments pass. "If Ned doesn't come home shortly, and I can't change your mind right now, please give my offer some consideration. You can't wait too long. It won't be safe for you."

Barbara closed her eyes. "I'll think about it, but I don't believe I could go through with . . . ."

"Lies have a way of coming out." She moved next to her daughter and took her hand. "I love you, Barbara. You have a sharp mind. Think for yourself. Don't let Hillary, or her handsome son, make your decisions."

Tension lined Barbara's face. Judith knew her daughter wouldn't ever agree to end the pregnancy. Yet she knew nothing good could come from her deception.

᪥

It took Ned and Donald a couple more days to convince Ross to join them. The trio constructed the still in the back corner of the machine shop's supply closet. While they were building it, Ned had closed his shop for a *safety inspection*, the only excuse he could come up with to clear the shop. When they finished, they used boxes and spare parts to camouflage his prize. This was risky, but Ned felt the still was his one hope for survival.

Ned stood back and began sizing up their camouflage. "I think you'd better add a few more boxes on your left." He paced back and forth, holding the left side of his belly while Donald and Ross wrestled with the boxes. *Fourteen days, that's it. I can do this. I can.* He casually opened his bottom desk drawer where he'd stashed several mouthwash bottles and other jars full of amber liquid. He felt a sense of relief knowing they were there until the first batch was distilled.

From the storeroom, he heard the ten gallons of distilled water being poured into the still, followed by the plop of what must've been the cake of ale yeast. Donald and Ross stayed in the supply closet long enough to make sure the connections didn't leak.

"Okay, ladies, you need to watch this little beauty every day." Donald said when he and Ross came out.

Next, Ross arranged Ned's desk so he could keep an eye on who went into the closet. Catching anyone who was poking around was crucial. Noise wasn't a problem. The one thing he couldn't fix was the smell.

"There's one other person besides me who has a key to the shop," Ned said, rubbing the back of his neck.

Ross ran his hand through his hair. "Who?" Sweat poured off him and he looked spent, but Ned ignored his cabin mate's question.

Donald walked back to the store room, seemingly satisfied all was well. "Now, in fourteen days, or when the bubbling stops, it should be ready. Keep the door open for as long as possible during the day for air flow."

"Fourteen days," Ned grinned. He turned to Ross. "Hey, did you hear? Fourteen days." His stash should last that long.

Ross said nothing.

"We ship out tomorrow, so I'll let you know how it goes when we get back." Ned placed his hand on Donald's shoulder. "Now, Donald, keep your fuckin' head down."

"Will do. Same goes for you girls." Donald brushed off his pants and adjusted his hat. "We'll both be back in port eventually, so save me a jar or two."

"You need not ask. There'll be jars with your name on them."

"So, who else has a key?" Ross asked again. Arms defiantly crossed over his chest, he stepped in front of Ned, and he wasn't budging until he got an answer.

"The Maintenance Officer. His section keeps duplicates of all the keys of the ship. It's a safety rule. I'm surprised you didn't know. Ross, you said you were good with this. What's with all the paranoia?"

"You realize if he gets a broom up his ass, he could check out your closet."

Ned knew Ross was right, and it was something he'd deal with if it happened. "I'll say you played no part in the still. Now, can we move on? You're becoming a royal pain in my ass." Ned leaned back against his desk. He hadn't felt well for weeks.

Ross stared at him. "You could get a dishonorable discharge. Hell, we could all get a dishonorable discharge." Ross threw his arms in the air. "Great for résumé reading."

"Then it's my problem, Ross." Ned stood a foot taller than Ross and loomed over him to intimidate his cabin mate. "I will take complete responsibility. Is there anything else I can do to get you off my back?" Ned glared, and he felt his palms begin to itch. He wanted nothing more than to punch his cabin mate. His patience had stretched to the point he couldn't handle any more bitching. Ross didn't understand how important this was to him.

Ross glared. "You're becoming a real prick." He turned back to Donald on his way out. "It was good to see you again, Donald. Leave your visitor's pass with the duty clerk when you leave the ship."

Donald laughed at the exchange. "I'm out of here. Hope you two little girls make up soon." He picked up his uniform jacket and slapped Ned on the shoulder. "See you on the back side. Stay safe."

"You too, Donald." Ned hated to see him leave.

Before they started to construct the still, Ned had memorized all the instructions down to the last detail. Fourteen days from now, that's all he had to wait, and the shine would be ready. Now, if the ache in his side and Ross would both give him some relief, he'd have it made. Fourteen days kept running through his mind. *I can do this.*

As the sun broke over the horizon, the USS *Cowpens* headed out to join in the Pacific raids. Each of the battles lasted several days. When downtime came, boredom set in. Raw nerves mixing with the anticipation of what might be about to happen made life aboard ship increasingly unstable. Ned noticed he and the crew were bickering and fighting over insignificant issues. As he reached for his coffee cup, his hands were shaking. Ned had almost consumed his entire stash of booze. He tried to stretch out his supply by drinking anything with a high volume of alcohol, including his cabin mate's aftershave. He was desperate, but the shine was almost done.

The night before the shine was ready for testing, unexpected orders came down to make the ship secure because a massive typhoon was about to descend on them. Ned instructed the crew to make sure all tools, machinery, and manuals were secured. He struggled with a dull pain near his navel and knew he needed to see the medic. Every lift or strain caused his discomfort to increase. The pain became sharp, and seemed to move toward the lower right side. He sat down and mopped the sweat off his face, not sure he could handle this razor-sharp agony inside his body.

"Chief, you okay? You don't look so good," one of his crew asked. "Want me to get you water or—"

"Stop worrying about me and get your ass moving, or we'll have a mess down here." He leaned back against the wall and resisted the urge to double over.

The young sailor shook his head. "Yes, sir." He picked up more webbing and saluted as he hurried past.

With his crew redirected to the front of the shop, Ned took the opportunity to tie down the still without drawing attention to what he was doing. He wound straps around the still, then took webbing and tied down the boxes he used for concealing his prize. He was about finished when he heard someone call his name. "I'm coming." He leaned against the wall and groped his way out, but started to vomit before he could close the door.

By the time his men got him to sick bay, his fever had climbed to one hundred and one degrees. His belly looked as if it belonged to a woman six-months pregnant

"Chief, let me help you onto the table," the young doctor said. "Tell me what's going on. When did it start?" The doctor bent his knees as he tried to keep his balance while the ship rode the waves.

"I've had pain for the past few months." He gasped as the doctor felt around his right side. "It's a sharp pain, but it usually goes away. I probably just need to take a dump. I'm fine. I need to get back."

As the doctor pressed on his stomach, Ned yelled out in pain and slapped the doctor's hands away. "*Stop!* You trying to kill me?" Ned tried to sit up, but the pain wouldn't let him move. "I need a bucket. I'm going to throw up." He leaned over, causing a razor-sharp pain to shoot through him.

The doctor signaled to the young corpsman, and Ned felt a slight pinch as the needle slipped into his shoulder. "This should settle things down," the doctor told him.

"What in the hell is going on with me Doc?" Ned used his T-shirt to mop the sweat off his face. "Whatever it is, I can't take much more."

"Chief, I believe your appendix is about to burst. We have to operate now, or you won't be here tomorrow."

"What about the typhoon? You're going to open me up during a fuckin' storm? I don't mind dying for my country, but I'm not dying on a damn operating table." Ned tried to sit up, but the pain became too intense. "You're fuckin' crazy, Doc."

"To be honest, Chief, you have no choice. You won't survive if I don't get this out of you. I don't have the knowledge or experience in this area to save you if it does burst. You won't survive. Do you hear me?" The doctor grabbed the table and wall to brace himself as the ship pitched forward. "So, what's it going to be?"

Ned held his hands up in surrender. "Have at it, I guess."

"Don't worry, Chief," the doctor said. "I'll do my best."

Waves crashed over the bow of the ship while the Cowpens groaned and strained against the wind and ever-growing force of the ocean. Supplies the crew hadn't yet secured flew off the shelves. Both the doctor and corpsman had to brace themselves to stand.

Several hours later, Ned woke up in the ship's recovery room groggy, but the pain was more tolerable, and the ship wasn't being tossed about as badly. He put his hands up to his pounding temples, trying to rub the throbbing away. He didn't know if it was from the anesthesia or from the lack of alcohol his system had come to expect. After taking a moment, Ned knew he was lucky to be waking up, then his next thought was about his still. Had he protected it well enough?

Ross poked his head through the open doorway and waved. "Hey, how're you feeling?"

"Better." He checked around to make sure no one was within earshot. "Have you been down to my shop?"

"Well, that's the big question of the day, isn't it? I've good and bad news for you." He shook his head. "Ya ready for the bad news?" Ross leaned down and whispered, "The still—smashed to smithereens." Ross waved his hands in an all gone motion. "A couple boxes broke from their ties and ultimately took it out of production. A huge mess, from what your crew told me."

"Ah shit!" Ned turned his head away. Waiting for this shine to cook had felt like the glue that held him together. Now what would he do? "Ross, did you see it? I mean any chance at all?" Ned arced his head back into his pillow. "I have to rebuild, it's my only hope. This can't—"

"No way. You're out of luck, my friend." He leaned back against the wall. Ned's lack of understanding aggravated Ross. "Ned, your men spent a good bit of time cleaning up that shit, saving your ass and mine." Ross stared at him. "Do you understand what I'm telling you?"

"What? The crew cleaned it up?" Ned tried to sit up, but winced immediately in pain. "We can start over when we get back to port."

"Sorry, buddy, but my days of moonshining are over. You're in this alone. I'm not risking getting caught."

"What the hell, Ross. I need your help."

"Your shop has a very odiferous odor." Ross laughed so hard he couldn't stand up straight. "Got any sailors from hillbilly country in your crew? They'll get what nearly went down."

"Damn." Ned reached for the glass of water next to his bunk. "Oww," he groaned. "Can you get me water? My mouth feels like an army marched through it." *How in the hell will I survive?*

Ross moved around the bed and handed Ned a cup. "Hurt much?"

Ned eased back after a small sip. "Yes. Damnit, Ross, the shine was almost done. You said good and bad news. What's the good news?"

"You're one lucky son of a bitch to be alive to tell the tale." Ross leaned back against the wall. "I hear when we get back to Pearl you'll be on leave for at least a month."

A great relief washed over Ned. "Are you sure about this? A month? Seeing my wife will be just the ticket." Getting booze wouldn't be a problem once he was stateside. "Damn, Ross, you should've started with the good news."

Ross laughed again. "Yeah, well, I had to mess with you first."

⊱

After an emotional weeklong visit, Barbara kissed her mother good-bye and watched the taxi pull away from the curb. Back in her apartment, Barbara was putting their breakfast dishes in the sink when she heard a sharp rapping on the door. *Mother?*

At her door was a man in a Western Union uniform holding a clipboard. A fear she'd never known before shot through her body. *Was Ned . . . ?*

She couldn't talk. The words the man said didn't register. She stared at him. Her heart raced, feeling like it might explode.

The deliveryman cleared his throat. "Ma'am, I've a telegram for you. Sign here, please."

Her hands shook as she signed her name. She took the thin yellow envelope as if it were breakable. For a moment, her world stopped turning. She stepped back into her apartment and closed the door, allowing the wall to support her. She opened the envelope.

Arriving at San Diego Naval Air Station this Thursday at 0900. Had minor surgery. All fine. Home for four weeks. Love, Ned

Relief washed over Barbara as she wiped her eyes. *Thank God, Ned's okay.* She walked into the living room and sat down. There was a good chance her plan would work. Rubbing her belly, she reread the telegram. There was no information about the surgery. What would happen if he couldn't have sex with her? The anxiety made her morning sickness worse.

Barbara called Hillary to tell her Ned was coming home. He'd had some kind of surgery was all she knew, and promised to be in touch soon.

⊱

On Thursday morning, she prepared to meet the transport plane from Pearl Harbor. Her hair was in a low bun at the nape of her neck. Staring into the mirror, she turned one way then the other. There was no evidence she was pregnant except her very tender breasts. And only she knew this.

The plane was late. For what seemed like endless hours, Barbara stood behind the wire fence that separated the tarmac and the covered waiting area. She was advised not to leave. She was told planes were often late, but that did little to put her mind at ease.

Two hours later, the plane finally arrived. She watched two hospital orderlies bring Ned down the plane's cargo ramp in a wheelchair. Barbara felt she might be sick facing him. Could she do this? Her cheeks were hot to the touch, and she felt sweaty, even though it was sixty degrees. His coloring told the story—he wasn't well. Ned smiled and waved as soon as his eyes found hers.

Ned squeezed her hands and brought them to his lips. "You look so good."

Barbara bent down and hugged him. Her eyes filled with tears and she struggled to speak. "Come on, let's go home."

"You don't know how good those words sound." Ned held her hand as he was wheeled through the hanger and out to a line of waiting taxies. "Thanks, guys. See you in about a month, unless the lady talks me into going AWOL."

The orderlies smiled and helped Ned into the taxi. "See ya, Chief." They placed his duffle bag in the trunk.

Once inside the taxi, Ned pulled Barbara into his arms. "How far is the apartment from the base?"

"Only five miles, not far."

Ned pushed his hat back. "Wow, so close—"

Barbara cut in. "So how're you feeling? Tell me what happened."

His arms tightened around her. "I'm fine, really. The craziest thing—I had appendicitis, and the doctors had to operate during a little storm."

"Oh my stars, Ned—during a storm?" She smoothed out

the hem of her dress, unable to look at him, ashamed of her first thought. *Can he have sex with me?*

When the taxi pulled up to the apartment, the driver scrambled to help Ned.

Walking gingerly toward the steps, Ned stopped and glanced around.

Barbara held out a five-dollar bill, but the driver shook his head. "Your husband paid the price ma'am; I won't be accepting no money." He pulled Ned's duffle bag out of the trunk, tipped his hat, and drove off.

Barbara had turned around, astonished by the driver's act of kindness, when the doorman appeared. She saw what her mother had predicted. Ned was a taken aback—almost speechless.

"Let me get the bag for you, Mrs. Johansen." He turned to Ned. "Glad to have you home, sir. I'll have the bellboy take your duffle to your apartment."

Ned thanked him. "Wow, this is some kind of star treatment for sure."

Barbara could see his confusion as Ned's forehead wrinkled, his eyes going from her to the doorman leading the way. He stopped and glanced down the street, then back at her.

Barbara kept talking about how he needed some good, home-cooked meals. As they walked into the building, she went on about what she wanted to show him after he had rested. She knew her chatter did little to hide the opulence or distract Ned from it.

After the bellboy had closed their apartment door, she watched Ned, trying to gauge his reaction. "How're you feeling? Are you hungry or thirsty?"

Ned took in the apartment without answering her question. "What's the rent on this place? I hope you haven't used all our profit from Pa's house to live here. Is this new furniture? I don't remember ever seeing it before."

Barbara heard her mother's warning. "Of course I didn't. I'll show you the rental lease agreement. You can see for yourself, it's affordable." She walked over to the desk and pulled out a thick envelope. Even though she'd practiced saying these words, the tone of her voice wouldn't have convinced anyone. "And no, that's not new furniture. I found a few pieces in second-hand stores and refinished them."

"Yeah? When did you start refinishing furniture?" He walked to the window and stood there for a minute. "Where's the booze? I sure could use a drink."

"Let me get it for you," she said, grateful she dodged the explanation that Art showed her how to refinish furniture.

"Sure. Let's not talk about rental contracts right now. Are you going to join me?" Ned asked when Barbara handed him the glass.

Barbara shook her head. "It's a bit early for me."

Ned shrugged. "How about you give me the cook's tour around this sky-high palace?"

Barbara laughed a little too loud. "Come on and I'll show you around." More than anything, she wanted to be honest with Ned, but knew it wasn't possible. When she opened the bedroom door, he put his glass down on the dresser. He pulled her to him and kissed with pent-up passion. Ned held her in a tight embrace as they fell back on the bed.

She resisted the urge to recoil from the taste and smell of his drink. This was exactly what she needed to happen, but she felt so guilty. "Ned, are you sure? Now? What about your incision?"

"It's been weeks. Let's see what this ole dog can do." He got up, closed the bedroom door, and turned off the lights. "I've needed you more than you'll ever know. Come here."

"Wait, I'm not sure." Her heart felt as if it might burst—it pounded so hard.

Ned sat up long enough to drain his glass. "No worries, I'm better than ever now."

Several hours later, she lay in his arms listening to the rhythm of his breathing. She stood up and slipped on her robe, then left the room. She wanted to get a shower, but didn't want to wake her sleeping husband. He'd never been rough when he made love to her before. She rubbed her breasts. Both were red, and touching them hurt. In the kitchen, she put on a fresh pot of coffee and sat at the small dinette table she and Arty had restored. *By the time Ned goes back to Pearl, I'll be over two months pregnant.*

The phone rang, startling her back to the present. She jumped up, knocking over the sugar bowl to answer.

Hillary's voice sounded excited. "Barbara, is my son home? I've been dying to call, but didn't want to interfere with his homecoming." She giggled as if she knew the punchline to the joke.

"Yes, he's asleep right now." Barbara leaned against the kitchen doorway.

"How does he look? What kind of surgery did he have?"

"Believe it or not, he had his appendix out during a storm." Barbara rubbed her forehead. "He looks like he needs some rest and a few home-cooked meals."

"Gracious sakes, surgery during a storm. I think you should expect him to be a little puny. Take care of my boy." She hesitated. "Call me, dear, and let me know when I can come over. Oh, be sure to talk to him about having dinner with us, pretty please."

"I will, Hillary. I'll be in touch soon." She hung up the phone as the door to the bedroom opened and Ned walked out.

"Who was that, my mother?" He opened the liquor cabinet and poured another glassful of the bourbon. "Do you have more?" He held up a half-empty bottle.

"Should you be drinking and still taking pain medicine?"

"Don't play Nancy Nurse with me. Anyway, I'm not on pain meds." He took a sip from his glass. "I drink when I want to. Are you becoming a nag?"

Barbara pushed her hair behind her ears. "You might not like it, but I know a great deal about medicine." She watched him stand looking out the window with his back to her. She didn't care for his attitude. "Ned, your mother wants to visit with you."

"What?" He added two ice cubes to his glass and went back to the window. "I hope you said no."

"No, I told her I'd get back to her when you were up for company. Ned, your mother has been there for me this whole time. I don't know what I would've done without her."

"Well here's a newsflash for you. I'll never feel any desire to see her. Got it?"

Barbara had never heard him use such a hateful tone. She felt that if she said anything, he'd explode. She now knew for sure that she couldn't tell him the truth about the apartment, or the baby. His whole demeanor had changed. Maybe he still hadn't recovered from his surgery. "I'll let her know we aren't coming for—"

Ned gave her a cold stare, stopping her mid-sentence. He picked up the bottle of bourbon. "Go get me another bottle or two." Then he shut the bedroom door.

&

After two weeks at home, Ned got restless. Something didn't feel right to him, and he'd a hunch Barbara wasn't telling him the whole story. One morning while Barbara was at the grocery story, he decided he needed to investigate more about their swanky apartment.

He pulled out the paperwork Barbara had tried to show him when he first came home. It seemed okay, but it didn't say who owned the apartment. He held a small glass of bourbon and ice in one hand, and with the other, he flipped through Barbara's address book till he found his mother's phone number.

A young man's voice answered.

"This is Ned Johansen. May I speak with my mother?"

"Uh—sure. Hold on and I'll get her."

"Ned? Is that you, Ned? How're you feeling, dear? I'd love to come over and see you, if you're up to a visit."

"Mother, I've a question for you." He gripped the phone with one hand and held up his glass to the light.

"Sure dear, what?"

"Is this apartment yours?"

"Mine? Oh my stars, Ned, no. I helped Barbara find the apartment, but it's not mine. Are you unhappy with the place? I'm sure—"

Ned heard Barbara coming in the door. He discontinued his call with his mother, but didn't put the phone receiver down. He wanted Barbara to see him on the phone. He was going to get some answers.

"Hey, Ned, I'm home," Barbara said when she entered the room. "Who're you talking to?"

"I was talking with my mother."

Barbara kept walking into the kitchen with the groceries. "Oh . . . uh, what did she want?"

"She told me this was her apartment and that you'd been lying the whole time." Ned turned just in time to see Barbara waver and start to fall into the cabinets. He pushed his chair back, and in few quick steps, he scooped her up in his arms.

As Ned placed her on the couch, he asked, "What's going on, Barbara?"

Barbara sat up. "It's true Ned. This is your mother's place." She cried. "I didn't tell you because I was sure you'd move out, and I had been looking for months. I couldn't find anything and . . . ." Tears spilled down her cheeks. "I'm sorry."

Ned sat back. "You didn't have to lie. This place even smells like my mother. I sensed it the minute I walked in here." He sat still, staring at her. "Mother didn't tell me anything. But I knew you were hiding something from me." He saw the pain in her eyes at being tricked, but he'd been justified.

She said nothing, then jumped up without warning and ran to the bathroom and vomited.

Ned walked in, picked up a washcloth and handed it to her, then sat down on the edge of the tub. He didn't mean to upset her this badly, but you don't lie to Ned Johansen. "It's okay, Mother owes me. The truth from here on out, and we'll work out the rest. Okay?"

Barbara turned around, put her arms around his neck with regretful tears falling down her cheeks.

Ignoring the pain in his side, Ned lifted Barbara up from the bathroom floor and carried her to the bed.

❧

The four weeks of leave passed quickly for Barbara. Ned would be going back to the ship. He was leaning against the doorway to the bedroom, watching her brush her hair back into a long ponytail. Barbara took a second to check out her profile. *Has he noticed the extra weight I've put on?* She looked up to find Ned smiling at her. She could feel her cheeks grow hot.

"What?" Flustered, she turned around, picked up her purse, and held it in front of her.

"You're beautiful. You know that, don't you?" Ned walked over and wrapped his arms around her. "It'll be harder leaving you today than when I left the first time. Please stay home."

"Ned! No. Please, don't . . . ."

"All right, but no tears. You hear?" He held her face in his hands. "Leaving you will be hard enough."

Barbara turned away and slipped on her shoes. "This month has gone by so fast. It seems like you just got here." She wiped her eyes and smiled. "Sorry, I know—*no* tears."

A few hours later they were in the same hanger he had arrived in, but this time Ned was walking. Their hands were entwined.

"I've got to go. Please keep those cards and letters coming." He was much better than when he had first arrived.

"You keep your head down." She tried to hide her sadness, but couldn't. "I love you."

After a long, passionate kiss, Ned walked out to the plane. She watched him until he ducked into the plane's doorway.

∽

Back at home, the empty apartment smelled of Ned's Aqua Velva aftershave. That afternoon, to stay busy, Barbara went into the bedroom and pulled off the bedsheets. An empty whiskey bottle rolled out from under the covers. *What?* Then, in the bathroom, she picked up his towel and brought it to her face to breathe in his scent. Instead, it smelled of alcohol. She checked the usual places for an empty bottle. Instead, she noticed her mouthwash and several other bottles were missing off her bathroom shelves. *What is going on?*

When she pulled fresh sheets from the linen closet, two more empty bottles crashed to the floor. A splinter of glass flew into her leg and blood began to trickle down. Barbara quickly pulled out the glass and wiped her leg, then swept up the broken bottle. She'd no idea he'd consumed the last four bottles she brought home the day before. *When did he drink all this? He hadn't seemed drunk.*

His excessive drinking during the last month had scared her. They'd always had a drink or two in the past, but this was different. Ned had displayed quick explosions of temper, and for the first time, she found herself afraid of her husband. At one moment he'd be his usual self, then something, anything, could set him off. Was it the war, or something else?

The doorbell rang, yanking her back into the present. When she opened the door, there stood Art.

"What do you want?" Barbara stood in the slightly open doorway.

"May I come in?" He stood with his hands behind his back, looking like a lost child.

Barbara didn't want to deal with Art. "No. Go away and leave me alone. Your brother knows nothing."

"Uh . . . half-brother, if you please. Come on, doll, I'll make it worth your while." A gleaming white smile crossed his face.

Barbara stood back and opened the door wider, but blocked him from going into the living room. "I doubt that. You better make this fast. I'm not in the mood for your antics."

Art walked in and tried to give her a kiss, but she pulled back. "Doll, did you do the deed with my evil half-brother? I don't want details. Well uh, yes, I do—but not really. You get me, don't ya?"

"If you're asking if I made love to my husband, the answer is, it's none of your business." She perched her hands akimbo. "I've taken care of our mistake."

"Ouch!" He shook his hands as if they had scalding water poured on them. He turned and opened the door. "I'm leaving. Never to return." She saw the sorrow in Arty's face as she pushed the door shut.

Barbara made sure she turned the lock. Emotionally exhausted and no longer able to hold back her regrets, she sobbed.

CHAPTER 12

# PEARL HARBOR & SAN DIEGO, 1944

**WEEKS AFTER NED** left, Barbara decided she should be honest with Hillary and tell her she was pregnant with Arty's baby. Her mother told her the fewer people who knew the truth the better, but she needed someone to share this with. And who better to confess to than Hillary?

The Villier's invitation for a cookout that Sunday came at the perfect time. Hillary would pick her up, and the forty-five minute drive would give them uninterrupted time to talk. Convinced Hillary would understand, Barbara tried to relax as she got ready.

Checking the mirror for any visible changes in her body, she saw her belly protruding, but whether anyone else could see it was the question. She chose a full skirt with a bright pink and green floral print and a white, cap-sleeved blouse. Barbara felt she had another month or more before she needed to get maternity clothes. In the meantime, large safety pins would take the place of the button on her skirt.

At noon, Hillary knocked on her door. "Yoo-hoo, it's me. Are you ready to go?"

Barbara picked up her purse and opened the door. "Yes, ma'am."

"My dear, you're radiant today." The two women hugged, then rang for the elevator.

Barbara tied a scarf around her head as Hillary steered her convertible onto the highway. The sun felt good as she leaned her head back to soak in its warmth.

"Barbara, I simply can't wait to tell you." Hillary tilted her head from side to side with a full, toothy smile.

Barbara glanced over at her mother-in-law. "What's that?" She turned her head back toward the sun while waiting for a juicy bit of gossip. Her mother-in-law always had tales to tell on her bridge partners. Someone was always getting surgeries they wanted to keep secret.

"Arty has a serious girlfriend." Hillary's voice came out with an uncommon squeal. "We will get to meet her today."

"A girlfriend?" Barbara sat up. "They're joining us today?" She'd known she would have to face Arty again, but not this soon. The two hadn't spoken in weeks. It sure didn't take him long to find her replacement.

"Yes. I'm anxious to see what you think of the new couple. My bridge partners tell me her family is very wealthy, and I believe they're out of San Francisco." Hillary bounced in her seat as if she were an excited child. "I hope this is the relationship for him; he needs to settle down. Don't you agree?" She turned to Barbara with a please-say-yes kind of look.

"He's still pretty immature, I mean young. I'm not sure he's ready for anything lasting." Barbara had a flashback of their visit to the doctor's office, then shook her head to get rid of the image. "Where did he meet her?"

"Oh my, I don't know. We must ask. Her name is Rita Cummings. Lovely, don't you think?" Hillary giggled like a teenage girl.

"Best of all, her family owns several upscale department stores." Hillary's face lit up with delight. "Hope we get in on the family discount. I'm sure Rita's out of college, but maybe not. So much to find out, don't you agree? What fun we'll have today."

Barbara didn't respond. This change ruined her entire plan for the day. How could she tell Hillary about the baby now?

"You know, I have to admit I thought something was going on between you and Arty." With a little rock of her head from one side to the other, she said, "Silly me, I know."

"It's understandable, Hillary. We did become close." Barbara wanted to say more, but Hillary interrupted with more tidbits about Rita's family. There would be no confession today.

The afternoon went well, and to Barbara's surprise, she liked Rita. She was a striking redhead with an athletic body and vivacious personality. She was older than Arty. They seemed made for each other. She was rich, which was enticing for Arty. He'd never have to work if they married. Barbara thought she might feel a little jealous, but Rita's charm was contagious. The three women sat next to each other, laughing at Arty's antics and enjoying Philip's cooking.

By the end of the evening, Hillary had had one too many cocktails and couldn't drive Barbara home, so Philip offered. Arty had left to take Rita home, without even a goodbye or a glance her way. Barbara couldn't get over how the day played out. Her time was running out. She had to tell Hillary.

Philip opened the car door for Barbara. "If you don't mind, I'll put the top up."

"Arty showed me how. Do you want any help?" As she turned toward Philip, she saw him smirk. *What was that?*

"No, I've got it."

Once the top locked into place, he started the car. "Well, speaking of Arthur, what do *you* think of his latest and greatest?"

Barbara wondered if Philip had suspicions about her relationship with his son. Was he fishing for her reaction? "I like her. The two of them make a striking couple. More importantly, what do *you* think of Miss Rita?"

"They'll make beautiful babies. If he's smart, he'll grab this one up. There's a lot of family money, according to Hillary. But Arthur's a playboy, in my opinion, and won't realize the prize until it's too late. He's a spoiled and self-centered young man." Philip sounded regretful.

Barbara decided not to comment and wanted to change the subject. She shifted in her seat, but couldn't think of anything to say.

"Oh, we forgot to ask, have you heard from Ned?" Philip glanced over at her. "This war can't last too much longer. Now, what's the name of his boat?"

"It's a ship, not a boat, and the name is the USS *Cowpens*." She had to take a deep breath to hold back her hurt feelings. The lack of genuine caring by Ned's family tended to overwhelm her. "I write every day, but our letters get held up. Reading the paper makes it worse, especially when I haven't heard from him. Then, as if by magic, a bundle will show up." She drew a deep breath, hoping to stop the lonely feelings that were welling up.

"Oh, yes, I've read about the battles in the Pacific. Sounds intense, but he's safe down in the *ship's* belly." Philip kept talking about the war, telling her how some friends of theirs had received word their son had been killed. "I don't know which is worse, hearing your child is missing, or is dead. What do you think?"

Barbara turned her head and stared out the side window, hoping Philip would notice she wasn't paying attention. It did nothing to deter him as he went over battles and news articles he'd read. His voice became so irritating she put her hands to her ears.

"*Please!* Stop talking about the war. I can't stand to hear any more. Don't you understand, I'm pregnant and—" Barbara's hands flew to her mouth as if she could snatch back her words. Tears spilled out faster than she could wipe them away.

"What? Why didn't you tell us this afternoon? Hillary will

be ecstatic with this news." Philip turned and stared at Barbara. "Why're you so upset? Is it my talk about the war?" He jerked the car off the road and skidded to a stop. "I'm sorry, Barbara. I didn't mean to upset you. It was a party today. You should've said something."

Barbara couldn't say anything and stared at him as she tried to pull herself together.

"Why are you crying? Barbara?" Philip tilted his head toward her when he spoke.

Barbara could only shake her head. "I'm so . . .

"You're so what?" Philip sat back in his seat. "I've got to say I'm a little relieved. There for a while there I thought you and Arthur . . . might of—

*I can't tell him.* Barbara couldn't look at him and braced herself for what she knew was coming.

Philip sat unmoving, his words slowly came out. "It is Arthur's baby—isn't it?" He turned away. "*I knew it!* I warned Hillary you two were spending too much time together. Does Arthur know?"

Her head jerked up, and she glared at Philip. "Yes, of course he knows." She'd heard from Gertrude how he'd treated Hillary when he found out she wasn't married when Ned was born. "I had planned to talk to Hillary today, but—"

"And Ned, have you said anything to him?"

"Yes, I told him he would be a father, nothing more. He hasn't replied. I'm not sure he's gotten my letter."

Philip stared at her, then slammed his hand down on the steering wheel, accidentally hitting the horn, causing them both to jump. "Are you telling me you're going to let your husband think it's *his* child? Taking the easy way out, aren't you?"

"How dare you!" Barbara couldn't stop herself. "Did you expect your son to assume the responsibility?"

"I honestly don't know what to think. Is my son aware of what *you've* done?"

She cocked her head to one side, not believing what she had heard. "What *I've* done?" Her eyes dug into him. "*Arthur* dreamed up the idea to let Ned think it was his child, and I, like a fool, I agreed." The words came out in a hiss, and she could feel her heart slamming against her breastbone.

Without another word, he started the car and pulled it back onto the highway. When they arrived at Barbara's apartment, Philip kept his eyes straight ahead as he spoke. "I'm sure Hillary will contact you tomorrow. I want you to know I expected more from you. I'm disappointed."

"And your son. Are you disappointed in the spoiled boy you raised?"

Barbara could see the muscles in Philip's face tighten, but he remained silent. She got out of the car and watched as he left tire marks when he sped away.

ↄ

During 1944, the USS *Cowpens* was a part of the navy's Third Fleet, whose orders were to obliterate the stronghold the Japanese had in the Pacific Islands at any cost. This enemy didn't comprehend the meaning of surrender; the price for freedom would be higher than anyone imagined.

The Third Fleet attacked the Marshall Islands in January 1944, then took part in operations against the Truk Island, and against Mariana Islands. The USS *Cowpens* had been in and out of action for the past six months.

Ned sat on his bunk and reread Barbara's letter. He never wanted children. The letter floated to the floor as Ned took a sip from his flask. *Me? A father?* He pulled his feet up onto the bed, tucked his flask under his mattress, and fell asleep.

In the morning, Ned found his cabin mate on deck. "Hey, I got news from home." He handed Ross the letter and waited for his reaction.

A wide grin broke out on Ross's face as he finished reading Barbara's letter. "Damn! You're gonna be a dad! Hope the kid looks like your wife."

"Yeah, isn't that the God's honest truth. I'm a little nervous."

Ross laughed and handed Ned back his letter. "I'd say let's go celebrate, but it will have to wait."

"Do you have any idea when we'll be back in Pearl?"

The roar of planes taking off silenced their conversation. It had been quiet of late, but they knew the Third Fleet was gathering support for a major offensive. Ross shook his head, and Ned interpreted it to mean they were in for a huge battle.

Ross heard his name being paged. "We'll talk later, Papa Johansen." He reached out and slapped Ned on the shoulder. "Congratulations."

Hearing Ross's words, Ned began to expect the worst was yet to come. He needed a drink. *Now I have a damn kid to worry about.* With his hands shaking, he could barely unlock his bottom desk drawer. He poured half a cup of bourbon, then topped it off with coffee. His booze supply was running low, and he knew he didn't have enough to last until they got back to Pearl. Sweat droplets popped out on his forehead and dripped down his face.

In the late afternoon, Ross came down to the machine shop looking for Ned. There were orders to prepare for the crossing of the equator. The brass had the idea to create a distraction for the crew before they went back into battle.

Ned glanced up to find Ross leaning in his doorway like he was a pin-up model. "What're you doing down here? Slumming?"

"Hey, I've good news to share with you."

"Yeah, what?" Ned asked with a goofy grin. "War's over, and we can go home?"

"Nope, not that kind of news, but something I think you'll like. We're to cross the equator, which means we'll have a little ceremony, in other words a party planned for all you pollywogs who haven't made the journey across. We shellbacks will show you pollywogs the way."

Ned brightened at the thought. "A party? Any liquid refreshments available?"

"I've heard there might be, but no one's saying for sure. The brass think it'll give the crew a much-needed diversion. We've been on this tub for months."

"Hot damn! I like the sound of that." Ned rubbed his hands together.

Ross smiled and shook his head at Ned. "Before we cross the equator, all you pollywogs will receive a subpoena to appear before King Neptune and his royal court. But first, we have to have a beauty contest."

Ned couldn't stop grinning. "A beauty contest? What the hell?" He leaned back in his chair and wrinkled his nose.

"Each department must choose one of their own pollywogs to represent their section in the pageant, and the highest ranking wog, which in your case is you, will be introducing your group's beauty contestant. Ross doubled over laughing and had to sit down. "This beauty contestant, whoever he is, has to dress in his best drag queen finery."

"When's the contest?" Ned laughed.

Ross searched the paper he was holding. "Says here the ceremony is set up for this weekend. What do you think? Got any beauties in your motley group?"

The sailors in the shop collected around Ned's doorway and yelled out names of possible contestants.

"Hell yes, we do!" Laughing, Ned pointed to one of the men standing at his door. "Hey Jonesy, you can do this, can't ya?" The young sailor blushed and shook his head.

"Hey, Ned, I've got to run," Ross interrupted. "I wanted to give you the news myself." Ross turned to leave, then stopped and walked back to Ned's desk. He leaned in so only Ned could hear him. "You'll need to be on guard; a lot of brass will be around. Watch your refreshments don't get out of hand." Ross sniffed. "By the way, I can tell you've had your daily quota already—slow down."

The two men locked eyes for a moment. Ned, sensing the warning was serious, gave Ross a slight nod. He knew he owed them all an enormous debt. "You're an old mother hen. You know? Get out of here. I've a beauty contest winner to pick."

∽

After her disaster of a conversation with Philip, all she wanted to do was get into bed. She tossed and turned before she fell into a fitful sleep. The next morning, she paced the apartment floors waiting for something to happen. Countless times she picked up the phone to call either her mother, or Arty, or Hillary, only to put the phone back in its cradle. What should she say? Surely Philip told Hillary what had happened. She sipped her coffee and was trying to force herself to relax when the doorbell shattered her resolve.

Barbara opened the door, and Hillary walked in without saying a word. Her eyes were red and puffy, but Barbara wasn't sure if this was from crying or booze. "Would you like some coffee?"

Hillary turned to Barbara. "Yes, please. I would've called, but I was afraid you'd tell me not to come." She planted herself in a nearby chair. "I talked to Philip, and I have to say you got his, well—I mean our—attention regarding Arty."

"What do you mean?" Barbara asked while she wrapped her bathrobe around her and headed toward the kitchen to make a fresh pot. She turned and looked at Hillary. "I said nothing he didn't already suspect or know."

Hillary turned away, her lips pursed together. "Philip ordered Arthur home last night so we could sort this out. What we want to know is what you want to do at this point." She hesitated a moment, almost as if she didn't want to ask the next question. "Do you love Arty?" She pulled out a handkerchief from her purse and patted her eyes.

Barbara placed her hands akimbo. "Are you crying because there's a chance your son might not marry a wealthy woman, and you'll lose out on the family discount? Or are you upset because of the hurt Ned will feel when he finds out? Which is it?" She stood still, waiting for Hillary to answer. Heat radiated from her body, and her eyes bored into her mother-in-law. "No one even asked how Ned was yesterday. He's in a damn war, and everyone acts as if it's not happening."

Neither spoke for several moments.

"You're being unfair, Barbara. I love my sons and want the best for them. I, uh—we want to do what you want because after everything is said and done, you're carrying our grandchild."

Barbara continued into the kitchen and finished making coffee. As she walked out, she shook her head. "No, Hillary, I don't love Arty. You know how homesick and lonely I was when I arrived. I'd never been without Ned, or my family. Your son was fun and made me forget how much I missed everyone. I messed up, which is no excuse. Ned will never understand." She walked over to the window. "What I'm sure of is that I love my husband, and if he finds out the truth, he'll never get over the betrayal. You can make wedding plans for Arty and Rita. I expect nothing from anyone."

"That's not fair either. Barbara, Arty cares a great deal for you and is sick about well—you know. My fear is that Ned will find out and turn this all around to where it's my fault. I'll never get the chance to make up for all the things."

"Honestly, Hillary, do you really think you can make up for the past?" Barbara raised her voice. "You can't. It's impossible." She waited for her words to register with Hillary.

Both women stopped talking. Barbara went to the kitchen and poured two cups of coffee. She handed one to Hillary, then sat down on the sofa.

"Barbara, please don't tell Ned. I know from experience the

truth won't relieve your guilt. You have my family's promise never to speak of this again." She took a deep breath and seemed to hold it, waiting for her daughter-in-law to speak.

"Keeping the truth about Ned's father from Philip hurt you when he found out, right?" Barbara turned her head enough to see her mother-in-law's reaction.

Hillary's head was bending down. "Yes, but this will be worse if you tell Ned. It won't be just another man's child. The fact the father is my son and Ned's half-brother will be more devastating to him." Hillary lifted her head and faced her daughter-in-law. "But—I think you already know this."

Barbara couldn't disagree with her mother-in-law. It made her sick to think about what a disaster she'd made of her life. "I've told Ned I'm pregnant, and I haven't heard from him, but it's not unusual. The one thing we have is time. Let's think this through. We only have one course to take."

Hillary tried to smile, and the tension in her face seemed to relax. "Oh, Barbara, honey, we need to buy you some clothes. I thought you were getting, uh . . . well, you know, eating too much, but now I know."

Barbara closed her eyes for a moment. *Unbelievable.*

❦

The beauty contest turned out to be the perfect venue for tension relief. The laughter and hooting from the men encouraged more outlandish behavior from the contestants. Ned's group chose the youngest sailor in his crew. He was nineteen years old and right out of boot camp, with the peach fuzz barely off his face. They fashioned long hair from a mop, then using a sheet and clamps, they designed a very revealing gown for their beauty queen.

Liquid refreshment found its way into the punch, and to Ned's delight, he found the booze the ship's officers had stowed away. After helping himself to a healthy number of bottles, he locked his treasure safely away in his office. There was no doubt in his mind now he'd make it until they got back to Pearl. He quickly made his way back to the contest, hoping he hadn't been missed.

After announcing the pollywog beauty contest winner, King Neptune and his entourage concocted a truth serum made of hot sauces and aftershave. Each wog had to swallow a shot, then the King and Davy Jones began to interrogate the pollywogs.

The party ended when the pollywogs, on their hand and knees crawled forward in a line to kiss the King's bulging gut, which was covered in axle grease and their hair-clippings.

With everyone in high spirits, Ned left the party and headed back to his office for a drink. When he opened his door, he found his office ransacked and the booze gone. All the bottles had been taken. Ned stood in his doorway, unable to move. Raw panic set in. How would he survive? Someone had found his stash. If they turned him in, his career was over. Everything was crashing down on him and he had nowhere to hide.

For days Ned waited to be thrown in the brig, but no one said anything to him. Nothing happened, and it drove him crazy. Then he started experiencing the physical effects of alcohol withdrawal, even though he drank anything he could find with any alcohol content.

Two days after crossing the equator, it was back to business aboard ship, and the Third Fleet roared out in full force to mop up the islands. The noise of exploding shells echoed in Ned's ears long after the battle had ended. He stayed in his office listening for the sound of torpedoes whizzing past the ship's hull instead of going to eat or rest. He expected to see hell at any moment. Every sound made him flinch. Drenched in sweat, he waited to die.

One of his crew knocked on his office door. "Hey Chief, the Maintenance Office is screaming for your reports."

Ned gazed up, weary and disoriented—he knew he should recognize the sailor, but nothing would register in his brain. He had to get a damage report ready, but his hands wouldn't move. He hadn't seen Ross in days and worried something bad might have happened to him. Even though he wanted to leave his office, his legs didn't move. His men attempted to help him, but Ned needed help they couldn't provide. In Ned's mind, he kept hearing the warning sound of approaching enemy planes. He saw nonexistent flames flashing in front of him, and to stop the ungodly screams that were coming from everywhere, he pushed his hands against his ears. One of Ned's men caught his eye, then slipped out of his office.

A short time later, Ross stood in his doorway. "Hey, buddy, what's going on?" Ross took a seat on Ned's desk. His uniform was filthy and there were lines of dried blood running down his left arm from an untreated wound. "Why don't we go to the mess hall and get something to eat. I think you've been drinking too much of your coffee." His voice was calm and natural.

Ned squinted. "No, someone took it all. Gone. Vanished. What do you know?" His hands shook. "You're bleeding." He pointed to the dried blood on Ross's arm.

"It's a scratch, nothing serious. How 'bout you come with me and we'll get something to eat?" Ross stood up and moved toward the door. "You coming?"

"Eat? No. I need a drink, and badly. You got anything?" Ned looked up, praying Ross could come through for him. "That's what I need. Help me, Ross. Please." Tears formed in Ned's eyes and the shakes racked his body.

"No, I think you need some rest and food more than you need a drink. Let's go." Ross waited at the door. "I'll go down to sick bay and get something to take the edge off. But first, let's get food in you."

Ned's men stood back as he got up and followed Ross out. "I can't eat, Ross, and I can't exist like this any longer."

"No, buddy, you'll be all right. What you need is food in your belly to soak up all the mouthwash you've been drinking." Ross motioned for Ned to follow. "Things have quieted down for a while, a perfect time to eat, then grab a few winks."

"No, I'm not interested in food." Ned turned back. "I'm going to stretch out for a bit first." He climbed the stairs and headed toward their quarters, where he passed out for a few hours of restless sleep.

The lull in the fighting ended and sirens rang out; enemy planes appeared on the horizon. Ned jumped up, banging his head on the bottom of the top bunk. Blood trickled down his forehead. He grabbed his shoes and shoved his feet in them, then raced down to his crew. Orders were blaring out of the loudspeakers. Men were dashing around to get to their duty stations. Ned seemed to come out of the fog. His uniform was soaking wet with sweat, and he felt like his skin wanted to peel off his body, but his short rest seemed to revive him enough to take charge.

Ross had a source in sick bay that supplied him with muscle relaxers and sleeping pills to get Ned through till they got to back to Pearl. In the meantime, Ned snapped and yelled at his crew for any infraction. After eight months at sea, the USS *Cowpens* returned to Pearl Harbor for repairs, supplies, and company replacements. As soon as the wounded left the ship and his reports were completed, he and Ross left for the O Club.

Ned and Ross each held a package of correspondence from home. They found a booth with a decent light above them and ordered a whiskey shot with a beer chaser. While Ross put his letters in order by date, Ned downed his shot and beer, spilling some as he raised the glass. Then he quickly ordered a second round.

Ross handed Ned a napkin. "Go easy on that stuff."

"Go fuck yourself, mother hen."

Ross stared at him, but didn't say anything. After two more shots, Ned began reading his letters. Neither spoke as they caught up on what was happening back home. When Ned came to the letter telling him he had a son, he put the page down.

Ross stopped reading. "Well, what is it, Papa Johansen, a boy or a girl?"

"A boy, Luke Johansen." Ned wiped his face. "I have a son." He was thrilled and scared at the same time. How would he cope now that he had someone else depending on him? He raised his hand and ordered another round.

Ross leaned across the table and clinked his shot glass next to Ned's. "Sounds as if it's time for shore leave."

Instead of shore leave, the navy sent Ned to Mayo Clinic in Rochester, Minnesota with battle fatigue and severe ulcers in his stomach. After six months, Ned was released from Mayo and given leave for a month to see his wife and son.

When he returned to duty, he learned that the navy had assigned him to the USS *Kula Gulf*, where he would be transferring supplies and cargo for the navy throughout the Korean War. He never saw fighting action or Ross Paxton again. Ned had more to offer the navy than being an errand boy. This change of duty was a slap in his face, but he was a good solider and did what he was told.

From 1954 to 1957, Ned alternated nine-month deployments with three months of shore duty. Each time he came home, he had to reintroduce himself to his son. As the years went on, Ned saw the problem. Barbara wasn't providing the discipline his son needed. The gap in their relationship became more obvious every time he returned. In 1957, the navy moved Ned to a desk job. He'd heard there would be military cutbacks, and a year later, Ned was told to retire.

⤸

The evening of his retirement ceremony, Ned stared out of his living room window at the lights blazing from the naval base. His medals hung heavy on his chest. Ned poured another shot and went back to the window. He realized he would never know how many sailors and officers he owed his career to. Would any be at his ceremony? Ned downed a couple more shots before Barbara joined him in the kitchen. He'd rather be back in the war than attending this farce of a ceremony.

Ned and Barbara entered the banquet room of the Officers' Club at Naval Base San Diego and were escorted to a table in the front. His crew and other officers attending his retirement ceremony slapped him on the back as he passed by. Military life was all Ned had known for thirty years. He smiled and hung on to Barbara.

After a dinner had been served, Ned's commanding officer stood at the podium. He waited for the group of men who had assembled to quiet down. He gave a synopsis of Ned's navy career, then called Ned to address the group.

As Ned stumbled toward the podium, he broke down in tears. He heard the murmurs and raised his arm. "I'm fine." Trying to pull himself together, he looked out to Barbara's worried face. She seemed to will him her strength as she sat forward in her chair.

"Sorry, emotions took over. Guess that means I'm going to miss all you sorry bastards." The audience laughed. Ned smiled and stepped to the podium, wiping his eyes. "I don't have much to say except that's it been my absolute honor to have served with you. I've met some of the bravest men in this man's navy. I will miss this group more than I want to admit. The navy has been my whole life, and to walk away is harder than I realized it would be." He wiped his face. "I hope you'll stay in touch. We're heading back to Boston to buy a home and start a civilian's life. Whatever that is." He stood at attention and gave the commanding officer his last salute, all the while knowing you weren't supposed to salute indoors, then went back to Barbara.

There was applause, and well wishes were yelled out as the commanding officer dismissed everyone. Ned's men gathered around him, shaking his hand. He saw Barbara step back and smile as his friends surrounded him, sharing their stories and best wishes.

As the last man shook Ned's hand, the couple got into their car and headed back to their apartment. They didn't speak on the car ride home. Ned didn't want to hear from someone who would never know, or understand, the depth of his feelings. No one understood. The pressure and insecurity of how he would provide for his family was closing in on him. He could sure use a drink.

It was his time to move on, but to what? He felt a desperate need to get back to Boston. Maybe he shouldn't have sold Ma and Pa's house. He wanted to get back to where he felt at home, and California wasn't home. When they arrived back at the apartment, Ned went straight into the kitchen and pulled his whiskey bottle out from under the sink, then collapsed in his recliner.

Their move to Boston was delayed by several weeks due to Ned's drinking.

࿐

Weeks later, fourteen-year-old Luke stood in the living room watching as the moving van pulled out of the parking lot. California was the only home he'd known, and leaving his friends was the last thing he wanted to do. Luke dragged himself into the bare kitchen looking for his mother. "Mom, what do you want put in the car?" The thought of being in the car with his father for the two-week trip made him sick. The two clashed every time they were together for any length of time. It had to be his father's way of doing things, or he'd get flicked on the head.

"Get the suitcases I have set out. I'll do another walk-through to make sure we didn't forget anything. And don't be so down. You'll love Boston."

"So you say. But because of Dad's binge, I'm going to be starting school late. I hate being the new kid."

Ned walked into the kitchen right behind him and flicked him hard on the back of his head.

"Ouch." Luke ducked away.

Before Barbara could react, Ned whirled his son around to face him "You have it so rough don't you—starting school late." Ned mocked Luke in the sound of a girl's voice. "You whine like a little girl." The vein in the center of Ned's forehead pulsed as he stared at his son. "Go and get the damn suitcases."

Luke had tears in his eyes, but he didn't say a word as he left the room. His mother followed him out of the kitchen. They both carried the suitcases to the car.

Once they were outside, Luke turned back at the apartment to see if his father was watching. "We were a lot happier when he was aboard ship. He's taking his anger of being made to retire out on us. I've heard your fights and seen the black and blue marks he's left on you." Luke threw the suitcases into the trunk.

"I'm fine, Luke." Barbara turned her son gently around to face her. "This is a very hard transition for all of us, Luke. You need to watch your comments and be respectful."

"Is Dad always going to be so strict with the military crap? You know it's his fault that I'm going to start classes late."

"Picture this—you'll be that handsome new boy walking into class, and all the girls will swoon." Barbara smiled. "This will be a good move. I promise."

"Yeah, right."

"You have to realize you two haven't lived together for very long stretches of time, but be polite. It's 'yes sir' or 'no sir' when you answer him, or there will be problems. Your dad is used to having men under him who jumped when he said to jump." Barbara reached out and put her hand on Luke's shoulder. "Right now, he doesn't see the difference in his crew and his fourteen-year-old son. Your attitude will get you into trouble. I'll do what I can, but you have to try harder than you've been."

Luke closed the trunk of the car. "Okay, if you say so." Luke checked again to see if his father was watching them. "Do you think we'll ever see *Grand-mère* Hillary and *Grand-père* Philip again?"

"My guess is no, but you never know what's going to happen." She reached up and pushed his hair out of his eyes. "Let's go get Dad and get on our way." With arms around each other, she and Luke headed back to the empty apartment. "It'll be good to see Gram again, don't you think?"

"Yes, ma'am." Luke tightened his arm around his mother.

~

Nearly two weeks later, the Johansen's pulled into Judith Barron's driveway.

All Luke wanted to do was get out of that car and away from his father. As he opened his door, Ned yelled, "Halt." With the car door open, Luke turned back to face his father, giving him a *what the hell?* kind of look.

"What?" Luke asked, his tone sullen and disrespectful.

"That's not how you answer me." Ned's face hardened.

Barbara turned back to Luke, shaking her head. "You two need to stop this now. Everyone is tired from this trip. Not in front of my mother—please."

Ned glared at his wife and smirked. "You're the reason he's like this. You didn't teach him any manners."

Before Barbara could respond, Luke stepped out of the car as Judith came out of the house clapping her hands. "You're here! Wonderful! Please come in—I've food and drinks waiting for you. It's so good to see you!" She open Barbara's car door. "Hello! How was your trip?" Not waiting for Barbara to reply, Judith turned and hugged Luke. "Oh my, you've gotten so tall."

"You always say that, Gram." Luke hugged his grandmother, laying his head on top of hers.

Ned shut his door with a shove that rocked the car, then he forced out a smile. "Hello, Judith."

Judith came around the car and held her arms out for a hug

from Ned. At first he didn't move, then smiled and wrapped his arms around his mother-in-law.

"How was your trip? Bet you're glad to be out of the car." She gathered them all up to the house, the whole time talking and asking questions. They were home.

## CHAPTER 13

# BOSTON, 1960

**BOSTON HAD ITS** first snowfall of the winter, and the neighborhood shimmered with tiny icicles that dangled off the tree branches and the edges of roofs. Bright sun rays bounced off the snow, but by late afternoon, the snowfall turned to dirty, wet slush. The mud-splattered school bus stopped two blocks from Luke's house.

"See you tomorrow," he told his friends, and jogged home.

Luke bounded up the red brick steps to his front porch. The two-story home resembled every other house on the block. His father had closed in the front porch, adding a touch of personality to the otherwise dull row home.

Today he felt invincible. That new blonde-haired girl had made eye contact with him at lunch. He'd never had a girlfriend, and definitely wanted her to be his first. He stopped at the front door and knocked the snow off his boots. When he opened the door to the living room, his excitement from the day evaporated.

Ned sat in the old, brown recliner watching television. The air in the living room smelled like a mixture of sour body odor and cigarette smoke. Next to the recliner stood a small oval side table dotted with cigarette ashes and a coffee cup with multiple rings around the rim. With no exchange of words, Luke knew his father's drinking had started again, which meant he'd lost his job. It'd been less than a month since Ned's last binge, and Luke dreaded what the next few weeks would bring.

His father turned as Luke opened the door. "You back?" Ned wore the same clothes he'd worn the day before. His face had yesterday's stubble, and his bloodshot eyes were vacant.

"Where's Mom?" His jaw tightened, and the words came out more as if a demand than a question.

"Who knows where the bitch is." Ned took a drag from his cigarette, causing him to cough.

Luke watched as a long ash fell on his father's bulging stomach. *Keep smoking, old man.* He pushed open the door to the kitchen. His mother, sat at the round dinette table. Her once jet-black hair now had gray running through it like silver Christmas tree tinsel. Her porcelain white skin had turned dull. Luke pulled out a chair and sat down. "You okay?"

"I'm fine. Your father is what you kids call *blitzed*."

Luke glanced at the different envelopes piled on the table. One stack was old, another stack had Second Request stamped on them, and the third stack was from a different company. Luke knew his family continued to struggle financially due to the navy losing his father's pay records and not paying him for six months after he retired. With no money coming in, they had to use money saved for a new home to rent and get reestablished. If his father could stop drinking long enough to work, they wouldn't have bill collectors after them. Luke's anger didn't help his family's situation, but he couldn't understand why it had to be this way.

"Mom, I'm sixteen. I can drop out and get a job." Leaving

school wasn't what he wanted to do. He was a straight A student and had a future, if he could survive his father's drinking.

"Thanks, hon, but you're right where you need to be." Barbara twisted her wedding rings. "How was your day?"

Ignoring her question, he asked. "What about a job after school?"

Barbara reached for her son's arm and gave it a pat. "Let's hold off for right now. I'm talking to personnel at Massachusetts General Hospital to see what's required so I can go back to nursing."

Barbara had worked as a registered nurse before Luke was born. Because she'd been out of nursing for eighteen years, attending classes would be necessary to learn the new medicines and procedures.

Ned shoved open the kitchen door. Barbara and Luke swung around in their seats. "Well, well, isn't this cozy—the fucking bitch and her whelp." His voice vibrated in the kitchen as he teetered back and forth, but he held firmly to the doorway. Even drunk, Ned Johansen was stronger than most sober men. Both Luke and his mother understood the danger they would face if they reacted to Ned's taunts.

"Ned, you scared us." Pulling her sweater tight around her chest, Barbara stood up and moved behind her chair.

Luke saw a dark blue bruise on his mother's neck as she wrapped her sweater tightly around her body. He wanted nothing more than to beat the life out of his father.

"Ned, why don't you turn on the news, and I'll bring you something to eat. Aren't you hungry? You haven't eaten anything today."

Ned stared at both of them as he rubbed his stomach. "Yeah, fix me something." A burp escaped his mouth as he stumbled back to the living room.

Barbara took a deep breath and turned back to her son. "It will be all right, Luke. Go do your homework, and I'll call you when dinner is ready."

"I love you, Mom."

"I love you more."

Luke had opened the door to his room when he realized he'd left his books and notebook in the kitchen. As he came around the corner at the bottom of the stairway, Luke saw his mother pulling something out from under the sink. *What?*

Barbara pulled the bottle of booze from Ned's under-the-sink liquor hideaway. She filled a glass halfway with the amber liquid, then took a medicine bottle from her pocket and removed two pills. Using spoons, she smashed them until they were fine particles, then she dumped them into the glass of whiskey. She added crushed ice, stirred, and when she turned around, Luke was staring at her.

"Mom?"

Barbara jumped back, spilling part of the doctored drink. With wide eyes, she stared at her son. "We'll all get sleep tonight," she whispered. Then, being careful not to spill more of the drink, she hand-delivered the glass to Ned.

The next morning Luke couldn't wait to get to school to see his soon-to-be girlfriend. He stepped in front of the mirror with a grin. His parents' door was open, but the bedroom was empty. He needed to talk to his mother, without his father around, about what he hoped would be his first-ever date this weekend. The kitchen lights were on, the coffee made, but he was alone. Luke peeked into the living room and saw his father asleep in his recliner.

On the table sat a note from his mother. *Luke, I've gone to Massachusetts General Hospital. Have a good day, and I'll see you tonight. Hugs!* He jammed the note in his back pocket and got his breakfast and lunch ready. More than anything else, he wanted his mother to divorce his father. This new job should give her the confidence and independence to make a move.

Luke was finishing breakfast and making last minute changes on his homework when his father came staggering into the kitchen.

"Where's your mother?"

"I don't know." He wouldn't tell this drunk anything. Taking the last gulp of milk, Luke shoved his papers inside his books. All Luke's instincts told him to leave.

His father went over to the coffeepot, poured a cup, and sat down at the table. Silence filled the room. Luke clenched and unclenched his fists. All he wanted was to get out the door without getting beaten. He got up, put his glass in the sink, then reached for his books. Ned grabbed his arm and shoved him back down into the chair.

"*WHERE* is your *MOTHER*, I said!"

"I just got down here, Dad. I don't know." Last year, his father nearly broke his arm when he smarted-off.

Ned stood and glared at his son, then slapped Luke across the face so hard Luke had to grab the table to keep from falling out of his chair. "Where is your mother? She wouldn't leave without telling her little sissy boy."

Luke righted himself in the chair, a little dazed. "I wouldn't tell you if I knew." Luke braced himself for another assault. He stood head to head with his father. Ned outweighed him by sixty pounds, so antagonizing his father wasn't a smart move. He had to leave before his hatred shoved common sense out of the way. He stood up and moved toward the back door.

Ned took two quick steps around the table. He pushed his son, knocking him against the wall. His nostrils were flaring, his face red. "You're not worth the effort, little piss ant." Ned's saliva splattered against Luke's face and his breath reeked. Ned turned, bumped the table, spilled his coffee, then staggered out of the kitchen.

Luke rubbed his cheek as he leaned forward, one hand on his thigh. His breathing rushed in and out. He couldn't understand why his mother didn't divorce this asshole. Luke grabbed his books and slammed the back door. *I hate you!*

As he walked to the bus stop, the icy air stung his face. When he got there, he stood off from the other kids. This wasn't how he pictured this day. His fear of what would happen to his mother drove him back home. Just as he turned, he vomited his breakfast.

A few minutes later, Luke opened the back porch door. A lounge chair in the corner was out of view from inside the house. He tugged on his gloves, then pulled his coat around himself, trying to block out the freezing weather. Luke looked at the sky and realized another snowstorm was brewing. His teeth chattered, and his body shivered as he watched the snow fall. He plugged in the electric heater they stored on the porch. Bringing the heater as close as he dared, he grabbed the packing blanket from the floor and covered up with it, but nothing seemed to block out the cold. Luke felt like a human Popsicle. While he waited, snowflakes collected in the porch's screen, creating a curtain of white that would spread across the windows as the day wore on.

It was afternoon before his mother came through the gate to the backyard. When she opened the screen door, Luke said in a loud whisper. "Mom, don't go in the house."

Barbara gasped and her hand covered her mouth. Her eyes darted from Luke to the house, then back to her son. "Luke, what're you doing here? Why aren't you in school? Did something happen to your father?" She put the grocery bags down and sat on the edge of his chair. "What happened to your face? Why're you out here? It's freezing."

"Before I left for school, Dad insisted on knowing where you were. I wouldn't tell him anything, and he got bent." He placed his hand on the bruise. "I couldn't let you come home without some backup, so I skipped school and waited out here."

"Let's get you warmed." She stood up. "Be sure to unplug the heater." Then they quietly opened the kitchen door. Like two little mice, they entered the warm house, making no noise.

Luke sat down at the table and watched her scurry around the kitchen. He couldn't get over how happy she seemed.

"I've so much to tell you." With a smile, she heated milk in a small saucepan, along with cocoa and sugar. Constantly stirring the mixture until it had all melted together, Barbara handed Luke a cup of steamy hot chocolate. Then she continued to put the groceries away. "I thought your father would sleep while I was at my interview. I'm sorry."

"It's my fault for mouthing off."

Barbara reached out and touched Luke's face.

"It's cool." He pulled his head back from her hand. "What did you find out at your interview?" Luke wanted to hear something good that might get them away from his father.

Barbara pulled out papers from her purse and sat down at the table. "It's back to school for me. I have to learn new procedures and medicines. Recent hires work the eleven to seven shift, which is perfect for us." She glanced at the pieces of paper on the table. "Nothing they mentioned was a surprise, except having to take a state board test. I haven't been in a classroom for a long time. Kinda scary."

"Does it cost anything? Do you have to pay?" He watched her, and could tell going back to school worried her more than she would admit.

"I do—somehow." She held out her hand and straightened out her rings. "I could pawn my wedding rings. It wouldn't be the first time they've been off my finger. Nothing is ever easy. Is it?" Barbara looked up, but the joy that Luke had seen earlier had vanished.

## CHAPTER 14

# BOSTON, 1960

NED'S VOICE CAME thundering in from the living room. "Barbara, where in the hell are you?" A piece of furniture smashed against the floor.

The crash made both Barbara and Luke flinch. Luke snatched the hospital file and shoved it into his pocket as Ned pushed open the kitchen door.

"I'm here, Ned. What do you need?" Barbara turned around as her husband staggered through the door.

Ned glared at Luke and pointed his finger. "Send that piss ant out of here."

"I'm not leaving." Luke moved away from the table. His eyes tightened, and his hands clenched into fists.

"That's enough from both of you. Stop it now!" Barbara stepped in front of Luke. "Luke, please go up to your room. I'll call you when dinner is ready. Now, please."

Ned sat at the table with a thud when Luke left.

"Would you care for something to eat?" Cautious around Ned, Barbara stayed out of reach. "Some food in your stomach instead of alcohol might make you feel better."

"NO! I need a drink. Where is it, bitch?"

Taking another step away from her husband, she said, "I poured it out this morning. We've got problems, Ned. You need to sober up. We're about to lose the house." Barbara hesitated. "I heard from the bank yesterday, and we need to come up with the past three months' mortgage payments, or they will foreclose on us."

"You fuckin bitch! This is all your fault." Ned got up and shoved back his chair. He went over to the sink and jerked open the bottom cabinet doors. "Where is it, Barbara?" He dumped cleaning products, scrub brushes, and dust rags onto the kitchen floor.

"Down the drain. Didn't you hear me? We have serious problems. You've got to get sober." She knew this wouldn't make any difference to Ned, but she was desperate.

"Get a fifth, or I'll go myself."

"There's a snowstorm. Nothing's open." Barbara knew that in Ned's fogged brain, getting his next drink was all that mattered. "I went to the store today and bought groceries with what money we had in our bank account. There's no more booze and no more money, Ned." She wiped her tears away. She couldn't do this by herself. Ned had to help. "And the phone has been turned off."

"There's no more money, Ned," he mocked her voice. "I'll get it myself." Ned pushed himself away from the sink and wobbled out of the kitchen.

"*NO!* Listen." She followed Ned, stopping to pick up the wooden chair he'd kicked over. "You can barely walk without falling. Please let me help you."

"You lying bitch." Dark circles were outlining the bags under his eyes, and his skin had a yellowish tint. The greasy hair plastered to his head begged for shampoo.

"You're not well. Please—I have sleeping pills. I can help you get through this. You'll be feeling like your old self again in two or three days. We've done it before. You'll be better in no time. Ned, please." Her hands pressed together as if she were praying. "Do it for us."

Without another word, Ned grasped the railing and climbed the stairs, rocking back and forth, then knocking against the wall. She stood immobile, uncertain he'd make it without falling backward. When he turned the corner into the bedroom, Barbara went back to the kitchen to clean up the mess. The family had learned that each drinking binge had to run its course, or he would be back in the bottle sooner rather than later. There was nothing she could do or say. If she could entice Ned to eat, she could sneak a sleeping pill into his soup. She had to try.

Barbara remembered the first time she had made this soup for Ned. It was shortly after he came home on leave to meet his son. Ned sat in the kitchen while she cut up vegetables, holding Luke with one arm while the baby snuggled to his chest. Luke's tiny head rested in his broad palm, and his feet stretched out nearly touching Ned's bicep. She remembered Ned telling her he never thought he could love another human being as much as he loved Luke. She took a gulp of air to dam back the hopelessness.

After the soup had simmered and the table was set, she went upstairs to get Luke and Ned. "Luke, supper's ready," she said as she tapped on his bedroom door. "I'll get your father if he isn't asleep."

Luke opened his door and went down the stairs.

Seconds later, she called from the stairwell with a panicked edge to her voice. "Luke, is your dad downstairs? Hurry!"

After a quick check, he yelled, "Mom, he's not down here. What's going on?"

Barbara ran down the front stairs and pulled open the porch door. The driving snow erased any trace of footprints down the walkway. Panic roused ugly possibilities in her mind. This was her fault.

"Go next door to Mrs. Watt's. Call the police. He said he was going to the package store, but I didn't think he'd go." Barbara ran into the kitchen, grabbed her boots, and shoved her feet inside them. "Tell them your father's been drinking."

"How long since he left? It's a couple miles to O'Malley's package store, Mom. You'll never get him back here by yourself. You go next door to call the police and I'll walk up to the liquor store. And," he paused, "why can't we use our phone?"

"The phone company shut off the service, Luke." She held up her hand to stop any more questions Luke might have. "I don't know how long. Maybe forty-five minutes to an hour at the most. I heard a noise like a door closing, but thought it came from upstairs." She put her hand to her throat, feeling the pounding fear. "It must've been when he left. And I'll walk up to the package store. You make the call, then come find me."

When Luke grabbed his scarf and hat, he saw his father's dark winter coat still hanging on the hook. "Mom, Dad's coat is here."

"Oh my *GOD*," she said. "Hurry! Luke, call the police."

"Wait, you'll need a flashlight."

"I won't go too far. Here, give me Dad's coat in case I find him." Barbara snatched the coat out of his hands. "Tell the police to hurry."

Luke bundled up in his winter gear and raced out the back door. The icy wind bit at his face and slithered inside his unbuttoned coat. He shivered from more than the cold.

It took Mrs. Watts an excruciatingly long time to answer. "Who's there?" The door opened only as far as the chain allowed.

"Mrs. Watts, it's me, Luke Johansen. Our phone is out. May I use yours?"

She unlatched the door. "Luke, come in." She stepped back as he swept past her. "Let me close the door. We're letting all the heat out. Now, what is it, dear?" she said. "Oh my goodness, Luke, what happened to your face?"

Luke didn't answer her. He rushed over to her hall phone and dialed the operator. "I need the police department. Please hurry," he said, without taking a breath. His heart pounded. He knew he shouldn't have let his mother go alone. He tried to keep his mind on what he had to do, and nothing more.

Mrs. Watts stood in the hallway watching Luke. She wrung her hands as she listened to the phone conversation. "Oh my sweet Jesus, is your mother all right?"

He held up his hand for her to wait as the operator asked Luke for his name and address, then patched him through to the police department.

"South Boston Police Department, Sergeant O'Keefe speaking," the police officer answered in a voice that told Luke he wasn't interested in a long story.

"Sergeant, this is Luke Johansen. We need help. My father left the house maybe forty-five minutes to an hour ago. He's been drinking. We found his winter coat, not sure what he has on, and my mother is out searching for him." Luke's fear bled through the phone lines.

"Whoa, son, slow down," the officer said with an edge of irritation in his voice. "What's it now? Your father's drinking and driving? What kind of car is he in? What's your address?"

"4363 Maple Avenue. No, he's walking. We don't have a car."

"Walking? In this weather? What's your father's name?"

"Ned Johansen."

"You got any idea where he headed?"

Luke turned his back to Mrs. Watts. "I think the package store on Main; it's a few miles from our house." He hated to say anything in front of a neighbor, but he had no choice. He turned back to her in time to see her hands cover her mouth.

"You say your mother went after him? In this weather?"

"Yes. My dad's sick, Sergeant. She'll go a few blocks, and if she doesn't find him, she'll come back."

"Son, you realize we're in the middle of a storm? I'm not sure if a patrol car can even get to your area of town. We got snow plows heading out—"

Luke squeezed his eyes shut. "Pleeeease! I, we need your help."

"Hold on." The officer put the phone down. Luke heard the officer giving numbers over the intercom. "Hey, kid, where're you now?"

"I'm at a neighbor's house. Our phone is out." He kept his head down, but he was sure Mrs. Watts suspected the truth.

"Okay, I'll have dispatch send out a call to the beat officer. We've also sent out a call for an ambulance. Give me a phone number where we can reach you. I can't tell you how long it will take, what with the weather getting worse."

"Hold on while I get my neighbor's number." Luke put his hand over the mouthpiece of the phone. "Mrs. Watts, what's your phone number?"

"Oh, um, 555-9899. Oh, wait that's wrong, 555-8999. Sorry." She appeared frazzled, and her hands shook. She picked up one of her cats as if it were a security blanket.

Luke repeated the number to the officer.

"Okay, got it. Good luck, kid. Help's on the way, and I would suggest you stay with your neighbor. Don't go out, or we'll be looking for you too."

"Thank you, sir." Luke set the phone down in its cradle and turned to Mrs. Watts. "Thank you."

"Luke, wait. Is, um . . . is your dad drinking again?" she asked as she put the cat down on the floor.

"Yes, ma'am. He is." Luke kept his eyes averted from her face and moved toward the door. Luke knew not to air dirty family laundry. "I have to go—Mom might need help. Thanks again."

"Let me know if I can help, Luke. Your mother and I are good friends, and we've climbed a few mountains together over the years."

Luke escaped out the front door. He hadn't been in her house for years, and he thought it still smelled as if she'd rescued one cat too many. Though the snowy night air felt like shards of glass blowing against his face, Luke took a deep breath, relieved to be out in the clean air.

When he got home, his mother wasn't there. Not waiting any longer, he turned on the porch light and was about to leave when Barbara pushed open the door.

"Mom, did you find Dad?"

"No, I could only make it to Washington Street. The snow blinded me. I could've walked right past him. There must've been two-foot snow drifts next to the sidewalks already. Did you talk to the police?" she asked as she dropped into a nearby chair. "What did they say?"

"Yes, they'll send a patrol car out, and an ambulance, just in case. Mom, the snow will slow everything down. I left Mrs. Watts's phone number, so they'll call there if and when they find him."

"Okay, let's eat something, then I'll go over to Mrs. Watts's house in case they call. You can stay here. I'll come get you if they call, or you come get me if the police come to our house."

"Mom, I can't eat."

"But we need to warm up. Come on, a small bowl. Keep me company."

She drew a deep breath, removed her coat, gloves, and scarf, then hung them up in the kitchen. Within a few minutes, they were sitting down at the table with steaming bowls of soup. Luke scanned the room, and everything seemed normal, but normal was so far from their reality. Neither of them spoke.

After they'd eaten, Barbara cleaned up the kitchen and threw in a load of washing. She and Luke both kept checking the time. They paced around the house, going from one window to another.

"Mom, do you think I should go over to Mrs. Watts? It's been almost an hour."

"No, let's wait a little longer. The storm is getting worse." Almost to herself, Barbara asked, "Where could he be?"

"No telling, Mom." He went to the living room window and watched the wind send the snow whirling. "Let's see if there're any weather updates." He walked over to the television console, pulled the knob, and waited for the picture to come to life.

The sound of the doorbell sent Barbara and Luke scrambling to open the door. Mrs. Watts stood covered in snow. "The police found Ned and have taken him to County General."

"Oh, Patricia, did they say if he was okay? County General? That hospital is a dump. Are you sure they took him there?"

"Yes, dear, I'm sure."

Luke reached out and put his arm around his mother's shoulders. She sagged against him.

"Did they say anything about his condition?"

"No, they said nothing except they found him and were on the way to County General. But they're sending a car around to get you and Luke," she said. "Please, keep in touch. I worry about you both."

"Thank you, Patricia. You're a wonderful friend. So sorry you had to come out. Would you like Luke to walk you home?"

"No, the police should be here soon. Keep in touch, dear. I'm only as far as next door." She turned and held on to the railing for balance against the wind. Luke and Barbara watched as she melted into the swirl of snow.

"I'll get some of your Dad's things together. I'm sure they'll keep him for a few days."

# CHAPTER 15

# BOSTON, 1960

THE STORM'S GALE seemed determined to keep Luke and Barbara from reaching the front doors of County General Hospital. For most of the nerve-wracking drive, the police officer who picked them up had to follow behind a snowplow.

Snow covering her head and shoulders, Barbara ran up to the information desk asking for Ned's room number.

A hospital volunteer scanned her papers for Ned's name. "I don't see a room number. Ma'am, if you'll take a seat in the waiting room. It's around the corner. I'll call the admitting nurse for information."

"What?" Barbara leaned over the counter, trying to see if she could see anything the volunteer wasn't sharing. "Isn't there any information on his condition?"

"No, my records have nothing on him except that he's here." Luke and Barbata glared at the woman in disbelief.

"I'll let you know, but there's no other information. You must wait. I'm sorry there's nothing more to tell you, Ma'am."

With frustration building, Luke stood in the waiting room doorway. Lovers' initials decorated chair arms, and the room reeked of cigarettes. Between the tattered magazines, nicotine-coated schoolroom clock, and the stained carpet, nothing resembled a place of healing. He and his mother took a seat near the hallway.

After an hour had passed, Luke said loud enough for a passing nurse to hear, "Mom, something isn't right. They should tell us how Dad's doing. We're family."

Barbata let out a sigh and shook her head. "I don't understand why they don't have an update on his condition by now. Keeping families in the dark is not routine practice for any hospital."

"Mom, I've a question." He stared down at the floor and wondered whether he should ask anything, but he couldn't hold back. "What's keeping you from divorcing Dad? Pleeease don't tell me you're sticking around for my sake. Why do we have to exist like this? I've seen your bruises, and I know about the broken bones." Saying the words out loud made him sick. "I've heard—" Luke used his fist to erase his tears.

Barbata readjusted her scarf. "Luke." She glanced around the room.

"What's next? Mom, I'm terrified that one day I'll get home and find you . . . ." Luke sat forward with his hands clamped together. He couldn't say it out loud.

"Luke, your father has a disease, and can't help himself." She brushed a stray piece of hair from his face. "We're all he possesses in the world. You understand how he feels about his mother and her family. Things will be better once I start working."

"What happened to him? Why does he drink?"

"Let's talk about this at home. This isn't the time or place. Okay?" She shifted in her chair and glanced up at the clock.

Luke blew out a puff of air, then sat back hard in his chair. There was more, and he felt it, but he knew she was right. Frustrated and cold, he stopped trying to make his case.

"Let's go get coffee or hot chocolate. I'm freezing. We need to move around. I bet we can see our breath if we turn our heads the right way." Barbata reached for his hand and stood.

At that moment, a nurse interrupted them. "Mrs. Johansen, Dr. Damron, the doctor who has been treating your husband, and a police officer, want to talk to you in the conference room on the third floor."

"Police officer?" Her eyes squinted, then she glanced at Luke. "Why?"

The nurse shrugged. "I'm delivering the message, that's all. May I show you the way? Sometimes these halls get confusing."

"Yes, thanks." She reached for the bag she'd brought for Ned.

Luke raised his hand as if he were stopping traffic. "Mom, this doesn't seem right. First, the hospital hasn't let us see Dad." Luke stared into the nurse's face. "We've had no word on his condition, and now the police want to talk to you." Addressing the nurse, Luke demanded, "Tell me about my dad."

"I'm sorry," the nurse replied. "My supervisor asked me to deliver this message. That's all I know. Mr. Johansen isn't one of my patients."

"Luke, think about the situation. It makes sense the police would want a statement. We sent them out on an emergency call in the middle of a snowstorm. Let's see what they want. Come on."

His mother sounded confident, and her reasoning made sense. "Yeah. Let's go." All Luke wanted was to be home.

They went up to the third floor, where the doors opened to a massive foyer with a nursing station in the center. They turned left, following the signs to the conference room.

"Mrs. Johansen, would your son like to sit in the waiting room? It's warmer than this hallway."

Luke gave the nurse a *what the hell kinda question is that?* look. "I can speak for myself, and no, I want to stay with my mother."

"Go ahead Luke. I'm sure it's a police formality."

"Are you sure I shouldn't go in with you?" He hesitated to leave. "I think I should stay with you."

"No, this shouldn't take too long. Then we can go home."

"Okay." Hesitating, Luke turned to follow the nurse.

"Mrs. Johansen, please take a seat in the conference room. They should be with you shortly."

Barbata opened the door to the conference room, her mind whirling. Could Ned be in trouble, or hurt, or—dead? Nothing made any sense to her, and a panicky feeling eroded her confidence. Maybe the police wanted to give her the bad news in private. She wished Luke had stayed after all.

After waiting for more than half an hour, the physician and a police officer entered the conference room. "Mrs. Johansen?" the doctor asked.

Barbata stood up. "Yes." Her voice wobbled.

"Please sit down. I'm Dr. Damron, and this is Officer Reed. He found your husband."

"Thank you for your help officer. We were afraid the snow storm—"

"It's my job to protect the public, Mrs. Johansen," Officer Reed said, interrupting Barbara. He didn't make eye contact, and headed to the other side of the table.

The policeman's gruff demeanor caused her to lean away. Barbara wasn't certain what to make of him. "Doctor, can you tell me how my husband is doing? We've been here for hours, and no one will let us see him, or talk to us about his condition."

Dr. Damron had sparse white hair and a Santa Claus belly. His face had a pink flush, and his glasses sat perched near the end of his nose, requiring him to raise his head to peer out. It seemed uncomfortable, but he didn't change the position.

"Mrs. Johansen, you need to answer a few questions before we discuss your husband's condition," the police officer interjected. He removed his hat without looking at Barbara.

"Yes, of course. What do you want to know?" Barbara said, glancing from the doctor to the police officer. She felt something wasn't right from the tone of the police officer's voice. "Please tell me about my husband? Is he . . . ." Barbata couldn't say the word, and she could feel her heart pounding.

The officer ignored her questions. "Did you try to give your husband sleeping pills earlier tonight? Just before he went missing?"

"What? Well, uh yes, I've given them to him so he could sober up. The medicine helps him to sleep through the worst of the withdrawal symptoms." Her hands left moisture prints on the table.

Dr. Damron leaned against the table. "Do you realize the potential problems you could cause by giving someone who has consumed a large quantity of alcohol prescription *sleeping pills*?" The pink in the doctor's face turned a shade deeper.

Barbara didn't understand their attack. "What?" She rubbed her forehead, trying to figure out what they were doing. "Doctor Damron this is the only way I can help him sober up. We have some serious financial problems right now." She'd never talked back to a doctor before, but the implications scared her. "I'm very careful."

"No, Mrs. Johansen, you aren't careful. What you are is very lucky you didn't kill your husband. You're in serious trouble," the police officer growled at her.

Barbata blinked, and for a second, her mind couldn't assimilate. "Serious trouble?" She peered at the police officer. "Wh, what—are you suggesting?"

"Is it correct you took all the cash out of the bank recently? You don't work outside the home, do you, Mrs. Johansen?" the officer asked, once again interrupting. "Planning to get rid of your husband and run off with all the money?"

"No! All what money? I need to speak to my husband."

Dr. Damron again leaned against the table. "Mrs. Johansen, you're in no position to demand anything," he warned her. "Giving prescription sleeping pills to someone like your husband can have a fatal outcome, but you already knew that, didn't you? We know you're a nurse."

Barbara's mouth opened to reply, but the words of protest froze in her mind. She couldn't imagine what Ned had told them, or why he would do this to her. How could they believe him over her? Nothing made sense to her.

Officer Reed slammed his fist down hard on the table. "Dr. Damron, if you would please let me handle this investigation. She is my suspect. I'll do the questioning here if you don't mind."

The doctor glared at the officer, veins in his forehead pulsing out, but he said nothing further.

"What? *Suspect*?" She fell back into her chair as if someone had punched her. "I wouldn't hurt Ned. Are you serious? Both of you think I tried to kill my husband?"

"Mrs. Johansen, you're being charged with the attempted murder of Ned Johansen. Do you understand what I'm saying? I've spoken to your son, and he tells me a different story. In fact, it sounds a lot more in line with your husband. Why don't you stop this innocent act?"

She gripped the arms of the chair as if they were a life preserver. "I don't believe you. Luke would never say that. I, or rather we, have serious financial problems. I, uh—we needed Ned sober. You're lying." With each accusation, she became more frustrated and panicked. "Bring Luke in here so I can see he is okay. Please."

Dr. Damron stood; he looked annoyed with the situation. "Your son is leaving with his father, and you're going to the psychiatric ward for evaluation. I've got patients to see."

"*Doctor*," the police officer said through his teeth. "Let me run this investigation."

Barbara glanced at the police officer, but turned her attention back to the doctor. "Ned will hurt Luke if they get into a fight." She pressed her hands together. "At the very least, let me call my mother or my neighbors so they can get Luke out of the house. You don't understand."

Officer Reed's face tightened, and his jaw muscles twitched. "I'm afraid it's you who don't understand, Mrs. Johansen. You'll be in jail as soon as we get through with this charade. In my opinion? Lady, you need to be in prison now, not this cozy hospital."

"Jail? Give me a chance to tell you what happened." She grabbed on to the table. "Let me explain."

The doctor stood up and signaled to a nurse who stood outside the door. She brought in a tray covered with a cloth. Barbara turned around when she heard the door open and recognized the young nurse. The feeling of betrayal caused her to gasp. The nurse kept her eyes down.

Dr. Damron took out a syringe and filled it with a clear liquid, then walked around the table to administer the shot. "This will calm you down, my dear."

She stood up when a male aide entered the room. He wrapped his arms around her as quickly as one would hold a squirming animal.

"Don't touch me!" Barbata screamed.

The doctor inserted the needle into her neck and stepped back. "You can let her go." He wiped his hands as if he'd touched something foul. "Mrs. Johansen, you'll be fine. Sit back and let the medicine do its job."

"Please! Let me call my mother to get Luke," she begged. "Someone, please help me. You need to listen! Ned's a violent man."

"Ma'am, your son has already left the hospital with your husband. He's okay. And you'll be fine in a few minutes. Please, settle down," the young nurse tried to reassure her in a quiet voice.

"Oh my God, you've got this all wrong." Barbara's head spun as she tried to stand, but her legs didn't move and her vision went black.

When Barbara woke up, she was in a hospital gown with an IV bag hooked to her left arm. Her panic returned as the conference room memories flooded back. She scanned the room. There were five other beds, but none occupied. A glass wall allowed the nurses to keep a constant watch on the ward. An eerie quiet sent a shiver shooting down Barbara's back. Her mouth was as dry as cotton. She tried to sit up, but a blinding dizzy spell forced her back down.

The door to the ward opened and a smiling nurse entered. "Good morning, Mrs. Johansen. I'm Nurse Cane, and I'll be your nurse while you're with us. Happy to see you awake. How're you feeling today?" She walked over to the right side of the bed and raised Barbara's arm to take her pulse. "You seem a little confused. Do you know where you are?"

"What time is it? How long have I been here?" she asked, but the words didn't sound like hers. She wiped her mouth. "May I have water?"

"Yeah, of course. It's Wednesday. You've been with us since last evening," Nurse Cane said, holding out a paper cup of water. "You need to eat something. Dr. Damron will be by to talk to you this afternoon."

Barbara's mind couldn't fathom she had been there overnight. It felt as if only minutes had gone by since her nightmare started. The realization that Luke was with Ned alarmed her. She understood she had to figure out her next move, but everything was moving in slow motion. There had to be a way out. *Mother!*

"Let me help you sit up, then I'll get your breakfast tray."

"I'm not hungry, but I need more to drink." Her head throbbed.

The nurse pointed to the back of the ward. "There is a bathroom through that door. Take it slow and easy if you get up." Then out the door she went. Moments later, she returned with a tray of food consisting of a bowl of oatmeal with no steam, along with a paper cup of orange juice, dry toast, and another paper cup of coffee with rings around the inside of the rim. Barbara turned her head away to fight the queasy feeling that was coming over her.

After the nurse positioned the bed, she gave Barbara a big smile. "Ok, sweetie, you eat up big for me. I'll be back to check on you."

The nurse left the room, and as the door closed, Barbara heard the distinctive click of an automatic lock. She tried to drink the orange juice, but she couldn't handle the sour taste. The oatmeal was a congealed gray lump. Not even trying to eat it, she covered it up with her napkin. After she rested a minute, Barbara tried a few bites of the dry toast and sipped the cold, black coffee. At least it was wet.

One thing she knew from her nurse's training was that not eating was a sign of depression. The food had to go. Barbara used the IV pole to support herself, and with her bedclothes, she hid the napkin full of uneaten oatmeal. As she crossed the room, the icy floors brought back some clarity to her thinking. She dumped the gruel in the toilet, then realized she needed to reduce the flow of medicine from the IV bag. Checking to see if anyone was watching, she made her adjustment, then headed back. With much of her energy drained, she struggled to get back in bed.

Later that afternoon, she woke up to find Dr. Damron reading her chart at the foot of her bed. She glanced at the IV bottle; nothing had changed.

"Dr. Damron, I have to call my mother so she can check on my son." Her voice sounded foreign. "Mother will be worried if she doesn't hear from me."

"Mrs. Johansen, I'll consider a visitor after we complete our evaluation," he said, looking over the rim of his glasses. "I've ordered the IV to be removed. If you cooperate with us, we'll be able to wrap this evaluation up in a day or two. I've arranged a session with the head of Psychiatry. Behave, and I'll see if your husband wants to see you—no one else."

"Please, listen. Ned has turned the situation all around." Talking made her head hurt. "You people have this all wrong." She knew she had to find a way to contact her mother.

The doctor left the room without another word, and she

watched as he spoke to her nurse on his way out. Barbara wanted to scream, but knew that reaction would be used against her. Instead, she bit the inside of her cheek as she struggled to hold herself together. She had to get help.

Sometime later that afternoon, a young aide brought in a tray of hot food for her. "Here you go Mrs. J," she said. "Can I help you sit up?"

"Thank you, yes."

Lunch consisted of an open-faced turkey sandwich with thick brown gravy, mashed potatoes, something green in a bowl, and a paper cup of watery tea. Barbara turned her head away, trying to hide the queasiness. She drank the tea. They used dehydrated potatoes, and the greasy brown gravy made them impossible to eat. She picked at the food, then took another trip to the bathroom.

Her nurse came in a few hours later, removed the IV from her arm, and checked her food tray. "Mrs. Johansen, you've a healthy appetite." The young woman gave her a thumbs up sign and turned to leave.

"Nurse, may I shower?" She held her breath—she had to get out of this room.

"Sure, I'll get someone to take you to the shower room. Oh, you've a shower bag in the bedside cabinet with all the items you'll need."

"Thank you." She rubbed the ache in her temples. "Something for my headache, too."

The nurse gave her a quick nod, and left.

Barbara climbed out of bed and got the shower bag out of the cabinet. It had shampoo, toothbrush, toothpaste, a small bar of Dial soap, and deodorant. Yes, everything she'd need, but what if something was missing? An idea became clear, but with a high risk of failure.

Her mother, Judith Barron, was a woman who got what she wanted in the most subtle ways. Barbara had to find a phone. She took out the toothbrush and toothpaste from the bag and hid them inside her pillowcase.

Not long after the nurse left, an aide entered the ward. She was older than Barbara, with tired, brown-green eyes, and hair tied back in a spiky ponytail. "My name's Johnnie Mae. Go on and get your shower bag and come with me," she said, pulling back the blankets and the tray table. "And get on these here slippers they give ya."

"I've got the bag right here." Barbara held up the bag. Her skin prickled with nerves; deceiving this woman wasn't right.

"Ya stay right with me, ya hear? Don't go runnin' off," Johnnie Mae snorted out as she unlocked the door. "I don't got no time for foolishness. No time, ya hear me?"

Barbara nodded. She paid close attention to the offices they passed. There were two more wards similar to hers with several more patients in them. As she walked down the hall, her hopes of finding a phone sank.

A black arrow pointed to the shower room. Barbara knew she had to make her move. "Johnnie Mae, my bag doesn't have a toothbrush or toothpaste." She held her breath. "I really need to brush my teeth."

Johnnie Mae grabbed the bag away from Barbara and quickly opened it. "No ma'am, they ain't in there. I knew they'd forget somethin'. Why didn't you tell me this right off?" She pursed her lips together. "I gots to do everyone's jobs and my own." She snorted, and her lips pursed together.

"Uh, I'm not thinking."

"I gots to go to supply, and you *has* to waits here. Don't be roamin' the halls, hear me?" Johnnie Mae gave her charge a stern look. "I gots no time for foolishness."

"I'll be right here waiting for you. I promise." Barbara felt a prickling all over her body. She knew she had to calm down and think. She had to find a phone.

Barbara waited until the aide rounded the corner, then hurried down the corridor in the opposite direction, using the walls for support. Her heart slammed against her breastbone as she tried opening one office door and then another. *Oh, please God let me find a phone.* Her head hurt, and her window of opportunity was rapidly closing. As she was about to turn around, Barbara watched a nurse leave an office without closing the door all the way. She flattened herself back against a shallow alcove until the nurse was out of sight. Hurrying down the hall, she peeked inside. The office was empty, and a black phone sat on the desk. Checking that no one was coming, she slipped inside and closed the door. Barbara fumbled her mother's phone number several times before she got it right. Judith answered her phone after four rings.

"Hello," Judith said. "Is anyone there? Hello?"

Hearing her mother's voice, Barbara almost couldn't speak while the tears flowed down her cheeks. She knew she had to calm down as she croaked out her words. "Mother, it's . . . I've little time. Ned's got—" her words shook as much as her body.

"Barbara? You sound terrible. What's going on?"

"Mother, he's accused me of trying to kill him, and he's convinced the police that I'm, uh, I'm insane. They want to put me in jail for attempted murder." Her voice sounded husky, and she had to hold the phone with both hands.

"What? Barbara. *MURDER?* Ned? Where are you?"

"I'm in County General Hospital." She felt nauseated saying the words. "In the mental ward. Oh, Mom, they won't listen." She pushed her hair out of her face and tried to breathe.

"A mental ward? Oh, my God! Barbara, I'll be there as quickly as I can."

"Mom, Mom wait." Barbara's head was throbbing, and the pounding refused to let up. "Ned has Luke at home. Please get him first, then get me out of this hellhole."

"Don't worry, I'll get Luke. And a lawyer too." The phone went dead.

Barbara put the phone back in its cradle. She felt weak, and worried she wouldn't make it back to the shower room. Opening the office door, she made sure the hall was clear before heading back.

Johnnie Mae met her at the door with her hands resting on her ample hips. "Whats you doin'? I tolds you no walkin' the halls." The aide leaned out of the doorway, then fussed in a high-pitched voice. "All I needs today is you causin' me trouble. Now git your shower and no mo' of your foolishness," she said as the door closed.

⌘

The next day, Barbara felt her nerves prickle every time the doors to her ward opened. Where was her mother? Why was this taking so long? She worried about Luke. Had she imagined her phone call to her mother? Many doubts raced through her mind. This place was playing with her psyche.

Nurse Cane brought in a wheelchair. "Hello, Mrs. Johansen. If you'll get your robe and slippers on, we will get you a quick physical with Dr. Marrow." She stopped the wheelchair by the bed, set the brake, and pushed down the footrests.

At first, Barbara couldn't speak. Her mind calculated that if her mother was fighting to get her out, this nurse was unaware. She tried to control her nervousness as she got out of bed.

Other than his being rude, Dr. Marrow's exam went as expected. Nothing was wrong with her physically or mentally. She knew the next thing they would do would be transport her to jail. *Hurry, Mom!*

After her dinner, she realized that Dr. Damron hadn't made his evening visit. She realized none of the nursing staff had been in her ward since lunch. She wasn't sure what was going on, but she hoped it was her mother raising hell.

Nurse Cane came in the next morning with the clothes she had worn into the hospital four days before. "Change into these clothes." All her perkiness had vanished.

"What's going on? Am I going to jail?" Barbara clutched the bedsheets as if they could save her. The nurse's attitude had made an abrupt change, probably her mother's handiwork.

"Mrs. Johansen, I don't know. Please, get dressed."

Barbara changed into her clothes and followed Nurse Cane to the third floor. She was fighting to keep her composure, knowing full well her mother and Luke were waiting for her.

As soon as Barbara saw her mother, she ran and wrapped her arms around her. "Mother, where is Luke? I don't see him." She stepped back, searching up and down the hallway.

"I couldn't contact him. Your phone must be out," Judith said, wrapping her arms around her daughter. "Come on, let's fix this fiasco."

Barbara's arms dropped to her sides, and she stared at her mother.

Judith took her daughter by the arm and steered her into the conference room where the nightmare had started.

Seated at the table were Dr. Damron and Police Officer Reed. New to the group were two other police officers, her mother's lawyer, and Dr. Marrow. The two women sat next to Judith's lawyer.

A tall, gray-haired officer pushed back from the table and stood. "Mrs. Johansen, I'm the Assistant Police Superintendent, Paul O'Keefe. Your mother and I are old friends. When she told me about your situation, I did a *small* amount of detective work, and I believe we owe you an apology."

Mr. O'Keefe circled the table before retaking his seat. "The officials here didn't check with your neighbors, your mother, or your doctor. If they had, they would've known something didn't add up. Your doctor believes the injuries he's treated you for over the past two years have resulted from beatings, instead of the falls you reported. It also appears your husband is quite the manipulator. He convinced several seasoned, but gullible, officials that you tried to murder him." The Assistant Police Superintendent paused and surveyed the sour faces around the table. "What I want you to do is tell us what happened."

✧

Hours later, two police cars parked outside Barbara's house. Her mother and her lawyer parked in the alley, and an ambulance waited around the corner. The snow in the road had turned into a muddy slush pit. Barbara took in a deep breath of the icy air. She was grateful and scared all at the same time.

"Okay, let's go over the plan one more time." The lead officer turned toward Barbara's mother as he spoke. "Mrs. Barron and Officer Reed will check to see if your grandson's in the kitchen. *If* Mr. Johansen isn't in the kitchen and your grandson is, get him out. If Mr. Johansen is in there, don't engage." He paused before he continued with his instructions. "We'll go in the front and draw him out, and transport him to the detox center at Massachusetts General Hospital. If we have any problems, I want you ladies out of the way. Let's make this simple and painless, people."

Barbara stood alone out of sight of her home. Her mother and Officer Reed disappeared around the back of her house. Seconds felt like hours. When she spotted Luke with her mother, she ran and grabbed him in an *I'll never let go* hug.

"I knew I shouldn't have left you." Luke stepped back from his mother. "Are you okay?"

"I'm fine—now. How about you?" Barbara scanned him for bruises. "Ned's never done anything the easy way," she told her mother.

Luke turned toward the house as the police and ambulance attendant brought Ned out on a gurney. "Mom, he was too sick to fight back."

## CHAPTER 16

# BOSTON, 1961

NOW THAT THE holidays were behind them, maybe the new year would bring something good into their lives. With Ned in rehab and their bank account empty, Barbara had no other choice than to accept help from her mother. It wasn't the first time she was left to shoulder the problems he couldn't handle. Her anger sat near the surface. She and Ned had always kept their financial struggles private, but at least they weren't homeless.

Judith knocked on the porch door holding a can of paint and brushes. She planned to keep the family busy and their house from falling apart. "Time to give this house a freshening up," she said with her normal enthusiasm. She hired two men to refinish the floors and help with repairs. Soon the old house rang out with the banging of hammers and the buzzing of sanders. The smell of linseed oil from the refinished wood floors floated throughout mixing with fumes from the freshly painted walls.

Barbara smiled. "This is the best this room has looked since we moved in." She clapped her hands and whirled around. "I believe I prefer paint fumes to cigarette smoke."

"Well, Mom, it's a toss-up for me," Luke continued to roll paint on the walls. "After I finish this section, I'm going to the library to get away from the stink."

"Okay. Thanks for your help, dear. You've worked hard." She worried how Ned's drinking would affect Luke in the future.

Judith pulled off her headscarf and plopped down in a chair full of newspapers. "We did super spring cleaning this winter." She chuckled at her joke. "Luke, you missed a spot at the top, to your right." She watched her grandson. "Yes, you've got it." Judith turned to her daughter. "It will be Ned's new beginning. You'll be out of school and working, and the extra income should take the pressure off him while he looks for work. What've you heard from the doctors?"

"They're concerned about his liver function. I don't have all the information because all the test results weren't available." Barbara wiped a droplet of white paint from the floor. "He is talking about searching for his biological father. It seems to be one of his hang-ups, along with Hillary's abandonment."

"How did you get that information? I was under the impression therapy sessions were kept private, between doctor and patient."

"Evidently, Ned gave his permission. I'm sure I'm not privy to everything, but it's nice to receive a little insight into his problems."

"Yes, it is. Hope the doctors will share more." Judith put her hands behind her head and leaned back in the chair. "I liked Hillary when I met her, but I never got to know her very well. What I can't fathom is how a mother gives up her child."

Luke left the room without a word.

Judith looked up in surprise. "What? My grandson leaves and doesn't say goodbye to his grandmother? What's gotten into him?"

"Mother, Luke just learned what happened to his father, and it's bothering him. I'll talk to him later, but let's not discuss this in front of him until I do. Okay?"

"Sorry, I should've realized he didn't know. It's hard to be compassionate when you've been so angry and hurt."

Barbara hoped her mother was wrong. Luke and Ned both needed answers to their questions. She did too, but her number one concern right now was getting herself through school and passing the state board nursing test, which was rapidly approaching. She took in a deep breath, reminding herself of how much she'd accomplished. Their future rode on her making it through these classes, but doubts played havoc with her confidence. *Why did life have to be so hard?*

That evening, Barbara pulled out her books and class notes, hoping to get her mind off the new financial situation with her mother. Ned wouldn't be happy. But if he had stayed sober, she wouldn't be in this pickle. She slammed her book shut.

The heavy footsteps down the back stairs caused her to turn her head as Luke burst into the kitchen. "Mom, I have a date Friday!"

"What?" She swiveled in her chair. "A date?"

"Before all this stuff started with Dad, I had met a new girl at school. Well, I asked her for her phone number, and finally had time to call her." He pulled the milk out of the refrigerator and began to drink from the carton, but his mother's arched eyebrows stopped him. Rolling his eyes, he reached for a glass. "We're going to the movies Friday. Okay?"

"How could I possibly say no? What's her name and where does she live?" Barbara couldn't stop grinning. It had been a long time since she'd seen him this excited.

"Her name is Claire Sims, and she lives two blocks west of here. The movie is a good first date, don't you think?"

"Sounds good." Barbara suddenly felt old listening to her son talk about dating. After Luke dashed upstairs, she tried to focus on her textbook, but even after reading the page twice, she realized she hadn't comprehended the material. She stretched her neck and groaned as the muscles fought back.

∽

It was Friday night, and Luke left the house at five thirty that evening. Barbara was watching her son head down the alley when the phone rang.

The operator's nasal voice boomed through the receiver. "Will you accept a call from Ned Johansen?"

"Yes, I will."

"Hey, how are you?" His voice was quiet.

"Ned? It's good to hear from you. We're fine. How 'bout you? Do you know when you'll be coming home?"

"We take one day at a time." He chuckled. "They won't give me a specific date. That's kinda why I'm calling. I'm worried, uh, worried about money and well uh—you understand?"

Now wasn't the time to go into all their financial details, but she couldn't let him worry. "Ned, we're fine." She hesitated, then squeezed her eyes shut. "Mother gave us a loan. I've paid the mortgage, the utilities, and things like that." She tried to gauge his reaction from his voice. *Damn phone, I need to see his face.*

"Um, tell your mother I'll pay back every cent, and thank her for me. Judith sure came through, didn't she?"

"Yes, she did." Desperate to tell Ned something positive, Barbara blurted out, "Oh, oh, Ned, guess who's on his first date." Barbara felt her laughter was a little high pitched, which may have given her nervousness away. "This dating thing makes me feel old." She braced herself, hoping he would think the news was good.

"How about that," he laughed. "A first date. Wow, time doesn't slow down, does it?" Ned remained silent for a few moments. "Well, glad you and Luke are okay. Better let you go. I'll call when I get a discharge date. I love you."

The dial tone buzzed in her ear as she replied, "I love you too." Ned had gotten off the phone a little too fast. She sucked on her bottom lip and held onto the phone, not wanting to break the connection. *Not sure that went well.* But she was relieved that Ned had sounded mentally healthy after six weeks without alcohol in his system.

Two days later, as Barbara folded laundry in the kitchen, her mother gave a quick knock on the door, then entered the house. "Hi, I wanted to drop by and see how you were doing."

"Hi, Mom. We're good. Ned called a few days ago—sounded strong and healthy." She gestured toward the coffee pot.

Judith took off her coat, then sat down at the table. "Does he know when he's coming home? Because I've something I want to discuss with you both."

"No, he said he'd call with that information. What do you want to discuss?" Barbara glanced sideways at her mother as she poured two mugs of coffee. She moved the sugar bowl closer.

"Well, I've been mulling over what you told us about Ned and his father." She stopped and picked up her purse. "So I did a little investigating on my own."

"Mother, I don't know if this is a good idea," Barbara said, fidgeting in her chair.

"Here are what we believe to be the facts." Judith ignored her daughter's skepticism and pulled out papers from her purse. "We have the name of the school Hillary attended, and I found out an old schoolmate of mine knows the headmaster."

She smoothed out the papers and slid them over for Barbara to read. "Hillary gave Ned his father's surname as a middle name. So, I can begin the research at this point. I also have the year she attended school. We can discreetly ask a few questions, get information on this man, whoever he is, then track him down." She sat back in her chair as if she'd just presented a case to a jury. "If Ned could meet his father, he might get answers he needs to heal."

"Have you thought about what would happen if his father didn't want to meet his long-lost son? From what I know, he wasn't thrilled when Hillary first told him she was pregnant." Barbara shook her head. "I'm not sure this is a good idea. Too, this might cause problems for Hillary that she won't appreciate. Maybe we should talk to her about this first."

"Sorry, but that woman doesn't have a vote in this decision. It's up to Ned. By the way, did you tell him you're going back to work?"

"No, it wasn't the right time. But I let it out you'd loaned us money to get the bills current. Didn't tell him about the home repairs you took care of." Barbara grimaced. "He said to thank you, and more importantly—he'll pay you back every cent. Not sure if he took the news all that well, but I'll fill him in when he gets home."

"He's got some redeeming qualities after all." Judith's left eyebrow arched. "I want to see him get answers to some of his nagging questions."

"This man may not want a reunion, and Ned needs positive events in his life. Let's wait for a while and see how he is when he gets home."

"Talk to his doctors and ask their opinions."

"That's a good idea. Mom, your offer is very generous, and I know where your heart is. But until I talk to his doctors, I don't want you to do or say anything."

"Okay, I'll hold off for now, Barbara. But this is something he wants, and the information might help." Judith stood up and slipped her coat on. "I'll be in touch. Kiss my grandson for me." She bent over and hugged her daughter.

After her mother was gone, Barbara leaned her head forward and rubbed her pounding temples.

∽

Two and half months later on a cool March day, Barbara watched as a yellow taxi pulled up in front of their home and Ned stepped out. Her skin prickled. One part of her wanted him to be home and the other was afraid.

Ned helped the driver pull his duffle bag out of the trunk. He stood on the curb and stared at the house as if seeing it for the first time.

Barbara opened the front door. "Welcome home, stranger."

"I've missed you so much." They hugged each other for several moments.

Luke stood back, watching his parents.

Ned released Barbara and stretched his hand out to Luke. "Good to see you, son."

"Good to see you too."

Ned surveyed the room. "Wow, everything is so different."

Barbara panicked. "Are you hungry? I've made your favorite— pot roast with carrots and potatoes." She smiled. "We've a lot of catching up to do. Why don't we go into the kitchen? I'll get you some coffee while I finish making dinner, and we can talk."

"Smells good." He followed them into the kitchen. "You've painted in here too?" He turned around, then grinned. "We should've done this a long time ago. It's amazing what a little paint will do to a place."

"Mother felt we needed to stay busy, so she showed up with two gallons of paint." Barbara handed Ned a cup of coffee. "She gave us some curtains and pillows she wasn't using too." A nervous giggle slipped out. Barbara didn't want her husband to believe they were better off without him.

"Your mother is something else." He sat at the table and sipped his coffee. "Luke, what's this I hear about a girlfriend?"

Luke's face lit up with a smile. "Yes, sir, she's Bill Sims's daughter. You've met her before. Her name is Claire."

"I don't remember her, but any girl that makes you smile like that must be a keeper."

Luke blushed and laughed. "Okay, that's enough."

"Man, it's good to be home."

⋦

The next morning, Ned pulled Barbara over to his side of the bed. "I'm sorry Barb, for everything I put you through. Please forgive me."

Barbara hadn't heard him use his pet name for her in a long time. It felt good to have him back. "Ned, true love is sharing an umbrella in the rain while waiting for the sun to shine."

"Yeah, kinda sums it up, doesn't it? Did you make that up?"

"You don't remember, do you? It was on the anniversary card you gave me a couple of years back. It meant so much, so I kept it."

"Barb, I want to make it all up to you and Luke." Ned kissed her bare shoulder.

"You can start by making love again, and we'll talk about the rest later." She reached out and brought his mouth to hers. Both were starved for the other's touch—they let the world fade away.

Luke's milk glass was still on the table when Barbara got downstairs. She plugged in the coffeepot and brought down two white mugs. By the time Ned had showered, Barbara had three fried eggs, several pieces of bacon, and toast waiting.

"There is nothing like the smell of bacon to welcome you home." He put his arms around his wife and kissed her again. "Thank you for loving me."

"I'll always love you." She kissed him quickly. "Let's eat while it's hot."

After breakfast, Barbara pushed her plate out of her way and took a sip of her cold coffee. Whenever Ned came off a binge, he was usually more accommodating. No better time to tell him than now, and get the truth out. "Before you got sick, I uh, I decided that I needed, no, wanted to go back into nursing." She paused and stole a glance at her husband. "Luke will be in college soon. And I, uh—I want to do more than cook and clean house." She could feel her pulse speeding up. "I've decided to go back to work." She stiffened, waiting for his backlash. "I've missed nursing." Worried Ned would see her true feelings, that she didn't trust him to stay sober and keep a job, Barbara moved from the table, busying herself with kitchen cleanup.

"I feel I'm the one that should provide for this family." He took a sip of coffee and wiped his mouth. "I assume your mother had a hand in helping all this come about." Ned gestured around at the repaired kitchen. There was a slightly aggravated tone to his voice.

"When you went into the hospital, Mother took over. You know how she is." *Well, there it is, the ugly truth.* Barbara pulled back her long hair and tucked the stray pieces behind her ears. "She got all our bills current, including your medical bills." She was mentally daring him to complain. "The basement leaked, and there were a few other repairs that wouldn't wait, so she did her usual thing." Feeling frustrated, she turned around and filled sink with water. She wasn't going to lie to him.

"Guess I need to see if I can find a job so we can start paying the ole gal back."

"Wait—I've an idea." She turned around and grabbed a dish towel to dry her hands. "What about starting your own business?" She waited to let the idea register in his brain. The idea came to her out of nowhere, but even without thinking it out, it sounded right.

Ned picked up his napkin and folded it over, then got up and poured himself more coffee. His face was a mask, hiding whatever thoughts must've been racing through his mind. "What kind of business would I start?"

"Home repair business. You're incredible at fixing almost any-thing. You build beautiful furniture, and your cabinets will be the best in town. Put your talents to work, Ned. Carl would be so proud."

"How would I get started? I've some of Pa's tools, but they were old when he used them. The shed is too small." He hesitated. "I'd need a truck or something to get around town. Where in the hell is *that* money supposed to come from?"

His agitation scared her. Nevertheless, she had his attention, and had given him the lifeline he needed. She pulled a binder from among her school books. "Here. Make a list of pros and cons, then just the essentials to get us started. It's time you were the boss. We can start out small, and once the business takes off, and it will, we can buy the things you want. What do you think?"

"Can I do this?" He sat back in his chair and crossed his legs.

"Yes! I know someone that could use a part-time job. I can keep the books, too. I'm excited. This will be our family business."

"Luke?" Ned rocked his head side to side. "Yeah, I'll need a helper, and he needs to learn how to do these things. I like the sound of *our family business*."

Before Barbara replied, Judith knocked on the door and walked into the house. "What are you two up too? What's going on?" She pointed to the list Ned had started.

Ned stood up and stiffly hugged his mother-in-law.

Barbara turned away, worried her mother would talk about finding Ned's father.

"Good to see you looking so well, Ned." Judith stood back, checking him over.

"Thank you, Judith. It's good to be home."

She hugged her daughter, then poured a cup of coffee for herself. "I wanted to come over and welcome you home."

"Mother, we were talking about Ned starting his own home repair business. What do you think?"

Judith said nothing. Barbara watched her mother mentally doing the good idea/bad idea scenario.

"Wow! I wish I'd thought of it first," she said at last. "I can't tell you how many times I've heard people asking if anyone knows someone who could change a lock, put up a door, or install a light. They want someone they can trust in their homes." She turned her focus on Ned. "This is right up your alley, young man. Once people see the perfection of your work, you'll be swamped. Yes! This is what the kids today call a cool idea. I'll bet I can get you more work than you can handle."

Barbara stood back, hoping her mother wouldn't interfere, and would allow her and Ned to find their way through this new enterprise. But that wouldn't be her mother.

Judith rubbed her hands together. "What say we get a business started today?"

"No, Mom, we'll do this ourselves. Small at first, then once Ned gets his reputation built, we can expand. We owe you so much now as it is." Barbara wiped the sweat off her hands.

"Don't be silly. Ned needs a truck and tools. I know you'll pay me back." Judith turned around to Ned. "Don't you agree?"

Ned glanced over to Barbara. "We need the help. So yes, I agree."

Barbara felt defeated. Did Ned do this to spite her? She sat back in her chair and her mother took over.

Judith left after lunch with a business plan in place.

❧

Later that afternoon, Barbara was to attend class. Leaving Ned so soon after he returned home didn't feel right. "I should be home by five o'clock or there about. We can talk more when I get back." She bent down to kiss Ned. More than anything else, she wanted to believe she'd given her husband hope for the future, and not more pressure.

With another hour and a half left in class, Barbara kept fidgeting in her chair and checking her watch. Worries of what Ned might do blocked out the entire lecture. During the class break she called home; the phone rang several times before she gave up. If this new business caused him to drink again, she would never forgive herself. She closed her book and her note binder, then turned to her classmate and asked, "Sally, would you call me tonight with the class assignment? I need to get home."

Startled, Sally looked up. "Sure. Anything wrong?"

"Probably nothing but my nerves. I'll see you tomorrow."

When Barbara opened her front door, she froze. The silent house scared her more than she wanted to admit. "Ned, where are you? I'm home a little early today." Her jaw clamped down tight and she ran to the kitchen. "Ned?" She called louder, then ran upstairs and darted in and out of the rooms. The house was empty. *Please don't let him be out drinking!* This was all her fault. She never should have suggested he start his own business. What was she thinking?

Shortly after five o'clock, Ned walked into the kitchen. Barbara was frantically pulling out everything under the sink. As an old booze bottle rolled across the floor, they both watched it come to a stop in front of Ned's feet. "What're you doing? I didn't think you'd be home yet." He leaned down to kiss her. She turned her head, but not before trying to smell his breath.

He stepped back, his hands on his hips. "Did you just smell my breath?" He glared at her and didn't back away.

"No—I didn't." Barbara pushed the cleaning products out of the way and stood up. Her heart pounding, she realized she'd let her imagination get the best of her. "I got worried, that's all."

He threw down the pad of paper on the kitchen counter. "Have a little faith, Barbara."

Barbara flinched. This wasn't how she wanted his first day home to turn out.

"Remember, this was your idea." Ned turned away, then ran his hands over his face. "I've been out pricing trucks. And determining what it would cost to enlarge the shed." He stood back. "I've got a good idea of the money necessary to get started." His hazel eyes bored into her.

"You're right." She took a deep breath and slowly let it out. "Would you like a cup of coffee or juice?"

Ned shook his head and picked up the pad of paper and dropped into a chair. He kicked the booze bottle away from him. "So every time I leave, you're going to freak out and search the house?"

"No, Ned." She took a second to collect herself. Tears puddled in her eyes and she quickly rubbed them away. "Let's try this again. Show me what you've found out. I want to make sure we only take what is necessary from Mother. I hate the fact we owe her so much now."

"So, let me get this straight. It's okay for you to put us in debt to your mother. *But*, when I need the help—it's not okay." He threw his pencil across the room, the vein in his neck pulsing.

Her intense fear that Ned would start drinking again had ruined their plans for a new life. "That's not fair. You left us with no money, and we were about to lose our home. I had no choice but to accept Mother's help." With anger so close to erupting, Barbara stopped. A screaming match wouldn't solve anything. "Let's agree to ask for only what's necessary to get started."

Ned seemed to accept her suggestion. "Here's what I've put together." The supply list appeared as though he'd used a ruler to measure each character's height and width. He'd drawn the exterior and interior of the workshop. Each diagram showed the tiniest of details, one for a retractable workbench, and pegboards for tools. Each of the drawings showcased his attention to perfection.

Maybe this would all work out. Still regretting the involvement of her mother, Barbara settled back and listened to all Ned's plans. Four weeks later, Ned had transformed the shed into a first-class workshop.

❧

By May, three months after starting his own business, Judith's predictions of more work than Ned could handle came true. The enormous debt they owed her mother still upset Barbara, but they planned to have her paid in full within two years.

Most nights, Ned fell asleep in his recliner before supper. His hands often cramped so severely he couldn't hold a pencil. Not a perfect plan, but Ned seemed to adjust by attending AA meetings, seeing his doctors, and working long days to build their business. Barbara continued to discreetly smell his breath, never completely believing life would remain normal.

After passing her state board exams six months later, Massachusetts General Hospital hired Barbara and put her on the graveyard shift.

❧

One very muggy August morning, exhausted from work, Barbara quietly opened the front door. She tried to remind herself why she wanted to be an emergency room nurse, then decided a hot shower was exactly what she needed before dropping into bed.

As she entered the house, a sudden chill washed over her body. A dreaded but familiar scent of stale beer and vomit filled her sinuses. *Oh my God!* She found Ned sprawled out in his recliner with a gash on the left side of his head and wearing a blood-stained T-shirt. His mouth was open wide and he was snoring loudly. Empty beer cans littered the floor next to his chair. The room looked as though a mini tornado had ripped through, breaking lamps and tearing down her new curtains. *Had there been a fight in here? Luke!* She dropped her bag and ran up the front staircase. When she got to Luke's bedroom door, she tried to open it, but couldn't. She pushed harder, and whatever was blocking it gave way.

Luke sprang up from his bed with a baseball bat in his hand as Barbara entered, his eyes open wide. He was still dressed in the shorts and T-shirt from the day before. His voice was full of sleep, but his words were deadly. "I'll kill you if you come near me!"

Barbara gasped. Her hand flew up to her mouth to stifle a scream. "Luke, it's me!"

Luke dropped back down on his bed when his mind realized who was at his door.

Unsure her legs would keep her upright, she sat down next to her son. "What happened? Why didn't you call me?" She checked her son over for any bruises. "Are you okay?"

He raked his fingers through his hair. "Yeah, I'm okay. He was drunk when I got home from Claire's." He bent over, put his elbows on his knees, and rubbed the sleep from his eyes.

"Did you hit him with the bat? His face is all bloody."

Luke propped the bat next to his nightstand. "No, I wish I had.

But he fell, and when I tried to help him, he took a swing at me. Guess what Dad told me—I'm not his son. Why would he say crap like that? I knew things were going too good to last."

She stiffened. This wasn't the time to go into the past. "I'm sorry Luke. He's drunk, and isn't aware of what he is saying. He won't remember what happened when he sobers up." She reached over and rubbed her son's back. "Does he have anything scheduled today?"

"We're supposed to build a bathroom cabinet to install on Monday." Luke paused a moment. "He has estimates he needs to write up, but nothing pressing." After a long yawn, he shook his head slowly. "That's all I remember."

"I'd better call his sponsor." She got up, then turned back. "You should've called me."

"What could you've done? By being gone, you saved yourself a beating. I wasn't about to bring you home to this."

Barbara knew she couldn't keep her son safe. So what was the point of him calling her? They stared at each other for a minute before she turned and headed down the back stairs. How was she going to go to work that evening and leave Luke? *Why, God?*

## CHAPTER 17

# BOSTON, 1961

BARBARA HUNG UP the phone after telling Paul Day, Ned's AA sponsor, that he'd started drinking again. She asked him to come over. Next, she poured a cup of freshly brewed coffee. Taking a deep breath of the caffeinated aroma, she heard her mother's voice in her mind, *And this too shall pass.* She was going to check on Ned›s head wound before she went back up stair to pack, then leave for her mother's. The sight of the torn curtains and broken pottery stopped her from going any further. The door to the living room silently closed.

With the last of her energy, Barbara walked upstairs and quietly opened her son's bedroom door. "Luke. I need—" He was sound asleep, and looked so peaceful she let him be. After a quick shower, she dressed, got clothes out of her closet, and placed them neatly in her suitcase, then placed them next to the door. Her body felt heavy, almost as if she were walking through Jell-O. There was no way she could live through any more of Ned's drunken binges.

When she turned around to get Luke, Ned stood in the doorway. Her hands flew to her chest as she gasped and stepped backward. How had he gotten up the stairs without her hearing him?

Ned saw her packed bags. "Where the hell do you think you're going?" His bloodshot eyes squinted as if he couldn't focus on any one thing. He leaned in against the wall to keep his balance. "Got some hot doctor waiting for you?"

The gash on his forehead had stopped bleeding, but she knew it required stitches. A wave of nausea came over her watching him sway back and forth. "Ned, you're hurt. Sit down and let me take care of your cut." She stepped backward instead of going forward, putting as much distance as she could between herself and her husband.

"You fucking bitch, leaving me here to take care of your bastard love child! I'll teach you!" He lunged at her, but his foot caught on the strap of her bag, causing him to fall. He hit his head on the side table, triggering fresh blood to gush down his face. "See what you did, you ugly *cunt?*" He tried to wipe the blood out of his eye, but couldn't keep up with the flow.

*Should I make a run for it, or stay put?* "Oh my Lord, Ned, let me get the bleeding stopped."

She heard a door bang open, and Luke ran into his parent's room. He held the baseball bat in his hands and stood over his father's sprawled body. "You son of a bitch, leave my mother alone!"

Barbara put her hands up. "No, Luke! I'm okay. Your Dad fell—that's all." Taking a deep breath, she had to gain control of the situation, or else Luke was going to kill his father. "Go get the first aid kit from the kitchen, and an ice pack. Hurry!"

Luke didn't move. He stood with the bat held high in the air like a batter getting ready to swing.

Barbara fought down her panic, stepping forward and placing her hand on his arm. "Go Luke, now! Get me the first aid kit and an ice pack."

Ned rested his head against the side of the bed. The blood turned the white sheets dark red. When his eyes rolled back, Luke lowered his bat. Then he ran down the stairs while Barbara grabbed a washcloth out of the bathroom to apply pressure to the wound.

From the kitchen, Luke called out, "Mom, Dad's sponsor is here. He's coming up."

Paul Day stood a stringy six foot two inches. His hairline drew back from his forehead, making his bloodhound eyes his most prominent feature. In a thick southern accent, he said, "Mornin' ma'am. Usually, I'd say *good* mornin', but nothing looks good here. What happened? He's out cold." Not waiting for a reply, he squatted down next to Ned. "Step back, ma'am, and let me get him on the bed for you." He lifted an unconscious Ned as if he were a sleeping child. "We probably need to take him to the ER to close up his head. Unless you can do it." He turned back to her. "I'm told you're a nurse."

Barbara took the first aid kit from Luke. "I am, but . . . ." Working all night and coming home to this mess had drained her stamina. "Let me get the bleeding stopped so I can have a better look." Her medical training kicked in despite her weariness, and she quickly had Ned's wound stitched and bandaged.

"Good job. Now, do y'all have a place to stay? I've got it from here." He turned around as Barbara picked up her bags. "Ma'am, please leave a phone number where y'all will be, and I'll call you when he's sober."

"I'll leave my mother's number on the kitchen table. Thank you, Paul." She watched Ned's breathing, then walked out. "Luke, you need to pack a bag."

⁂

Three days later, Barbara heard from Paul. "Your husband is in much better shape than when you last saw him. Do you have time to come over?"

"How did you get him sober so fast?" she said, not believing Ned could sober up so quickly. Usually, this meant he'd be back in the bottle sooner rather than later. Her instincts sparked an immediate distrust of Paul's assessment.

"He had the expected DT's and vomiting, but I have a concoction that helps stabilize the body. Anyway, I want to be here with you both. There're changes we need to speak about."

Later that afternoon, Barbara opened the kitchen door and found Ned and Paul sitting at the table drinking coffee. Ned appeared as if a train might have run over him. A dark purple bruise seeped out beneath the bandage and spread below his right eye.

Paul smiled and motioned for her to come inside. "Come on in and sit a spell."

She and Ned glanced at each other as she reached for her mug. "How're you feeling?" Barbara tried to sound as though she cared, but she didn't.

Ned hung his head. "Like a damn fool."

Barbara pursed her lips together. She so wanted to say, *What did you expect?* Silence hung in the air.

Paul stood up. "Ma'am, I think you and your husband have things to talk about, so let me give y'all some privacy." He walked out and closed the door.

Barbara wished she were anywhere but here. There was nothing new he could say. Still, she asked, "What happened, Ned? Things were going so well. I don't understand." She circled the rim of her cup with her index finger, then placed the cup on the counter. "I can't do this anymore—I can't." Her voice quivered.

Ned rested his head in his hands. "I know." He pushed out a breath. "It'd been a long, rough day, and I bought a beer on the way home. I thought I could handle *one beer*. Damn, it tasted so good. One thing led to another, and beyond that, I remember nothing till I came to, and Paul was standing over me."

"It's always one beer, one drink, isn't it, Ned? You should know you can't handle *ANY* alcohol." She rubbed her face with both her hands and pushed her hair back. "This can't happen anymore. Your business will suffer. And what about our family, Ned? You said horrible things to Luke—and me." She walked over to the sink with her cup. "I don't believe Luke can or will forgive you this time." Staring into her coffee as if it were a crystal ball, she hoped answers would float to the top.

Ned didn't reply.

Barbara turned around to see tears running down his face. "We can't go through this again. Do you understand what I'm saying?" She couldn't summon up any sympathy; Ned had disappointed her too many times.

Her husband nodded.

Paul walked back into the kitchen and poured more coffee into his cup, then sat down at the table. "Ma'am, did your hubby here tell you about making an appointment with his doc? He'll ask to be prescribed a medicine that'll make him violently sick if he drinks any alcohol. It's called Antabuse."

Barbara stared at Ned. "No, he didn't." She paused and drew in a long breath. "I've heard of the drug, but I thought if you drank alcohol at the same time there's a chance it could kill you."

"I'm pretty sure Antabuse won't kill you. You'll get disoriented, you'll sweat, and you might feel heart palpitations, but what you will definitely feel is bad—very bad," Paul said. "Kinda makes you *wish* you were dead."

To Barbara's surprise, Ned raised his head. "Sign me up."

Their history made her want to believe there was a magical pill that suddenly fixes everything. But it would take more than his agreeing to the medication before she'd have any faith in him. He was always more agreeable to anything after one of his binges. Barbara felt this was the same con game she'd listened to her whole married life.

❧

Three weeks later, Barbara and Luke moved back home. The family didn't melt into their old routines. Luke refused to work with Ned, and stayed at Claire's house most of the time. Barbara worked double shifts at the hospital, and used the extra money to restore the living room while continuing to repay her mother. Ned started his new medicine and got back to his home repair business, but now he worked alone.

Barbara came down the staircase to make lunch when her mother knocked on the porch screen door. "Hi, Mom, this is a surprise. What're you up to?" They hugged. "You're very dressy this afternoon. Going anywhere special?"

"Thank you, dear. Actually, I'm coming back from a bank meeting. I wanted to see how things are. You've been home for six weeks. Are you seeing any difference in Ned?" She pulled out a chair and sat down at the table. "Did you finish with your living room?"

"Something isn't right with Ned, but I can't figure it out. And the living room is almost done." She flipped her ponytail off her shoulder, then turned around to see if Ned's truck was in the driveway. "Mom, did you see Ned's truck when you pulled in the alley?"

"No. Where is he?"

"I think he's out working on some project. Did I tell you Luke has refused to help Ned?" Barbara leaned her head to one side and tried to stretch out the tight muscles in her neck.

"Bet that isn't going over very well." Judith shifted in her chair. "Don't you think it's time we talked about my suggestion of having a detective search for Ned's father?" Judith said after a pause, "You know Ned wants this done. The doctor told you months ago, and I can make it happen."

"I'm not sure this is the best time, Mom. It might be the Antabuse he's taking, or the pressure he's feeling working alone, but I don't understand what's going on with Ned right now." Not wanting to sound ungrateful, Barbara paused. She knew now wasn't the right time. "I don't want to take a chance of making our situation worse—"

"Or better," Judith interrupted, her perfectly shaped eyebrows arched.

Ned walked in from the porch. "What're you two talking about? Or better who?"

Barbara turned toward the cupboard and squeezed her eyes shut. She took a deep breath, allowing herself a few seconds to consider whether she should tell him or not. "Ned, Mother wants to hire a detective to find your father." She kept looking at the counter, not facing her husband. "I have to say, I am not in favor of this idea."

"What?" He shifted his glare from his wife to his mother-in-law.

Judith pushed out a chair. "Sit down, Ned, and let me tell you what I've been thinking about, and you choose what you want to do."

Ned refused to sit, and instead stood with his arms crossed, staring at the two women.

Judith pulled papers from her purse. She seemed to ignore his refusal to sit down. "I remembered the name of the boarding school your mother attended. It turns out that an old schoolmate of mine knows the headmaster." She slid the papers closer to Ned. "I want to ask my friend if he'd give us contact information on the man we believe is your biological father. We know his name, and the approximate time of his employment. We would do a little investigating. Assuming he's still alive, we'd reach out to him and see where it leads."

Barbara set two cups of coffee on the table and pushed the sugar bowl toward her mother. Both mother and daughter were silent.

Ned leaned over the documents. When he finished reading, the vein in his forehead was pulsating. "How'd you get your information about me wanting to find my father?" His cheek muscles twitched. "Judith, why are you doing this?"

Judith glanced over at her daughter, then back at Ned, and quickly said, "Ned, I care about you and my daughter. If I can play any part in helping you with this issue, well, I just want to." Judith sat back in her chair and folded her hands in her lap. "You deserve to have your questions answered."

His eyes were cold and hard. "My wife shouldn't be running off at the mouth telling you *my* business. Thank you, but *NO!* You need to back off, Judith, and find another charity case." He turned back to Barbara. "I need to have a talk with my wife."

Barbara gasped, and her hand went to her mouth "Ned, wait, I—I'm sorry. I should've told, uh, asked if it was okay to tell Mother about this." Nothing she said came out the way she wanted, and she wasn't making any sense in her panic.

"You're damn right you should've. Where do you get off telling anyone my business?" He took a step toward his wife, his hand forming a fist, then releasing it.

Judith jumped out of her chair and held up her hands. "Whoa Ned, think about it. I'm not someone just off the street. I care about you, and want to give you something your mother didn't—answers. I've the funds to make this happen, and we won't know until we try. Think of the possibilities."

Ned stepped closer to his mother-in-law. "I would prefer you to stay out of my business, Judith. Do I make myself clear?" He stood towering over her.

"All I ask is that you settle down and think about my offer." Judith didn't move back.

Ned glared at the two women, then walked out of the kitchen, letting the door slam on his way out.

Barbara's legs felt weak, and she slid to the floor.

"I've never seen him like that before." Judith's eyes glistened as she reached out toward her daughter. "Why don't you come with me and let him cool off? I'm so sorry. I should've listened to you."

Barbara couldn't say anything. With a deep breath, she struggled to sit in one of the kitchen chairs. "I'll be okay. And if I were to leave, it would be worse when I came home." She brushed her hair away from her face. "Mother, he needs time to think about your offer."

At first, Judith didn't move. "Barbara, I want you to come home with me. I've never been so scared in my life, for both of us. What about calling his sponsor?"

"That's a good idea. I'll call Paul and see if he'll come over." Barbara's whole body trembled.

"Honestly, you're making a mistake staying here." Judith gathered her coat and purse. "Please, for your sake, come with me."

"Thanks Mom, but he'll cool off." She didn't believe her own words, and wanted to leave, but felt she was wrong to have said anything to her mother in the first place. Hopefully, he would cool off so they could talk, and she could apologize.

Barbara watched Judith drive down the street. She stayed at the door for several minutes before she went back to reach Paul, but got no answer.

⁂

Ned worked in his workshop for the rest of the afternoon. Near dinner, Barbara felt she needed to check on him. She had to make him understand her mother's intentions. With the table saw roaring away, Ned didn't hear or see her enter the shop. The sawdust fell like snow, dousing Ned with a pale-yellow coat instead of white flakes.

Ned finished the cut he was working on. He looked up to find her in the doorway. "What?" His voice was flat, and he sounded as angry as he had a few hours before.

"Thought I'd come see if you were at a stopping point. Dinner is almost ready." She tried to sound cheerful, but her voice betrayed her.

"Don't rush me. You're always nagging." Ned brushed the sawdust off his pants. "Is Luke home? It's about time for him to carry his weight around here. You coddle him too much."

"No, he's still at Claire's house. I'm sure he's eating dinner with her family." A chill ran through her.

"He's there a lot these days—too much." Ned slammed the

219

board he'd cut on the workbench, causing it to splinter. "Shit! See what you made me do?" He snorted out a breath as he stared at the board. "You don't listen to me. Maybe you should call your fuckin' mother. She can fix Luke too, while she's at it." His words sounded like the snarl of a dog warning an enemy to back off.

Rooted to the ground, Barbara didn't think she could get her legs to move. "Mother only wants to help you." Her voice vibrated the words.

"I don't need her kind of help. What I need is for your damn child to get off his lazy ass and help me. Got it?" He turned around and threw his tool belt on the workbench.

"Yes. Please don't be mad. Mother is family, and has your best interest in mind."

Ned kept his back to her and did not reply.

Barbara went back to the house. She knew there was more to his agitation than her mother's offer and Luke not working with him. He must have started drinking again. But he wasn't having the same symptoms Paul said he would have if he drank while taking the Antabuse. She went upstairs to their bathroom and pulled out Ned's medicine bottle. Fumbling with the cap, several pills tumbled out. The pills were aspirin, not Antabuse, but they were almost the same size and color. *This is bad.* He wasn't taking the Antabuse, so his aggressive behavior made sense now. She had to contact Paul. She closed the cabinet door, then turned to find Ned standing between her and the hallway.

"What in the hell are you doing?"

Barbara hesitated, her heart pounded so loudly she was sure Ned could hear it too. "Nothing." She didn't look at his face as she eased past him.

With his arms crossed over his chest, he poked her chest hard with his elbow.

"Oww!" The hair on the back of her neck rose. Stepping down

the stairs at what she hoped appeared to be a normal pace, her entire body was screaming, *Leave!*

With Ned coming down at any moment, Barbara was afraid to call Paul and have him catch her. She went about setting the table with glasses and plates. The whole time trying to maintain calm.

Ned took a seat at the table. "What do you think about how much time Luke is spending with that girl?"

At least Ned wasn't talking about her mother. She wanted to tell him it was because of him that Luke stayed away, but now wasn't the time. "As long as we know where they are and what they're doing—it's his first real relationship. Puppy love is pretty powerful."

"I think we need to have a sit-down with him. He needs to work with me again if he wants money to date this girl."

Barbara placed the bowl of mashed potatoes on the table and turned away from Ned so he wouldn't see her fear. "Let's hold off. You and Luke might want to get together and talk. Like you used to."

"Not going to happen. I'm making the kid tougher so he can deal with life. You're too easy on him. You've made him into a sissy momma's boy."

His words startled her, causing her to spill milk on the counter. "Ned, please let's talk. What's going on? You don't talk like that unless you've been—"

"All I ever hear is you nagging me. Don't do this. Don't be like that. Well—I'm sick of it. Think you're so high and mighty, but you're not," he said, glaring at her. "Maybe you should tell your mommy? Or better still, I should tell her how you're always telling me what I'm doing wrong." With every word his face got redder and the veins in his forehead pulsed out his anger.

Anything she said would only aggravate the situation. Silence was wrong too; he would think she was ignoring him. Her chest hurt. She glanced at the porch door. Could she make it past him? Sweat droplets rolled down her back.

Ned pounded his fist on the table making the dishes rattle. "I'm never doing what you think is *right!*"

Barbara made a mad dash toward the door, but Ned, unexpectedly agile, grabbed her and threw her against the counter. "You're not going anywhere." He pulled his arm back, then slammed his fist into her stomach.

⌘

When Luke came home later that night, the kitchen light wasn't on. *Mom's slipping, no light.* He felt something hard under his shoe and turned on the light to see what he'd stepped on. There on the kitchen floor lay his mother's unconscious body. She had mashed potatoes ground into her hair and face. Shards of broken dishes, spilled milk, and food lay scattered across the kitchen. A trail of blood flowed from her nose down to her throat. Cuts from the shattered glass were on her face and arms. Luke could tell the swelling and ugly purple bruising were from the punching fist of his father. At first, he couldn't believe what he was seeing. It was a scene out of a horror movie: chairs knocked over, blood mixed with food, and a nearly-dead body.

"Oh my God, *Mom!*" He squatted down next to her. "It's okay, it's okay—I'm here." He gently touched her throat to feel for a pulse. "*Oh, God!* Mom, what'd he do to you? I should've been here." He wiped her face gently. "I'm calling for help. You're safe now."

Barbara moved her arm, faintly acknowledging Luke.

Luke called for an ambulance, then dialed his grandmother. "Gram, he's beaten Mom. Meet us at the hospital."

"Oh my God. She should've come with me. Luke, is your father still in the house?"

"No, I don't think so. I didn't see his truck." He stared down at his mother. "I hope he wraps it around a tree."

⌘

At the hospital, Luke paced back and forth, waiting for news from the doctors. He couldn't stand the stares he got when he explained what had happened.

An hour later, Judith came pushing through the double doors of the emergency room. "Luke, have you heard how your mother is doing?" They clung to each other. "It's my fault. This is all my fault."

Luke led his grandmother away from the other families. "Gram, you had nothing to do with this." He didn't want their conversation overheard, and kept his voice low. "Mom's in surgery. I heard the doctors say something about her spleen, several busted ribs." Luke wiped his eyes. "I'll kill the son of a bitch. He doesn't deserve to live another minute."

Judith scanned the waiting room. "Have the police been here? Have you called his sponsor? I can't think of the man's name right now." She walked over to the water fountain and wet a handkerchief, then handed it to Luke. "Dear, wipe the blood off your face."

"Someone told me they were on their way, but that was a while ago." He wiped his face and hands, then stuffed the handkerchief in his coat pocket. "His sponsor? No, I haven't called him, don't know his number or name."

Judith closed her eyes. "I'm afraid this is all my fault." Judith rubbed her temples, then placed her coat and hand bag in a nearby chair. "I should never have—"

"What? Gram, you had nothing to do with this crap." He took her hands in his. "What're you talking about?"

"I offered to help track down your dad's father." She took a deep breath. "Your mother told me how agitated your father had been. She knew something was wrong, but didn't know what. I didn't listen to her, and made my offer to find his father anyway. He was furious." She paused. "I've never been more afraid of anyone in my life."

Before Luke could respond, a nurse came up to them. "Luke Johansen?"

"Yes. How's my mother?" He put his arm around his grandmother.

"Please come with me. Your mom is out of surgery, and her doctor will be in to talk to you," she said.

"May my grandmother come too?"

"Yes, of course."

Judith picked up her purse and coat. "Can you tell us how the surgery went?"

"I'm sorry, I don't know. But her doctor will be in shortly." She opened the door to a small office off the main hallway. "Please, take a seat. It should only be a few minutes."

The nurse came back moments later. "There's a Paul Day in the waiting room. He said he's your father's sponsor, and needs to talk to you."

Judith grimaced. "If you will, ask him to wait. We'll be out as soon as we meet with the doctor."

The nurse nodded and left.

"How did he know where to find us?"

"He must've talked to your dad."

A few minutes later the doctor knocked on the door, then entered. "I'm Jack Hagel." He reached out to shake hands with Luke.

Luke stood, shook his hand, then turned to his grandmother. "Yes. And this is my grandmother, Judith Barron."

Judith stood and shook hands with Dr. Hagel. "I want to reassure you both that Barb came through surgery just fine." He gestured toward the chairs and waited until they were settled. "We had to remove her spleen. She has three broken ribs, and a broken nose."

Judith put her hand on Luke's arm. "How long will you keep her here?"

"I need to observe her for three or four days. She also suffered a concussion. She'll be in some discomfort until her ribs heal."

Luke tried to take in all the information, but it had to be about someone else. How could this be about his mother? "Can we see her?"

"Once she's in a room, the nurses will come get you." He stood up and put his hand on Luke's shoulder. "I've worked with your mother since she came to MGH. I promise you, we'll take good care of her."

"Thank you, Dr. Hagel." They shook hands and walked out to the waiting room.

Paul stood up when he saw Luke open the door. "How is she?" He shuffled his ball cap from one hand to the other.

Judith explained what the doctor had shared with them. "So what rock is Ned hiding under?"

"He's in jail for DUI. He'll be in for a rough couple of days."

"Mr. Day, I hope it's horrible for him," Judith said.

"Gram, nothing will change. Mom needs to divorce him before he kills one of us."

Paul held up his hands. "Whoa. I realize y'all been through hell, but Ned isn't a bad person. He was under the influence, and didn't have any idea what he was doing. Please don't be talking divorce—the man needs help. He needs y'all."

Judith and Luke stared at Paul as if he'd just appeared before them. Judith dropped into the nearest chair. "Mr. Day—right? Don't you dare stand there and tell us what a good person Ned is. Do you understand me?!" She glared into Paul's blue eyes. "My daughter, Luke's mother—" her voice broke. Judith had to stop and regain her composure. "My daughter nearly died tonight at the hands of this . . . good person," Judith said as she stood up.

Paul nodded. "Yes, Ma'am."

## CHAPTER 18

# BOSTON, 1961

BARBARA LEFT THE hospital five days after she'd suffered a brutal beating from her husband. With Ned in jail, she had comfort that at the least, he wouldn't show up at her door. There wasn't a part of her body that didn't hurt, and every time she looked in the mirror, the reflection startled her. Physically she would heal, but the damage to her soul was beyond repair. She dreaded going back to work with everyone knowing her husband had almost beaten her to death. And poor Luke, would he recover?

Within days of her hospital release, Paul Day surprised her with a call asking if he might come for a short visit. Barbara agreed. She lay on the couch as if an Egyptian mummy, wrapped with elastic material around her chest that supported her three broken ribs. No matter how she positioned herself, nothing stopped the pain. To treat her broken nose, the doctor taped it and stuffed it with cotton. The bruising, a royal shade of purple, spread around both eyes. She thought it created a Halloween horror mask appearance.

She made no attempt to cover it up. Barbara wanted Paul to witness the aftermath of Ned's handiwork.

Paul knocked on the living room door as he entered. "May I come in, ma'am?" He held a milk glass vase full of white and yellow daisies. "Where do you want these flowers? Ned told me you like these little petal pickers."

She ignored his reference to her husband. "How nice, they're beautiful. Put them on the television. Thank you." She grimaced in pain. "Please sit down."

"Feeling rough?"

Barbara didn't want his pity. "The medicine they gave me helps, but there's not much you can do for broken ribs except wait for them to heal. I'm out of commission for a while." She shifted her head a little so she could see Paul better, causing pain to ricochet throughout her body. She had to squeeze her eyes shut to keep from moaning. When she opened them again, she caught him grimacing in sympathy. "What's going on with Ned?"

"Well, he has to appear in court next week for drunk driving. The plan is for him to move in with me and my family after rehab. By the way, he volunteered to go."

"Really? I'm surprised."

Paul was quiet for moment. "I'll work with him, and hopefully get the home repair business going again. I'm good with my hands, and Ned, well, you know. Money might be tight."

"Keep him away from Luke and me, and we'll be fine." Barbara had no emotion in her voice. "Money is the least of my concerns right now. Keep him away from us."

Paul stood up. "You be well, ma'am. I won't take up any more of your day." He turned away, then back to her. "You or your boy need anything, let me know." He grinned. "Don't get up; I'll see myself out."

Barbara smiled at his attempt at humor, but she knew his intentions were to get the family back together. She would fight that fight when the time came.

❧

With the holidays over, college loomed right around the corner. Luke's time at home was coming to an end. Barbara couldn't dwell on this now as Paul had insisted the family meet. He'd convinced her it was necessary for Ned to complete his current step of the AA program in order to make progress. Ned needed to reconcile his mistakes. This included her mother; they all needed a pathway to heal. He swore this was an essential part of Ned's recovery, and hers. She wasn't sure. The thought of seeing him again made her sick.

On the day of his visit, Barbara knocked on Luke's bedroom door. "Luke, your dad will be here soon. We all need to talk. He wants to make amends."

"I've heard it all before, Mom. How long before he falls off the wagon and kills one of us? You can listen to him if you want, but if you insist on me talking to him, I'll leave. I'm not buying all his sorry shit again."

Barbara rested her head against the door. She wished she hadn't agreed to this meeting. She wasn't ready emotionally. The closer the time came, the more nervous she became. What had she been thinking? "Luke, I expect you downstairs when your father arrives. No arguments. If I can do this, you can too."

Without waiting for his reply, she headed to the kitchen to make coffee. She wasn't sure she would ever be ready to listen to Ned's apologies.

There was a knock on the porch door and Judith walked inside. "I was afraid I'd be late to this little soirée." She grimaced.

Barbara stared at her mother's appearance. She'd dressed in a radiant pink dress and matching shoes. "Uh, hi, Mom. You're a little overdressed for the occasion, don't you think?"

"Sorry. But I'm headed to a bank board meeting after we're done here. Wanted to make a statement with this dress and wouldn't have time to go home to change." Judith pulled out a chair and sat down.

"I'm not looking forward to this, whatever it is." She rolled her eyes. "Where's Luke? Isn't it supposed to be the whole family?"

Barbara didn't want to argue with her mother about this meeting again. "Mom, Luke doesn't want to be a part of this discussion, but he'll be down." She rubbed her forehead—she'd been experiencing constant headaches since her beating. Today's tension seemed to make the pain unbearable. "I understand where he's coming from."

They both turned as the porch door opened and Paul and Ned walked into the kitchen. The tension in the room was like an arcing live wire throwing sparks of lightning into the air. Everyone stopped and waited for someone else to make the first move.

Barbara wiped her hands on a nearby towel. She avoided facing Ned. "Uh . . . sit down. The coffee should be ready in a minute. Let me get Luke." Her hands shook while sweat began to drench her body.

Paul held up his hand. "Let's wait on getting Luke, if you don't mind, ma'am." He took a seat next to Judith. "It's good to see you again, Mrs. Barron."

"Paul, good to see you too. How're you doing?" Judith gave a slight nod to Ned, but said nothing.

"Ma'am, I'm better than a frog's hair in the rain," he said, smiling. "Ned, why don't you sit down too?"

Barbara's fear didn't allow her to come any closer to the table. She took down five white mugs for coffee, then realizing what she'd done, put one cup back up. She tried to maintain control, but being here again with Ned was more like a repeating nightmare. Her breathing came in shallow breaths. *I'm going to be sick.* She turned around and found Ned staring at her. She leaned back against the kitchen counter. "Uh . . . I'm not ready for this. I, uh—I thought I, but . . . I can't." She picked up a dishtowel and wiped the sweat from her face. "You almost killed me, Ned. *Right here in this room.* Our son found me unconscious and bloody. He wasn't even sure I was alive." Her voice came out louder than she meant and her nervousness made her words sound like they weren't hers when she spoke. "And I have constant headaches now because you kept smashing my head on the floor."

Ned's face contorted. His mouth opened. "Oh God! Oh God! I'm, uh, I'm so sorry Barbara. I am. Please." He covered his face with his hands. "I can't believe what I did to you."

"Take your hands down and look at me. You nearly killed me in this very room." Her heart was now pounding on her breastbone to escape.

Judith got up and put her arms around her daughter. "Paul, this, whatever *this* is—is over."

Paul stood up, laying a hand on Ned's shoulder, signaling him it was time to leave.

There were sounds of pounding footsteps on the stairs as Luke burst into the room.

"What's going on?" Luke asked, looking from his mother to his father. "You son of a bitch, *leave* us alone." He moved to stand in front of the women as if to shield them from his father's presence.

Paul helped Ned to his feet, not responding to Luke. As they passed, Paul tried to put his hand on Barbara's shoulder, but Luke blocked him. She saw their eyes lock: Luke blazing, Paul unchallenging. Barbara's mind couldn't function. She was paralyzed by fear. The pounding in her temples refused to subside while she hung onto her mother and son.

When they reached the door, Ned turned back. "It will never happen again, Barbara. Never."

Luke yelled, "*Get out of here! You piece of shit!*"

Paul pulled the door closed behind them.

⁓

In the weeks following the failed family meeting, Judith made an appointment with a private investigator at a restaurant down by the pier. She felt partially responsible for her daughter's beating and wanted to make her own amends by giving Ned closure. At night, Barbara's bruised face haunted her dreams. Would she ever be able to forgive herself? She had located Mr. Arbour through an under-cover police officer she knew, but his warning about the PI had caused her to second guess what she was doing. *He floats just above the law. Be careful, and don't get sucked into his mild manners and appearance. He's dangerous, but he gets results.* She sat by the window and watched the fog roll in off the water as the boats bobbed in the gray swirl.

Judith knew the moment Mr. Arbour entered the restaurant. A chill shot through her body while she watched as he spoke to the hostess. What was it she didn't like, or perhaps trust, about him? He was an unassuming man with thinning hair and thick glasses. On guard and ready, Judith smiled as he approached the table.

Mr. Arbour removed his coat. "Mrs. Barron, it's a pleasure to meet you." They shook hands and ordered two Bloody Marys. "Your story sparked my bloodhound senses."

Judith was surprised by his cultured voice. "Good. We'll need them to track this man down." She pulled the paperwork from her purse. "I want to fill you in on a few details about the man you're going to be hunting. But let me be clear on one point. I want to *see* what information you gather to confirm you have the right person. Before or if *I decide* if contact is to be made—I want pictures of him, too." Particular as always, Judith took her time giving Mr. Arbour the family history.

After she finished, Mr. Arbour sat back in his seat. "Mrs. Barron, I'm good at what I do. If I wasn't, you wouldn't have hired me, right?" Richard Arbour shrugged, causing his eyebrows to come together. "If I tell you I have the right man—I've got him. It'll save me time and you money. Just let me do my job."

Judith held her temper. This was a serious family matter, and she wanted control over the investigation. But she could see it was slipping away. "Mr. Arbour, I appreciate your concern about my finances, but I don't want any interference in this man's life unless I say so. Are we clear?" She paused. "I want your report showing proof, along with photos. I'll call you once I have the information. The decision will come from *me* as to whether you're to contact him. Are we clear?" Judith glared at Mr. Arbour.

"It's your money." Mr. Arbour shrugged. "You're the boss, lady."

Judith didn't care for his reply, but attempted to hide her feelings. "Mr. Arbour, I have your plane ticket, reservations for a hotel near the school, and I've booked a Peugeot through Hertz Rental Car Company." She pulled out a brown envelope. "I've all the paperwork organized for you in here. Also, I've enclosed the money we agreed to, and our contract." She looked up from the paperwork, questioning her sanity for hiring this man, but it was too late. "If you will, sign the last page, then we can let the dogs out." She smiled and sat back in her seat, swirling the ice in her empty glass. Judith could see his mind working. He would do it his way, she was certain.

Mr. Arbour picked up the contract and spent a few minutes reviewing it, then signed and dated the document. "Mrs. Barron, I'm very impressed. Looks like I have everything I need. I'll be in touch with you soon."

"Have a safe trip, Mr. Arbour."

He stood, shook hands with her, and left the restaurant.

Once Richard Arbour was out of the door, Judith tucked the signed contract into her purse, then called the waitress over. "Alice, did you get clear pictures of him?" At least with a signed contract and photos proving they'd met and money was exchanged, she would have the proof if she had to take him to court. Not sure it would do her any good. She picked up her coat and purse.

"Yes ma'am here's your camera."

"Good doing business with you." Judith handed the waitress a twenty-dollar bill and turned to leave, then as if on the spur of the moment, turned back around. "Let me know if you see him again." She took the bill and jotted her phone number on it. "Thank you."

Alice smiled. "Yes ma'am."

Once settled in her car and on the way home, she couldn't shake the uncomfortable feeling she had made a serious mistake.

∽

During the month that followed the failed attempt to make amends, Paul convinced Barbara to let them use the shop to regenerate Ned's home repair business. They all needed the income. Barbara's one requirement was that they didn't come into the house. Both men agreed to her stipulation. At first, the sounds of the table saw and sanders made her nervous. But in time, she adjusted to the noise, and noticed the quiet when they didn't work in the shop.

After Ned and Paul had left one evening, Barbara, curious to see what they'd been building, went out to the shop. As soon as she opened the door, the smell of fresh-cut lumber greeted her. Sawdust covered the floor, and the footprints of Paul and Ned were everywhere. There were skeletons of cabinets crowding the center of the shop. She'd reached out to touch one when she heard something behind her, and whirled around. Ned stood at the door watching her.

Barbara jumped, and her hand flew to her mouth, muffling a scream. "You scared me," she said, her voice exposing her raw nerves.

"Sorry, I didn't mean to, uh . . . I forgot to get our work schedule and need to set up some new jobs." He walked in and picked up a folder from the workbench. "How're you doing?"

Taking a few steps backward away from Ned, she bumped into a stool. "I'm, uh I'm healed up." She pushed back her hair. "I like to see what's being built. I, uh—well after you left . . . ." The walls were crowding in on Barbara and she tried to fight the panic building inside. "I have to go."

"Wait. Please don't." Ned held out his hand to her, but moved no closer. "Can we talk? How's Luke doing? And you how're you?"

To a stranger their conversation would sound normal, but there was nothing normal about their relationship. "I'm fine. Luke's fine, visiting colleges with Claire. You seem healthy and . . . ." Her mind was in a flurry. She didn't want to be this close to Ned. She desperately wanted to get back in the house. This had been a mistake.

He pulled over a stool and sat down. "College. Damn, it's already time to be looking at colleges? Time has slipped past me." He shook his head. "Well then it's a good thing the business is booming, with college tuition coming up. Paul is unbelievably talented. He kinda draws in customers with his southern accent and *gentlemanly* ways." Ned laughed. "We've more work than ever. At least I didn't mess this up." He brushed the sawdust off his jeans. "I miss you."

Barbara backed up again, putting more distance between them. "I don't know, Ned." She lied. She knew exactly how she felt. Her fear was mounting as she tried to figure a way out. Who would hear her if she screamed? Her body was shaking. "I'd better go." As she made her way out past him, Ned stood up, caught her arm, and pulled her into his arms. Her body felt as if it had turned to stone. She couldn't scream, or move, or run. Fear paralyzed her.

"Barbara, I'm so sorry for hurting you." He placed his forehead on the top of her head. "I can't believe what I did. I love you more than I can tell you." Then he kissed her forehead. "Please forgive me. I can't lose you."

Barbara closed her eyes. She was sure he could feel how hard her heart was beating. "Ned, I don't know how I can't take . . . ." Nothing was coming out right. "Luke . . . ."

Ned lowered his arms and sat back down on the stool. "What can I do?"

"Nothing, other than to give us both time." Tears ran down her cheeks. "Stay sober, Ned."

"I understand." He reached for her hands and brought them up to his lips, but she pulled away. "I know the treasure I could lose. We'll go slow and steady."

"We can try, Ned." Her mind flashed back, and she could almost feel his first punch that broke her ribs. "But if you drink again, we're done." Another lie. She didn't believe him capable of keeping his word.

Barbara watched as Ned drove off, then closed the shop door, relieved he'd left. With Luke so wrapped up in Claire, she'd become envious of their relationship. Hopelessness engulfed her as she went back to an empty house.

Entering the kitchen, she was still thinking about Ned. *Would anything with him ever work?* When she looked up, she saw Luke was staring at her. "Oh, hi, uh . . . I didn't realize you were home. Are you staying for dinner?"

"What in the hell are you doing even talking to him? Are you letting him con you again?" Luke said. He pushed the chair into the table, causing the cups on it to rock back and forth. "You'll get sucked into his lies and promises. I can't believe this after the beating you took. What're you thinking, Mom?"

"It's not what you think, Luke."

"Mom, I am leaving for college next August." Luke's eyes glistened. "I don't understand you. Do you want to be his punching bag?"

Luke stormed out of the house. Barbara watched the screen door bounce as he left. She pulled out a chair and sat down with her head in her hands.

∽

It had been three weeks since Mr. Arbour left and Judith had received no communications. She wasn't going to wait any longer. She picked up the phone and dialed the operator. "Yes, I want to put in an overseas call to Montpellier, France, the Hotel Franco, and speak to a Richard Arbour."

The operator asked her to hold while she made the connection.

After a minor language barrier, Judith reached Richard's room. The phone rang several times before a voice thick with sleep answered.

"Is this Richard Arbour?" she demanded. The thought of him ignoring her was infuriating.

"Mrs. Barron?"

"Yes, remember me—the person who's paying your bills." Judith heard a woman's voice, but didn't understand her words. "Who's that?"

"A new friend of mine, if you must know," he paused. "We were sound asleep. Why're you calling? Is everything all right? Did you get my report? I've been waiting for your approval to contact our friend."

"I've gotten nothing. That's the problem." She snorted out in disgust. "When did you send me the report?"

"I sent it a week ago; you should get it any day now. I'm waiting for you before I contact him. I told you I was good at what I do, Mrs. Barron. I got him."

She hesitated, not sure of anything. "I want to see the pictures and your information first. If I don't have the report in two days, I'll call you back." She hung up before Mr. Arbour replied. Waiting wasn't one of Judith's strengths.

# CHAPTER 19

# BOSTON, 1962

THE MONTH OF May came fast. Luke's high school graduation had been a blur for Barbara. Now it was August, and her only child was leaving for college. The Sims had volunteered to drive Claire and Luke to the University of Massachusetts. Standing at the street, she handed her son a carefully packed box full of towels and linens. He'd never grasp how much thought and care she'd put into packing so he'd have everything he needed.

Luke shoved the box in alongside his and Claire's bags, crushing in the sides. The back of the Sims's red and white station wagon could hold nothing more. Conflicting thoughts crowded Barbara's mind. She wanted him to follow his dreams. She had to let go. But what would she do without him? Barbara had to swallow hard.

Claire poked her head out of the car window. "Bye, Mrs. Johansen. See you during Thanksgiving break."

"Bye, Claire. You'll do well, I'm sure." Barbara smiled and turned back to Luke. "You'll beat the worst of the heat by leaving this early." She held her hands behind her back, digging her nails into her palms. "Remember to call me when you get in your dorm room. Just one ring and I'll know you got there safely. Okay?"

"Mom, you've told me this a hundred times already." Luke closed the tailgate of the station wagon. "I love you, Mom."

"Love you more," she whispered. The tears made her eyes sting. "Be safe, Luke."

"Mom, please don't let Dad move back. Promise me." After a hug and a quick kiss on the cheek, he gave her a smile. "I'll remember to call."

Barbara touched Luke's face. "You need to get on the road. Don't worry. I'll be okay, I promise." The words sounded hollow to her, and she was sure they did to her son too.

Barbara stepped back from the car as Luke got in, but she watched and waved until they turned the corner. As she stood on the sidewalk, the memory of last night's dinner ran through her mind.

Claire's parents had invited her over for a cookout to celebrate before their children left for college the next day. Their sculptured backyard was lit by small, colorful party lights. Everything was perfection— such a stark contrast to their home and family life. Claire had the upbringing Barbara had wished for Luke.

Sitting quietly, she watched the Sims joke back and forth with each other. She was lost in thought when Luke pulled a patio chair next to hers.

"Mom, why such a faraway look?" Luke asked. "What are you thinking?"

"Nothing, really." Getting serious right now would only cause tears she refused to shed.

"Claire's family is pretty great, don't you agree?"

Luke and Barbara watched from the patio as the Sims family cleaned up the kitchen after dinner. Their close relationship made Barbara jealous. *Watch out Ozzie and Harriet, here come the Sims.*

"Claire's an extraordinary girl, but please don't rush into anything. You've plenty of time. Enjoy your college years. Take your time."

"I've got it under control. If I get into medical school—"

Barbara her raised eyebrows. "If?"

"Let me finish. It'll be eight years before we can even consider taking this relationship to the next level. So, don't worry. Plus, I use protection."

Barbara gave him a fake, wide-eyed expression and pretended to check around to see who might've heard their conversation. "Don't talk like that. Claire's father might hear you." She shook her head. "You'd better be careful." They stopped talking and watched as Claire walked toward them.

Claire smiled. "What're you two talking about?"

"What a lovely evening we've had." Barbara squeezed her son's hand. "Thank you."

❧

Barbara rubbed her arms and pressed her lips together in a bittersweet smile at the memory. She stood for a moment longer, but her chest ached, and she just wanted to be alone. But instead, she found Ned watching her from the living room windows. *Not now!* She blew out a long breath as she opened the front door. "Oh, Ned I, uh, I didn't expect you."

"Do I need to call for permission? It's my house too." Defiantly, Ned crossed his arms over his chest. "Sorry, but I wanted to see Luke off."

"Well, he's gone." Barbara walked into the kitchen. "Want a cup of coffee, or are you in a hurry?" She picked up the breakfast dishes and put them in the sink. The house still smelled like bacon and pancakes, Luke's favorites. "You ever notice how maple syrup makes everything sticky?" She said as she scrubbed off the syrup, dismissing him. She hoped he would take the hint and leave. With her son gone, she was alone and vulnerable.

"Barbara, now that Luke is out of the house, I want to come home." Ned stood with his hands on his hips and his feet spread apart.

She closed her eyes for a moment. His comment needed a reply. She hoped the silence spoke volumes.

He walked over to the doorway and leaned against the side. "I've been sober for a long time, and I deserve a second chance. We need to get back together and . . . ."

She still had headaches and couldn't stand to eat mashed potatoes.

Barbara dropped the plate back into the sink and turned around. "A second chance, Ned? You put me in the hospital for a week. Do you want me to tell you about the pain you caused by breaking three of my ribs, or the pain I had when you broke my nose, or . . . ."

Tears spilled out, and she struggled to regain control. "Stop! I don't want to talk about you getting a second chance. It's not a second chance. It's the one-hundredth chance." Barbara unleashed her pent-up feelings about Luke leaving home on her husband. "Ned, right now I need to sleep before my shift starts. Leave. Me. Alone." Her mouth filled with saliva. She would throw up if she had to say more.

"This conversation isn't over, Barbara. If you'll *excuse* me now, I've got to get to work so I can *pay* for your son's college tuition." The screen door slammed so hard it bounced and banged several more times.

Barbara sank down onto the floor and wrapped her arms around her legs. Would she ever feel safe again? Luke was right. She never should have allowed him back into her life.

∽

A week after Judith spoke to her private investigator, Mr. Arbour, she received the package he swore had been sent. She wasn't sure she wanted the information after all that had happened. She didn't want to risk any more trouble. Even though it'd been over a year, the image of her daughter's swollen face, covered with black and blue bruises and wrapped in bandages, haunted her dreams. She walked into her office, picked up the letter opener, and sliced opened the brown envelope.

As the photos tumbled out across her desk, Judith sucked in a deep breath. "Oh my stars, that's Ned. Older, but it could be him," she said to herself. She sat down and began to read the report Mr. Arbour sent, then glanced back at the photos.

After debating with herself for two days, Judith knocked on Barbara's back door. "Hello? Anyone home?" she asked, walking into the empty kitchen. She had to tell Barbara what she'd found out.

"Hi Mom, I'm getting dressed, be right down. Help yourself to some coffee."

Judith filled a white mug with coffee and stood by the stairs. "Did Luke get off okay? Thought you might want some company. Hey, how about lunch today?"

"Yes, my boy is in college. Can you believe it? Lunch sounds good, but I have to work," Barbara said as she came down the stairs. "I need to get my beauty sleep before my shift starts." She gave her mother a hug, then filled a mug with fresh coffee. "Oh, did you see Ned's truck in the alley? He's supposed to be working in the shop this afternoon."

"No, it wasn't there when I drove up." Judith took a second to discreetly scan her daughter's arms and neck to make sure there were no suspicious black and blue marks. Satisfied, she sat down at the table.

Barbara took a small sip of coffee. "He and Paul must be working late today. I thought he'd be back by now."

Judith reached into her purse and brought out the brown envelope she'd received from Mr. Arbour. "I got some pictures of the man we think might be Ned's father, and a report from my private investigator." She hesitated, not sure of her daughter's reactions. "You need to see the pictures," Judith said as she arranged them on the table.

When Barbara didn't reply, Judith turned around. Her daughter stood still with her arms hanging at her sides as if she were a puppet, waiting for someone to pull a string so she could move. She paused. "I wouldn't share this information with you if I didn't think you needed to see it."

"Mother, I don't want to see anything that remotely relates to Ned's father, or his past. I still wake up at night drenched in sweat. In my dreams, I'm getting beaten all over again. When I wake up, my bed, my nightgown, everything is soaked, and it takes hours for me to get back to sleep. If I can. Now Luke's gone." In defiance, Barbara crossed her arms over her chest, her voice vibrating with emotion. "Ned wants to move back."

Judith swung around in her chair. "No! Barbara, I don't trust him. Please don't let him come back." Judith held up her hand. "I'm sorry. It's none of my business. But . . . ." She felt this wasn't her battle to fight. "You know me. If this information weren't necessary, I wouldn't say anything." She turned back to the table, her heart still racing. "Does Montpellier, France, ring any bells for you?"

"What?" Barbara approached the table. "No, why should it be familiar to me?" She stopped. "Yes, wait a minute. I believe it was either the town, or near the town where Philip grew up. Something like that—I could be wrong."

Judith pointed to two of the pictures. "Look at these."

Barbara pulled out a chair and sat down. She fingered through the pictures, then suddenly stopped. "Oh my God, Mother!"

"What? You look shocked."

"Mom, have you ever seen pictures of Hillary's husband or her in-laws?" She covered her mouth with both hands. "Wait a minute."

Judith watched as Barbara got up, ran into the living room, and pulled an old photo album out of the coat closet. She flipped to the back of the album and took out a wrinkled picture of a family.

"Look at this picture," she said, handing it to her mother. "This is Hillary's husband and his family. The newlyweds, Hillary and Philip, went to France to meet his family after they got married. Ned tried to destroy this photo when he first saw it, but Carl stopped him. I always thought there was more to the story, but figured Gertrude didn't know." She paused. "But maybe she was keeping Hillary's worst nightmare a secret."

"Oh my stars, do you think?" Judith held the old photo next to the new snapshots. She studied the posture, the smiles of the men, then looked up. "Are Hillary's father-in-law and the boarding school teacher one and the same? He'd have to be in his late eighties or early nineties. Wouldn't he?" Her hand went to her throat and she sat back in her chair. "How can this be?"

Barbara picked up the new pictures and the old photo. "It depends on how old he was when he got Hillary pregnant. But the resemblance is unmistakable. That crooked smile, even the physiques are the same."

"Wait. Hold on. The last names are different. Something isn't matching up. We must have the wrong man." Judith rubbed her lips together. "What's missing?"

"Gertrude told me that Hillary insisted the biological father's last name be given to Ned. It's Moreau." Barbara lined up the pictures one by one. "When I lived with Hillary in San Diego, she never talked about her past, or her in-laws."

"Right. So far, this information matches up with what we knew. Mr. Moreau is a cook of some kind. If I remember, all of Philip's family is in the food business. So where does this teacher come from? And how does it connect with Philip and the last name of Villier?"

"Evidently, we don't know the whole story." Barbara rubbed her forehead. "The last names have me confused. They sure have a family resemblance. What's the connection, cousins maybe?"

Judith squinted at her daughter. "It's possible I guess. I would've liked to have been there when Philip introduced his new bride to the family." Judith's eyebrows arched. "Clearly we are missing some facts. I'll ask Mr. Arbour to check this out."

Barbara stopped flipping the pictures. "Gertrude told me she thought it was odd the couple never went back for another visit. Equally curious, Philip's family never came over here to visit them either, even after their two boys were born. They certainly had the money. Maybe we know why now." Barbara rubbed the back of her neck and stretched it one way then the other. "So Mother, does this mean your investigator thinks Mr. Moreau is Ned's father?"

"Yes, but more importantly, I think Mr. Moreau could be Philip's father too." Judith picked up her purse and stacked the pictures on the table.

"So wait a minute. Philip, Hillary's husband, and Ned . . . are half-brothers? What's going on here?" Barbara tilted her head as she tried to make sense of this new information. "No. This isn't right, is it? Again, where does the last name of Villier come from?"

"Mr. Arbour seems to think we have the right man. I think the best thing to do here is to burn these little gems and drop the whole subject." When Barbara didn't respond, Judith turned around. "Don't you agree?"

At that moment, the porch door banged and Ned came into the kitchen. "Don't you agree to what?" He scanned the table and pointed. "Who's this?"

Barbara closed her eyes for a moment. "Ned, Mother went ahead and hired a detective to find your father. These are some pictures her investigator sent."

Words eluded Judith as she watched her daughter handle her husband. All she could think of was the last time Ned walked in on them while they were talking in the kitchen. She hated to admit it, but she was afraid of her son-in-law.

"Judith, I, uh, I'm okay now. You may not believe me, but I'm better than the last time we saw each other, and have been sober for a long time now. Right, Barb?" Ned looked at his wife, seemingly embarrassed.

"He's doing well, Mother."

Judith decided to keep her doubts to herself.

"Is this the man you think is my father?" He began flipping through the stack of pictures on the table.

Judith could feel her skin begin to prickle. She didn't know how much of their conversation he'd heard. "Uh, we, uh—we aren't sure. I expect to find out more soon." She watched Ned's body language as he leaned over the table. There was nothing there to alarm her. Ned flipped over one picture after another when he found the old wrinkled one of Philip's family. He seemed better, but she'd seen him begin drinking again after long sober stretches.

He cocked his head to one side. "Why is this picture here?"

Ned hadn't heard the entire conversation. Relief loosened the grip Judith's muscles had on her neck. "I wanted to see a picture of your mother when she was young," she said, as she maneuvered her purse to cover Mr. Arbour's report. "Barbara found this old picture. Hillary was quite beautiful."

Ned picked up the old photo. "I guess she was, if you like the slutty type." He glanced up, then turned his attention back to the pictures. "So what's the skinny on this guy?" Ned held out the picture he was holding of Mr. Moreau.

"We aren't sure." Judith glanced at her daughter. "My investigator is still working on the case. He should be wrapping up his investigation shortly." The two women's eyes met for a second. "Well, I do hate to leave, but I have an appointment, and I'm going to be late if I don't go now." She lied. Then gathered all the pictures and placed them back in the envelope. Ned reluctantly gave her back the picture. When she picked up her purse, her fingers scooped up Mr. Arbour's report at the same time. "You two don't work too hard. Barbara—I'll be in touch."

Ned put his hands on his mother-in-law's arm. "Get back to me when you find out, Judith. And, uh, thanks. I haven't told you how much I appreciate what you're doing for me. I mean us." He turned back to Barbara. "I've been a jerk, and well, I'm . . . ."

Sure that her son-in-law could feel her increased anxiety, Judith pulled her arm from Ned's hands. "Ned, let me be clear. If you ever hurt my daughter again—" Her eyes were cold and hard.

Barbara gasped. "Mom, please, Ned's been sober."

"No, your mom is right to feel this way. I would too." Ned stepped back. "It won't happen again, Judith."

"Ned, for your sake, it better not." Judith opened the door and turned back. "I'll be in touch."

In the car, Judith took a minute to settle down before she drove home. She'd never said anything to Ned before, but felt it was over-due. She was more determined than ever to have Mr. Arbour find out about the Villiers and their connection with Mr. Moreau before terminating the investigation.

After she arrived home, she pulled out the report to study it more. She needed time to think before she decided her next move.

It had been over a week since Richard had heard from Judith, and he wondered what the old bag would decide to do. Sitting outside the café across the street from the Moreau's apartment and res-taurant, he continued to watch all who came and went. The plaza had various shops and outdoor vendors lining the main street. The weather was warm, and with the sun on his back, he suddenly felt very drowsy. After two weeks of his investigation, Richard had no doubts Mr. Moreau was the biological father of Ned Johansen. His job was done, and he was in no hurry to go home. Judith Barron would have been smart if she'd let him handle the investigation his way—the right way. Richard took a sip of his coffee, then went back to reading his newspaper when a shadow fell across his table. He looked up to find Mr. Moreau standing over him. *Holy shit.*

"Excuse me, sir," Mr. Moreau said, speaking perfect English. "May I sit? I think we need to talk."

Richard smiled and extended his hand. "Yes, please sit down. I would love to have company." Mr. Moreau resembled the picture of Ned that Judith had given him. Both men were built tall and lean. Their small eyes were set too far apart and they had the same hairline.

Mr. Moreau did not smile as he pulled a chair out away from the table. "Sir, have we ever met before?"

"No, not that I'm aware of." *Shit!*

"Then why are you following me and asking questions about my family and me? Montpellier is a small village, and we all watch out for each other." Mr. Moreau's face hardened.

*What the hell, Judith. I'll just ask.* "Mr. Moreau, I've been hired to find out if you had a child with Hillary Dearborn. She went to the boarding school where, I believe, you taught many years ago."

As he watched Mr. Moreau glance around the café, there was no doubt in Richard's mind this man knew his past had caught up with him. Somehow, the man seemed to age right before his eyes. "Sir, do you know her?"

"Yes, unfortunately, I did," he said after a long pause. "What will it take for you to forget what you have learned and leave me in peace? What happened was long ago and almost ruined me."

*Scoring on both ends of this job—oh, hell yes!* "Sir, you have a son who wants and needs to meet you." Richard watched beads of sweat break out on Mr. Moreau's forehead. Richard leaned back in his chair and waited. He needed to know what the old fucker would pay to make him go away.

"No, this is too public a place to discuss such a sensitive subject. Please meet me at this address." Mr. Moreau handed Richard a card. "Noon tomorrow is the earliest I can get away without raising any questions."

Richard jotted down the time on the back of the card and put it in his shirt pocket. "I'll be there."

⁓

The next day, Richard arrived a half hour before the agreed upon time to get the lay of the land. He didn't want any surprises, and felt better after he patted his gun in its shoulder holster. The building had once been an old monastery, now converted into a winery. Behind the main building were rows and rows of fruit-bearing grape vines.

Richard felt he'd stepped back in time, and at any moment he'd see knights racing their horses through the countryside to save a damsel in distress. The dark green of the vineyards contrasted with silvery-gray leaves of the olive orchards. There were no billboards, or any evidence of modern-day civilization to spoil the view. Richard could see himself living here in peace.

As Richard slowly walked back to the monastery, he saw Mr. Moreau sitting at an outside table waiting for him.

"Please have a seat. Er, you know my name, but I didn't get yours," Mr. Moreau said. He waved at one of the winery's servers. "We'll have a carafe of our cabernet sauvignon reserve, please."

"Richard Arbour." He extended his hand.

"Ah, another Frenchman." Mr. Moreau shook Richard's hand and quickly let it go.

Richard pulled out a chair and sat down.

After the wine had arrived, the two men sat quietly until the server was out of earshot.

Richard swirled his wine. He brought the glass to his nose, taking in the full body of the cabernet. Watching Mr. Moreau, he felt the man had never been in this position before and needed some small talk to relax. "This wine is excellent. Tell me about the winery. My family is originally from Canada." He smiled. "This is my first trip to France. How long have you lived here?"

"We've won a few awards for our wine. I'm pleased you appreciate its bouquet." He took a deep breath, apparently aware of what Richard was attempting to do. "My family has lived here for many generations. I found this monastery more than twenty years ago and bought it for the wine and the beauty of the vineyard. I find peace here unlike anywhere else I've been. I've found this place to be an invaluable retreat when I've problems to solve." He hesitated, as though trying to resolve this situation. "We have serious business to discuss. What will it take for you to leave and report back that you couldn't find me?"

Richard watched Mr. Moreau's hand tremble as he lifted his wine glass. "Sir, you're asking me to double-cross my client. No can do." *Like hell I can't.* "My reputation would be ruined." *So what. I'll be rich.*

"I'm sorry, but my youth and poor judgment nearly caused me to lose everything I love and hold dear. I'm assuming you're aware of what happened." His drooping eyelids nearly closed as he hesitated. "Miss Dearborn's parents came to the school and accused me of rape. Fortunately for me, no one backed up their accusation. The school had no choice, and terminated my employment. I had no income, and a reputation that barred me from ever teaching again. I was stupid." His eyes were veiled as he slipped his fingers up and down the stem of his wine glass.

"Is that when you went into the restaurant business?"

"Yes. It was by accident really, but I always had a flair for cooking, so it seemed natural. My family supported me, and they bought me my first restaurant. Luckily, we were very successful. I was able to let go of the past." Mr. Moreau leaned back in his chair. "Give me an amount that will buy your silence."

"Sir, what you're asking would be my ruin." He'd get as much money as he could get from the old man.

Both went silent as Mr. Moreau stared down at his gnarled hands and seemed to be reliving a moment in his past. "Mr. Arbour, you've met with Hillary?"

"No, I've never met her." Richard sat quietly, whirling his wine around the glass, waiting for more of the story to unfold.

"I see." Mr. Moreau's wrinkles gathered on both sides of his eyes. "Who is it that has you looking for me?"

"Actually, my client is the mother-in-law of your son. She feels if you two could meet and talk to each other, it might help him with some problems he has." Richard paused and waited to see if this sparked any reaction. "Would you like to see a picture of him?"

Mr. Moreau raised his head. "No. I have four sons only, and they are all I need or want. Do you understand?"

Richard picked up his wine glass and took the last sip. "Let me leave this with you, sir." He pulled out a small envelope of photos and laid it on the table. "I feel you need some time to think before you say no. You know where you can find me."

ஒ

Judith spent the next few days agonizing over what she'd learned. Should she push this issue more? Something inside her wanted the whole story, and yet the pain it might cause those involved—was it worth knowing? Finally, she picked up the phone and put in an overseas call to Montpellier, France. After several minutes, the call went through. "Mr. Arbour."

"Mrs. Barron, good to hear your voice. Did you get my report?"

"Yes, I did, and I want you to do a little more research. But I don't want you to make contact with the man." She paused and picked up the report Mr. Arbour had sent her. "I want to know why this gentleman left his teaching career and what he did afterward. One more small item, I want you to investigate a family by the name of Villier and see if there's any connection between the two families. Then we need to close this case."

"Villier? Isn't that Ned Johansen's mother's married name?" he asked. "Wait, what? You're closing the investigation? Why?"

She hesitated, not sure how much information to give him. "Yes, that's her married name. Your memory is very good. Hillary Dearborn married Philip Villier, and he's a chef and restaurant owner in San Diego. I think there might be a connection between Mr. Moreau and the Villier family. I'm not sure what it is, but that's what I want you to find out. Remember, I don't want any contact. I feel digging up the past might be too painful for everyone involved. We need to close this issue and leave well enough alone."

"Okay, you're the boss. I'll see what I can find out, then head back."

Judith paused. Richard's answer didn't sound right. "Give me a call when you return, and we'll meet back at the pier." He'd agreed too quickly.

"Okay, will do, Boss."

⧫

Two days later, Richard was outside the café drinking a glass of wine when Mr. Moreau walked up to his table. "Please sit down." Richard raised his hand to order a glass of wine for Mr. Moreau.

After the server had left the wine in front of him, Mr. Moreau spoke. "Sir, we need to finish our business."

"I've given your situation serious thought. I will accept fifteen thousand dollars, not francs, to keep my silence, and will leave France as soon as the money is in my account." He picked up his glass of wine and took a sip. "By the way, my client has also asked me to find out about a family with the last name of Villier. Do you know them?"

What little color the old man had drained from his face. "Yes. You need to drop this investigation now, Mr. Arbour."

"If you don't want to tell me, I'm sure there is someone in this village that will." He saw Mr. Moreau's face tighten and knew he'd hit a nerve.

"I'm sure there is, but it won't further your investigation. Drop it now." Mr. Moreau drank half his wine in one swallow.

Richard sat back in his chair and stared at the old man. "Let me be the judge of that. I think we need another glass of wine." Raising his hand, Richard signaled to the waiter to refill their glasses.

Mr. Moreau inhaled deeply and kept his eyes downcast. He waited until the server was gone. "What I share with you today must remain a secret." He hesitated, then with what seemed his last resolve, spoke. "My first wife left me after she found out about my indiscretions. She took back her maiden name of Villier." His hands shook as he picked up his wine glass and lifted it to his lips.

Richard's mind began to whirl. He couldn't believe what he was beginning to piece together. *Yes, I'm going to be rich.* "Mr. Moreau, you have my word. I will only tell my client what you tell me to."

Mr. Moreau gave a slight nod. "And she changed our young children's last names as well. She didn't want them to be connected with the house of Moreau." He reached for his wine. "After she died in a carriage wreck many years later, I found my boys and we were reunited. By this time, they were on their way to becoming notable chefs under the name of Villier. And I had remarried.

"Your current wife—does she know?" Richard leaned forward, not wanting to miss a word.

"No, my wife doesn't know about Hillary." His shoulders seemed to round more, and his head hung as if it were too heavy to lift. "One night's frivolity, that's all it was. Do you understand? I lost the love of my life and my sons. I've worked so hard to regain Philip's trust. We were a family again. And then Philip brought home his new wife. *Quelle dommage.* Of all the women in America, he had to marry her!" Mr. Moreau drank the rest of his wine in one swallow. "*Mon dieu!* Must I die to be free of this woman?"

Under the table, Richard rubbed his palms together. "So let

me get this straight. Hillary is your son's wife, and also the mother of your . . . bet you were shocked when you saw her again." He wasn't sure how this had happened, but as long as he would profit, he didn't care.

"Mr. Arbour, there is no way to describe my reaction when I saw who Philip had chosen to be his wife." Mr. Moreau took a deep breath. "Now you know why it is so imperative that this remain a secret." Mr. Moreau slipped his fingers up and down the stem of the empty wine glass. "Philip must never know."

"And Hillary never told Philip?"

"What? And lose her wealthy new husband?" He snorted out a breath. "No, she and I spoke only once, and we agreed never to reveal this to anyone."

Richard sat still for several moments. "I can keep your secret, but I will need a bit more." He paused. "Say, fifty thousand to keep my silence." Richard sat back comfortably in his chair. "Once the money is in my account, I will leave France and will keep yours and Hillary's secret. You've my word as a Frenchman." Richard knew he had the old man by his hairy balls.

Mr. Moreau stared with disdain at Richard. "I will see the money is transferred to your account." He pushed back his chair and stood. "Mr. Arbour, you are a man of no honor to take advantage of my unfortunate situation. The only reason I will agree to this is I doubt I will live long enough for you to demand more."

Days later, Richard received notification of his new account balance. He made reservations and took the next flight back to Boston. He buckled his seatbelt and leaned back in his first-class seat. Smiling to himself, he imagined what he would do with this new windfall— perhaps go shopping for his own winery. All that was left to do was meet up with Mrs. Barron and sell her this new story. It shouldn't be a problem. He ordered a glass of champagne. When it came, he held it up in a silent toast. *To the folly of others.*

CHAPTER 20

# BOSTON, 1962

AFTER FLIGHTS FROM France that lasted three days, Richard Arbour's plane landed at Logan International Airport in Boston. He was jet-lagged and wanted to get home to his own bed. If Judith Barron found out about his double-dealing, his ass would be trash. One thing he knew he had to do was move the money Mr. Moreau had put in his account. Mrs. Barron had a lot of friends in the banking business. The money couldn't stay in his account. It wasn't that Richard didn't trust Judith Barron; he figured that if he were on the other end of this deal, he'd check.

The next afternoon, Richard walked into his bank and transferred the fifty thousand to a Swiss bank account. He now felt secure. She would never find out, and the money would be there when he was ready to buy a vineyard and retire in peace. For now his career was essential, and he wasn't ready to hang up his guns yet. Retirement would be great, but it had to be on his terms. He had a few more years and a couple of scores to even up first. He'd taken a financial shine to Mr. Moreau and wanted to keep that avenue of future installments for his silence open.

All he'd left to do was schedule one last appointment with the bitch, and their business was over. He had to spin his version of the truth so that no holes were detected. But in reality, he was confident in his acting ability. He was ready.

The phone rang as he walked into his apartment, and he knew she'd beaten him to the call. *Damn!*

"Mr. Arbour, so you *are* home safe and sound. Fantastic, when can we meet?" Judith asked, with a sarcastic edge to her voice.

"Actually, I was writing up my final report for you. How does tomorrow at the pier sound to you? Say about one-thirtyish."

"I'll see you soon." She hung up before he replied.

Richard arrived at the pier early and walked down the dock daydreaming about yachts and vineyards. The wind rippled the water into tiny white caps, and the sun blazed through holes in the clouds. More than any other client, Richard wanted to be done with this one. Maybe it was his conscience that was bothering him, but he was ready to move on to a new case. He turned to go back to the restaurant when he saw that Judith had arrived, and she was early.

Handling Mrs. Barron would be no problem. His experience had prepared him to deal with all kinds people. After all, she was just an old broad; he could wrap this case up with a bow, a big *fifty-thousand-dollar* bow. He laughed to himself.

"Mrs. Barron, nice to see you again," Richard said as he held out his hand. "It's good to be back in the US."

Judith shook hands with Richard. "Glad you're back safely, Mr. Arbour." They walked into the restaurant lobby.

Richard waited to spin his tale until drinks had arrived. "You're looking well, Mrs. Barron." Build the bitch up and get the hell out was his goal.

"Let's get to the meat of this meeting, shall we Mr. Arbour?"

Judith pushed off her coat onto the back of her chair and placed her purse in the empty chair next to her. "Tell me what happened after the last time we talked."

After listening to Mr. Arbour, Judith leaned back in her chair. "I don't understand a couple of issues. Let me recap, and correct me if I've misunderstood." She put her hands together as if doing finger push-ups. "Even though I instructed you not to have contact with this man, *you* went ahead and told Mr. Moreau that *you* were investigating him. Is that right?"

Richard's jaw tightened. He wanted to reach across the table and slap her. *She's so smug.* He'd saved her time and money. She should be appreciating his talents, not accusing him of some horrible act. "Yes, as I said, Mr. Moreau confronted me. It was natural at the moment to ask him if he knew Miss Dearborn. The old guy knew who I was before he approached me. Why lie?"

"How honest of you not to lie, Mr. Arbour." Judith glared at him. "For a seasoned investigator, I'm a little surprised you allowed yourself to be identified. Sloppy work, in my opinion." She sipped her drink, but kept watching him. "Moving on, after a second meeting, he later confessed to being Hillary's lover, right?"

Her words irritated him more than he realized. "Yes." Richard smiled, leaned away from the table, and glanced down at his watch.

"Some place to be, Mr. Arbour?" she smirked at him. "You said he became a cook, is that right?"

As soon as those words left Judith's mouth, his whole body tensed. He knew he had to hide his increasing dislike for her, but it was getting harder to do. "Excuse me, I said he became a chef, and his family bought him the restaurant since he was barred from teaching. Miss Dearborn got him fired." He immediately realized his voice had hardened. "Excuse me, let me make myself clear. Her parents got him fired. They accused him of rape, and we both know it was consensual. It usually is." He snorted out his reply.

Judith's eyes stayed locked on his. "Now what about the Villier family? Go back over their connection with Mr. Moreau."

Richard hesitated. He had to be careful. "From what I got from Mr. Moreau, this was a family that lived for a while in his village. I believe he said they were friends with his late wife. Nothing special, they knew each other of course. It's a small community." He lowered his chin and rubbed the back of his neck.

"Nothing special, Mr. Arbour?" Judith drummed her fingers on the table, one finger at a time in a slow and non-rhythmic manner.

"No, sorry, let me be clear. I followed all the leads, but couldn't make any substantial connections between the two families—other than the fact they were friends of his late wife's. What's the big deal?"

Judith was quiet for a few seconds. "So, that's all?"

"Yeah, that's about it." His eyes darted away from any direct contact eye.

"I think there's more. You're lying." Judith sat forward in her chair.

"Wait a minute, no one talks to me like that! I did what you asked me to do." Richard picked up his napkin and wiped the sweat from his hands. "I might have messed up when I talked to Mr. Moreau ahead of what you instructed, but I got the information."

"No, you gave me part of the information. There is more." Judith stopped, then as if she'd just placed the last puzzle piece in the picture, she said, "You got paid off!"

"You crazy old bat! No one accuses me of double-dealing. Our business here has ended. Keep the balance of your payment. I don't need it." Richard pushed his chair back, making a loud scratching sound, and stood up.

A few of the waiters and customers turned to see what was happening.

"Sit back down." Judith said in a calm, low voice, "You don't need the money?" Her eyebrows arched as she glared at him.

Richard pulled his chair back to the table and lowered his voice.

"You're mistaken. Mr. Moreau is a fine man, and he has suffered enough because of your family."

"A fine man? Really?" Judith's eyebrows arched once more. "Excuse me, you do realize you're defending a man who cheated on his wife, took advantage of a young schoolgirl, then refused to take responsibility for a child of his making." Her words were hissing through her teeth. "I think you'd better start over, and this time, I want the truth."

✧

On the train ride home for Thanksgiving break, Luke tried not to think of his mother and the possibility that his father might have moved back home. Being away from home had been a relief. He found himself not thinking or worrying about his parents for the first time in his life. Now with the holiday here, he was dreading the next four days. Life took on a natural feel with Claire. They both made Dean's List that semester, and he was thinking of applying for a part-time job at a small county hospital. Everything in his life was coming together without the constant strain of his father.

Claire's parents' red and white station wagon pulled up to the train station, and the two students piled their duffle bags full of dirty clothes in the back. The weather had that crisp, autumn feel, and the trees had begun to change into their fiery-colored foliage. Luke felt a warm sense of familiarity as they drove through streets he'd traveled most of his life. Surprised at his feeling, he reached over and took Claire's hand.

The car stopped in front of the house, and he saw his mother waiting outside. They waved as she walked down to the car.

"Hello, strangers!" she called out. Barbara leaned down to the passenger window. "Thank you, Bill, for picking up my boy."

"Our pleasure, I assure you," Claire's father replied.

Both Claire and Luke got out of the car.

Luke smiled and gave his mother a quick once-over, checking for any bruising. "Hey, you!"

"Hi, Mrs. Johansen, it's good to see you again," Claire said, standing at the back of her parents' car. She gave Barbara a hug.

"Hi, Claire, so glad you and my boy are home. Missed you both."

Luke pulled out his bag and opened the car door for Claire. "I'll see you later. Okay?" Claire got out and he gave her a quick kiss and hug, then he threw his bag over his shoulder.

"Sure," Claire said as she got back in the car.

Luke and Barbara walked arm in arm into to the house. He dumped his duffle bag in the living room before they went into the kitchen, where his father sat at the table. At first, neither of them moved, then Ned got up and held out his hand. For a split second, Luke couldn't believe his father had the nerve to face him. His anger began to build.

"Good to see you son. Anxious to hear about—"

"Wait a minute," Luke interrupted, then turned to his mother. "What's he doing here?"

Barbara put her hand on Luke's shoulder. "Slow down. Your dad has been sober now for over a year. He's here to welcome you home."

"What made you think I'd want him to welcome me home?" he said, glaring at his father. Luke's fists kept clenching and unclenching. He stepped toward his father. "I found my mother nearly dead. You nearly killed my mother—right here in this room. What in your fucked-up mind made you think I'd ever want you to welcome me home?" Luke wanted to tell his father how much he hated him, but stopped.

Barbara gasped and covered her mouth.

Ned glanced over at Barbara. "Don't forget, son, who's paying for your fancy college." He picked up his jacket and walked out.

Barbara stood staring at Luke. "I can't believe you. He's worked very hard so we'd have money to keep you in college. He's been going to meetings and staying sober. Give him a—"

"Give him a *break*?" Luke interrupted his mother. "He nearly killed you, or did you forget?" Luke's face reddened, and his heart felt as if it was ready to leap out of his chest. "You could've at least warned me he'd be here. Has he moved back?"

"No, he hasn't moved back." Barbara rubbed her temples. "I wasn't sure you'd come home if I told you he wanted to see you," she said as she pulled out a chair and sat down. "We all need to forgive and move on. If I can do this, Luke, you can."

Luke shook his head. "No, I can't. Your idea of a happy little family isn't real." As though all his energy had left him, he dropped into a chair. "Mom, things are going so well for Claire and me. I can see a good future and enjoy a happiness I haven't felt before. Living like we have with Dad, well honestly, if it weren't for you— I'd never come back."

"Please, don't say that, we're family." She stopped and took a deep breath. "There're things I haven't told you that you're old enough to know." She rubbed her arms and stood. "I want you to hear the truth from me."

Luke watched her. "What truth? Don't tell me what a rough life he's had again." His jaw muscles twitched. "I've seen you get beatings protecting me. Don't tell me about Dad's pitiful life." His voice caught, and he couldn't continue.

Barbara held up her hand. "Stop. You don't—"

"Maybe not, but I'm not going to stay around this house and witness another one of your beatings so we can pretend as if we have this fairy-tale family." Years full of hate and disappointments couldn't be held back any longer. "Because the truth is, we don't." Luke walked out, slamming the porch door behind him.

◈

Judith didn't have to make excuses not to have Thanksgiving dinner with Barbara and Luke since they were having dinner with Claire's family. She hadn't decided how much to reveal to Ned and still have the report sound convincing. The one thing she knew for certain was she'd have to lie better than Mr. Arbour did when she gave Ned her version of the investigation. She had waited to talk to Barbara until she knew Ned would be there working in the shop. This wasn't going to be easy. "Hello, anyone home?"

"Mom?" Barbara called from the basement. "I'm doing Luke's laundry. He leaves tomorrow."

"That wasn't a very long visit," Judith said, standing in the basement doorway. "Is it okay if I make a fresh pot?" She didn't wait for a reply and poured out the morning coffee.

Ned opened the kitchen door and leaned against the door jam. "Hey, Judith, I thought that was your car."

"Hi, Ned, come have a cup of coffee." Her hands trembled, and she hoped he didn't notice. "How was your Thanksgiving?"

"Not great, but it was okay. Had dinner with Paul and his family. His wife's a southern cook. It was tasty, but not what I'm used to eating." He seemed to rock back on his heels waiting on her news. "Hey, have you heard anything more from your investigator?"

"That's why I'm here, actually." She plugged in the pot and turned around. "Let's wait till Barbara joins us, okay?" She could feel her blood pressure rising. "How's Luke doing?" she asked as she brought the sugar and spoons to the table.

"I don't know. Luke's still holding a grudge against me for, uh . . . well you were there. I guess I deserve it," he said as he brushed off his jeans. "I'd probably feel the same way." He pulled a chair out from the table and sat on the edge.

"Ned, those days are behind you now." Judith hoped she sounded confident, but she wasn't sure of anything when it came to Ned. She picked up a nearby towel and wiped the counter. Anything to keep busy. She still didn't like being near her son-in-law.

Barbara walked into the kitchen and hugged her mother. "What's up?"

"Well, I've had the wrap-up meeting with my investigator, and he has confirmed most of what we already knew, with a few exceptions." Judith hesitated a moment. "The man Mr. Arbour took pictures of wasn't your father. The gentleman was your dad's second cousin, or something like that." She glanced over at Ned. He appeared as if he was holding his breath. "Your father passed away about fifteen years ago, but his cousin wasn't exact on the date.

"This cousin explained that Hillary's parents came to the school and accused your dad of rape. The scandal ended his teaching career. And I would think the humiliation Hillary's parents suffered justified their actions. The English are prudish when it comes to sex—before marriage. It would have been a black mark against the whole family. Anyway, your father was struggling to find work after the word got out about his affair."

"My father is dead?" Ned fidgeted in his chair. "Surely your investigator found out more. If not, you wasted your money, Judith."

"No, I don't think I *wasted* any money. Now you know for sure that your father cared about you and your mother. He didn't have the wherewithal to find you, and if he had, he couldn't have supported a family." She looked at her daughter for a split second. This would be closure for Ned, something Judith believed he needed.

"This investigation did a lot of good, didn't it?" Ned said with a sarcastic tone.

Barbara interrupted. "Mother, I guess we'd begun to hope Ned's dad might be willing to meet with him." She rubbed Ned's shoulders. "This is very disappointing. We don't mean to be unappreciative of Mr. Arbour's efforts, or yours."

"What about the cousin?" Ned asked. "Did he tell your investigator any more about what my father died of? What did he do after he stopped teaching? There has to be more."

Judith shook her head. "Mr. Arbour found out your father's wife died in a carriage accident. They didn't have other children—"

Ned's head jerked up. "What? I was his only child. What happened to his estate? Maybe I inherited something."

"From what Mr. Arbour told me, there was no estate. In fact, your father left nothing but debt." Judith got up and poured the coffee. With her back to Ned, she took a second to take a breath. This had to work for her daughter's sake. "Anyone care for milk?"

Ned's foot bounced unconsciously on the floor. "Well Judith, thanks for trying. I assume the investigation is closed, right? It kinda feels anticlimactic." Ned stood and shoved one hand into his pocket. "Barbara, I'll see you later. I have to get some supplies for Paul." Ned opened the door. "Thanks again, Judith."

"This information should at least close one door for you, Ned. If you want to talk more, let me know." The last thing Judith wanted was to have another discussion with her son-in-law about his father.

"Naw, nothing left to discuss, but thanks for trying." Ned closed the door and walked out.

When the door closed, Judith took a deep breath. She held out her hands and watched them shake.

Barbara looked out the kitchen window and watched Ned get into his truck. She turned to her mother. "Mom, why are you shaking? What's wrong?"

Judith pulled out the report she'd received from her investigator. "You might want to read this one day, but it's all fiction."

"What do you mean?" Barbara took the report her mother held out.

"My investigator got paid off to lie to me."

"What?" Barbara stared at her mother.

"His report is nothing more than the fairy tale. I've a friend in the banking business. He confirmed that Mr. Arbour moved a significant amount of money to a Swiss bank account. He wouldn't verify how much." Judith shook her head. "I had a funny feeling about him, but I've gotten the word out to my contacts in the police department. Our Mr. Arbour won't be a private anything for much longer. Hope he got a lot of money—he's going to need it."

"So what's the truth?" Barbara pulled out a chair and sat down.

"Pretty much what we already knew." Judith raised her cup and took a sip. "Ned and Philip Villier are half-brothers." Judith held her coffee cup, then placed it on the table. "Ned's father is alive and well, he couldn't care less about Ned or Hillary. Cooking is the family business."

"I could've sworn Gertrude told me there were other children. Or was that a lie? Oh, and what about the difference in the last names?" Barbara asked.

"Yes, there is a good-sized blended family. The connection between the Villiers and the Moreau's family is Mr. Moreau's first wife was a Villier." A smirk crossed Judith's face. "Turns out he'd been cheating on her. She divorced him early on in their marriage. She changed her name back to her maiden name of Villier, and somehow she got their two young sons' names changed too." Judith arched her eyebrows and her lips pressed together. "When he married his second wife, they had two boys."

Barbara pushed her hair out of her face. "I didn't know you could change your children's names too. Wow! Talk about vindictive. Guess the saying is true about a woman scorned."

"Wouldn't you be? His wife wanted nothing to do with him. Can't say I blame her. This makes me wonder how many times he got away with messing around with young girls before getting caught." Judith paused a moment. "Now we understand why Philip's name is different than his father's." Judith traced the handle of her cup with her finger. "Sad, don't you think?"

Barbara nodded. "How did Philip and Hillary ever meet up?"

"Philip married when he got out of culinary school. They came to America. He wanted to make a name for himself by bringing French cooking to America. They picked Boston. His wife died from the flu after he'd bought his first restaurant."

"Of all the places he could've gone. I assume that Philip doesn't know any of this?"

"No, not as far as I know. Only Mr. Moreau, Hillary, and now us. Hillary and Philip never returned to the family home, and his father stayed in France. According to Mr. Arbour, the old man had no idea who his son was bringing home. Mr. Moreau paid off Mr. Arbour to make sure Philip would never know. My guess is Hillary will take this secret to her death bed."

Barbara rubbed her arms and looked back out the window. "I can't imagine what Mr. Moreau thought when Philip introduced his new wife to the family. Oh my stars . . . what a shock."

The two women sat in silence.

CHAPTER 21

# BOSTON, 1965

**THREE YEARS LATER,** Ned moved home, and he and Barbara began a normal enough life together. Luke's graduation from college was the big event now as Barbara held the ladder steady for Ned while he pushed open the attic door. "Barbara, which suitcase? You've got three up here."

"Get the largest one." A strong, musty scent floated down to her. Unexpected memories, welcome and unwelcome, washed over her. After Ned's adoptive mother Gertrude died, Barbara had spent weeks cleaning out the old house. Surprised by the emotions the attic smells brought up, Barbara wiped her eyes. Explaining her feelings to Ned was useless. He would never understand. Her life had taken on so many changes throughout her round trip from Boston to San Diego, then finally home again.

Luke told her he had a surprise. Time had gone by too fast, and she wasn't a fan of surprises.

"I still don't see why we can't see the kids get their diplomas, have dinner, then hit the road home." Ned lowered the suitcase, then closed the door to the attic. "Two days, maybe three at the most."

"Ned, the fact that you and Luke are on better terms is so important. Enjoy a few days off from work." *Will he ever just go with the flow of life?*

"I've a business to run, and being gone a week isn't good." Ned shook his head as he took the ladder downstairs. "Call me when dinner's ready. I'm hungry."

❧

The two graduates, Luke and Claire, had requested both their families attend the graduation ceremony and celebration dinner afterwards together. Barbara felt the sting of jealousy. She wanted this special time with her family alone. Determined to make the best of this day, she said nothing.

At the graduation dinner, the group of six was sitting around the table talking and laughing when Luke tapped his water glass. "We've an announcement," he said as he stood up. "Claire and I've applied to the University of Massachusetts Medical School. Hopefully," he and Claire glanced at each other, "hopefully we'll get accepted."

Barbara sat back in her chair. "Now this is excellent news. You both can live at home." A genuine smile brightened her face. "What do you want to study?"

Luke shook his head. "I'm not sure."

Claire spoke up. "I want to go into medical research." She glanced at her parents. "To find a cure for pediatric cancers. I became passionate about this field of study after we volunteered at a children's clinic. I feel this is the right direction for me."

Claire's mother, Alice, looked startled. "I don't understand. You want to go to medical school?" She glanced over at her husband, then back at her daughter. "I thought you wanted to be a mother and housekeeper—like me."

"Mom, I uh, I want more." Claire kept her head down.

Barbara glanced at Luke to gauge his expression, but he didn't react. She watched with interest at this revelation. Luke never discussed Claire's relationship with her parents. Maybe everything wasn't as perfect as it appeared.

Bill Sims raised his wine glass. "Well, congratulations to our future doctors. Better put off retirement if you're going to medical school. A doctor! Well, we couldn't be more proud. Right, Alice?"

Alice reached for her water glass, but offered no words of encouragement.

The two graduates didn't raise their glasses. "We've one more announcement." Luke sat down and took Claire's hand. "We've decided to stay in Lowell this summer to continue working at a rural clinic where we've been volunteering." Luke paused and looked at his mother. "We'll be living together."

Barbara listened to an audible sucking in of air from the other three parents. She knew she wasn't the only one who wasn't ready for this next step. So this was Luke's surprise: he wasn't coming back home now, or in the future.

Luke didn't let their reactions stop him. "Marriage is on our horizon, but we wanted to wait until we graduated from medical school. The clinic has agreed to hire us for the summer, so we'll earn a little money. But the experience we'll gain is worth much more."

Barbara refused to react. She had made her feelings clear from the beginning that getting into a relationship right now wasn't smart. She watched Claire's parents, hoping their reactions would slow down this train wreck of an idea.

Bill Sims's eyes squinted and the lines in his forehead deepened. "I don't agree with this free love bullshit. You kids are—"

"Whoa, Bill." Ned held his massive hands in the air. "These two finished a four-year degree in three years. They're at the top of their class. I think they have their act together. Let's give them some space to grow."

Bill Sims took a deep breath, but did not respond.

Barbara wanted to scream at her husband. She didn't want her son living with Claire; she wanted him to come home. But she realized it would never happen.

Luke and Claire nodded their appreciation to Ned. "Mr. Sims, we knew this wouldn't be a popular announcement, but we wouldn't go behind anyone's back."

Claire sat quietly next to Luke.

Barbara watched red blotches appear on Alice's throat. She felt she might have an ally in Claire's mother. With six to eight years more of school ahead of them, Barbara felt it was a long time for a relationship to last. She took a quiet breath, then lifted her glass and said, "To our future daughter-in-law."

Three months later, Barbara was out watering the plants on her front porch while she watched a group of neighborhood children play kickball in the street. Not too long ago, Luke would have been in the thick of that very game. Where had the years gone? She sighed. Judith would have been by her side. Losing her mother last year had shaken her to the core. Judith had been her champion and best friend. Sometimes she'd forget Judith had died and would go to tell her mother something, only to relive the loss.

The telephone interrupted her daydreaming and she ran to answer.

"May I speak to Ned Johansen?" the voice asked.

The accent was familiar. "May I tell Ned who's calling?"

"I'm David Villier, Hillary and Philip's son, Ned's half-brother."

"David, it's me, Barbara. How're you?" Barbara glanced at the clock. "Something has to be wrong, or you wouldn't be calling at this time of day. What's happened?" Her hand went to her chest.

"Barbara, I thought it was you. I'm sorry, but my news isn't good."

"What? What's happened?" She pulled the kitchen chair over so she could sit down.

"Barbara, Father died yesterday in a car wreck. He shouldn't have been driving. Dad's such a stubborn old fool."

"Oh, David. I'm sure your family is devastated."

He hesitated for a moment. "There's more. Mother suffered a massive stroke this morning, and the news I'm getting is not hopeful." His voice broke with emotion.

"I'm so sorry. Philip and Hillary were so kind." She rubbed her temples as the tension increased. "What do the doctors say about your mom's condition?"

"The doctors have done everything they can. She doesn't have long."

"Is there anything I can do to help you?" Barbara was ready to fly out to help the family. She was sure that's why he'd called.

"Barbara, Mother wants to see Ned before . . . " he hesitated. "She has to talk to him. It's been this way too long. A lifetime wasted, in my opinion. If you can't afford the plane ticket, Mother will pay."

"David, thank you, but it's not the money. You know their history." Barbara took a deep breath and let it out slowly, giving herself a moment to think. The request made sense. Ned needed this closure and so did Hillary. "Give me your phone number and I'll call you back after I talk to Ned."

After they had hung up, she paced the kitchen. She wasn't sure how Ned would react. They hadn't talked about his mother or her family in some time. It was almost as if they didn't exist. If he wouldn't go, should she fly out? Did they even have the money for one ticket? She didn't want to see Arty, and of course, he would be there. Why didn't he make the call? The rest of the day, she stewed about how to approach Ned. Should she call Paul, his AA sponsor and business partner? Would Ned drink again, or let go of his hatred? The day proved exhausting as she imagined all kinds of scenarios of how their conversation might turn.

Later that evening, Ned dragged into the house. The strain of the day showed in his stooped shoulders and grimy clothes.

"Did you have a rough day?" She wasn't sure if now was the right time to talk, as worn out as he looked, but they didn't have the luxury of time. "Please sit down. I've bad news for you."

Ned's metal lunch box dropped on the table with a loud crash. He rubbed his face with both of his hands. "What? Don't tell me something else has broken around here. I just don't have the time or energy right now." He closed his eyes for a few seconds as if bracing for impact. "What now?"

"No, it's nothing like that, although I wish it were . . . Philip died yesterday in a car crash." She studied Ned to read his reactions. "There's more. Hillary wants you to come to California—"

Ned interrupted her, blurting out, "Mother must've called today, drumming up sympathy, no doubt." He walked over to the fridge and pulled out the water jug. "I'm sure she's crushed, but I'm not the one to hold her hand. She has two other sons to do that for her. Hell—Philip didn't even like me."

"Ned, let me finish. There's more. Your mother suffered a massive stroke this morning. She wants—"

Ned turned around. "Wh, what happened again? How'd you find out?"

"Your brother David called and told me."

"David? What's the deal with Mum again?" He cocked his head to one side as if to hear her words better. "Say it again. What happened?"

Barbara went over the phone conversation again, but this time with more details, giving him time to absorb the reality of what he was hearing. "I'd go with you, but we can't afford for us both to go. Ned, this might be your last chance to see your mother." Tears built up in her eyes. "There've been too many lies and secrets. It's past time to forgive."

Ned stared down at the floor and didn't move. "I knew this day would come." He leaned against the counter. "I can remember the day when she moved to California. My birthday was in a few weeks. I watched as Philip handed their new baby to Mum after they boarded the train." He raised his head. "I could never get that image out of my mind. Her face lit up when she took the baby. I stood rooted to the ground." He placed the water jug on the counter.

"I didn't think she'd leave me." He faltered. "I wanted to go too." Unblocked tears streamed down his face.

Barbara put her arms around him. Ned had always kept his real feelings for his mother buried, protected by an angry guard. She felt his pain so sharply, and there was nothing she could do to shield him from it.

For several moments, they stood holding each other before Ned pulled away. "Better get me on the next flight out."

◘

Two days later, Ned arrived in San Diego. The landing went smoothly. Ned never enjoyed flying, and coming back to California added to his anxiety. He picked up his luggage and went out to hail a taxi. When he reached the exit, he saw a man holding a sign with his name printed out in large letters.

"I'm Ned Johansen."

"Nice to meet you. I'm your brother David." He held out his hand. "Don't believe we've met before."

"No, I don't think we have." Ned stared at his brother and saw a younger Hillary in his face. "Have there been any improvements in Mum's, uh, I mean Hillary's condition?"

David shook his head. "There won't be any improvements."

Emotion overtook him and he couldn't finish. "Sorry, Ned. I've just lost my father and the news isn't good for *our* mother."

Ned felt as if his whirling world fell off its axis. He knew he should say something comforting, but no words came out.

The drive to the hospital took an hour and the men said little. Ned kept remembering the day Pa died. He felt shattered, as if the world had ended. Nothing about seeing his mother for the last time stirred that kind of emotion. Whether she was in his life or not ceased to matter to him.

David pulled up to the hospital's entrance. "The room number is 407. Uh, Ned, I love my mother more than you'll ever know. She wasn't perfect—but who is?" He looked down for a moment. "I'll give you two time alone."

Ned couldn't find the words he needed to say, so instead he gave a little nod and got out of the car. He stood at the bank of elevators and thought about turning around. Now, more than any other time Ned could remember, he craved a drink. One drink. Could he handle only one? The stark white hall and glaring lights seemed to go on forever. When he reached her room, he waited for a split second, then knocked.

A young nurse opened the door. "Are you family?"

Surprised by the question, he stammered out, "I, uh . . . yes, I'm her son." He heard himself say the words, but it didn't seem real.

"Her condition is critical, so please don't stay long." The young nurse stepped aside as Ned entered.

The room was dark and had an antiseptic smell. His vision needed to adjust to the soft lighting. A vase with a single, white, long-stemmed rose sat on her bedside table. He assumed it was her favorite. Unable to move closer, he stood at the foot of her bed and looked down at the shriveled woman before him. He'd never seen a person in this condition before. Without warning, his stomach rolled and excess saliva filled his mouth. He swallowed and turned away, fighting the overwhelming desire to rid his body of this feeling.

Hillary's eyes opened. "Neddy, is that you?" Her words slurred.

"Yes, ma'am, it's me." He hadn't heard her nickname for him in decades. Tightness spread across his chest. "How do you feel?" Surprised by his feelings, he wiped his eyes.

"Come closer." She moved her hand closer to the edge of the bed. "It's been a long time."

"Yes, ma'am." He moved the metal chair closer than he wanted.

"You know about Philip?" Tears slipped down her cheeks.

"David told me." Without thinking, Ned lifted her hand and held it with both of his. Instead of the soft, warm hand he remembered, it felt like a bag of cold bones. He fought the urge to pull away.

She took a labored breath. "I need water."

Ned picked up the plastic cup on her bedside table and guided the straw to her mouth. The task felt foreign to him, and he wished Barbara had come. He noticed his hands were shaking and tried to steady them. He had adjusted to the low light, and realized the right side of her face sagged. In fact, nothing on the right side of her body seemed to move.

"Thank you." She closed her eyes for a moment. "I need your forgiveness before—" she stopped. "We should've talked, but you were so angry." Her voice sounded strained.

"I was just a kid. How could you leave me behind?" The tears slipped down his face. "What did I do wrong?" This was his last chance to tell her how he felt, but at this moment, it no longer mattered.

"I thought I was protecting you. Philip was a very jealous man." She closed her eyes. "I couldn't let him hurt you. Then, I did the unthinkable and left you. Carl and Gert tried to tell me." She seemed to get weaker before his eyes.

When she didn't move, he panicked. "Mum?" He started to get up and find her nurse, but he felt a slight pressure from her hand. He turned back to his mother.

Hillary took a shallow breath, and Ned bent his head closer. "Neddy, I've always loved. . . ."

Hillary took a shallow breath, and Ned bent his head closer. Her eyes closed and her mouth sagged open. The struggle to hang on was over.

Ned stood up, yanked open the door, and called for a nurse. Several people came running into the room, pushing him out of their way. He stepped out into the hall and found David.

"She's gone, isn't she?"

Ned nodded and wiped his eyes.

The two men stood apart from each other in the hallway.

Their mother's doctor walked into the hall. "David, I'm sorry for your loss. Her journey is over, and she's with your dad."

David shook hands with the doctor. "Thank you for all your help." He turned back to Ned. "Guess there's nothing left for us to do here. I think you'll be comfortable at Mother's." He pulled out a handkerchief and wiped his face. "I don't know about you, but I could use a drink."

"Sounds good." He felt sure he could handle one drink, as most people did every day, and no more. He hadn't had a drink in years. Considering what he'd been through today, hell he deserved a drink.

❦

It'd been over twenty-four hours since Ned left, and Barbara hadn't heard a word. She had to find out about Hillary's condition. She picked up the phone and called the number David had left. There was no answer. She pulled out her address book and called the home number for Hillary. There was no answer.

Next, she called his AA sponsor, Paul Day. "I don't want to bother you with this, but I haven't heard from Ned. I have a terrible feeling."

"Listen, I'll be there after I run a few errands for this customer. Find out what you can from the hospital, and we'll pick it up from there." Paul took an audible breath. "I've a few people we can call for help."

Two hours later, Paul Day knocked on the kitchen door, then wiped his feet on the rug before he entered.

"Glad you're here, Paul. I found out that Ned's mother died the day he arrived. I don't know if he got there in time or not." She dropped her head in her hands.

Paul pulled out a chair and sat down. "When's the funeral?"

She lifted her head and pushed her hair back. "I don't know." The phone rang, causing them both to jump. Barbara got up to answer it.

"Hey, sexy lady, how the hell are you?" Ned said.

She motioned for Paul to come to the phone so he could hear what was going on. "Ned, you're drunk. Oh my God." She wanted to get mad and yell at him, but couldn't. "Hold on, someone here wants to talk to you." She handed the phone to Paul.

"Hey buddy, how're you doing?" Paul asked. He held on to Barbara and shared the phone so she could hear.

"That BITCH—I knew she'd drag you into this. I knew it."

Paul shook his head. "I'll call a friend of mine who'll help you climb back on the wagon. Give me the address of where you're staying, and a phone number."

"Forget it. I can handle this myself. You're nothing but a killjoy, and I'm not gonna let you spoil my family reunion. It's my mother's funeral, after all." Ned slammed the phone down.

Paul hung the phone up and placed his arm around Barbara's shoulder. "Stay strong, Barbara. I realize you're worried, but it's not over yet." He walked to the door and turned around. "I've a particular customer I have to take care of. In the meantime, get me the address of where he's staying. I'll be back as soon as I can." Paul's hound-dog eyes seemed to droop more than usual. "I've gotten to know Ned, and I can promise you this. He's in hell right now. He'll kick himself when he sobers up."

Barbara wasn't sure she agreed. After Paul left, she went to her desk and pulled out her address book. After several failed attempts, she called the long-distance operator and explained the problem. Moments later, Art's phone was ringing. She hadn't spoken with him for many years, and really didn't want to now.

Art's phone rang several times before a young woman answered.

"Hello, my name is Barbara Johansen, and I'm calling for my husband's brother, Arthur Villier. Is he available?"

"Oh, I've heard Dad talk about you. I'm his daughter, Emma."

Barbara stammered. "I, um, I didn't know he had children. May I speak to him?"

Emma laughed. "Sure thing. Hold on and I'll get him."

Barbara heard his daughter call him to the phone while she braced herself. She fought hanging up the phone.

"Well, well, as I live and breathe, doll, it's been a while, hasn't it?" Art laughed into the phone. "Guess you've heard about Mom and Dad. Hey, your husband is on his way over, and we're going to enjoy some brotherly bonding over a few cocktails. From the call I got, he may've gotten a head start."

Barbara heard his voice and couldn't believe she'd made such a terrible mistake. "Hi Art, sorry to hear about your parents. They were good people."

"Thanks, doll. Do you want to talk to *Neddy* when he gets here?"

"No." Her hands shook. "Listen, Art, Ned's an alcoholic, and he hasn't touched alcohol in years—till now. I need the address of where he's staying so we can get him sober before the funeral." She could feel the heat on her face.

"I thought something wasn't right, but hell, who am I? This is kinda weird isn't it . . . you and me talking after such a long time."

"Arty, please give me the address of where Ned is staying so we can get him sobered up." *What a jerk.*

"Sure thing, doll, but first," he paused. "My long-lost brother, does he know I'm the father of his kid?" Art laughed. "Sorry, I couldn't help but throw that grenade at ya. Kinda like a gotcha."

Barbara froze. *Oh God, can his daughter hear him?* Art's cavalier attitude stunned her. "No, please, keep your voice down. All I want is the address and phone number of where Ned's staying."

"Emma wouldn't mind having a brother," Art laughed again. "He's staying at Mother's. How 'bout that after all this time? Should I tell her?"

Barbara hung up the phone without responding. She needed her mother more than anything right now. What would she do if Art told Ned the truth? She paced the room.

⌁

Three weeks later, Ned returned home from California. When the city cab pulled up to the front of the house, Barbara walked out to the porch. Her mother had always said having secrets between a husband and wife would ruin a marriage. She had to tell Ned the truth.

When Ned entered the house, his shoulders slumped and he kept his eyes adverted. His behavior didn't surprise her. "Did you have a good flight?" She didn't offer any form of affection.

Ned put his suitcase down. "Yeah, it was okay."

"I've some coffee made. Would you like a cup?" She was uncomfortable, but knew this conversation had to take place. "Come in the kitchen and let's talk."

Ned nodded and followed Barbara without comment.

After setting two cups down on the table, Barbara sat across from her husband. "We've a lot to talk about." She was ready to clear her conscience. This was the best time to talk to Ned. He was usually very willing to appease her. She felt she had an even playing field. They were both guilty.

Ned sat forward with his hands clasped together. "If you're going to tell me about you and Art—don't."

Barbara wasn't expecting Ned to be so blunt. She was surprised, yet relieved at the same time. "What?"

"I already know. I figured it out years ago. Now after seeing Art, well, it was even more obvious to me. Luke's his double."

Barbara sat still and could feel tightness spread across her chest. She knew he'd always suspected, but how did he connect Art? "What do you mean you figured it out?"

"Let me back up. I . . . uh, I didn't know it was Art, but I knew Luke wasn't my blood." Ned's eyes were hooded. "When I was in rehab, I talked with the psychiatrist and came to grips with the possibility that uh, maybe Luke wasn't my son. I don't blame you Barbara. I was miserable to live with, then on top of all the uh, the uh . . . well, the abuse you took from me." He ran his hand through his hair. "I was pissed at first, but the doc straightened me out. He helped me kinda understand your side of things."

"It's never happened again, Ned." Barbara was ashamed that she hadn't talked to him before, but she'd always been afraid of his reaction. "Saying I'm sorry is so inadequate. But I am."

"You had every reason. With all I've done to our family."

"We both made mistakes, Ned. We should've talked long ago. But you aren't always the easiest to talk to. Luke is your son, not by blood, but through love." She stood up and walked to his side of the table. Barbara lifted his chin so his eyes finally met hers. "I love you, Ned Johansen. I always have and will." The weight of being guarded when it came to Luke and Ned's family was gone. She hoped Ned felt the same way.

Ned stood up and wrapped his arms around her. She listened to the pounding of his heart, then she heard him let go of a sob.

CHAPTER 22

# BOSTON, 1985

THE PREACHER AND Luke walked into the back of the chapel together. Luke headed to his seat with his mother and Claire. The preacher walked to the podium next to Ned's casket, then he welcomed and thanked everyone for coming on behalf of the family. The service began with the reading of the twenty-third Psalm.

He asked if anyone had thoughts or memories they wanted to share about Ned.

John Preston, Ned's old friend and a longtime neighbor, stood up and came to the front. He was tall, and his skin had a leathery appearance with deeply etched worry lines across his forehead. "Barbara, Luke, I want to tell you how sorry I am for your loss."

Luke and Claire nodded while Barbara turned away with no expression of acknowledgment. Seeing John again brought back memories of how he would sneak whiskey to Ned when he was trying to get sober. Luke could feel the tension in his neck tighten.

"My friends, Ned was a jokester, and this story proves he could take it as well as dish it out. Which he did." John smiled.

Luke shifted in his seat, then checked to see if his mother was okay.

"See, it was like this. The city was working on the sewer lines and had to tear up roads and sidewalks to get to the pipes. They worked at night mostly." He paused and sipped from the cup he'd brought with him.

Luke was pretty sure he knew what John was sipping.

"Well, this particular morning, I see a big ole "danger" sign in front of Ned and Barbara's house. So when I see Ned come out that morning for his paper, I decided he might need help. So, I went over all neighborly like." John smiles again. "I said to him, 'Hey Ned, what's going on? Need any help?' Well, my friends, Ned tells me nothing's going on and how the hell did that sign end up in front of his house? So we decided it was either a mistake, or someone's pulling a joke. Ned came up with the idea to move the sign down to Richard's house. He lived a couple of doors down. He and Ned weren't the best of friends, if you get what I mean. So we moved the sign. 'Let Richard worry about his sewer lines,' Ned tells me. We had a big ole laugh. I said to him, 'I'll tell ya what Richard does, 'cause I can see his driveway from my front window.' "

Luke chuckled at his own involvement with this story. Because what John wasn't aware of is that Luke and his friends had put the "danger sign" in front of his dad's house in the first place.

John took another sip. "Friends, it turns out, Richard wasn't even home. He'd gone on vacation. The sign sat in front of his house for days. Then it was gone. We figured the city picked it up. Ole Ned starts laughing so hard he farted. That guy could take it and give it." A polite laughter rippled through the audience.

Luke tried to smile, but John had touched a nerve. *Yes, he could.* He watched his mother to see if John's memory of Ned had upset her. It didn't appear to.

"I'll miss you, buddy." John nodded as if he was tipping a hat toward the family, then sat down.

The preacher asked if there was anyone else who wanted to share their memories. When no one came forward, Luke stood up and took a quick glance around the gathering. He was a little surprised that more of Ned's drinking buddies hadn't come forward, but maybe it was for the best. At the podium, he wiped his hands, pulled out his notes, and with a deep breath he began. "Let me begin by thanking you all for coming. My mother, my wife Claire, and I appreciate your support."

Luke forced a grin. "Dad always liked a party." A few people laughed. "And was a pro at telling and playing jokes on you. Thank you for sharing that memory, Mr. Preston. I'd completely forgotten about the sign.

"But Dad also had another side that was creative. He built beautiful pieces of furniture. Give him an idea of what you wanted and he'd create a piece better than you could've imagined." Luke took a step back, then put his hands in his pants pockets. He watched his mother, who seemed to have collapsed into her own world and didn't appear to focus on any one thing, and wondered if she'd heard any of his words.

"Carl, who was Dad's adoptive father, he and Dad had as close a relationship as any natural father and son. Pa Johansen got Dad into a tool and die shop as an apprentice shortly after he graduated from high school. Then he had him join the navy as a reservist. This background turned out to be exactly what the navy was looking for when the war broke out. Dad retired after giving our country nearly thirty years of service. But the war left Dad, like many men, broken and unable to find peace. He shared little with me about his experiences. What he did tell me was that even years and years after the war, he could still hear the sounds of the torpedoes as they narrowly missed the ship's hull." Luke paused and took a sip of water from the glass the preacher had left for him.

"Pa Johansen and Dad both loved baseball and were loyal fans of the Boston Red Sox." From the back of the sanctuary, Luke heard, "Go Reds." He grinned.

"On their way home from a game, Pa Johansen died of a heart attack. Losing his father had a devastating affect on him." Luke took a deep breath and mopped his forehead with his handkerchief.

"After Dad retired from the navy, he settled our family in Boston. He had a hard time fitting into civilian life. Finding a job that suited him proved impossible." His voice wavered, and he saw Claire wipe her eyes. Visions of the abuse his mother endured flew through his mind. "Finally, my mom suggested that Dad start his own home repair business." Luke felt his emotions taking over. Gathering his notes cards, he put them in his coat pocket. Looking down at his family, he paused for a moment. *I have to let the past go.* "My father's talents were as incredible as his demons." Luke took another sip of water.

"My father was shaped by events he had no control over." Luke's eyes filled with tears. "But today his troubles are over. Now we celebrate Dad's life. He's in a better place. That's what's important now. Rest in peace." He looked down at his wife and mother, then over to the casket where his father lay. "I love you, Dad." Words he hadn't spoken since he was a child. Luke turned back to the preacher, gave a brief nod, then left the podium.

As Luke took a seat next to Claire and his mother, he let out a sigh, not of relief, but of satisfaction and acceptance. For the first time, he felt an unaccustomed sense of peace when it came to his father.

The End

# AUTHOR'S NOTE

In the real-life story, there were five of us kids instead of one child. We each remember things a little differently from one another. We protected the family. No one talked about Dad's drinking. I was well over fifty years old before I could tell anyone my father was an alcoholic.

We created a strong family bond. My older sister, Pat, took care of the four of us from the time she was nine years old. She took my younger brother Philip for his first haircut, his first day of school. She was the one who taught him to cook. She was our second mother, always there to listen or help in any way she could. Pat passed away on March 25, 2019. She was seventy-seven. We miss her wisdom and good cooking.

Our youngest brother Philip passed away on July 5, 2012, at the age of fifty-nine, due to cancer. We always told him he was adopted because he didn't look like the rest of us. We all had brown eyes, but he didn't. We thought he was Dad's half-brother's son, although he did have the same creative abilities as Dad. Philip became a master carpenter. The truth is we'll never know, but that's okay. We miss those sparkling blue eyes.

Dad died from a stroke and leukemia on August 30, 1995, at the age of eighty-one. I believe my mother's background as a nurse helped him. They were married for fifty-four years at the time of his death. We do miss him. The man who was sober, funny, and so talented.

Mom died on December 19, 1999, on Dad's birthday. She was eighty-four. She had dementia and had developed bone cancer. I always thought that once Dad died, Mom would have a calmer, more peaceful life. But it didn't happen. Pat made the ultimate sacrifice when she and her husband Bud moved in with Mom not long after Dad died. Due to the bone cancer, Mom had to have a rod placed in her femur. The Alzheimer disease proved to be a blessing as it seemed to block the pain from the cancer. Mom was placed in a nursing home after the surgery. She lived four more months, then joined Dad. We miss our mom everyday.

My story is based on events I heard my mother, aunts, uncles, brother-in-law, older brother and sisters tell about Dad. I used his naval service records to sketch out a small portion of his career in the navy. Pat's husband, Bud, found Dad's birth certificate and his adoption papers for me. My brother, Don, and sister, Jane, are all that's left of our family. We text each other every night staying in touch and loving each other.

Through the early mornings when I got up to write and research, I wove a fictitious story around these bits and pieces of his life, and ultimately found peace with my father.

Made in the USA
Monee, IL
21 November 2021

82511870R00173